WHAT'S COMING TO YOU

SHIVANI JAI

First Edition (August 1 2025)

Print ISBN: 979-8-9995584-0-4

www.ShivaniJai.com

 Formatted with Vellum

Behind every woman is a bunch of other women who supported her, encouraged her delusions, and reminded her that what she wants matters, and that she's deserving of success.

Thanks to those women.

CHAPTER 1

Marilys Daniels prided herself on being a highly punctual person, but even she had to admit she might've gone overboard this time. Her dinner reservation wasn't until eight, but she'd been parked outside the restaurant since seven-fifteen, fighting the urge to turn around and go home.

Her friend, Amanda, had convinced her to come out for a blind double date with her, her fiancé, and one of his single friends. Mari thought arriving early might help her get over her nerves, but the longer she sat there, the more nervous she felt. She wasn't really the "blind date" type. She was practically allergic to small talk, let alone small talk with a stranger she'd never seen before under the pressure of a date, but Amanda was not an easy person to say no to.

"You are so great, and Greg has *great* friends!" she insisted as they left yoga together one day. "And I'm dying to get more female energy in the group. It's a total sausage fest!"

Mari laughed at that but remained unconvinced. "So, basically, misery wants company?"

"Exactly!" Amanda exclaimed. "And what better company than my very best friend and new girl in town, Mari Daniels?"

Mari rolled her eyes, but Amanda soldiered on.

"Girl, trust me! When you meet Mason, you will be thanking me. He's charming, he's sexy, he's ambitious, *and* he's a really good guy!"

"Then why does he need you to fix him up?" Mari countered.

"Bitch, becauuuse!" Amanda groaned, tossing her braids. "Despite being one of Greg's smartest friends, he makes the dumbest dating choices. He's a sucker for blonde, big-boobed, big-lipped Insta-baddies. And even though we graduated years ago, he keeps going after these community college girls. It's embarrassing…we need to save him!"

Mari laughed again, but internally, she was cringing. Amanda's description of Mason was intriguing, but a man pushing thirty who was exclusively attracted to college-aged blondes didn't sound like her type in the slightest. Being the same age as him, she doubted she'd even have a chance if that was his preference. Plus, she had dark hair, brown skin, and pretty standard B-cups. The odds were not in her favor.

"He doesn't sound like he wants saving," she pushed back.

"Then save *me*!" Amanda threw her hands in the air. "I can't talk to these girls! I mean, they're fine or whatever. I'm sure they're good people, but there's never much below the surface, and Mason always ends up in some annoying, immature drama that Greg and I get sucked into. It's so annoying. I swear, sometimes it feels like we're back in college, you know? Plus," Amanda leaned in. "I think he's bored with the women in this town, and you're new and exciting! You're fresh meat! I think he's going to like you. You're just what he needs."

"How do I not already know this friend of Greg's if he went to Wazzu with us?"

"He didn't go there with us," Amanda clarified. "I just mean it feels like we're all back in undergrad when he brings those girls around. He's actually an Eastview townie. He and Greg grew up together. But don't worry, he's not a deadbeat," she added quickly, noting the look on Mari's face.

"Greg actually said he was kind of a big deal around town when they were younger. Super popular and all that. He just, you know, has a little growing up to do."

"Amanda, I don't want to date someone who isn't a grown-up already," Mari replied seriously. "Why would you want that for me?"

"Just meet us for dinner and see for yourself," Amanda insisted. "It doesn't have to be a double date; think of it as us helping you make new friends in town. If you don't like each other, you can go home after, and you never have to see him again. And you can tell me to fuck off if I'm wrong... but I'm not," she grinned.

Mari knew her friend well enough to understand that any further resistance would be futile. "Fine. You win. For now."

Despite her misgivings, it was worth saying yes for Mari to see the way Amanda lit up. Between excited squeals, she gave Mari the date, time, and location but refused to say anything more about Mason or even show her a picture of him.

"And don't try to look him up online, or I'll kill you," she warned. "I don't need you talking yourself out of it before you even meet him like I know you will."

Since then, Mari had done her best to be cool about the whole thing, especially after Amanda shamed her so accurately for her potential premeditative misbehavior. She told herself whatever would be, would be, but now double-date night was upon her, and she was spiraling faster with every passing minute. As she reached for her phone to recheck the time, it buzzed with an incoming call. She saw the ID and answered immediately.

"Hi, Mom."

"Hi, lovey," Meena Daniels replied. Her voice was slightly more wavery than usual.

Mari sat forward, instantly alert. "What's wrong? Are you okay?"

"Of course, baba, of course! Everything is fine!" Meena answered brightly, then paused. "Actually, I was just feeling a little bit down, so I thought I'd call and see what you were doing."

"Oh. Well, I'm good. Everything's fine here," Mari replied, allowing herself to relax a little. "Why were you feeling down?"

There was a long pause. "Did I ever tell you Mikul was conceived on this date?"

Mari smiled and shook her head. Mikul was her older brother who'd been killed by a drunk driver when she was little. Meena's grief over the loss of her son shaped the rest of Mari's childhood, and to this day, Meena often relied on her daughter for grounding whenever memories of her son threatened to unmoor her. Mari was twelve the first time Meena shared this particular story, and she'd heard it enough times since to get over the weirdness of it. Most people would probably rather die than hear about the night their parents made a baby, but patching her mother up right now was a welcome distraction from Mari's own current anxiety. "Tell me again," she said warmly.

"Well, when we first got married, your dad and I were working a lot, but we made a deal that every second Tuesday of every month, no matter what, we'd have a date night. We went to this beautiful little old-school Italian restaurant... you know, the kind with the candles that melt down all over the wine bottles? Anyway, we had dinner, and then... well..." Meena faltered. "I guess that's all. Just a regular date night between your dad and me, and then there was Mikey..." she trailed off absently, lost in her memories.

"It's a nice story, Mom," Mari smiled into the phone. "Do you feel a little better?"

"Yes, I—I think I do," Meena replied, returning to the conversation. Her voice was stronger. "Thank you, beloved."

"You're welcome, Mom." They sat silently on the phone for a long time, feeling their feelings together.

"So, what are you up to, darling?" Meena finally asked.

"Actually, I'm about to go on a date," Mari declared, sounding much more excited than she felt.

Meena gasped with delight. "A *first* date?"

"Mmhhm."

"Oh, that's wonderful, baba! On a second Tuesday! What a good sign. Maybe he'll be your forever person, just like your dad and me! Who is he?"

"I don't know. It's a blind date. Amanda set it up. All I know is his name is Mason."

Meena gasped again. "Another M! Oh Mari, he'd fit right in with us. I like the sound of this."

"Easy, Mom, let's not get ahead of ourselves, okay?" Mari kept her voice level, but her mother's reaction sent a fresh shot of panic through her system. She'd been so worried about the threat of rejection by this mystery guy that she'd failed to consider the opposite possibility. What if Mason was 'The One'? Was she ready for that? At first, the idea was as terrifying as the possibility of rejection, but the longer she considered it, the more excited she began to feel.

"I didn't know you were dating again," Meena replied. Mari could practically hear her mother pouting through the phone. These were the kinds of updates she was used to getting without having to ask. "I thought you were taking a break after the last few didn't work out."

"I was," Mari replied. "I mean, I am..." she added, cringing at memories of her most recent dating disasters.

It had been so long since she'd last gone on a good date that Mari swore off the practice a while ago, choosing to focus on herself instead. It wasn't a happy choice. Moving to Eastview, Washington was supposed to be the beginning of Mari's fairy-tale—an idyllic Pacific Northwestern nesting ground for her to build the domestic life of her dreams—but so far, trying to date here was a dismal experience. She tried dating apps for a little while, but everyone she met was either painfully dull, creepily over-sexed, acting utterly insane in her DMs, or ghosting her entirely. Mari did her best to play the game, but she always came away pining for the good old days when you'd bump into someone great in a store or at a bar.

Or through mutual friends, she thought. The butterflies in her stomach fluttered excitedly.

"This is just a one-off because Amanda wouldn't take no for an answer," she told Meena, shooing them away.

"You know, you could always come back to Chicago," Meena offered. "The city is full of nice young men who would be great for you! You don't have to stay with us, of course, but you could until you find your own place. In fact, Mr. and Mrs. Rocco around the corner are selling their house! It could be a nice starter home for you. Your dad and I could help out with the down payment."

"Nice try, Mom," Mari smiled ruefully.

Leaving her parents in Chicago to go to Washington State was one of the hardest things she'd ever done, and while she often felt guilty about separating from them, it wasn't enough to compel her to return. After grad school, they'd tried to entice her back home, but once Mari had gotten a taste of independence, there was no going back. Instead, she had allowed Amanda to convince her to try out Eastview, a small but fast-developing town near Portland that was attracting lots of recent grads ready to jumpstart the rest of their lives, just like her.

"No, really," Meena persisted, "I can call the Roccos in the morning. I bet they'd be happy to sell to us!"

"Don't call the Roccos, Mom." Mari kept her voice gentle but firm. "I don't want to move back to Chicago. My life is here now, okay?"

Meena sighed. "It would just be nice to have you close again."

"I know, Mom, but I'm right here, aren't I?"

"Yes. Yes, you are, beloved," Meena conceded, changing the subject. "So, what time is your date?"

Mari's eyes darted anxiously to the dashboard clock. "Ten more minutes."

"And you have no idea who he could be? What about Amanda's Instagram?"

"I promised I wouldn't look."

"Well, I didn't promise. Let me see…"

Mari listened indulgently while her mom went through her social media. Meena was linked with all of Mari's closest friends online, but it didn't bother Mari at all. She liked having all her loved ones connected.

"Hmm, there isn't any Mason tagged in her pictures," Meena murmured as she examined Amanda's profile.

"Well, he's Greg's friend, not hers," Mari explained. "They grew up together here in Eastview."

"Oh, her fiancé?" Meena asked. "I don't think I've met him. His profile is private… there."

Mari chuckled quietly as her mother added Greg as a friend and made a mental note to explain the random request when she saw him.

"Oh, he's very handsome, good for Amanda," Meena continued. "I didn't realize he was from Eastview… and this Mason is, too… ah, I see."

"See what, Mom?" Mari sat up straighter. "Did Greg add you back already? You found Mason?"

"No, I see that if this works out, you really aren't ever coming back to Chicago," Meena clarified wistfully.

"Oh, Mom," Mari laughed, feeling her tension dissipate. "Listen, it's time for me to go. Wish me luck, okay?"

"Okay, good luck, baba. I love you."

"Love you too, bye." Mari waited until her mom disconnected the call before she put the phone down. Her nerves returned in full force as soon as she was alone with her thoughts again.

"Get a grip, Marilys," she whispered as she flipped the sun visor down to check her makeup in the mirror one last time.

A moment later, her phone pinged with a text from Amanda, letting her know they'd arrived. She checked the time—7:57 p.m. —just long enough to take a few deep breaths, touch up her lip gloss, and walk in casually late.

Gathering her purse under one arm, Mari stepped out of her car and turned resolutely towards the restaurant. It was an unusually warm night, and as she walked across the parking lot, a full moon shone brightly overhead. In her mind, she heard her mother's voice declaring it yet another good omen. She noticed jasmine flowers spilling out of planters near the restaurant's entrance, filling the air with their romantic scent. With each step forward, Mari felt an increasingly powerful sensation of being drawn in like a magnet; she had the strangest feeling that she was walking toward her destiny.

Her stomach lurched when she noticed a tall man with a broad, handsome face and wavy, golden hair approaching from the opposite direction. His piercing green eyes gave the impression of a hungry tiger stalking toward her. Mari nearly stopped in her tracks. She wondered if this was Mason, and if so, should she introduce herself? Then again, what if she did and it wasn't him? Even if this wasn't her date, Mari had absolutely no desire to embarrass herself in front of this... specimen.

While she was busy stewing about the impending interaction, he reached the door first and held it open for her with a dazzling smile. She smiled back and thanked him politely as she went past, hoping she didn't look as nervous as she felt. Inside the restaurant, she spotted Greg and Amanda waiting near the hostess stand.

"I see you two found each other!" Amanda beamed.

Mari glanced back at the man, who had followed her closely into the restaurant. He was taller than she realized; she had to tilt her head back to look at his face.

"You're Mason," she murmured. It was meant to be a question, though it came out more like an awed statement. Her face flushed with embarrassment. She was sure her cheeks were glowing neon red.

Mason graciously pretended not to notice. "Guilty," he replied with an easy smile. "Mason Goodridge." He took her in boldly from head to toe. Mari was so busy melting under his appraisal that she forgot her own name. She started to put her hand out, but he surprised her by leaning in for a hug. His scent made her dizzy. "It's great to meet you, Mari. You look great; I like your dress."

Mari barely had time to mumble her thanks before the hostess announced their table was ready. As they followed her through the dining room, Mari felt Mason's hand on her lower back, guiding her forward. At the table, she eased herself into the chair he pulled out for her, grateful to be off her legs, which were quickly turning to jelly. As Mason settled beside her, his arm brushed against hers, sending a crackle of electricity through her.

While everyone busied themselves with their menus, Mari used the next few moments to calm down and think of something interesting to say. By the time the server left with their drink orders, she was back in control. She turned to Mason, prepared to strike up a conversation, only to find him gazing intently at her. She stared back, determined to keep her wits about her.

"So, Marilys. That's an interesting name." His voice was deep and assuring, and his eyes were such a mesmerizing shade of green that, for a moment, she forgot she was meant to respond.

"What? Oh, thanks, my dad picked it. It means 'shining sea' or 'beautiful sea'? Depends, I guess. My parents had this deal that since my mom named my brother, my dad could name me. My mom's name is Meena. It means 'fish' in Hindi, or, um, 'eyes that are like a fish'? Beautiful like a fish, not weird. Unless you think fish eyes are weird… I guess they kind of are. Anyway, my dad thought it was a nice pairing—the names. And since my brother had an Indian name, they gave me an Anglo one. My brother was named Mikul. It meant 'friend.' My mom is Indian, my dad is white. We all called him Mikey. My brother, I mean, not my dad. Mikey was my brother." Mari cut herself off, finally realizing the horrifying extent of her ramble.

At that moment, their drinks arrived, and Mari accepted hers gratefully. She sipped from her glass and forced herself to get a grip. Mason seemed like a great catch so far, but she reminded herself that she was, too. There was no need to be this flustered, just because he was beautiful.

"Sorry, that's a much longer story than you asked for, isn't it?" She laughed and shook her head, feeling more like herself.

Mason smiled. "That's okay. It was a nice story." They were the same words she'd offered her mother earlier on the phone; his tone was the same, too. He was trying to put her at ease. Mari melted all over again.

"So, half-Indian," Mason continued. "I guess that explains why you're so beautiful."

It was a complete line, one she'd heard a million times before, but it felt different coming from him. Blushing again, she retreated into her wineglass for a much-needed break from his intense charm, but his attention didn't waver from her face.

"You said your brother *was* named?" Mason asked.

"Oh. Right." Mari set her glass down gently. "He, uh... he died when he was fifteen. Drunk driver. I was ten."

Mason's expression softened. "I'm so sorry."

"Thanks. It's okay. It was a long time ago."

"Even so. You must miss him a lot."

"I do, but... it's weird. He was my brother, and obviously I knew him, and I loved him, and I miss him, but... I was so young. I'm just as accustomed to living without him as I was to him being here. Does that make sense?"

Mason nodded. "Yeah, it does."

Mari nodded back, encouraged. "My parents took it a lot harder than me. That was the worst part. My mom completely disappeared."

"Your mom left you?" Mason asked, horrified.

"Oh, no, not literally," Mari replied quickly. "I mean, she disappeared into herself. She went kind of catatonic. It took a while, and it wasn't easy, but my dad and I managed to get her back eventually. She's okay now."

"That's a lot to ask of a ten-year-old," Mason observed. "You must be incredibly strong."

"Well, I can't lift a bus, but I could probably kick your ass if I needed to," she joked.

Mason smiled with understanding. "I promise I'll never give you a reason to." There was so much care in his voice that, even though they'd only met a few minutes ago, Mari had the disorienting feeling that they'd known each other for years.

"That's a big promise to make on a first date," she mused.

"Well, if I break it, you'll kick my ass, right?" Mason winked.

Mari considered him, feeling suddenly skeptical. "You know, most men would find that off-putting."

Mason frowned. "Find what off-putting?"

Mari shrugged. "Most men seem to lose interest if a woman comes off too strong."

"Weak men," Mason snorted, then looked her up and down appreciatively. "You shouldn't have to hide yourself like that. You certainly don't for me. So far, I like you in all your glory." The twinkle in his eye nearly knocked Mari off her chair. She felt a strange and sudden swell of emotion threatening to overtake her. She needed to change the subject.

"Do you have any siblings?" she asked.

"Nah, only child," Mason obliged, easily picking up her cue. Mari marveled at his sensitivity. "Unless you count that idiot over there," he added, grinning at Greg, who was wrapped up in conversation with Amanda. Mari had almost forgotten they were there.

"Ah, so you're a big brat, huh?" she teased. Something dark flickered across Mason's expression, so fleeting Mari wasn't even sure she'd seen it, but it was enough to send a small jolt of alarm through her. "I'm just kidding," she added quickly, but the damage seemed to have been done. The atmosphere between them chilled.

Mason had leaned closer as they were talking, so his face was now only inches from hers. Mari held herself still while he studied her with an unreadable expression. She smiled uncertainly, but he didn't smile back. She scolded herself for speaking so carelessly. Just when she was sure she'd blown the entire evening, as suddenly as clouds parting to reveal the sun, Mason morphed back into himself.

"Well, let's just say I've pretty much always gotten whatever I wanted," he laughed. Those green eyes twinkled mischievously.

Mari was speechless. Mason's change in demeanor was so sudden, she felt as though she were witnessing two people in one body. A vague instinct tugged at the back of her skull, but it was drowned out by relief flooding her heart. She had the sense that she'd just narrowly escaped being devoured by him, and as she took in his glittering smile, she realized a part of her wanted to be.

"Well, first time for everything, right?" she parried.

Mason didn't reply, but the way he looked at her was electric. Mari began to feel overwhelmed by his intensity again, and though she didn't want to be the first to look away, she was forced to break eye contact in order to breathe. She caught Amanda watching them from across the table with a victorious grin.

For the rest of the evening, the conversation flowed effortlessly among the four friends. Mason and Mari got to know each other easily. Everything Amanda had told her about him was true—he was intelligent, funny, engaging, and totally at ease with her. Occasionally, the light scent of his citrusy cologne would drift past Mari's nose, and her stomach would growl with a hunger that had nothing to do with food. Over and over that night, she caught him studying her intently and was startled by his attentiveness.

Mari was used to fighting for connection with guys who were barely half-interested. This was so unlike any date she'd ever been on before that she began to fear Mason was too good to be true—too smooth, too gorgeous, too... into her. All she'd ever wanted was to be seen back by someone, to be attended to, and now, here was Mason, looking at her like some buried treasure he'd just unearthed. His appreciation for her was intoxicating.

As the evening drew to a close and Mason kissed her by her car under the full moon, Mari realized two things: first, she'd spent her whole life searching for a connection she didn't actually believe existed until she felt it with Mason, and second, that her search was finally over.

CHAPTER 2

"Y"ou know, if you weren't so full of yourself, you'd be the perfect boyfriend," Mari lamented. "Why is it so hard for you to just *not* do this? It's like you need attention from other women to survive. Is what we have not enough for you?"

"Mari, of course it is," Mason replied wearily. "That was nothing. I was literally just talking to her."

"You were flirting your ass off with her," Mari corrected.

Mason sat back at the table and folded his arms, his eyes tracking his girlfriend as she paced back and forth in her kitchen. Mari was spilling over with emotion, tears falling from her eyes, but he refused to be swept away alongside her. He was tired of having this discussion.

"I had zero romantic intentions with that woman," he declared.

"That doesn't make it okay, Mason. It's not appropriate when you're in a relationship with someone, and you're out on a date with them, to go and buy a drink for someone else. Even though you had no romantic intentions, it still feels disrespectful to me. Do you get that?"

Mason fixed Mari with a tedious glare. He hated it when she

talked to him like he was incapable of understanding human emotions. He understood her perfectly; he just knew she was wrong.

Mari was behaving irrationally. Never the type to sit and pout, she had voiced her displeasure as soon as the woman was out of earshot, after which they'd spent the entire ride home disagreeing about what actually happened. The discussion started calmly enough, but the more Mari spoke to Mason so condescendingly, the less inclined he felt to apologize, which only made her more upset, and around they'd gone for the last hour.

"What do you want me to say, Mari?"

"You haven't even said sorry yet, Mason."

"Fine. I'm sorry. Can we be done with this now?"

Mari processed this for a moment, then deflated. "Are you?"

Mason resisted the urge to roll his eyes. He was sorry to have upset her, but he didn't see the problem with his actions, nor did he care to be lectured. It's not like he'd snuck off and bought the woman a drink behind her back. She'd sat beside them at the bar and chatted with them for a while, and when her tab came, Mason told the bartender to add it to their own. He didn't even remember the woman's name—or if he'd even asked for it.

"Fine, Mari, I will never buy another person a drink ever again. Would that make you happy?"

Mari collapsed against the kitchen counter, massaging her temples. "Mason, that's not the point."

"So, what is the fucking point?" Mason returned, raising his voice. All this dramatic sighing and moaning was getting on his nerves. "A woman I barely remember sat beside us at a bar for a while, and we paid for her drink. The end."

"No, not 'the end,'" Mari replied, matching his volume. "She sat beside *you* so she could hit on *you*, and instead of demonstrating that you were with *me*, you encouraged her...*and* rewarded her with a drink!"

"Do you see her in the room with us right now?" Mason

demanded, gesturing around. He watched with satisfaction as Mari's mouth fell open, dumbfounded. "Exactly. No, you don't. Because I didn't encourage shit."

It was a bald-faced lie—he had definitely encouraged it, but not for the reasons Mari was accusing him of. He was loyal to her, a fact she conveniently forgot at times like this, but he'd had the same effect on women his whole life. How they chose to behave around him wasn't his problem, but it was nice to know that that power hadn't diminished, especially since his girlfriend seemed to be growing immune to it the longer they were together.

It was on the tip of his tongue to remind her that the part of his personality she was complaining about now was the very thing she'd fallen for herself the night they met, but he knew that would only prolong this argument, and he was beyond ready for it to be over. Mari loved to hash things out endlessly, down to exhaustive detail. Once she got going, it was nearly impossible to shut her up.

When Mason was first introduced to Mari, he wasn't quite sure what to make of her. She was hot, of course—they wouldn't have lasted this long if she wasn't—but with her dark features and compact, curvy figure, she wasn't what he typically went after. He could tell that she was also a much more complex person than he was used to, which was intimidating at first. Once he sensed her attraction to him, though, it was easy to deploy his usual 'charm and disarm' routine. Watching her eyes light up every time she felt his attention on her at that first dinner was fun. It became an amusing game for the evening, seeing how easily he could undo her. He didn't expect to fall for her in the process, and by the time he realized it was happening, there was no going back.

He could see why Amanda thought they would get along. Not only was Mari incredibly cool and confident, but she made a concerted effort to see and understand him on a level no one else had attempted to before. In exchange, she offered him such raw vulnerability, exposing parts of herself that he could tell she usually kept hidden. The first time they slept together, she got so lost in the moment with him—it made him feel powerful to know he could elicit such a reaction from someone like her. In the year they'd been together, it still never failed to excite him, seeing how his every little move affected her so profoundly... except in instances like this.

"You're making a mountain out of a molehill," he insisted. "Can we please just move on?"

Mari wrapped her arms around herself and studied Mason without saying anything. He withstood her appraisal impatiently, watching her eyes focus and unfocus with every passing thought. He couldn't tell what she was thinking, which only made him more annoyed.

"Well?" he pressed. She still said nothing. He watched a single tear roll down her cheek. "You know, even when you cry, you're really beautiful." He cracked a disarming half smile, but it didn't work. In fact, the comment seemed to upset her. Mason's irritation surged again. "What now?" he sighed.

Mari seemed to snap back to attention at the change in his tone. Her expression lifted slightly, then fell again, as if she'd just been given new eyes and was disappointed by what she saw. Finally, she whispered, "I don't think I can do this anymore."

Mason sensed a fresh argument simmering and felt weary all over again. "Gimme a break, Mar," he groaned.

"No," Mari persisted. There was a seriousness in her tone that he didn't like the sound of. "We've been together for a year, Mason, and we've been having this same argument for a year. I love you. And I hear you say you want to be with me, but you make me feel like... I don't know if you love me."

She paused, leaving an opening that Mason sensed he was supposed to jump into, but he was too busy trying to work out where she was going with this to respond as quickly as she seemed to want him to. A look of profound disappointment passed over her, confounding him further. She gathered herself and continued.

"I never wanted to be someone whose self-esteem was based on their relationship, Mason. I'm not that person! But you make me feel so much doubt. You make me feel like I'm creating problems when I know I'm just pointing them out. I'm not the problem."

Mason felt a chill creeping through his body as she spoke, but his mind still struggled to comprehend the direction of their conversation.

"What exactly are you saying?" he demanded.

Mari fixed him with a strange, sad expression.

"Spit it out," he insisted, but she stayed mute.

Mason pressed his lips together and zeroed in on his girlfriend, trying to read her. As they looked at each other, understanding solidified in his gut, gathering heat until it was glowing white hot and burning an angry hole through his stomach. It dropped lower, deeper inside him, igniting a pool of anger he'd never felt before.

"You're saying you want to break up," he clarified darkly.

Mari looked away, the gesture confirming what she was unwilling to say. Mason stared her down. He was still seated, and although she stood above him, she appeared to shrink under his scrutiny.

"Is that right?" He heard the growl in his voice and did not attempt to control it. It was clear Mari heard it too, by the way her brow furrowed nervously.

"No, Mason, that's not what I'm saying," she protested, her voice shaking. "That's not what I mean." She sat beside him and reached for his hands, but he pulled them out of her grasp. Wounded, she reached for him again, but he stood up, putting distance between them.

When he faced her again, her expression was riddled with regret. It occurred to Mason then that she had been bluffing. For one brief moment, his anger was replaced with relief, only to return in a fresh wave at her audacity for thinking she could manipulate him with such a cheap ultimatum. She didn't want to leave him, of course not. She was trying to control him.

Mari was eyeing him carefully as he processed his thoughts. He narrowed his gaze at her and was satisfied to see her shift uncomfortably, confirming his suspicions. For a moment, he felt like laughing. She should've known better. It was time to teach her a lesson.

"You just said I'm a problem for you," he began, amping up the hurt in his voice. "Do you have any idea how mean that is? I've been nothing but loyal to you, Mari. I'm here having this argument with you now instead of back at that bar with anyone else because I love you. But you're saying all that means nothing."

"No, Mason, that's not what I'm saying," Mari repeated. She was starting to panic—his plan was working.

"So, what are you saying then?" he challenged.

Mari faltered. "I'm saying... I don't know. Sometimes, I feel like my only choices are being with you or being happy."

Mason blinked, feeling a swell of offense, but he pushed it aside. As much as that hurt to hear, it was more ammunition for him to work with.

"Well, that's no choice at all, is it, Mar?" he exclaimed. "Fuck me, right? You're saying you'll be happier on your own? Then go be happy. Or do you think I don't want that for you either? 'Cause I'm such a bad guy, right?"

"Mason, I want to be happy *with you*," Mari pleaded. "Please! Slow down for a second."

Mason ignored her and barreled forward. "Well, I *was* happy with you," he bit back. "But if you haven't felt the same, then I guess there's only one thing left for you to do."

"Mason, I—"

"No." He waved his hands, cutting her off. "If that's what you think you need to do, then do it. I don't want to be the reason you're unhappy. That's not fair to me. We can end this right now."

Mason began storming around the apartment, gathering his things while Mari followed him like a puppy, begging him to stay and talk things through. He had to give her credit; she was trying her damnedest, and he couldn't deny it might've been nicer to resolve this night in bed instead of going home alone, but there was no going back now. No matter what she said or did, he held her at bay. He would leave her here tonight to feel his loss, and in a few days, he'd let her come crawling back. The look on her face as he walked out told him she'd already learned her lesson.

As he marched down the hall to the elevators, he didn't have to look back to know she was standing at her door, gutted, watching him go. When the elevator doors finally closed, concealing him from her view, he leaned against the paneled walls and basked openly in the afterglow of his victory.

She'd be back.

CHAPTER 3

"Mari's on her way," Amanda announced, hopping off her bar stool. "I'm going to the bathroom."

Mason gripped his glass tightly, but kept his eyes glued to the football game blaring overhead without comment.

"Nice, how far away is she?" Greg replied.

"Ten, fifteen minutes. Probably less. So don't include me in this next round."

"She's not coming in?" Greg asked, sounding surprised.

"No, honey." Amanda gave her husband a meaningful look. "She's just picking me up."

"Oh. Right. Okay," Greg accepted this with an awkward glance at Mason, who pretended not to see it. "Well, where are you guys gonna go?"

"We're going to check out that new rooftop bar downtown and then see where the night takes us."

"Downtown, huh?" Mason finally chimed in. "You gonna let your wife go out downtown looking like that?" He winked at Amanda. She rolled her eyes, but he could tell from her smirk that the compliment had reached her.

"Eh. She's looked better." Greg winced playfully at the punch

Amanda landed on his arm, then leaned closer to Mason. "I like to keep her humble so she won't think about leaving me." He also winked at his wife, who made a throat-slitting gesture. "Besides, I've found it's better to let the women gather once in a while, to blow off steam. Keeps them from getting out of hand."

"Joke's on you because I plan on coming home later and getting completely out of hand." Amanda smiled, pressing herself against her husband.

Greg nuzzled her neck. "I'll be sure to stretch."

Mason watched his friends paw at each other with a mixture of appreciation and disgust. "I see the newlywed phase is going well."

"Could've been you," Amanda replied dryly. "Mari did catch the bouquet at our wedding, but since you dropped the ball, I have to find someone else to keep her on track."

Mason ignored her and returned to the television overhead, leaving Greg to deal with the uncomfortable silence that followed. It had been nearly two months since he walked out of Mari's apartment after that last fight, and things had not gone according to plan. The following morning, she had texted asking if they could talk, but he didn't answer, intending to wait for a second message before responding. To his surprise, it never came, and he hadn't seen or heard from her since, except at the wedding, where they'd both kept their distance.

"So, when is she getting here?" Greg asked again, awkwardly trying to mend the moment between his wife and best friend.

Amanda kissed him with a small, appreciative smile. "Any minute now."

"Well, I'm sure you guys will have fun," Mason said. "How's she been?" He leaned back in his chair, allowing Amanda to study him. She was trying to make him uncomfortable, but he refused to give her the satisfaction. He grinned as her eyes narrowed in irritation.

"She's doing great," Amanda replied. "She got a few big commissions on some properties she sold recently, and we've been going to yoga a lot. I swear," she said in an aside to her husband, "I'd give anything for an ass like hers."

"That feels like a trap, so I will not respond, but good for her," Greg smiled, pumping his fist in good-natured solidarity.

"That *is* good for her," Mason agreed. "I'm glad to hear she's doing well." He drained his glass, his throat suddenly dry, then signaled to the bartender for another round for Greg and himself. He felt Amanda's eyes still on him and wished she would leave and go to the bathroom already.

"Mmhmm," Amanda hummed deviously. "Actually, I'm glad we're finally doing this tonight. We were supposed to go out last weekend, but she had to cancel because of some last-minute dinner invite. She wouldn't say who with, though, so I plan on getting all the details about him—I mean it, tonight."

Despite himself, Mason shot a sharp look at Amanda and found her beaming at him with sly satisfaction.

"You okay there, Mase?" she asked. "You look a little green."

Mason glared at Amanda, silently wishing his best friend had never met this stupid bitch. Over the years, he'd seriously considered breaking them up. From the moment Greg brought her into their lives, she'd been a meddling nightmare who talked too much and paid far too much attention to what he was doing. He knew Greg better than anyone, and he knew just what seeds to plant in Amanda's mind to end this relationship, no matter how long it had gone on. He considered exercising that power now but ultimately decided not to for Greg's sake. Instead, he smiled back.

"Never better," he replied, enjoying her discomfort at his unexpected reaction.

"Huh?" Greg asked, suddenly tuning in.

"Don't worry about it, babe," Amanda replied, smoothing his hair affectionately before sauntering off to the ladies' room. "Be right back," she called over her shoulder.

When they were finally alone, Mason turned to Greg with an accusing glare. "I know this is a setup," he scowled.

"Honestly, it's not," Greg insisted, then thought again. "Or, if it is, I'm not in the loop," he added. While Mason grumbled, the bartender dropped two fresh beers in front of them as he passed by. Mason and Greg drank silently and watched the game side by side.

"Do you want to see her?" Greg finally asked, keeping his eyes on the screen.

Mason searched for the answer in the bottom of his glass. "I don't know."

"Do you want to know what I think?"

"No."

"Okay." There was another long pause. "But what I was going to say was—"

Mason groaned loudly.

"No, no, really," Greg persisted. "Come on. I normally wouldn't say anything, but I feel like I've learned a few things since getting married. You're my brother, and I want to help you."

Mason begrudgingly fell silent and let his friend continue.

"I think you should try to see her tonight." Mason opened his mouth to object, but Greg kept going. "I think you should try and see her tonight, and you guys should really talk. I've been your best friend since we were ten, Mase, and I know you don't like to hear it, but you were different when you were with Mari. I think she was good for you. She made you more…I don't know. Grounded, I guess. And you're not going to like this part, but she's not like other girls you've dated, but you treated her like she was, and I think you took her for granted."

"Are you insane—" Mason tried to interject again, but Greg was on a roll.

"No, I'm not kidding. Come on, man. I love you, but you know I'm right. I watched you. You would have your arm around Mari, and your eyes would be all around the room looking for something better, but I don't think you'll find it, Mase. Maybe before Mari, you would've, but not now."

"So she's this incredible angel, and I'm just the piece of shit who got lucky with her. Is that what you're saying?"

"No, that's not what I'm saying."

"I never would've cheated on her. Do you seriously think I'm that kind of guy? Really, Greg?" Mason challenged, raising his voice.

Greg refused to take the bait. "I know you're not," he replied patiently. "I'm saying you're the best guy I know, and you've finally found someone who is a match for you. You shouldn't let that slip through your fingers. That's all." Having said his piece, Greg shrugged and turned his attention back to the TV, leaving Mason to stew in silence.

As annoyed as he felt about being talked to like this by his sidekick, Mason knew Greg was right. He had touched on feelings Mason thought he had stuffed so deep down that nobody could see them, but now that Greg had spoken them out loud, they were impossible to ignore.

He did miss Mari and the way she used to make him feel. They should've been back together by now, and if she had just played her part, they would've been. Instead, she had defied him—abandoned him!—and made him feel like a fool. He couldn't just forgive her for that. She needed to do something first to prove she wanted him.

"Uh oh, what do we have here? You two having a little lovers' spat?"

Mason's already sour mood worsened as he recognized the male voice behind them. Exchanging tedious glances, he and Greg turned around as Mari's real estate partner, Ryan Marsden, draped his arms over the backs of their chairs, enveloping them in a haze of cologne.

"Oof, gentlemen," Ryan purred, pretending to shiver. "It's chilly over here. How about a scotch to warm you up?" He signaled to the bartender with a heavy black credit card balanced loosely between his fingers.

Greg chuckled, nodding at the card. "Go ahead and tell him

to move our whole tab over to that thing. I'm not above it. I'll take the scotch, too."

"My man," Ryan laughed, thumping Greg's back with his fist. "You know I got you." He turned to Mason next. "Goodridge," he nodded civilly.

Mason returned with a smile that felt more like a grimace, but otherwise stayed silent.

Ryan was a longtime friend, though that was a term Mason used generously. They'd been acquaintances in high school, but when Ryan and Greg both went off to Washington State, Mason was forced to accept him as part of their inner circle.

After moving to Eastview, Mari had teamed up with Ryan on a real estate venture which proved highly successful. Friends had assumed they would end up together, but Mari hadn't been interested in him that way. Mason was proud of her for having better taste—personally, he always thought Ryan had a sort of rodent-like quality about him. Still, even after Mari chose Mason, Ryan remained protective of her, which had only added to the ongoing tension between the two men.

"Oh my god, Ryan! What are you doing here?" Amanda exclaimed, returning from the ladies' room. She greeted him with a warm hug. "Oooh, you smell nice," she observed as they separated. Mason suppressed a gag.

"Thanks, babe," Ryan grinned, oozing his trademark salesman charm. "Mari mentioned she might be passing through here with you guys tonight, so I thought I'd come say hey," he explained, eyeing Mason.

It took every ounce of patience Mason had to remain unbothered by this.

"Ah, I see," Amanda grinned back. "Well, she'll be here any minute, but we're not staying. We're going downtown… actually, do you want to come with us?"

Mason snorted into his glass. "You two are pathetic," he muttered.

"What was that?" Ryan asked, gently moving Amanda out of the way.

"Okay, guys, come on now." Greg got to his feet, sensing the change in the atmosphere. Ryan held out a hand to stop him.

"We're okay," he replied in a deceptively easy voice. He offered Mason a friendly smile. "I just wanted to make sure I heard him right. You said Amanda and I are what, Mase?"

Mason bristled internally at hearing his nickname come out of Ryan's slack mouth, but he kept his cool. "Oh, I said you two are pathetic," he repeated with a friendly smile of his own. "This setup is pathetic. Your thirst for my ex is pathetic. It's all just… well. Honestly, it's kind of adorable how stupid you guys think I am."

"Wait, what setup?" Amanda asked.

"Mase, nobody is calling you stupid," Greg cautioned. "Let's all just chill out for a sec."

"No, he's right," Ryan agreed. "I do think he's stupid. You can call me pathetic if that'll make you feel better, but that doesn't change the fact that you had a good thing and were stupid enough to blow it. You're just upset now because you're worried, and you should be. I've been with Mari almost every day for the past two months, and you know what we haven't talked about *at all*? You. She's moving on, and I'm not stupid enough to waste the opportunity."

Mason knew Ryan was just trying to get under his skin, and was annoyed to admit it was working. He had no desire to sit here and argue with this weasel of a human being any longer. It was time to end this, so he reached for the one trigger he knew would shut Ryan down immediately.

"Tsk, tsk, tsk," Mason shook his head sadly. "All this swaggy bullshit," he sighed, gesturing at Ryan's clothes, "and you're still the same little rat from high school, chasing after my scraps. You've been with Mari almost every day for two months and haven't managed to catch her rebound? Pathetic," he chuckled. "Go home, dude. She doesn't want you."

With that, Mason returned to his beer. Out of the corner of his eye, he could see Ryan's shoulders heaving. Mason listened for the familiar huff that indicated he was about to storm off, but he was surprised to hear laughter instead.

"What's pathetic is that you still think that old high school bullshit still works on me," Ryan chuckled. "Look around, dummy. Everyone's all grown up. Except you."

Despite himself, Mason glanced at Amanda and Greg, who were stunned to see Ryan standing up for himself like this. Mason opened his mouth, but without a response prepared, it appeared to just fall open in surprise.

"Hey, I get it," Ryan squeezed Mason's shoulder encouragingly. "You're a charming, beautiful man. You've probably never had to compete for anything until now." He leaned closer.

"But I have. And I'm good at competing. I read people for a living. Do you want to know what I see in you?" He paused to let his eyes wander across Mason's face.

"I see an unfinished stint at the local community college and a mediocre career in hardware sales. I see a pretty, insecure loser who uses charm to hide the fact that that's all he'll ever be." Satisfied that he had Mason sufficiently off balance, Ryan straightened and spoke so Amanda and Greg could hear him again.

"You may have been a catch before Mari, but now that you've lost her, people are going to see you for what you really are. And regardless of what happens between us, I know I'm going to be in her life much longer than you'll be, because she knows I actually give a shit about her."

Despite the ambient buzz in the bar, the silence among the group as Ryan finished his scorching delivery was deafening.

Mason's heartbeat pounded furiously in his ears. He felt his blood come to that familiar simmer and savored its heat while he stared his opponent down. Ryan held his position for a long time, but eventually faltered. Mason smiled.

"You know, Mari told me what happened with you," he

began. "We were in bed, exhausted…" He paused to appreciate Ryan's flinch. "And she told me all about how you confessed your love for her, but she didn't feel the same." He watched Ryan's face redden with the realization that Mari had disclosed this private moment to Mason.

"She tried to let you down easy by saying she wanted to focus on herself for a while. It was a total lie, but you knew that, didn't you? You accepted it because that meant it was her, not you. But then, *our* friends," he waved at Amanda and Greg, who were still frozen, "introduced her to me, and all that went out the window. She didn't want to focus on herself. She just couldn't stomach the thought of you." Mason cuffed Ryan's shoulder. "You go ahead and have fun with her tonight, bud. It's not going to change a thing."

Ryan's face was a gratifying mottled purple by the time Mason finished speaking. Out of the corner of his eye, he sensed a twitch in Ryan's shoulder. Mason ducked the punch easily, silently thanking him for swinging first. In a flash, his knuckles connected with Ryan's teeth, eliciting a satisfying crunch. Greg and Amanda dove after Ryan as he tumbled over barstools on his way to the floor. Grabbing his jacket, Mason called out a cheerful goodbye, and walked out the door.

The cool night air felt incredible on Mason's skin as he stepped outside. Every cell in his body was electrified. He closed his eyes, relishing the feeling as he walked toward his truck. He was so caught up in the moment that he failed to notice another person moving in his direction until their shoulders impacted, jarring him out of his reverie.

"Mason?"

Even before he heard her voice, he recognized her perfume— fresh, floral, and seductively familiar—but he didn't slow down. Mari called out to him twice, but he kept going, listening to her voice recede behind him. She sounded distressed; he was glad to hear it. He contemplated turning around at his truck and letting her run to him. Part of him wanted to lure her somewhere private where they could kiss and make up and put this whole thing behind them, but he decided against it. Punishing her felt just as good. He hoped their near miss ruined the rest of her night.

As he drove off, he decided enough was enough. The way everyone was sticking up for Mari and the fact that she and Amanda had gone to such lengths to put her in front of him tonight confirmed to Mason how desperately she wanted him back. He was tired of playing games now. They'd all had their fun, but tomorrow, he'd put an end to this nonsense.

———

The next day, Mason stood outside Mari's door, ready to play his hand. He was confident things would go his way, but he felt nervous all the same. Pushing those feelings aside, he adopted a confident, earnest stance and knocked on her door.

After an eternity, he finally heard the locks turn, and then she was there, looking utterly confused. "Mason? What are you—"

"Wait," he said quickly. "Just let me get this out." For a moment, it looked like she was going to argue, but she let him continue.

"I'm sorry," he began. "For last night, and for what happened the last time I was here. I thought I was happy before you came along, but you made me think differently about the future. You bring out something in me that I've never felt before. You make me feel seen. I wasn't ready for that, but I am now. The last time we were together, you said you didn't know where you stood with me, and I'm here to tell you. I love you. You made me feel strong, and I promise to never take that for granted again."

Mason lowered himself to one knee, then pulled out the ring he had purchased that morning.

"Mari... Marry me.

CHAPTER 4

On the morning of her third wedding anniversary, Mari stood alone in the spacious kitchen of the idyllic home she shared with Mason, drinking her coffee and feeling dissatisfied. She twisted her wedding rings around her finger while she thought about the early days of her marriage.

After she and Mason were engaged, life seemed to unfold like a fairy tale. She had no idea what to expect when he showed up at her door that day, but the things he'd said to her before dropping to one knee with that stunning diamond were so close to what she'd been yearning to hear that it was almost uncanny, like he was reading them straight from her mind. Mari knew her answer before he even finished popping the question.

When they shared the happy news, their family and friends surrounded them with joy and support. Even Ryan had accepted the development with a sincere gentleman's handshake and best wishes. Their wedding day was like a dream—Mason looked every bit the part of Prince Charming, and she was glowing with happiness.

Am I still *happy?* The question popped into her mind, surprising her.

"Of course you are," she answered out loud. Her voice

echoed as she stood alone in this massive kitchen, in this cavernous family home, in this bustling family neighborhood. The silence surrounding her was deafening. Mari had hoped that by now, she and Mason would have gotten started on a family of their own. Their marriage so far had been a happy one, except whenever the subject of children came up.

One year after the wedding, Mari knew she was ready to take the next step and start a family with Mason, but sensing he wanted to enjoy their newlywed phase a little longer, she waited another six months to broach the subject. As they climbed into bed one night, after days of rehearsing how she would bring it up, she turned to her husband and blurted, "I've been thinking about something."

Settling in beside her, Mason turned those hypnotizing green eyes on her and indulged her with a simple, "Tell me."

Even after all this time, Mari's insides still melted when he looked at her that way. "Well…" she began, suddenly shy, "we've been married for almost two years… and I know we haven't talked about it seriously, but…"

"But?" he prompted.

Mari struggled to find the words.

"Mrs. Goodridge, are you about to break up with me again?" he asked, feigning shock. "Because I don't have any more diamonds handy…" Since their last breakup before getting engaged, this had become Mason's favorite inside joke. It was just the right thing to diffuse Mari's tension.

"The opposite, actually," she laughed. "I want us to have a baby."

"Ahh. A baby," he repeated, nodding slowly. The way he said it made her feel like a kid trying to convince her parents to get a puppy. Frowning, Mason leaned back against the pillow and folded his hands. Mari chewed her lip anxiously, trying to read his mind.

"Well?" she finally asked. "What do you think?"

"Mar," he said carefully. "I don't know if kids are in the cards for me."

Mari blinked once. "What do you mean?" she asked. Mason merely shrugged.

"Is it related to your health?" she pressed. "Was there something…You never mentioned anything before. I mean… it… seems to work…fine," she faltered. "Not that I would care, of course. You know I love you no matter what. In sickness and in health, right? You just never mentioned anything," she repeated dumbly. "What is it? We can see a doctor. There are all kinds of specialists now—"

"Mari, stop," Mason cut her off sharply. "My health is fine."

"Then what is it?" she asked.

"I don't want to have kids."

Mari felt herself grow prickly hot, then cold. "What do you mean?"

Mason looked at her plainly. "It means what it sounds like."

"I don't understand. We're married. You never said this before."

He shrugged again. "It never came up."

"Of course it came up!" Mari insisted, raising her voice. "You—" she stopped to sift through conversations they'd had in the past. She knew she had brought up kids before, but in hindsight, she couldn't remember what he'd said in response. "We've talked about this," she finished lamely.

"No, *you* talked about it," he clarified. "You never asked me what I thought about it."

"Why was I supposed to *ask*?" Mari countered. "If *we* were talking about it, you could've shared your point of view. This isn't a dictatorship." Mason snorted, but she ignored it. "If this is how you felt, you should've told me before we got married."

"Or what, you wouldn't have married me? Gimme a break, Mari. You were so desperate to get married that you rushed us to the altar six months after our engagement. You didn't give us time to talk about this."

"You showed up unannounced at my door on your knees with a ring, and *I* was the desperate one?" Mari felt herself getting wound up and paused to collect herself.

"This is silly. I love you, Mason. I wanted to marry you. If you felt like we needed a longer engagement to talk about these things, you could've said so."

"*Wanted* to, past tense? So, what, you want to leave me now? Just like that? Good to know."

Mari struggled to temper her frustration. He always did this when they disagreed—escalated things so far past the initial argument, and in such a different direction, that she was forced to stop and recalibrate to avoid a complete derailment.

"That's not what I'm saying, Mason. Please. I love you. I'm just trying to talk about this."

Mason was quiet for a beat. "I love you too," he replied, softening.

"Well, good. At least we still have that going for us." She smiled, trying to lighten the mood. "But we're going to have to work through this now. I want kids. Why don't you?"

Mason shrugged. "I just don't feel that strongly about kids. I never did. It's not like I know any or enjoy spending time with them. I'm happy with the way things are."

"Okay, but that's different from not wanting them at all," Mari contended.

Mason shot her a tiresome look. "Look, I just know having a kid is not what I'm meant to do with my life."

"What the hell are you talking about?" Mari exclaimed, losing patience. "What are you meant to do with your life then? What is this great mission that I'm just learning about now?"

"I'm done with this conversation." Mason threw the covers off and swung his legs over the side of the bed. "I'm sleeping downstairs." Grabbing his pillow, he stormed off to the living room, leaving Mari to spend the night alone.

Mari was blindsided by Mason's revelation, but her instincts told her not to give up. His reasons for not wanting kids were thin, and she knew from their history together that he likely just needed a little push in the right direction. He was always resistant to change in their relationship until she took decisive action. It was the same when they got engaged—he didn't want to change, so she left him, and then he showed up at her door with a ring and all the right words. This time would be no different. The following morning, she began secretly flushing her birth control down the toilet.

She got pregnant fairly quickly. Mason was not happy with the news, but when she miscarried shortly after, her grief seemed to change his mind. He was supportive when she wanted to try again, but that pregnancy also failed, as did the next one. Eventually, they turned to IVF, but finances prevented them from going very far.

Much to Mason's annoyance, Mari disclosed their private struggle to her parents, who had moved to Eastview shortly before the wedding to be closer to their daughter and new son-in-law. Relations between Mark, Meena, and Mason were not always as warm as Mari had hoped, but they chilled significantly after they offered to foot the bill for another round of IVF. Mason couldn't believe his ears when Mari floated this to him.

"Are you crazy?" he shouted, standing up from the couch where they sat together.

"Is it *so* crazy?" she shouted back. "They know how much we want this. They want it for our family, too!"

"*Our* family, Mari. *Yours* and *mine*. This is an insane overstep! First, they move out here and insert themselves into our lives, and now they want to buy us a baby?"

"They don't want to buy us a baby, don't say it like that," Mari pleaded. "It's what family does!"

"My parents would never butt into our affairs like this."

"What is the problem?" Mari demanded through her tears. "You've accepted help from my father before. You didn't complain when he backed your landscaping business."

"And do you think he's ever let me forget that? Even after I paid him back? As far as your dad is concerned, I wouldn't have been able to get my business going without him, and I *could have*. It might have taken me longer, but I would've done it," he finished bitterly.

Mari watched her husband anxiously, unsure what to say next. She sensed the conversation crumbling into a separate issue she didn't want to get sidetracked into. Mason appeared to take her silence for judgment.

"Do you not believe I could've done that?" he asked incredulously.

"Of course I do!" she insisted. "And they don't think that—"

"I can't provide for their precious daughter without their help; that's what they think! I can't even give my wife a baby without their assistance. I mean, help me out here, Mari. You're killing me! What about my pride?"

Now, it was Mari's turn to be bitter. How many times in their relationship had Mason's pride held them back from finding happiness sooner than they could have? She bit back that response and sighed, defeated. "I'm just trying to solve this for us."

"Not like this," he asserted before storming out in typical fashion.

Mari knew her parents' offer was an overstep, but it was also a win-win in her mind. Mason's refusal to see it that way frustrated her to no end. They had struggled for so long. They were being offered such a rare gift, but in the end, she decided to let it go. Digging deep within for patience and acceptance, she assured herself what was meant to be would be.

For the next year and a half, time marched on, cycle by fruitless cycle. With every failed attempt, the distance between Mari and Mason grew wider and emptier.

Mason remained as dutiful as ever, but she began to sense undertones of resentment from him. He became increasingly distracted, throwing himself into his work and returning later and later in the evenings. Still, they kept up appearances and carried on like the Mari and Mason everyone expected. On the evening of their third anniversary, they celebrated by hosting a dinner for their loved ones at home, then retreated to their corners once the party was over.

As Mason slept beside her that night, Mari lay awake and stared at the ceiling, contemplating how to save their future. She loved Mason with all her heart; she wanted nothing more than to be with him forever. She'd have given anything for a family of her own, and she beat herself up about not being able to carry a child for her husband. It was that desire that had driven her to take matters into her own hands in the first place, hoping to cement them together as a family.

She began to wonder if her initial act had cursed their journey from the beginning. She knew it was wrong to lie about her birth control, but she fully believed at the time that it was the wrong thing for the right reasons, and in the end, once they had their baby, she'd be absolved. Instead, she had dragged him down this wretched, grief-stricken road with no idea how to even begin to turn things around.

Mari looked at her husband, breathing softly beside her, without a single worry line etched into his handsome face. He looked so different in the daylight, so disappointed, so weary. She blamed herself for their misery. How long before he blamed her, too?

CHAPTER 5

Now in its fifth year, the Goodridge marriage remained suspended in icy limbo. The once-smiling Marilys Goodridge now wore a perpetual frown as she struggled to solve her problems at home while her husband remained ignorant to the platonic chasm that widened between them with every passing year. Every day, Mari went through the motions while her mind constantly worked on the problem of how to be happy again. The sickness in her marriage was also leaching into other relationships outside of it. She could feel herself changing into a person she never wanted to be—someone who hid their private life out of shame.

She knew her closed-off demeanor was alienating to friends and family. She'd never felt so lonely. Though she wasn't ready to admit it, she feared her marriage was over. It pained her to realize how bad things had gotten between her and Mason. These days, they were more like polite roommates than husband and wife.

As she and Mason got ready side by side one morning, she tried to make eye contact with him in the mirror to strike up a conversation, but he was so deeply engrossed in his routine that she wondered if he even realized she was in the room.

"Have a good day... love you!" she called out half-heartedly from downstairs as she left the house.

"You too," he shouted back. It stung Mari's heart to hear his lack of interest. She'd rather he told her to fuck off. At least if they were fighting, it would mean some passion remained, but instead, there was nothing but cool, quiet apathy. It hurt so much more.

When her car wouldn't start in the garage, it was enough to send Mari spiraling into the depths of despair. She pressed her forehead against the steering wheel, trying to hold back tears.

The last thing she wanted was to go trudging back into the house looking as pathetic as she felt. Sniffling, she dug out her phone and swiped into her rideshare app to arrange a ride to work. To her relief, a driver would be there to rescue her in less than five minutes.

Grabbing her belongings, she exited the car and headed outside to wait, closing the garage door behind her. She was halfway down the driveway when Mason came through the front door, heading for his truck. He stopped short at the sight of his wife, who stood there like a deer in headlights.

"Mari? What are you doing out here?"

Mari shifted awkwardly as he approached, color rising in her cheeks.

"What happened?" he asked again.

"Car won't start," she muttered, doing her best to appear nonchalant.

Mason looked to the garage, even more confused. "So, you're walking?"

"No, no... of course not. I called a car."

"Why? I could've taken you. Why didn't you come back inside?"

Mari shook her head. "I wasn't sure if you'd be ready yet. This just seemed faster."

"Well, cancel it; I'll drop you off."

It's okay," she said quickly. "It's already, like, a minute away."

Mason studied his wife skeptically but thankfully yielded. "Alright, well, gimme your keys. I'll call a tow truck and get it over to the shop. Hopefully, it's a simple fix. I can pick you up after work, and we'll go get it."

"You don't have to do all that," Mari protested. "I can handle it once I get to the office."

"Don't be silly," Mason insisted. "Let me help you."

He was being so kind, but for some reason, it made Mari uncomfortable. She hated the way she felt. She hated what they had become. She wanted to take Mason up on his offer, but it felt strange to rely on him.

"Mar?" Mason prompted. "Keys?"

Mari glanced away, trying to hide her discomfort, and was relieved when she spotted her ride advancing slowly up the street.

"Okay…okay," she agreed, hastily digging her keys out of her purse and dropping them in his outstretched palm. "I gotta go." She gestured towards the car, which had stopped in front of their driveway. "I can be ready at five?"

"Okay then, I'll see you at five," Mason turned back to the house without so much as a peck on the cheek, Mari noted with a wistful stab. "I'll text you after I talk to the mechanic. Have a good day," he called over his shoulder.

"You too," she sighed, turning in the opposite direction.

Now, as she sat outside her office building waiting for him, Mari replayed the morning's interaction while she stared at the pavement, regretting every second of it. These were the moments she dreamed of—waiting for her husband to pull up like a knight in his shining white pickup, the way he used to for their dates, way back in the beginning.

She should've been warmer with him this morning, more affectionate, less apprehensive. She should have felt excited about this upcoming time with him, but instead, she dreaded the thought of an awkward and silent car ride home. She was so sick of herself.

"Aww, you look like you lost your puppy." A candy-scented shadow fell over Mari as a woman's cheerful voice interrupted her wallowing.

Mari looked up and suppressed a groan. Jeanine Alder, the irritating new assistant she shared with Ryan, stood over her with her lips pursed in a glossy, patronizing frown.

They hadn't needed an assistant, but Ryan insisted after noticing Mari's increasing despondence, hoping it would help take some pressure off her at work. Mari would've liked the opportunity to interview Jeanine first, but Ryan already had her prepped and ready to go as soon as she agreed to the idea. Once he introduced her, Mari understood his eagerness. Jeanine was tall, slim, leggy, and curvy in all the right places, with blonde hair and big, brown, doe eyes. She was biologically designed to weaken the average man and seemed to know it, but that wasn't why Mari disliked her.

Her first impression of Jeanine was that she was very friendly and bubbly but a little too familiar, bordering on inappropriate. She struck Mari as rather desperate. It was clear that being liked by people—and men in particular—mattered more to Jeanine than anything else, including competence, which was evident in the meager support she provided as an assistant. Mari was patient with her for Ryan's sake, though, guessing he probably had a crush on her. She owed him that much.

"Hey, Jeanine." Mari returned to her brooding, hoping Jeanine would take the hint. She didn't.

"Penny for your thoughts!" Jeanine plopped down beside her, tugging a strip of fabric Mari assumed was meant to be a miniskirt over her slim thighs. Her perfume was strong and smelled like cheap bubble gum with a hint of something sour underneath. Mari fought the urge to slide away from her.

"You know... long day," she murmured kindly.

"*Oof.* Tell me about it," Jeanine rolled her eyes dramatically.

She crossed one long leg over the other, sending her skirt so high again that Mari felt the need to avert her eyes. "My diary entry tonight is going to be a doozy."

"Diary?" Despite her desire to keep the conversation minimal, Mari's curiosity was piqued. She was surprised to hear that someone like Jeanine would have such an introspective practice. Perhaps she had misjudged her.

"Oh, absolutely," Jeanine nodded, reaching into a large, pink, designer tote bag. "I've journaled every day since I was thirteen. That's when I got my first one... for my birthday, get it?" she grinned. Mari didn't get it, but she didn't interrupt.

"I got this cute, matching pen for it, too. See?" Jeanine added, brandishing a pink, glittery, hardcover journal and matching pink, fluffy, feather-tipped pen. "Just like Cher from that old movie, *Clueless*? You know it? It's such a classic. Anyway! Cute, right?"

"Mmm." Mari nodded, eyeing the accessories cynically. She considered asking Jeanine what she wrote about but decided she didn't have the energy for the answer. "Well, that's a good habit."

"Oh, absolutely!" Jeanine agreed. "I don't know what I'd do without it. Keeps me sane, you know?"

Mari nodded again but kept her thoughts on Jeanine's sanity to herself. With nothing to add, she went back to brooding. Jeanine leaned closer until Mari could feel her breath tickling the side of her face.

"Hey!" she nudged Mari with her elbow. "Cheer up, Buttercup!" she chirped, tucking the journal and pen away again. "The good news is the day is done, right? Mind if I smoke?"

Mari wanted to say yes and point out that it was inappropriate and annoying to be addressed as "Buttercup," but that would take more energy than she had to give, so she left Jeanine to interpret her silence.

Rummaging in her bag, Jeanine pulled out a pack of cigarettes and lit one between such perfectly pouted lips that Mari got the impression she'd rehearsed that move many times before. Jeanine closed her eyes and took a long, deep, theatrical drag, exhaling loudly and collapsing against the bench.

Mari felt a migraine coming on as she sat through this performance. She kept her eyes down, trying to ignore Jeanine, but she could feel the young woman glancing furtively at her, searching for another opening.

"This weather's just gorgeous, isn't it?" Jeanine finally managed.

Mari glanced at the sky. "Yeah, it's getting warmer."

"*Finally*, right?" Jeanine exclaimed, grabbing onto the interaction. "I've been *dying* for it to get warm again. I don't do well in the cold; I'm a hot-weather girl. Like, when can I stop wearing these boring clothes and get into my swimsuit? My tan lines have totally disappeared *everywhere*. I might finally get to lay out this weekend. My complex has this amazing pool and hot tub, and it's so much better when it's warmer out. Hey! We should have a pool day together!"

Mari had zoned out while Jeanine prattled on, but she snapped to attention at this last part. "What?"

"A pool day!" Jeanine repeated excitedly. "We could have the whole office over."

"We?" Mari repeated dumbly.

"Oh yeah, it would be so fun. We could lay out by the pool, have some margaritas… We should do it!"

"I don't think I can this weekend…"

"Oh, well, what about next? I'm serious; we should get together!" Jeanine insisted. "What about Friday? I can put out the word. Nobody likes working on Fridays anyway. Let's do it! We can kick off the weekend at the pool and celebrate that it's finally warm!"

Mari began to feel overwhelmed. "I don't know, I have to see…"

"Oh, come on!" Jeanine pleaded. She was practically wriggling with enthusiasm. It was borderline obscene.

Mari wrestled with herself, trying to put her finger on why this woman was so irritating to her. She was just being friendly, but it felt too forced. Jeanine was so hell-bent on connecting that Mari got the feeling she was after something from her that went beyond friendship. Approval? Validation?

Whatever it was, Mari sensed a fervor in Jeanine that made her want to put distance between them. As she struggled to find the words to fend her off, she saw a white pickup truck rounding the corner. Relief flooded through her, washing away all previous dread about riding home with her semi-estranged husband. She stood up quickly.

"That's my ride, I'd better get going."

"Oh," Jeanine nodded, deflating.

"See you tomorrow!" Mari called over her shoulder as she hurried to the passenger door and hopped inside. "Hi," she breathed to Mason, "I'm glad to see you."

He returned her greeting with a smile, but his expression was somewhat puzzled as he looked past her out the window. Mari turned and stifled another groan when she saw Jeanine, who had followed her to the truck and was now standing at her window.

"And who is *this* handsome devil?" Jeanine exclaimed.

Mari masked a pained cringe. Trading glances with her husband, who was sizing Jeanine up with a bemused expression, she replied briskly. "This is my husband, Mason."

"Well, hello there," Jeanine purred. She reached across Mari to offer her hand through the open window, resting her cleavage on the frame in the process. "Mari didn't tell me she was married to a supermodel."

Mari pressed herself back to make room for the handshake, smiling tightly. Was Jeanine flirting or talking to a 5-year-old? It was hard to tell. She glanced at Mason, who appeared delighted as he took Jeanine's hand.

Of course, she thought bitterly. It had been a while since Mari witnessed Mason in action with another woman, but he seemed to slip into his former character with ease. She eyed their clasped hands uncomfortably.

"Very nice to meet you as well," Mason replied, "Miss…?"

"Jeanine. Jeanine Alder… but you can call me Jeannie." Jeanine pressed her hands together in a prayer position, lifting her elbows to mimic a genie pose. "Your wish is my command."

Mari guffawed.

"Jeannie, then," Mason obliged. He glanced at Mari with his lips pressed together in amusement. "Good day at the office?" he asked.

"Oh, fantastic!" Jeanine jumped in. "I was just telling Mari here that my complex has this great pool set up. You guys should come check it out sometime! We can have a little office pool day, soak up some sun and all that."

Noticing his wife's stiff posture, Mason demurred graciously. "Well, that's a really nice offer. We'll have to think about that."

"Yeah. Hey, we've got to go, but I'll see you tomorrow," Mari interjected, signaling to her husband. "Have a good one!"

"You too, enjoy your evening. Ciao!" Jeanine stepped back, waggling her fingers at them as they drove off.

Mari stared miserably out the window, feeling like she'd jumped from the uncomfortable frying pan into the awkward fire. Eventually, she closed her eyes, surrendering to the silence. She sensed Mason frowning in her direction occasionally, but she had no idea what he was thinking and precious little energy left to find out.

"Are you okay?" he asked.

Mari's eyes snapped open. "Hmm? What?"

"What was that back there?"

Mari straightened uneasily in her seat. "What was what?"

Mason raised one eyebrow. "Mar, we've been together a long time. I've never seen you actually flee from someone," he chuckled. "Who was that?"

It was embarrassing, but Mari felt the tiniest ember spark to life inside of her upon hearing Mason refer to them as "we." She paused to savor it, forgetting that he was still waiting for an answer.

"Hello, you still there?" He waved his hand in front of her eyes.

"Sorry. Yeah."

"So? Who was that?"

Mari sighed again. "My assistant," she grumbled.

"Assistant?" Mason repeated, surprised. "You have an assistant? Since when?"

"Oops." Mari realized that she hadn't told her husband about this new development. "Ryan hired her a few weeks ago... I guess I forgot to mention it," she added guiltily.

Mason paused to process this. "I didn't realize you guys had gotten that busy."

Mari held back from explaining that Ryan did it because he thought she looked so miserable.

"But you don't like her?" he asked.

Mari grimaced. "I don't know..."

Mason took his eyes off the road to study her for a moment. His expression light up with understanding. "Oh, no..." he breathed. His smile widened mischievously. "You *hate* her."

"No!" Mari protested. "Well... not exactly..."

"Yes, you do!" he laughed.

"Hate is a strong word," Mari insisted.

"It's okay, just say it, Mar," Mason urged. "Go on. It might make you feel better."

"Well, can you blame me?" Mari finally blurted. "She's awful!" She pressed her hands together, mocking Jeanine's genie impression. Mason laughed harder. Mari allowed herself a smile. It felt good to make him laugh. It felt good to laugh together.

"Yeah, that was... something," he agreed. "Seems like she's just being friendly, though."

"I suppose," Mari acquiesced. "But she's so 'in your face,' you know? And she's not a very good assistant. I swear, she cares more about everyone liking her than she does about being..." she trailed off, searching for kinder words.

"... yes?" Mason prompted

"... than... being... good at her job?"

"So, she's incompetent?" Mason cackled. "Oh boy. Why don't you just fire her then?"

Mari shrugged unhappily. "Ryan likes her, I guess."

"Ah ha," Mason replied, understanding. "Well, then she's probably good at *something*," he mused suggestively.

Mari shot a challenging look at her husband. "Care to elaborate?"

Mason pretended to zip his mouth shut, green eyes twinkling. "So, you have to put up with a shitty, annoying assistant because your partner is fucking her," he summarized.

"Well, I don't actually know if they are," Mari admitted. "I don't know what he's doing. I just assumed he liked her, but now that I think of it, she's not his usual type."

"Maybe he just brought her on to make you jealous," Mason offered, his tone flattening.

Mari scoffed. "Don't be silly."

"What's silly about that?" Mason countered. "We both know he's only had one type for years." He looked at her pointedly.

"Mason, please. Don't start." Mari sighed, though his jealousy stirred something in her.

"Fine." Mason shrugged, then added, "Maybe he's just a giant pussy who knows he doesn't have a shot in hell with a woman like that."

Mari looked at him sharply. "A woman like what?" she asked. Mason glanced at her, surprised by the sudden bitterness in her tone.

"Hey, you want me to kill her for you?" he asked, trying to disarm her. "I bet she's still back there. We could swing around and run her over with the truck. No one would know."

"Ha. Maybe," Mari snorted without thinking. Surprised at

herself, she quickly covered her mouth with her hand. Mason was laughing, scandalized.

"Whatever," Mari grumbled. "I saw the way you looked at her. Let's not pretend that that wasn't exactly your type, once upon a time."

"Maybe physically," Mason chuckled, "but I preferred my blondes a little less desperate and a little more sane." He met Mari's questioning eyes. "You can smell the crazy on that one a mile away," he explained.

Mari looked out the window as she considered this. She had thought similarly about Jeanine, but if Mason also noticed it, she wondered if Jeanine was worth more concern. Mason suddenly reached for her hand.

"Hey." He waited for her to turn back around. "Jealous?" he grinned.

Mari rolled her eyes but failed to hide her smile. "Please," she smirked out the window. "If that's what you prefer, by all means, set me free and go for it." She spoke defiantly, but her stomach twisted at the thought.

"Nah, I don't think so," Mason declined breezily, squeezing her hand. "Turns out I prefer hot brunettes." Mari looked back and found him giving her an appreciative once-over that made her insides quiver.

"How do you feel about buying dinner for a hot brunette before you take her home tonight?" she asked, emboldened.

The answering gleam in Mason's eye made her heart skip a beat. "Honey," he replied. "I'll take you anywhere you want to go."

Suddenly, it was as if all the ice that had built up between them over the last few years melted and evaporated at once. For the first time in a long time, things felt familiar between them. It filled Mari with so much hope. She would've rocketed into the sky if Mason wasn't sitting there, holding her hand.

"On second thought," she replied. "Dinner can wait. Take me home."

CHAPTER 6

The warm evening air ruffled Mason's hair as it blew through the open window. After a long day of work, these long drives home in the summer twilight were like a balm to his soul. Tonight, he opted for the scenic route, gliding along the dusky Eastview Highway that wound through the nearby forest around a vast, abandoned quarry lake. He drove in silence, allowing the cicadas in the woods and the air rushing past his ears to drown out his troubled thoughts.

Today marked the halfway point of his wife's pregnancy. He still couldn't believe it was happening.

Things had been going so well. He and Mari had finally broken out of the rut they'd been trapped in for years after trying to have a baby had almost destroyed them. The first time Mari brought up kids seriously after they were married, Mason knew it wasn't a good idea. They had a good life with just the two of them, and from what he'd seen, kids made everything complicated and unpleasant. Why would they do that to themselves? He had no interest in children.

Of course, by some cruel twist of fate, Mari ended up pregnant anyway. Mason was angry at first, but after seeing how happy it made her, and bearing her grief after the first miscarriage, he agreed to indulge her when she wanted to try again, thinking perhaps it might not be as bad as he thought. He had no idea what a long, exhausting journey the next several years would become. He grew weary of being pulled under every month by a wave of despair she seemed unable to control.

With every loss, the Mari he once knew disappeared into an obsessive, gloomy husk. He'd been right all along; having kids had made their life miserable—and they hadn't even managed to create one yet!—but Mari refused to give up.

After a while, Mason began to feel secretly relieved every time it didn't work out. He even contemplated ending things when suddenly, things changed between them. She stopped focusing on what they didn't have and started showing interest in him again. They were back to normal. He was happy... until a few months ago. Since he learned of this baby's existence, each month had passed like a long, ominous roll of thunder, filling him with dread.

Mason thought back to the day Mari broke the news. He'd gone away for the weekend, and when he returned home, she met him at the door with tears in her eyes and a positive test in her hand. Their official due date was October 31st, which he found ironic, given the horror he felt.

He was upset with himself for not being more careful. After all their struggles, he assumed it would be nearly impossible for her to get pregnant again, but he should have known better. He remembered the tremor that went through his legs as he took in her joyous expression. Every cell in his body told him to drop everything and take off running as fast and far as possible.

He realized then that he didn't want any of this anymore—this baby or this marriage—but he had no idea what to do about it. If he left, he'd look like an asshole. From that day on, he kept up the role of the devoted husband tending to his increasingly pregnant wife, while internally, he paced the perimeters of his confines like a caged animal, hunting for a way out.

Mason leaned his head out the window as he drove and took

a deep breath, inhaling the scent of the forest flying past him. At home, his lungs felt more constricted with every passing day, as if the baby was taking over his air supply while it grew. The closer they got to the due date, the tighter some invisible vice inside him squeezed.

Meanwhile, Mari's mood fluctuated wildly between glowing contentment and extreme anxiety that something could go wrong any minute, thanks to their previous struggles. Her feelings took up so much space that there wasn't room left for Mason to have any of his own. Enslaved by her maternal instincts, she'd even forced them to take in a stray black cat they'd found under the house, against his wishes.

"He's bad luck, Mari, and we already have a baby on the way. How are we supposed to take care of this animal, too?" he demanded.

"Look at this tiny face!" Mari ignored him as she scratched the cat's chin, entirely under his spell. "How could anything so cute be bad luck? Besides, he was already living here for who knows how long. This is as much his home as ours, so we should make him comfortable. I think you look like an Otis," she cooed to the animal. "He's part of our family now. We're a family, Mase!" That had been the end of that discussion.

Mason was tired of lying about how excited he was for all these changes. He was tired of doing everything and getting nothing in return. He was tired of coming in third in his home behind some dumb animal and someone who didn't even exist yet. He was tired of it all, and he wanted out. He had no idea how to do it, but he knew it wouldn't be easy.

Figuring out how to seize his freedom without giving up his reputation, business, or hometown was an incredibly frustrating riddle. He searched himself desperately for the answer, but he came up as empty as the darkening road stretched out ahead of him. Mason had a whole life here in Eastview, not to mention a flourishing local business, that he couldn't just detonate by up and leaving his perfect, popular, pregnant wife. People in their community would think he was a monster. It would be impossible to stay here and have a clean break, especially with a kid he wanted nothing to do with in the mix.

He thought about neglecting Mari to the point that she would want to leave him, but he hated that image, especially considering how everyone viewed her as his savior when they got engaged. The implication that he would've been nothing without her was still incredibly offensive to Mason; he'd never been nothing. He was Mason Fucking Goodridge! Didn't anyone realize how lucky *she* was to have ended up with *him* when he could've had anyone he wanted? And now, here he was, stalling on the way home, fighting against Mari's gravity. Sometimes, he really resented her for trapping him in this position.

The road ahead curved widely, and Mason drifted along with it, trying to release some of his frustration. To his right, a steep, tree-covered hill dropped down into the valley, offering a wide vista of the dusky sky stretched over the quarry lake below. For a moment, he wondered what might happen if he didn't follow the road's bend and went full speed over the edge. Would he fly?

He imagined the feeling of weightlessness as he sailed into the sky with nothing above or below him. What if he kept on flying and left his whole life behind? Exhilaration fluttered in his stomach at the idea.

His fantasy was shattered by bright headlights and honking from an oncoming vehicle. Mason snapped his attention back to the road, squinting as the other car's harsh beams shone directly into his eyes. He scowled and swore at the car's retreating taillights in his rearview, willing the driver to veer off the curve he'd just passed. As the other car disappeared around the bend in the road, Mason took another deep breath to settle himself back down, but it was no use. He'd never been so miserable. He prayed that the answer to his problems would present itself soon.

CHAPTER 7

"Mase, come look! Dad brought us a present!"

As Mason came down the stairs, Mari opened the front door to reveal her father, Mark, standing on their porch next to a box that was almost as tall as he was.

"Well, it's from your mother and me," Mark clarified, "but tadaa! It's the crib you wanted!"

While Mari celebrated with her dad on the porch, a wave of nausea nearly forced Mason to his knees. He gripped the banister tightly to steady himself.

"Wow," he replied, forcing a smile. "You didn't have to haul that all the way here. You could've just had it delivered."

"Or we could've come and gotten it with the truck," Mari added.

Mark waved them off. "Oh, I know. Your mother said to have it delivered, too, but I wanted to see your faces when you got it. I hope you don't mind. I know we promised to call before we came over, but I wanted to surprise you."

"Of course, we don't mind," Mari replied, glancing anxiously at Mason. "Right?"

"Right," Mason agreed, though he made no move to help his father-in-law as he struggled to haul the giant box over the threshold. Mark set the box down in the foyer and straightened to catch his breath.

"Your mother didn't feel up to it, but she sends her love," he said to Mari, then looked at Mason. The two men smiled awkwardly at each other. "I thought I could stay and help you put it together," he finally offered.

"Oh, that would be so great!" Mari exclaimed. "Thank you, Daddy. Mase can help you bring it upstairs…?" She looked at Mason, who nodded wordlessly with a smile plastered on. "Great, thank you, honey. I'll go clear some space in the baby's room." As she passed him on the stairs, she touched his arm. "You're okay, right?" she whispered.

Mason took in her worried expression. He did not appreciate Mark's unannounced visit or the thing he had brought with him, but he knew better than to object. Instead, he took comfort in the knowledge that one day soon, somehow, he would be free of all of them. He nodded again, caressing her cheek. "Totally."

Mari leaned into his palm and covered his hand with her own. "Okay, good," she breathed, relieved. "See you upstairs."

Half an hour later, Mason and Mark had unboxed the crib and laid its unassembled pieces around them on the nursery floor. They knelt together in the middle with instructions in hand while Mari rocked in the glider, looking on.

"I know it's been a few decades since I've had to do this," Mark mused, shaking his head in frustration, "but you'd think that in all that time, they'd have found a way to make this simpler."

"Don't fret, papa," Mari comforted him. "It's like a test. If we can figure this out, we can handle a baby, no problem. Right, Mase?" She grinned and nudged Mason with her foot.

"Mmhmm," he hummed distractedly. "Alright. Let's get this over with, shall we?"

Working together, Mason and Mark made decent progress for several minutes but reached an impasse when they disagreed about whether the crib bottom should be installed before or after the four sides came together.

"I told you it needed to go in before," Mason insisted, pointing to an adjustable mechanism in the frame's corners. "It'll get stuck on these if we try to do it now."

Mark shook his head. "No, son, look," he said, pointing to a different spot, "there's a notch here where the whole thing just slides and clicks in when it's done. I'm sure of it."

Mason's nostrils flared. He hated it when Mark called him 'son.'

"If it's supposed to just *slide* in there, I think that would've worked by now," he retorted.

Mari did her best to diffuse the escalating tension. "Maybe just try sliding it one more time," she suggested, "and if that doesn't work, you can take it apart and try it the other way."

"Thank you, honey," Mark said to his daughter, vindicated. He looked at Mason expectantly. Mason rolled his eyes but relented. They attempted to slide the board into place, and once more, it jammed in the same spot.

"It has to go in super straight, try it one more time," Mark insisted.

Mason shot an exasperated look at his wife.

"Dad," Mari intervened, "just go back and take it apart; this isn't working."

"It will take forever to do that," Mark complained.

"It won't," Mason sniped. "It will take five minutes. We've already wasted twice that much time arguing about it."

Mark pressed his lips together and glared at his son-in-law, but Mari interrupted before he could say whatever was on his mind.

"Dad, just try taking it apart; it's not like we're in a rush here. The baby's not going to show up and need a crib in the next half hour," she teased, patting her belly.

Mark was unyielding. "I think out of the three of us here, one of us has a little more experience with this kind of thing," he said pompously. "I'm telling the both of you, we do not need to go backward here. We would be wasting time." He sat back and crossed his arms.

Mari looked pleadingly at her husband. "I don't know," she began, "maybe—"

"No fucking way," Mason cut her off. He'd had enough, and watching his wife cave yet again to her whining parents was beyond his limit. "Why are we indulging this? This is the definition of insanity. We have tried this a million times, and it is not working." He glared accusingly at his wife.

"Would it kill you to back me up here? This is supposed to be for us, about us, and you're sitting here afraid to stand up to your dad over something this small." He shoved the half-assembled crib aside. "Where is it going to end, Mari?" he shouted. "Which family is your priority here, yours or ours?"

Mari sat frozen in the glider, taking in Mason's outburst. She opened and closed her mouth, trying to respond, but Mason could see he had put her in panic mode. Her eyes began to well up, but the sight of her tears only frustrated him further. Abandoning the crib, he stood up and declared he needed some air, then marched downstairs and out of the house without looking back.

Mason fumed as he walked. He was mad at Mari, and Mark, but also at himself for losing control like that. This tantrum certainly wouldn't help his case down the line. He was lucky he hadn't blown up and revealed his true feelings right then and there.

The accusations he'd lobbed at Mari about prioritizing her family over theirs were utterly hypocritical, and he didn't even know where they came from. He didn't care about having a family with her anymore. In the heat of the moment, he had instinctively reached for something he knew would hurt her. Mari constantly struggled with maintaining healthy boundaries with her parents versus neglecting them, especially now that she was pregnant, so it was an easy trigger.

Something suddenly clicked in Mason's mind. Everyone knew Mari's family was unusually close and that her sense of responsibility to her parents often clouded her judgment. On top of that, as her pregnancy developed, she had become increasingly pessimistic and paranoid about something going wrong, thanks to their previous struggles.

If Mason leveraged this just right, he could establish a pattern of behavior on her part that would eventually give him no choice but to leave her, driven out by her erratic behavior and negligence. The separation would probably have to happen after the baby came; the last thing he needed was to be blamed for any complications in Mari's pregnancy by leaving her beforehand. He resolved to stick it out until then and hoped the baby's arrival would help distract everyone when he finally broke free.

"Mase! Son! Wait up!" Mason's scheming was interrupted by by footsteps pounding on the pavement behind him.

"Fuck," he muttered. "What now?" With an unwelcoming scowl, he turned and watched his father-in-law jog toward him.

Mark was a tall, thin man who never quite outgrew the lanky awkwardness of his teens, as demonstrated in the gangly way he ran now. His longish, steel-gray hair flapped against his forehead, giving him the impression of a floppy, friendly dog. He was panting as he caught up and placed a hand on Mason's shoulder.

"Hey, look, I'm sorry about that back there," Mark huffed, gulping to catch his breath. "I know sometimes I can be a little overbearing, and I know that outburst was meant for me. I wish you hadn't taken it out on Mari."

Mason's jaw twitched at this, but he held his tongue.

"You're right," Mark continued. "Mari and me, and my wife, we are very close. Sometimes boundaries get blurred, and I know that's been challenging for you. You and I have never really talked about this before, but will you give me a chance to explain?" He waited for Mason's permission, but when it didn't come, he went on anyway. "You know, life hasn't been easy for Mari..." Mark began.

Mason reacted with grim skepticism but allowed Mark to continue.

"When our son died, her whole world got turned upside down. Nothing prepares you for the loss of a child, and I'm not proud to admit that I lost my way as her dad for a while after that. We both did—my wife and I. We relied on Mari far more than anyone should on a ten-year-old girl. She doesn't seem to think so, or at least she's never admitted it, but sometimes, I fear that we robbed her of her childhood years. We forced her to grow up because of the way we fell apart." Mark's voice wavered, but he recovered quickly.

"Anyway, after that, I vowed to make it up to her by being the most supportive parent I could be. And I guess sometimes I go a bit too far. Perhaps I get too involved." Mark smiled ruefully. "You'll see for yourself pretty soon. Becoming a dad will turn you into someone you never thought you'd be."

Mason couldn't help but grimace at the thought, causing Mark to pause and assess him for a long moment. Although he looked nothing like Mari, Mason noticed he had the same keenly perceptive expression.

"This must be hard for you," Mark finally offered. "I bet nobody has asked you how you feel about everything going on. I know when I was a new father, nobody asked me how I was doing."

Despite himself, Mason felt his anger toward his father-in-law recede. Mark was a stubborn, overbearing, passive-aggressive ass, but Mason forgot that he could also be incredibly empathetic, just like Mari was. He was never too proud to accept accountability or apologize when he hurt or offended someone. It was hard to stay mad at someone who had such little ego.

By asking Mason about his feelings, Mark had inadvertently given him a dose of some much-needed medicine. Mason had no desire to foster closeness with his father-in-law, especially now, but he did very much need to express his feelings, and here was a willing audience—not to mention perfect, fertile ground for him to begin seeding his newly formed plan.

"I have everything anyone would want right now," Mason began cautiously. "But it's coming at me very fast, and it is… overwhelming."

Mark nodded sympathetically, and they resumed walking together. "Sometimes, we can want things really badly out of life, and then when we get them, when they become real, it can be scary."

"I'm not scared," Mason said sharply. Mark didn't challenge this and waited patiently for him to continue.

Mason paused, unsure what to say next. He needed to choose his words carefully. As understanding as Mark was being, he likely wouldn't tolerate hearing Mason complain too much about his daughter.

Looking up at the trees above them, Mark scratched his stubble thoughtfully. "You know. My daughter is an incredible person."

Mason clenched his fists in his pockets, bracing for whatever lofty praise for Mari was coming next.

"She's always been so clear about what she wants," Mark continued, "and she's always had this ability to draw those things to her like a magnet, like the sun. When she was younger, there were plenty of times when she was ready for things before her mother and I were, you know? Dating, driving, wearing makeup, moving all the way to Washington, getting married," he chuckled.

"Don't get me wrong, we never wanted to stop her from doing any of it, but sometimes it would've been nice if our girl gave us a moment to go along of our own accord instead of charging ahead and forcing us to catch up with her."

Mason glanced sideways at Mark as they walked, on guard against the older man's uncanny insightfulness.

"You know, Mason, I'm always going to think my daughter is

perfect; I can't help that." Mark smiled helplessly. "But that doesn't mean I'm unaware of her imperfections."

"I do feel like I got hustled along this road faster than I would've liked," Mason admitted.

Mark nodded, understanding. "Mason, it's okay to question if fatherhood is what you want or if you'll be good at it. I'd even say it's normal. I certainly had some crazy, panicked ideas when Meena first got pregnant. But the moment I held my son for the first time, I never looked back. I found my happiness. It's easier said than done, but I know you can do it too."

Mason stopped walking and faced Mark. "Believe me, that's all I want," he replied ardently. Mark studied the fire in Mason's eyes and nodded, apparently satisfied with what he saw.

"Good," he affirmed. "Why don't we head back now? I'll get out of your hair, and maybe you can try to patch things up with Mari. She's probably pretty lonely back there."

She'll get used to it, Mason thought to himself as they turned towards home.

CHAPTER 8

Mari didn't know what was wrong with her. Everything was going perfectly fine. Her baby was growing strong and healthy, and she couldn't have asked for a more attentive partner, but something just didn't feel right.

A gnawing feeling had settled in the pit of her stomach since Mason shouted at her and stormed out after the crib incident a few weeks ago. His words that day had touched on one of her deepest fears—Mari hoped that this baby would bring everyone she loved closer together, but Mason had implied that he was feeling pushed out. She didn't know how to begin to fix that. She loved Mason more than anything; she was carrying a piece of him inside her! She felt closer to him than ever. How could he not feel the same?

She was grateful for whatever her father had said to bring him home that day, though neither of them shared what was discussed. Since then, Mason seemed much more relaxed. He encouraged her to spend as much time with her friends and family as she wanted without placing any demands on her; he was patient and kind when they spoke, but his words often left her unsatisfied. He was affectionate, but even wrapped up in his arms, she sensed distance between them. She couldn't shake the feeling that there was something troublesome simmering behind those dazzling, disarming smiles. She lived in a constant state of anxiety about what was going on in his head, pushing herself to the brink of insanity.

"I know something is wrong, Mason! I know it!" she screamed when she finally broke down. "Just tell me what it is! I can handle it. *We* can handle it! Please!" she begged, but he only looked at her with alarm.

"Mari," he replied, his voice soft but full of confusion. "I'm doing everything I can to be supportive, but somehow, it's still not enough for you. Why are you being so hard on me right now? What else do you want me to do?"

Mari didn't know how to answer that question. He wasn't doing anything wrong; she just didn't *feel* right. She wasn't trying to be hard on him, and she felt guilty for making him feel that way, but she couldn't turn this feeling off.

"I'm sorry, Mase. I don't know what's wrong with me," she admitted, covering her face with her hands. "I feel like I'm not in control of myself."

"I have to be honest, this version of you is new for me, too," he replied, looking her over with concern. "I know you're going through a lot right now between the hormones and the baby nerves, but the doctor said you're doing fine, right? I get why you're a little paranoid, but it's okay. I understand. It'll be okay."

His words left Mari feeling both comforted and strangely hollow. She was relieved to know he wasn't upset with her, but hearing him say he didn't recognize her was terrifying. She looked into his eyes, searching for answers to all her lingering questions, and saw him studying her back. What was he looking for? What wasn't he seeing in her anymore?

Mari felt herself unraveling all over again. She wanted to ask, but she feared doing so might push him further away. She didn't want him to think she didn't trust him. Maybe she *was* just paranoid.

"I don't know what's wrong with me," she repeated, burying her face against his chest. "I'm sorry. I know I've been off balance, but… don't leave me, okay?" she whispered, half-joking into his T-shirt. "I love you."

Mason wrapped his arms around her and squeezed affectionately. "I love you too. You'd have to go pretty far off the deep end for me to even consider that, Mar."

There it was again—that twinge of doubt that twisted her gut when he said something that sounded like love, but felt like a warning. They were holding each other, but she could feel him slipping through her fingers. She needed to hear him say he'd never leave her. She started to ask for it but quickly changed her mind. She'd only be casting more doubt, and being in his arms felt too good. She burrowed into him again without another word, tightening her grip around his waist.

By August, as long, hot afternoons stretched into leisurely, warm evenings, Mari did her best to relax into her third trimester and focus on the good in her life. At the end of every day, she rocked on her porch swing with Otis curled at her side and watched the neighborhood wind down while she waited for Mason to return home. She closed her eyes and imagined their future son racing up the driveway on his bike as the streetlamps blinked on, demanding to know if dinner was ready. She smiled at the memories yet to come.

Otis began to purr contentedly beside her as if he could feel what she was feeling. A warm breeze carried the heady scent of roses past her, and she opened her eyes to gaze at the trellis near the front door where she'd planted climbing roses when they first moved in. Mason had advised against it, telling her they'd be too high maintenance, but Mari insisted, arguing that they would be beautiful and invite good luck to their door. In the end, she had won out, and she was happy to see them blooming big and bright in the summer heat.

Glancing up, she noticed a large, round, russet-colored moon peeking through the treetops and thought back to the night she and Mason met. She remembered kissing him good-night in the parking lot under that full moon, feeling the same excitement and anticipation over what the future held for them. She marveled at how far they'd come together and felt the urge to celebrate all they had to be grateful for. Amanda and Meena had already thrown her a baby shower, but there hadn't been a celebration that included Mason, and he deserved something, too. Perhaps it would even help alleviate whatever was causing the shadowy undercurrent she still sensed in him.

It had been a while since they'd spent time with their friends like they used to, and she decided that when he came home that night, she'd suggest having a few people over for dinner tomorrow evening. Mari was making tea in the kitchen when he finally trudged in, looking completely exhausted.

"You're home!" she exclaimed, delighted.

"Hey," Mason mumbled, tossing his keys and backpack onto the counter.

Mari watched him settle in. His business had taken off considerably over the last year, but as the client list for Goodridge Landscaping grew, Mason was forced to work later nights to catch up on invoicing and paperwork. Once they found out she was pregnant, Mari tried to convince him to hire help, but he insisted on having complete control of his books. She was happy for him and his success, and she knew it was a point of pride, but she hated seeing him so depleted.

"I was going to drink this tea and watch a movie while I waited up for you. Do you want to watch it with me, or are you tired? Are you hungry? I can fix you something."

"I'm just tired," he muttered. His voice had an even thinner edge to it than usual.

Mari studied her husband closely. He looked drained and tense, with long shadows underneath his eyes. She wanted to ask him what was up, but there was a fine line between showing care and stifling him, especially at times like this.

"I get it," she replied delicately. "Are you sure I can't make you something to eat?"

"I'm good." He reached around her to get a glass from the cabinet, then moved to the sink.

"Okay…" She stepped warily out of his way. Mason focused on the taps as he filled his glass with water. She realized he hadn't looked at her once since he walked in. "Everything okay today?" she asked.

Mason shrugged. "Yeah. Why?"

"You just seem a little more than tired."

"It's whatever. Just work stuff."

"Are you sure?" she pressed gently. "Do you want to talk about it?"

"Nope," came his flat reply. He drank his water with his back to her.

Mari felt her patience slipping away. Mason might've had a bad day, but he was being rude, and she didn't deserve it. After months of trying to manage his delicate moods and her own anxiety, Mari was on the verge of giving in to anger. Mason suddenly turned around as if he, too, sensed the shift in her. They exchanged tense, warning glares for a moment before he dropped his shoulders with another heavy sigh.

"I'm sorry," he relented. "It was just a long afternoon and I'm tired, but everything really is fine."

Mari raised one skeptical eyebrow.

"Seriously." Mason came closer and kissed the top of her head. "I'm okay. Let's talk about something else," he suggested, adopting a brighter tone. "Tell me about your day."

The sudden switch in his demeanor was jarring, but Mari forced herself to move on with him. "Oh, you know," she replied breezily. "Just another boring day, cooking up a tiny person in my body."

Mason grinned and pretended to shudder. "Creepy."

They laughed together. Mari was relieved to feel the tension between them evaporate instantly.

"Actually, I wanted to talk to you about something," she said. "Do you think tomorrow will be another late one for you?"

Mason stiffened, then looked at her warily. Mari wondered again what could have happened today to put him so on edge, but she put it out of her mind, not wanting to drag them backward.

"I'm asking because I was thinking of inviting some friends over for dinner tomorrow night," she soldiered on. A grumpy shadow passed over her husband's beautiful, fatigued face. "Not a huge group," she added quickly. "Just Greg, Amanda, and maybe one or two others. It's such short notice, I'm not even sure who could come. I... I wanted to see how you felt about it first... before I invited anyone." She faltered, clocking the pensive frown on Mason's face. She paused to let him speak, but he said nothing.

"It's just been so warm out in the evenings lately," she went on. "I thought it might be nice. We could grill and do some wine; well, you guys can," she smiled, patting her belly affectionately. "And it's a full moon tomorrow, which I thought would make for some nice ambiance... it could be romantic..."

Mason's curious expression brought color to Mari's cheeks.

"Or it can just be Greg and Amanda... if you're up for it," she shrugged, backtracking.

Mari's heart sank as she watched her husband weigh her proposal in his mind with a distasteful frown. She was about to abandon the idea when his expression suddenly lifted.

"Yeah, that would be nice," he finally agreed.

"Are you sure?" Mari asked, unconvinced. "It's okay if you don't want to."

"No, let's do it," Mason replied with a smile. "It's a good idea, invite whoever you want. What time are you thinking?"

Mari stared at her husband, bewildered. She always knew him to be capricious, but his mood swings were especially unnerving tonight. Mason's expression was now completely smoothed over, but she knew there was more on his mind. He looked at her expectantly. Mari debated pressing him a little harder.

"I don't know, I guess... six?" she finally replied.

Mason nodded. "Okay, that sounds good. I'll come home by four to help you."

"Okay... great," she conceded.

"Great."

They stood on opposite sides of the kitchen, evaluating each other.

"Was there something else?" Mason finally asked.

Mari felt some vague instinct tugging at the back of her skull, but she couldn't articulate what it was. She opened her mouth to speak, but no sound came out. A million questions were stuck in her throat. She wasn't sure which one to ask first or which one would make things better rather than worse. She swallowed and shook her head. "No, I guess not."

"Okay, good. In that case, I'm going to take a shower and get some sleep." Mason smiled at her. It lifted his cheeks, but his eyes remained flat. Mari was reminded of one of those grinning Halloween masks with the eyes cut out. When he leaned in for a kiss, Mari was surprised by a sudden instinct to back away from him.

"Good night," he murmured against her forehead. His lips felt cool on her skin.

Mari closed her eyes and focused on enjoying his closeness. As he headed upstairs, Mason flipped off the lights, leaving her alone in their half-darkened kitchen to stare after him.

CHAPTER 9

Mari woke up the following day still feeling uneasy while her husband whistled through his morning routine. She hadn't seen him like this in a long time. Suddenly, he was his old self again—charming, affectionate, and completely irresistible. This was the Mason she'd been missing for months, but his sudden and unexpected return left Mari unsettled. Whatever was weighing on him yesterday seemed to have evaporated entirely from his shoulders overnight, while for her, that nagging feeling in the back of her skull grew more and more urgent as the morning went on.

Mari was annoyed with herself for being such an anxious pessimist. She chided herself for her lack of gratitude and forced herself to focus on the good: the weather forecast predicted a breezy, warm day with highs in the mid-eighties; there would be some clouds later and a rainstorm overnight, but nothing that would spoil their dinner plans; she had a wonderful evening with friends to look forward to, and her happy, handsome husband had woken up smiling at her. There was nothing to be nervous about.

Still, when she thought about the darkness that flickered across Mason's face last night, anxiety swelled up and threatened to consume her. She pushed it down defiantly. She and Mason were finally in a good place. It was probably just hormones, and she refused to let them derail her or dampen her spirits. Mari looked forward to the day when she was no longer pregnant and back in control of her emotions.

To distract herself, she got busy preparing for their guests that evening. In the end, only Greg, Amanda, and Ryan were able to accept her invitation at such short notice, and that was perfectly fine with her, although she worried that Mason's good mood might be spoiled when she texted him the final guest list and he saw Ryan on it. She debated uninviting him.

It was no secret that Ryan and Mason hated each other, but what Mason didn't know—and what Mari had kept from him— was how familiar Ryan was with the current ups and downs in the Goodridge marriage. Mari hadn't done it on purpose, but she and Ryan worked side-by-side every day for the last several years. He couldn't ignore the emotional rollercoaster she'd been on, and it was impossible for her not to open up about it. She'd needed a friend, and Ryan had appointed himself as her emotional guard dog. If he caught even a whiff of discord between her and Mason tonight, he might pounce in her defense. It certainly wouldn't be the first time.

Though she hadn't witnessed it, she knew all about the bar fight they'd had over her before she and Mason got engaged. That was the last thing she wanted tonight. Still, something about the way Mason smiled at her in the kitchen last night made her want Ryan around. She decided to keep him on the list and texted it to Mason as is. She braced herself for his reaction, but surprisingly, he didn't seem to care.

> Kk, lmk what you need from the store. See you at 4 x.

Breathing a sigh of relief, she texted him back with a short list of last-minute groceries. Mason returned home promptly at 4:00 p.m., as promised, with everything she requested. He helped her set up, gave the grill a once-over, and then, after one last check-in to make sure Mari was good, headed upstairs with a pregame beer to shower and change.

In the kitchen, Mari listened to upbeat music while she put the finishing touches on her appetizers. Every once in a while, she'd hear Mason singing along loudly and off-key upstairs and smile, basking in his good mood. When he returned to the kitchen, refreshed and ready to receive their guests, he wrapped Mari in a bear hug and waltzed her around the island before releasing her and going to the fridge.

"I know why I wanted to have this dinner, but what are *you* celebrating?" she teased.

Grinning, Mason cracked open a fresh beer, took a long swig, and let out a refreshed, "Ahhhh!" He sighed happily. "Let's just say I had a problem yesterday that I no longer have today, and that feels *great*!"

Mari laughed with him, but her instincts sharpened. "Care to elaborate?"

Mason prowled toward her with a mischievous look and pulled her close. He put his lips to her ear as if he were about to share a big secret. Mari shivered as his cheek brushed against hers. His scent, fresh from the shower and citrusy from his cologne, made her feel dizzy.

"Nope!" His lips popped against her ear, sending a tingle down her spine. He kissed her on the cheek, then squeezed her shoulder and went to start the grill. His golden hair gleamed in the afternoon sunlight as he stepped outside. Mari watched him go, spellbound.

"Something's gotten into you two tonight," Amanda teased as Mari settled beside her later that evening.

The two women were lounging on a cozy teakwood sectional under a pergola in their backyard, having a drink and watching Mason, Greg, and Ryan stand vigil over the grill. The sun was just beginning to set, but the wooden deck had absorbed the day's heat and still gave off plenty of warmth. Mari rested comfortably against the canvas cushions with her bare feet tucked underneath her. She returned her friend's grin, crinkling her nose mischievously.

"Ugh. You don't know how happy it makes me to see you like this," Amanda gushed. "So, spill! What changed?"

Mari couldn't stop smiling as she tried to come up with an answer. "I don't know! It kind of happened overnight. He just... woke up different." She paused to consider it some more. "I think something happened at work, but he hasn't said what."

Amanda frowned. "At work?" she repeated.

"He said some problem he had yesterday is gone today." Mari shrugged. "Honestly, whatever it is, I don't care. This whole time, I've been worried that the problem was us, but... I guess I was overthinking it, and it's just been work stressing him out. I've been so wrapped up in pregnancy stuff I guess I was a little tunnel-visioned," she sighed. "Things are still a little up and down with us, but the closer we get to B-Day, the more 'up' he is than 'down,' you know what I mean? So, I'm just grateful."

"I guess..." Amanda replied, then, seeing the worry in Mari's expression, added, "Don't mind me. My husband's a golden retriever trapped in a human body. I don't know what having a complex partner is like." She smiled reassuringly.

"Fair enough," Mari laughed. "I just mean, I think Mase and I are both seeing the end in sight and feeling the pressure lift. You know, last night when I suggested having you guys over, I was a little nervous he'd say no. I'm so glad he didn't."

"Why would he say no to us?" Amanda asked, surprised.

"Oh, I don't think he would've been saying no to *you*. I guess I was worried he might say no to *me*—to putting together a dinner and hosting with me. He's so hot and cold sometimes, and the preggo-anxiety doesn't help when I'm trying to figure out where I stand with him some days."

Amanda frowned again. "Mar, you should never feel unsure about where you stand with your husband…"

"No, I know," Mari replied quickly. "That's not what I meant. I just mean…Look, this pregnancy has kind of done a number on us. I know it's what we wanted, but it definitely hasn't been easy, and I think it affected us in different ways. I wasn't an anxious person before this, and now I feel insane with worry about everything all the time. I know he's struggled with it, too. I haven't exactly been easy."

"Nah, fuck that!" Amanda declared loudly. Across the deck, the men stopped talking and glanced over at them, concerned. Mari smirked into her ginger ale.

"We're fine!" Amanda called back, raising her glass. She waited for them to lose interest before turning back to Mari.

"Fuck that," she repeated. "You're pregnant! You are literally growing a human in the middle of your guts. Your body, your hormones, and your goddamned mind have been taking turns betraying you for the last seven months." She gestured at their husbands with her wine glass, sloshing its contents.

"They're never going to understand what that's like, and as women, we have the right to be as difficult and insane as we need to be to get us to the finish line and deliver a healthy little baby. They can fucking deal."

Mari grinned at her friend's candor.

"You're not even the worst Pregzilla I've ever heard of!" Amanda went on. "Not even close! God help Greg whenever we get there. I love him so much, but I will probably be a complete batshit-snack-monster-T-Rex, and there's nothing he or I can do to change that." Amanda shook her head resignedly while Mari cackled.

"Hmph. You haven't been *easy*…" she muttered. "Honestly? Fuck Mason. I love him. I love you both to death," she clarified, "but fuck him." Amanda concluded by finishing her wine.

"Yeah, maybe you guys should wait until our baby is a little bit older so we can all support Greg properly when the time comes," Mari laughed.

"That's probably a good idea," Amanda agreed.

"I appreciate the pep talk, though. And you're right. I should cut myself some slack." Mari sighed. "Thank you for reminding me."

"What are friends for?" Amanda asked as she reached for the nearby bottle to refill her glass. "Anyway, I'm not worried about you guys. Especially after seeing you together today," she smiled.

"Maybe it's this full moon making us feel a little wild," Mari joked.

"Oh, it's definitely the full moon," Amanda nodded. "I always feel like that."

"You do?"

"Oh, absolutely," Amanda chuckled. "Every time there's a full moon, I feel a little unhinged, but I think that's true for women in general. We're like werewolves. Some of the best sex Greg and I have ever had has been during a full moon."

"Makes sense for a werewolf and a golden retriever," Mari laughed.

"Go ahead and laugh, but you'll see," Amanda replied. "Based on how you and Mason are behaving, you two are in for a wild night." Mari rolled her eyes as Amanda let out a playful howl, but something stirred excitedly in her.

"Who knows," she sighed. "It's honestly been forever since we've done anything. I've been so gross and pregnant that neither one of us had been interested."

Amanda was undeterred. "Welp. You better dust that thing off because Greg and I already bet money that you're getting some tonight!"

Mari nearly choked on her ginger ale.

"Calm down, virgin, I'm just teasing," Amanda grinned, thumping her on her back. "But I hope I'm right. It sounds like you're long overdue for a little TLC. I'll even help you hide his phone so he doesn't get distracted."

"His phone?"

"Yeah, when he's not staring at you, he's staring at *it*. You haven't noticed?"

Mari shook her head. She'd been so starstruck by Mason all afternoon that she hadn't noticed at all, but as she looked at him now, he was engrossed in something on his screen. He suddenly looked up and caught her staring. Mari held his gaze. He winked at her, sending a flutter of anticipation through her insides.

"You ladies hungry?" he called out. Mari's throat had gone a little dry, so Amanda responded for her.

"Starving," she called back suggestively.

By the time they all sat down to eat, the sun had dipped well below the trees, but the air was still warm and hung heavy around them, thickening with humidity ahead of the approaching storm. Big, puffy clouds rolled in with the twilight, but between the candles on the table, the twinkle lights over-head, and the steadily rising moon, they had plenty of light.

All of Mari's senses heightened as evening fell. She sat next to her husband at dinner, feeling waves of heat roll off his body. As they ate, his arm occasionally brushed against hers. The contact sent shivers down her spine, making the little hairs on the back of her neck stand on end. In the humidity, his scent lingered around her so powerfully she could taste it, creating a hunger that the meal laid out before her couldn't begin to satisfy. When he laughed, the sound tickled her rib cage. Every time she looked at him, she felt a jolt of electricity go through her. She wondered if everyone else could see them, too, like flashes of lightning that accompanied the soft rolls of thunder that had begun to sound in the distance.

Since Amanda pointed it out, Mari couldn't help but notice that Mason kept his phone on the table, face down, for the entire meal. Every once in a while, it would buzz for his attention, and she'd watch him pick it up and glance at an incoming message with an irritated look before setting it back down without responding. It happened over and over—vibrate, distract, scowl, ignore. Mari did her best to ignore it, too, until it went off for what felt like the hundredth time. Mason's cell vibrated obnoxiously against the wooden table with an incoming call, attracting the entire group's attention. Mason's lips tightened to a grim line as all eyes turned on him.

"Everything okay?" Mari whispered, putting a hand on his shoulder.

Mason shook his head. "It's nothing."

"It doesn't sound like nothing," Amanda chimed in. "You've been blowing up."

"I know. Sorry guys. Just ignore it, it's nothing." Mason took his phone off the table and slid it into his pocket. "What were we talking about?" he asked, attempting to change the subject. Before anyone could reply, the phone vibrated again in his pocket.

"If it's nothing, why don't you just put your phone inside?" Ryan asked impatiently. Mari intervened before Mason could utter an icy retort.

"Is it work?" she asked gently. Mason pressed his lips together and nodded at her. She nodded back supportively. "It's okay, just answer it."

"I don't want to," Mason replied stubbornly.

"You don't want to?" she repeated, surprised. "What do you mean? What's going on?"

"Don't worry about it," he muttered. Mari and the others continued to stare at him with varying degrees of concern and confusion. "Seriously, guys," Mason insisted, looking around defensively. "It's no big deal. Let's talk about something else. What's for dessert?"

"*Excellent* question," Amanda seconded, happy to move on. Turning to Ryan, she added, "And speaking of dessert, Ryan, why don't you tell us about you and this Jeanine character I've been hearing about?"

Ryan shifted uncomfortably. "Thanks a lot, Mari," he muttered, looking betrayed. Mari shrugged, feigning innocence.

While Amanda grilled Ryan, Mari stole another glance at her husband. A thrill went through her when she found him looking intently back at her. They locked eyes, each attempting to read the other's thoughts while their guests faded away around them.

Mason suddenly raised his hand to her face, causing her to flinch involuntarily. He chuckled and brushed a hair off her forehead, tucking it behind her ear. Mari felt a familiar heat rising in her core. She wasn't drinking, but she suddenly felt drunk. A warm breeze carried the scent of jasmine past her nose, and she had a flashback to the night they'd met. He'd thrown her off-balance then, too.

Mari was suddenly overcome with a sense of déjà vu so powerful it made her nauseous. She felt like she was going to vibrate out of her skin—maybe Amanda was right about tonight.

The five friends sat around the table talking, laughing, drinking more wine, and savoring each other's company long after the meal was finished. With his belly full, Mason leaned back and stretched his arms overhead, allowing one to fall lazily over the back of Mari's chair. Greg watched them with a thick, tipsy smile on his face.

"It's good to see you guys like this," he said.

Amanda groaned. "Oh boy, here he goes."

Greg waved her off. "No, no, don't worry, I'm not going to say anything," he slurred. As his tablemates relaxed, he picked up again. "But what I was going to say was—"

Another round of groans erupted from everyone at the table, but Greg soldiered on. "No, no, no! Come on, guys! I just want to say, as your good friends, we've seen how hard things have been for you these last couple of months, and we love you, and we're happy for you, and we just want you to be happy, and we're happy to see you looking so happy. So, cheers… to happiness!"

"To happiness!" everyone replied, laughing as they clinked their glasses. Mari gazed lovingly at her friends, grateful that tonight was going exactly the way she'd hoped.

"Okay, Mr. Happy," Ryan muttered cynically as he brought his glass to his lips.

"Truly, slap happy," Amanda teased, reaching for her husband's glass. "You know Greg's had enough when he starts getting sentimental."

"Actually, I think I deserve a refill for my beautiful toast," Greg declared, fending Amanda off with one hand and reaching for the wine bottle with the other. He filled his glass and leaned across the table to top up Mason's. "Here you go, my friend; you deserve some too."

Once both glasses were full, Greg tipped his towards Mason's. "You're going to make a great dad, Mase."

Mason clinked glasses without a word and drank deeply, bracing as he swallowed his wine in one gulp. Across the table, Mari noticed Ryan eyeing them bitterly.

"Something wrong with the wine, Mason?" he asked. Mason's eyes flashed acid green as they flicked up to meet Ryan's shrewd gaze. "You look like you just swallowed a mouthful of nails."

The others glanced at Mason, who sized Ryan up thoughtfully.

"It's fine," he clipped. His suddenly chilly demeanor seemed to lower the temperature around them. Mari clenched her teeth to keep them from chattering.

"Are you fine?" Ryan asked. "You seem tense." The two men stared each other down.

"I'm fine," Mason finally replied.

"That's convincing," Ryan quipped.

"Ryan," Mari warned. Both men ignored her. A stillness had fallen over the group as everyone monitored the rising conflict.

"Is there something you want to say, Ryan?" Mason challenged, sitting forward.

"I think your face just now said it all," Ryan replied evenly.

"What is that supposed to mean?" Mason sneered, not helping his case.

"Greg just toasted to your fatherhood, and in response, you grimaced and chugged your wine like you have a stomach full of bees," Ryan scoffed. "Every time someone says something about the baby, your whole face falls."

"Ryan!" Mari exclaimed. "Stop it! What has gotten into you?"

"I'm sorry, Mar, but it's true. I don't know why you can't or won't see it for yourself, but for the last few months, Amanda and I have both listened to you doubt yourself nonstop, and there's nothing wrong with you. It's *him*!" Ryan pointed an accusing finger toward Mason. "This guy has you completely convinced that you are the problem here, and you're not."

Mortified, Mari looked at Ryan, who was heaving with frustration, then Amanda, who had covered her mouth in shock, and finally at Mason, who was looking at her with a betrayed expression.

"Been telling stories about me, Mar?" he asked quietly.

Mari's heart dropped into her stomach. "No! Mase, it's not like that. I'm sorry— "

"Don't apologize to him!" Ryan exclaimed. "He should be apologizing to you!"

"Ryan, would you *please* shut up—" Mari pleaded.

"No, Mari, let him finish." Mason's voice was honey-smooth, but his expression was murderous. "I know things haven't been easy for us, but I never thought you'd go running to him about it. I guess I should've, though. We all know he's been in love with you for years. Why don't you let him save you *now*, since he seems to be your big hero? I guess that would make me... the villain?"

Mari felt the blood drain from her face as she took in her husband's hurt expression. Hot tears pricked at her eyes. She looked around the table helplessly, unsure what to say next. Greg stood up and attempted to intervene.

"Okay. Alright, everyone, why don't we all just take a time out?"

"Mase, I'm sorry," Mari breathed, locking eyes with her husband. She heard Ryan make a disgusted noise.

"You've got to be kidding me," he groaned. "Mari, come on. He's got you like a yo-yo on a string, and you just keep falling for it!"

"Ryan, he's her husband," Amanda interjected. "They have a baby on the way; it's not that simple. It's also none of your business, so lay off. Guys," Amanda turned her attention to Mari and Mason, "don't worry about him. He's just a drunk, pent-up idiot."

Ryan showed no signs of remorse or backing down. "No, I'm not." He shook his head and turned back to Mason. "You may have everyone else fooled, Mason, but I can see you clear as day."

"Can you?" Mason asked coolly.

"Clear. As. Day," Ryan repeated. "Maybe I was in love with Mari once, but that was a long time ago. I never stopped loving her as a friend. I put her happiness first and tried to see you the way she did—as anything other than exactly what you are—but you keep proving me right! All you can ever think about is yourself. You treat everyone like they're disposable. You have one of the greatest people in the world for a wife. You had nothing before she came along and gave you all of this." Ryan gestured back towards the house.

"You're sitting here in this beautiful home, surrounded by friends and a good woman who loves you and is carrying your child, and when you think no one is looking, you are miserable. But I see you, Mason. I always have."

As Ryan delivered his tirade, rain began to fall, but nobody made a move to get indoors. Heavy droplets pinged against empty wine glasses, punctuating the stunned silence that hung around the table. Mari shivered as the raindrops hit her skin.

Mason's expression was lethal, but just as he opened his

mouth to speak, his cell phone buzzed again with an incoming call.

"Do you need to take that?" Ryan asked smugly.

Mari held her breath as she watched her husband. The rain was falling steadily on all of them now, and he seemed to find a sense of calm as it washed over him. To her surprise, he smiled. Mari glanced back at Ryan, whose grin wavered.

"Actually, I think I'd better," Mason purred. He stood up and squeezed Mari's shoulder, then bent to kiss her forehead. Out of the corner of her eye, she saw Ryan scoff, then look away in disgust. Guilt twisted her stomach both ways.

"We'll talk about this later, okay?" Mason murmured, caressing her face. "Why don't you see Ryan out?"

Mari nodded, eager to prove her loyalty. Mason nodded back with an encouraging smile. Mari's eyes filled with relieved tears.

"Do you two mind helping her clean up?" Mason asked, turning to Greg and Amanda. "I'll be back to help in a minute."

"Sure, of course... No problem," they answered quietly, pushing back their chairs.

With that, Mason walked away to take his phone call.

CHAPTER 10

Mari sat at her kitchen table and watched her husband through the patio doors while Amanda and Greg ran in and out, bringing the wreckage from their rained-out dinner party indoors. Ryan left without saying good-bye—not that Mari would've known what to say to him anyway. She felt like she might shatter into a thousand pieces if anyone so much as breathed in her direction. She had no idea where to begin sorting out her thoughts and feelings, so she focused on her husband's instead, observing him through the glass like an animal exhibit.

Mason paced back and forth under their shaded pergola, out of the downpour, and out of earshot. Mari had no idea who he was talking to or what was being discussed. Between the dark and the rain, she couldn't make out his expression, but she could tell from his body language that the conversation was heated.

Mason clenched his fist as he argued with whoever was on the phone. Finally, he halted with his back to Mari. She watched his posture sag in defeat. Still holding the phone to his ear, he threw his head back, then exhaled and dropped his chin to his chest. He stared at the floor and nodded, then ended the call.

Mason put his phone away and straightened, rolling his

shoulders. As he turned to the house, Mari averted her eyes and watched furtively as he joined their friends in clearing the rest of the table outside. They returned to the kitchen in silence. Amanda and Greg deposited the last of the dishes in the sink and came to join Mari at the table. Mason closed and locked the patio door, then finally met her gaze.

"Is everything okay?" Mari whispered. She heard the shaking in her voice, but she couldn't control it. Amanda took her hand and squeezed it reassuringly. Mari saw Mason eyeing the gesture and gently pulled her hand back.

"All good," Mason replied grimly. He paused, then added, "I have to go out tonight."

"*Tonight*?" Mari exclaimed.

Mason glanced self-consciously at Greg and Amanda. "You know how it's been this week," he mumbled. "Work's just driving me kind of nuts," he explained, acknowledging their friends.

"Sure man, but going to deal with work stuff now?" Greg asked, unconvinced. "Are you sure this is the best time?"

"I can't think of a better time," Mason countered bitterly.

"Mase, don't go," Mari spoke up, trying to reign things back to just them. "Please."

"I have to agree, Mase; I don't think this is the best time," Amanda chimed in.

"Well, that settles it then!" Mason exploded. "Why don't I put on some coffee, and we can all sit and talk about Mari and I's relationship together? In fact, let's get Ryan back here and ask him how *he* really feels about us. I've still got a few pounds of flesh left for you fucking vultures!" he snapped.

Greg quickly stood up and positioned himself in front of Mason, while Amanda put her arm around Mari, who was crying again.

"Geez, dude," she muttered. "Aren't we sick of this yet?"

Before Mason could reply, Greg dragged him outside for

some air. Amanda went back to comforting Mari, who drifted in and out of awareness, not registering a word her friend said.

Mari's eyes traced the natural patterns in the wooden tabletop while she sifted through her thoughts. For months, she had done her best to ignore her disquiet and live in the present, interpreting her husband's behavior with the most loving benefit of the doubt. Now, blurry memories floated to the surface of her mind like puzzle pieces that she couldn't quite fit together. The harder she fought for clarity, the more elusive it became.

When he returned to the kitchen with Greg, Mason knelt beside her and apologized for his outburst while their friends looked on supportively. He told her he loved her and promised her everything would be okay. Wanting nothing more than harmony restored, Mari accepted his words and his kiss, hoping it would break this spell of unease that was taking hold of her.

Instead, when he pulled away and she looked at his impossibly beautiful face, she saw the same mask he'd worn the night before—that perfectly painted-on smile with empty eyes.

As the storm began its crescendo, pummeling down on the roof over her head, Mari finally came to the realization that the feelings her husband once had for her were not just lost, but irreparably broken.

CHAPTER 11

"You guys should get going. This storm's only going to get worse," Mari insisted, ushering Greg and Amanda to the door.

"Are you sure?" Amanda asked. "You still have a lot of cleaning up to do. It'll go faster if we all pitch in."

"Don't worry, about that. I'll be fine," Mari promised. Amanda looked unconvinced, but Mari was adamant. "Seriously, don't worry! I've got this. Text us when you get home."

With that, Greg and Amanda offered quick hugs and ran to their car while Mari and Mason watched and waved together from the front porch. A clap of thunder split the air, hustling them back into the safety and shelter of their home.

"Oof." Mari winced at the noise and put a protective hand on her belly. "I hope they make it home okay."

"I'm sure they will," Mason replied. "Come on, I'll help you clean up."

Mari allowed Mason to guide her back to the kitchen. The sounds of the rain outside and the scraping and stacking of dishes filled the silence as they tidied up together. An impatient *meow* drew their attention to Otis, who sat beside his empty dinner bowl, looking offended.

"Oh shoot!" Mari turned to Mason. "Did you feed him earlier?"

"No," Mason clipped. "I was a little distracted, in case you forgot."

Too tired to argue, Mari ignored his tone and her subsequent flash of irritation. "I wasn't accusing you. I just didn't want to feed him twice accidentally."

"I didn't feed him."

"Okay. Fine." Mari dried her hands and went to fill Otis' bowl. "I'm so sorry, kitten," she said as she returned it to him. "Here you go. Eat up."

Otis accepted her apology with a slow blink and dove into his food. Mari scratched him between the ears and stood up, feeling a head rush as she straightened. She steadied herself against the nearby countertop and glanced back at her husband. Mason stood at the sink with his back turned, oblivious to her struggle as he dried and put away wine glasses.

A wave of exhaustion swept over her, accompanied by crippling nausea. Her neck felt stiff, and her limbs were suddenly too heavy to bear. Mari glanced down the hall past the kitchen, measuring the distance to the stairs. The thought of dragging her weary body up to the bedroom was overwhelming. She looked at Mason again and decided to extend an olive branch. Despite all that had happened between them that evening, she needed him right now.

"Do you want to watch a movie with me?" she asked. He didn't answer. "Mase?"

He cocked his ear in her direction. "What?"

"Would you like to watch a movie with me?"

Mason carefully wiped the glass in his hand, thinking it over. "Aren't you tired?"

Mari shrugged. "Yeah, but I'm not sleepy yet. Come sit with me?"

Mason put the glass in the cupboard, then closed it softly. "I'm going to go deal with that work thing," he said quietly.

Mari felt her heart speed up. Disappointment, anger, confusion, and exhaustion swelled up at once and threatened to burst from her in a scream, but she forced it all back down.

"I don't understand," she said, clinging to composure. "Why? What is going on?"

"It's complicated."

"Complicated?"

"It'll be quick."

"It's complicated, but it's quick," Mari repeated, raising an eyebrow. "What is it?"

"It doesn't matter—"

"It very much does," she fired back. "What could possibly be so urgent you have to run out at 9 p.m. on a Friday in the middle of a rainstorm to deal with? Explain it to me."

"I don't have to explain anything to you," Mason snapped.

Like a damn breaking loose, Mari's patience suddenly gave way. She'd tolerated Mason's mood swings for too long; being spoken to like this was the limit. All the feelings she'd been suppressing rushed through her, washing away her exhaustion and infusing her with a second wind of anger. She opened her mouth to put him in his place, but what came out instead surprised even her.

"Is this really about work?" she asked. She watched Mason freeze and knew she'd finally asked the right question.

"What else would it be about?" he asked, narrowing his gaze.

"This doesn't make sense," she said slowly.

"What doesn't make sense, Mari?" He scowled, but she was no longer intimidated. She felt her anger receding, replaced by a laser-focused calm.

"What exactly are you accusing me of here?" Mason demanded.

Mari couldn't say the words. She and Mason stood on opposite sides of their kitchen, facing off as the rain battered the roof over their heads. Otis had finished his dinner but remained crouched in his corner, monitoring the escalating tension.

Mari swayed on her feet. She was suddenly too tired for this fight. "I don't know, I guess," she conceded. "I'm going to bed." She started to leave the kitchen, but Mason stopped her.

"Hey, wait," he murmured. "Everything is fine. I'll be right back. Okay?"

Avoiding his gaze, Mari pulled out of his grasp and continued upstairs. Behind her, Mason made an exasperated noise.

"You're being paranoid!" he shouted. She heard him snatch up his keys and go out the front door, slamming it loudly behind him.

An hour later, Mason had still not returned from his "quick" run. Unable to quiet her mind, Mari paced the halls of her big, empty house. When her body got tired, she sat on their bed and stared into space, feeling the heavy mantle of truth settle on her shoulders.

Mason had been very distracted lately.

Mason had been coming home late a lot.

Mason's moods changed often and inexplicably.

Mason went to work at 9 p.m. on a Friday during a rainstorm to deal with an emergency… in landscaping.

Could he be…?

No. Mari shook her head as if she were trying to get rid of a disappointing answer in a Magic 8 Ball. She got up and took a long, hot shower to wash away her misgivings, but they would not budge. She stood naked at the vanity, surveying her reflection in the steamy bathroom mirror. The woman looking back at her was distorted by fear and anxiety. Her brows were knitted together, and the corners of her mouth turned down in a frown, creating deep worry lines all over her face. Misery seeped out of her pores.

Seven years ago, Mason had ridden into her life like Prince Charming to rescue her from the verge of loneliness, or so she thought. She realized tonight that she'd been dancing on that precipice this whole time, only now it was in the arms of someone who waltzed her back and forth from the edge like a game, threatening to throw her over her at any moment. Now, she was in free fall.

Mari's eyes stung with tears as they moved down to her rounded belly. She cradled her stomach in her hands, pressing lightly. She felt a tiny flutter in response.

"Hi, sweet boy," she murmured. Mari had spent years imagining what it would feel like to place her hands on her own body and feel the presence of another life growing inside her.

I'm not alone. Awareness dawned on her with a tinge of shame. How could she have forgotten? From the moment she learned she was pregnant, she had never been alone. She got so caught up clinging to her marriage, supplicating herself to preserve her tenuous bond with Mason, that she'd overlooked the indelible bond forming right there in her body.

"My boy," she whispered again. A surge of protectiveness went through her. This baby was coming into the world so small and fragile. It was up to her to keep him safe, to make sure he was loved. There was no way she would ever allow him to feel alone or neglected by the people he depended on the most—the way she'd felt in this house for so long.

Her son would grow up strong, secure in the knowledge that someone was always looking out for him, never doubting that he was loved. If she couldn't do that for him here, she'd take him somewhere she could, and if she had to do it by herself, she would. She was surrounded by people who loved and cared for her fiercely and would do the same for her baby.

Mari lifted her head and looked at herself through her baby's eyes, composing herself into the person he needed her to be. She had no idea what the future held in store from here, but she was no longer afraid to find out.

CHAPTER 12

Fueled by her newfound courage, Mari dressed quickly in a sweatshirt and leggings and began her search.

Starting with Mason's nightstand, she opened each drawer and rummaged through them carefully. In the closet, she searched all his pockets but found nothing. The scent of his cologne lingered on his clothes, threatening to suffocate her with grief. She felt crazy, tearing through his belongings like a bloodhound, but her intuition would not allow her to stop. Like a forensics detective, she slid her fingers in between stacks of folded T-shirts and balled-up socks, probing for secrets, but found nothing.

After exhausting every possible hiding place upstairs, Mari hurried downstairs to continue her search. She wasn't sure which would be better: finding something, or finding nothing. Finding nothing would mean that Mason was right. It would mean she was paranoid and that her instincts couldn't be trusted. It would mean she couldn't trust herself. She desperately needed to find some external validation for what she was feeling. On the other hand, Mari's heart pounded as she imagined the pain of what that validation would mean—that her husband no longer loved her, and possibly never did.

In the kitchen, she checked the mail slots and the junk drawer where Mason would empty his pockets at the end of the day—nothing. His gym bag and the coats and jackets in the mudroom and hall closets—nothing. His workbench and storage bins in the garage—nothing. Mari searched desperately but found no evidence that her husband was keeping secrets from her.

It was not a relief.

Suspicion tugged insistently at the back of her skull. Flipping the lights off in the garage, she retreated to the front hall, drained and frustrated. She plopped down on the stairs and buried her face in her hands. She was seven months pregnant, alone, and scouring her house like an FBI agent because she thought her husband might be cheating on her. It was the kind of thing she'd expect to see on a trashy reality TV show, not her real life.

Mari's cold, broken heart sank into her stomach. Hot tears filled her eyes for what felt like the hundredth time that evening. She watched them splash on the carpet between her feet. Something bumped against her hip—Otis had come to console her. She smiled tearfully as he nuzzled her side. Otis accepted a scratch between the ears and then moved down a step to weave between Mari's legs. His presence was a comfort. Mari felt her tears recede.

"Now, what?" she sniffled.

Otis gazed at her, his pupils dilating knowingly. He blinked once, then meowed and turned away. Without looking back, he trotted down the stairs and through a darkened doorway off the foyer that led to the home office she and Mason shared—the only room she hadn't searched yet. Mari watched him disappear, then listened to his collar jingling from inside the empty room, beckoning her to follow. She hesitated, then stood up obediently.

In the unlit office, a desk stood in the center of the room, in front of a wall of built-ins lined with books and framed photos from their life together. Mason's laptop sat open on the desk—the screensaver's pale glow drew Mari's attention like a moth to a flame. The empty desk chair was pushed back, facing her like an invitation. In a corner by the window was a chaise lounge where Otis sat, curled up in the watery, orange light coming from the streetlamps through the rain. He swished his tail patiently, waiting for Mari to take the next step.

Without turning the lights on, Mari moved toward the desk and sat down, brushing the mouse pad to bring up the password-protected login screen. She paused with her fingers outstretched over the keys. She knew Mason's password, but there was a reason she'd been avoiding this room. If there was anything to find, she knew it would be here, and there would be no going back. She wouldn't be able to unsee whatever was on the other side of this. She held her breath and let her fingers fly.

Mason's computer desktop was neat and sparse. Mari clicked through the folders—tax documents, client forms, old start-up paperwork—nothing unexpected. He rarely took pictures, but she went through his photos anyway, bracing for any images that might have been sent to him. There were none. His browser history was intact but revealed nothing incriminating. After several minutes of searching, there was only one place left to look: his messages.

His computer and phone were linked, so Mari knew any texts he'd sent or received would be on the laptop. She hesitated, partially from fear, but also the final vestiges of love that told her not to go any further, to trust him, and to respect his privacy. Heart pounding, she let the cursor linger over the icon for a few more seconds while she battled with herself.

If there was nothing here, then she had invaded his privacy for nothing, and *she* was the villain. She feared the pain of discovering an affair. The thought of a life broken apart—of starting over as a single mother—was a nightmare, but she'd come too far, and the stakes were too high for her to stop now. She didn't want to live in fear anymore. She double-clicked the mouse firmly.

Mason's affair was all there, laid out in soul-crushing black and white: an endless stream of intimate and explicit texts and photos going back to before Mari got pregnant. She struggled to breathe as she witnessed the evolution of this relationship from a brief encounter in a bar to an escalating attraction that led to a meet-up, and then another, and another, their cravings for each other intensifying with every rendezvous. Mari's heart stopped when she saw the other woman call herself his "girlfriend." It was the same weekend Mari found out she was pregnant.

Her hands shook violently when she saw "I love you" turn into "We should be together." Mason had sought solace in this stranger's arms after finding out his wife was pregnant, leaving Mari to beg for his affection for months while he was intimate with *her*. He confided in *her*, admitting he didn't want to be with Mari anymore, but felt he had no choice.

Mari felt as though she'd been punched in the stomach, but her torture was far from over. The other woman's appetite for Mason was insatiable. She begged him to leave his marriage and choose *her* instead, but Mason always evaded the subject. He finally attempted to end the affair yesterday. Mari realized this must've been the "problem" he was referring to this morning that he felt he had solved.

Finally, she reached this evening's barrage of texts from the woman, who was not handling the breakup very well at all.

I'm not letting u off this easily. We need 2 talk.

Baby, plz. Talk to me.

Please babe, I'm sorry. Will u answer?

Answer your phone.

Mason! Answer me!!

ANDSWER UR FUCKING PHONE

?????????????????????

STOP FUCKING IGNORMING ME!!!!!!

we need. to talk.

Mason. If u don't answer me right now, I'm telling Marilys.

Mari was startled to see the woman use her full name. Mason had sent one reply, right before he left the house that evening:

I'm omw.

Mari couldn't make it make sense. She wanted to weep and scream and sob. She wanted to throw his computer at the wall and smash it to pieces, then tear apart their home in a tornado of rage. Her insides caught fire, then turned to ice. She felt like vomiting. She felt empty and numb. She couldn't move. She could barely breathe. She had the sense she was falling down a deep, dark hole, watching the light disappear above her as she crashed to the bottom.

Eventually, Mason's keys jingling in the front door snapped her back to the present. From the darkened office, she watched him walk past her, heading for the kitchen. She listened to him empty his pockets into the junk drawer she'd just ransacked, then fill a glass of water and chug it. She heard his footsteps come back her way, passing her again as he went upstairs to their bedroom, where he paused for a long moment.

"Mari?" he called out.

Mari didn't answer. She listened to him walk around upstairs, calling for her.

"Mar? Where are you?" He jogged down the stairs again. "Marilys?" he called into the empty living room. "Are you home?"

Mari remained silent, knowing he'd find her eventually. He passed the office again on his way to the garage to check if her car was still there. Coming back, he finally noticed her sitting in the dark, lit by the soft white glare of his laptop. In one look, he knew she knew everything.

"Mar," he breathed softly. Mason stood in the darkened doorway, sizing up his wife, who glared at him out of the shadows.

"Mari?" he repeated, flicking a switch by the door.

Mari didn't flinch as the bright overhead lights came on. She sat like a statue in the office chair, elbows resting on the armrests, hands draped loosely over the ends. In the light, her dark eyes glittered with black fury. Mason eased into the room with one hand cautiously outstretched.

"Honey…"

Mari gasped like she'd just come up from the bottom of the ocean.

"How could you do this?" she shrieked. She slammed her fists on the desk, dropped her head between her arms, and began to wail. "How could you do this!"

Mason retreated a step, startled by her outburst, but recovered quickly. He stood there stoically, waiting for her to exhaust herself. Mari labored to catch her breath, eventually regaining composure.

"Mason," she began again, her voice back down to its usual register. "What *the fuck* is this?" Her sudden volume startled Mason again. His mouth fell open dumbly.

"Do you not have *anything* to say for yourself?" Mari demanded. "All this time? *All this time*! How could you do this? Who is she? *Say something*!"

"It's not what you think," Mason began lamely.

Mari's eyes widened. "It's not what I think?" she repeated. "It's not what I *think*? Oh my God!" She got to her feet and began to pace. "Oh my God. Okay… Okay. It's not what I think. Phew! It's not what I think." She laughed maniacally, then spun around to face him.

"Okay, Mason. It's not what I think. So, what is it? Because I *think* it looks like you have been having an *affair* while I'm pregnant with our baby. *Our baby, Mason*! Are you insane? Who is this woman? No—"

Mari cut herself off and began to pace again. "No. I don't

want to know. *I'm* insane. I'm insane. Oh, God, I'm so stupid."
She began to cry again. "I'm so, so stupid," she said, laughing
through her tears. "I loved you."

Mason took a cautious step towards her. "You're not stupid,"
he said softly.

"I am!" she wailed, pushing him away. "I am! How could
you do this, Mason? How could you do this to us? We're about
to be parents! My God. I've done everything—*everything* to be a
good wife to you... you... asshole! I don't deserve this!" she
wept.

"Mari, it was just a mistake."

Mari laughed between sobs. "A mistake."

"I went there to end it!"

Mari froze. "So did you?"

Her sudden calmness caught Mason off guard. He sized her
up warily.

"Did you end it, Mason?" Mari repeated.

Mason lifted his chin. "Yes, Mari, of course I did."

"Oh, of course you did. *Of course you did*?" Mari resumed
pacing. "Oh, thank God. Of course you did, Mason!" Her
laughter was brittle. "Gold star, buddy! Good job! What the fuck
is wrong with you?"

"What the fuck do you want from me, Mari?" Mason exploded.
"Nothing is wrong with me! Nothing is wrong with *me*! Do you
think things have been easy for me? I have been miserable—
fucking *miserable* with you in this fucking house! For years! From
the moment you said you wanted to have kids, you have been
downright unbearable!"

Mari looked at her husband as if he had slapped her.

"Don't look at me like that," Mason sneered. "I'm sick and
tired of feeling muzzled by you! Our whole relationship has
revolved completely around *you* and what *you* wanted. You
want to know the truth, Mari? The truth is that you were so
fixated on becoming a mother that you forgot to be a wife. I
deserve someone who cares about what *I* want. If you want to

know how this happened, look in the mirror. It happened because of *you*."

Mari flinched as Mason jabbed his finger in her direction.

"I didn't tell you to go looking through my shit tonight. That's on *you*. Honestly, I'm surprised it took you this long." He laughed. "You really thought all those late nights were work? I didn't even have to try to hide it from you; you *wanted* to be blind. You didn't care."

Mari felt her anger fading, replaced by guilt. Was he right? Had she neglected him? She didn't think so, but he had never snapped like this before. He was speaking with so much conviction that it made her doubt herself. Maybe she had driven him to this. The fighting spirit that possessed her just a moment ago was suddenly gone. Mari felt herself falling back into that black pit of despair, drained and wounded by Mason's words. She couldn't take it anymore. Suddenly, everything became clear.

"Maybe some of that is true, Mason. Maybe I was blind, and maybe I wanted to be. Who knows anymore? But I know I'm not the bad guy here. I did my best. And I don't want to do this anymore. I'm done."

With that, Mari walked out of the office, leaving Mason alone. She went up to their bedroom, grabbed a bag, and began to pack. Mason followed moments later, pausing at the threshold.

"What are you doing?" he asked, eyeing her things spread across the bed.

"I'm getting the fuck out of here, and I'm going to my parents." Mari went into the walk-in closet to retrieve more clothes. When she came out, Mason was still leaned against the doorframe, deliberating.

"Is this necessary?" he asked, finally entering the room. Mari ignored him and carried on packing. She sensed he was hurt by that, but she no longer cared.

"Mari... Mari, stop." He reached for her arm, but she yanked it out of his grasp. "You're acting like a child!"

Mari tried to cover her mouth before a hard, bitter laugh escaped her lips, but she wasn't fast enough. She recovered and went back to packing without acknowledging him.

Mason sighed. "Look. It's almost midnight, and we're both exhausted. I don't think this is smart, Mar. Hello? Mari! The least you could do is act like an adult and have a mature discussion about this!"

Mari couldn't resist rolling her eyes, but still said nothing.

"Look, I'm sorry you found out like this," Mason persisted. "Believe me, I didn't want that. I feel sick about it! I should have told you. But you can't just traipse off in the middle of the night in a thunderstorm while you're six months pregnant. I'm not letting you do that!"

"Mason," Mari chuckled, "I'm seven months pregnant. And you don't have the right to stop me from doing anything anymore. You've made your choices. Now I'm making mine. If you think I'm spending one more night in this house with you, or one more minute in this joke of a marriage, you're an even bigger clown than I thought." It was satisfying to see how her words had cut him, though he tried to mask it.

"What kind of mother are you?" Mason countered. "Have you even thought about how reckless this is? Putting yourself and the baby in harm's way? Throwing away your whole marriage before your child is even born? What will people think of you when they find out?"

"If anyone is confused about what drove me out of my home in my condition, I will happily set the record straight about my cheating, asshole husband without an ounce of shame. And Mason, let's get one thing straight. I haven't thrown away anything. You threw away our marriage. I'm just not diving to save it this time. Now get out of my way."

Mari attempted to sidestep Mason and retrieve her toiletry bag from the bathroom. As she reached the doorway, Mason grabbed her by the arm again, rougher than before. She whirled, attempting to yank herself out of his grip, but his fingers dug painfully into the soft flesh of her inner elbow. He pinned her against the doorframe and held her there. His face was a mask of cold fury.

Mari felt a flash of fear. Mason's expression softened as he looked her over. She held still, wondering what he was thinking. A million emotions seemed to pass through his eyes: anger, fear, something mournful... regret? Did he feel regret? Despite all that had happened tonight, Mari found herself hoping her husband would make one last plea. She already knew she'd accept it. She looked into those captivating, forest-green eyes, praying he would see the love she still had for him. Mason loosened his grip on her arm and rubbed it gently.

"Mar," he said softly. The sound of her name on his lips made her feel lightheaded. "Can we just stop for a second? I know this hurts, but it'll hurt more if you do this now. I guarantee you'll regret it in the morning."

No. I won't. The words sprang to her mind automatically. Mari suddenly saw her husband with fresh eyes. Of all the things he could've said to her, it wasn't "I love you" or "I need you," but "You'll regret this." Since he returned home tonight, all he'd done was attempt to shame, belittle, and gaslight her into thinking she caused a problem that she had merely discovered, just as he had for the last seven years.

Mari felt a peculiar laughter bubbling up in her throat and released it in Mason's face. The sound split the air like ice, cracking apart in a deep, old glacier. She shoved him away with a strength that surprised them both.

"No. I won't," she replied. Mason backed away as she advanced on him. "I won't regret a single thing, Mason. You're a coward. Everything that you've done tonight, and for the last few months, are the actions of a weak, pitiful man. For seven years, I loved you, cared for you, and fought for you because I believed you were something far better than what you are. I have given you and this marriage everything I had, which is far more than you deserved." Mari jabbed a sharp finger into Mason's chest.

"You're a grown-up, Mason. If you were unhappy or unsatisfied, you could have said so. But instead, you're saying... what? That I drove you to cheat on me because I was too busy investing in building a family with you? That's bullshit. You're bullshit."

Mason seemed to shrink under Mari's wrath, but she didn't let up.

"I have been running myself ragged trying to prove I deserve to be with you. You made me feel like I had to earn my place beside you, but now, *I see you*, Mason. I see right through you. The man I have been imagining this life with isn't real. He doesn't exist. The man I'm looking at right now?" Mari stepped back to appraise him.

"You are small, and weak, and empty, and I am done with you." She put a hand over her stomach. "*We* are done with you. My son will be a better man without you in his life."

With that, Mari retreated to the bathroom and slammed the door in Mason's face. Turning to the mirror, she braced herself against the vanity and studied her reflection. Her expression was a mixture of grief and victory, but unlike before, she recognized the person staring back at her. She bowed her head and let her tears flow, knowing she had just changed her life forever.

CHAPTER 13

From the kitchen, Mason listened to Mari's car start, followed by the hum of the garage door as it opened and closed again. She was finally gone.

Breathing a sigh of relief, he grabbed a beer from the fridge and chugged it on his way to the living room, bracing as the cold, bitter liquid hit the back of his throat. He set the empty bottle on the coffee table and collapsed on the sofa, cradling his head in his hands. He curled his fingers into his hair and pulled, hoping the pain would distract him from his racing thoughts. Mari had left him with a lot of damage control to do. Finally, he dropped his hands, took out his phone, and forced himself to make the call he'd been dreading. After a few long rings, a woman answered, her voice groggy.

"Hello? Mason? What's wrong?"

"Hey, Meena, I'm sorry to wake you."

"Mason?? What's wrong??"

Mason could tell by the rise in her voice that Meena had bolted upright in bed. He pinched the bridge of his nose wearily. His mother-in-law's instinct was always to panic first, then ask a million questions second.

"What time is it?" she asked. "Oh God… is it the baby? Is the baby coming? Where's Mari? Is she okay? Can I talk to her?"

"Everything is fine," Mason reassured her. "It's too early for the baby. She's only seven months, remember?" In the background, he heard Mark sit up and ask his wife what was happening.

"It's Mason," Meena explained. "Something is wrong."

"Nothing is wrong!" Mason insisted, struggling to suppress his impatience. "Look, I just wanted to call and give you the heads up that Mari is on her way over to you."

"What? Now?" Meena's voice sharpened. "Why?"

"It's a long story. We can get into it tomorrow, but could you please let me know when she arrives? I told her not to go, but she insisted." Mason could picture Mark and Meena exchanging worried looks in the silence that followed.

"Son," Mark began carefully, "did something happen between you two?"

Mason bit back the urge to respond irritably. "We just had an argument," he explained. "It…wasn't great. She packed up some of her stuff and said she was heading over to you for the rest of the night. I just thought you should know. She was really upset, and with this rain…"

"You didn't try to stop her?" Mark asked.

"Of course I tried!" Mason replied hotly. "You know there's no stopping her when she gets ready… it was a bad fight," he finally admitted.

"What happened?" Mark asked again.

"I…" Mason struggled to find the words. They'd find out eventually, but he wasn't ready to deal with that yet.

"Okay. That's alright," Mark relented, sensing his discomfort. "Mari is a careful driver. I'm sure she'll make it over here just fine. We'll figure this out together."

"She's going straight to voicemail," Meena whispered to Mark in the background. Mason could hear her growing distress.

"Try her from the landline, and maybe put the kettle on?"

Mark whispered back. "She'll probably want tea when she gets here." He paused, then added, "Don't worry, she'll make it."

Mason suddenly remembered that this was not the first time Mark and Meena had sat up late at night waiting for a child who ultimately never returned. He softened as Mark turned his attention back to him on the phone.

"We'll let you know when she gets here, Mase."

"Okay, thanks... Dad."

Mark hesitated. "Are you sure you don't want to tell me what happened?"

"I'd rather not right now," Mason replied, "but I'll come over first thing tomorrow, and we'll all talk, okay?"

Mark was silent a moment longer. "Okay, sure. We'll let you know when Mari gets here."

"Thank you. I'll see you tomorrow. Goodnight. Sorry again."

Mason hung up without waiting for Mark's response, then eased himself down on the couch. He held the phone to his chest with one hand, pinching the bridge of his nose with the other to stall the migraine blooming between his eyebrows. He lay there listening to the rain against the window until he finally succumbed to his exhaustion and passed out. As the rain dwindled, Mason's breathing softened in kind, the rise and fall of his chest growing increasingly shallow until it was no longer moving at all.

Mason lay still as a corpse, not breathing. His body jerked once, and then again, harder as it fought for oxygen. Finally, with a heaving gasp, he exploded off the couch, clawing at his throat with wild eyes. He landed hard on his knees, then pushed himself off the ground in a panic, gulping for air.

Sitting back on his heels, Mason worked to regain control of his breathing. As his heart slowed, he felt a vein throbbing in his head. Pressure receded from his temples. His lungs felt tight, as if something had been suffocating him.

A distant, soft *click* set Mason on high alert. He froze, cocking his ear toward the garage, and listened. There was nothing but the rain falling softly outside. He was alone.

Brrrrrrrrrring!

His cell phone rang, startling him all over again. Fumbling around, he located it underneath the couch and snatched it up, checking the time—it had been just over an hour since he called Mari's parents.

"Hello?" he answered, trying not to sound so out of breath.

"Mason? Mason, can you hear me?" It was Meena again. She was frantic.

"Yeah, yes, I can hear you. Is Mari there?"

"Mason?" Mark replied, on speaker with his wife. "She's not here yet."

CHAPTER 14

Mason tightened his grip around the mug of coffee in his hands and stared miserably at his reflection in its black surface. No matter how much he drank, the cup never emptied. He couldn't stomach another sip.

It had been nearly eight hours since Mari left for her parent's house, and no one had heard from her since. Mason and Mark had both tried to report her missing and were told nothing could be done for twenty-four hours. However, when the sun started to rise, and there was still no sign of her daughter, Meena pitched a fit so hysterical that the police finally caved and sent two detectives to the Daniels' home.

Meena had also called in Mason's parents, Kris and Steve Goodridge, who wasted no time joining once they were made aware of the situation. Like her son, Kris had wavy golden hair and stunning green eyes. She sat beside him on the sofa, mirroring his posture while she rubbed his back supportively. Near a large picture window, Steve, tall and broad with iron-gray hair and a steely gaze, paced back and forth with his arms folded and one fist pressed to his lips.

Out of the corner of his eye, Mason caught Mark approaching

with the coffee pot again and quickly covered his mug. "Please, no," he pleaded, shaking his head.

Mark blinked as if he'd been startled out of a trance. To Mason's relief, he nodded, set the pot down on the coffee table, and returned to his seat beside Meena, pulling her close. Their faces were gray as they huddled together. Meena suddenly glanced up and made eye contact with Mason. Her haunted expression set his insides churning—he quickly diverted to studying the room until his stomach settled.

Mason knew Mari had helped her parents decorate, but he never realized how eerily similar Mark and Meena's house was to theirs until now. Mari's touch was everywhere; the furniture was overstuffed and supportive, just the way she liked; the same soft carpeting from their house covered the floors here, and everything had been selected from the same palette of warm, soothing neutrals she favored. Despite the coziness of the setting, nobody in this room was relaxed.

Detective Cora Hoxton sat on the arm of the sofa with her body angled toward Mason. She had a kind but commanding presence; her elevated perch only added to her air of authority.

"So, you had an argument, and she stormed out," she recapped in an intense, gravelly voice. Mason wondered idly if she was a smoker. He didn't smell cigarettes on her—on the contrary, her perfume was surprisingly sweet for a woman who looked so stern. It was familiar, too, though he couldn't place it.

"What was the argument about?" Hoxton asked.

Mason studied the detective curiously. She seemed both young and old at the same time. Her piercing gold eyes stood out against her dark complexion and were trained intensely on his face, giving her the appearance of a predatory bird. Although she wore no makeup, Mason noticed her nails were long and painted an alluring, candy-apple red—a captivating contrast to her plain, conservative clothes. He'd never seen a woman who was so masculine and feminine at the same time. He got so distracted in his assessment of her that he almost forgot she was studying him with equal curiosity.

"Mr. Goodridge?" she prodded, lifting one eyebrow.

Mason knew it was time to come clean, but between the detective's formidable presence and his parents and in-laws surrounding him, he hesitated to reveal the truth about his disagreement with Mari last night. They had all been so supportive, but he knew that would change the minute they found out what he'd done. He also knew that if they learned the truth any other way, things would look much worse for him. Taking a deep breath, he set his mug down and prepared to rip off the proverbial band-aid.

"I'd been having an affair with someone. Mari found out last night."

The air went out of the room as Mason finished speaking. Beside him, Kris uttered a soft, sad "oh" as she removed her hands from his shoulders and folded them in her lap. His father stopped pacing and dug his hands into his pockets while he studied the ceiling. Meena gasped, then covered her mouth and stared at Mason in abject, tear-filled horror. He did not need to look at Mark to see the color rising on his face or feel his anger.

He noticed Hoxton recording all these responses and worried about what conclusions she was drawing. Mason watched her exchange a knowing glance with her partner, Adam Martinez, who stood at a distance, leaning against the living room doorframe.

Mason looked down at the carpet between his feet. His skin burned from all the eyes he could feel on him. His humble posture contradicted the resentment he felt inside. He felt a secondary flash of anger at Mari for leaving him in this position.

"Oh, Mason," Meena breathed, finally breaking the silence. Her voice dripped with acrid disappointment.

To Mason's relief, Hoxton resumed her questioning before anyone could say anything else.

"How did she find out?" she asked matter-of-factly.

Mason shrugged. "I don't know."

"You don't know?"

"I wasn't there."

"So, where were you?" Martinez demanded. Mason immediately understood that he was the 'bad cop' in this duo.

"I don't know how she found out," Mason replied to Hoxton. "I just came home, and she was crying at my computer. I'm guessing she saw my messages."

"Where were you?" Hoxton repeated Martinez's question in a less challenging tone.

Mason lowered his gaze to the carpet again. "I told her I was going to work, but I went to see... you know." He gestured lamely, inviting her to assume the rest.

Around him, there was another soft chorus of disappointed sighs. Hoxton carried on as if she hadn't heard it.

"What time was that?" she asked.

"What time did I leave? Or what time did I come back?"

"Both."

"I left around nine. I came back around... I don't know... ten-thirty? Eleven?" With every word Mason uttered, the atmosphere thickened with his family's displeasure. He felt sick to his stomach.

"That's a short rendezvous," Martinez quipped.

Mason glared at him. "It wasn't for that."

"What was it for then?" Hoxton asked, redrawing his attention.

Mason spared another contemptuous glance at Martinez before responding. "I told her a few days ago that we shouldn't see each other anymore," he replied. Meena scoffed, but Mason ignored her and continued. "She didn't take that very well. She was calling and texting me nonstop yesterday. I tried to ignore her, but when she threatened to go to Mari, I went to talk her down."

"You've got to be fucking kidding me," Mark muttered.

"We'll need her name and contact information," Hoxton replied, remaining focused.

Mason nodded sullenly.

"So, you left around nine and came back around eleven to find your wife in your office, where she's discovered your affair," Hoxton summarized. "Then what?"

"She was angry."

"Were you?"

"No."

"No?" Hoxton repeated skeptically.

"No."

"Okay. What next."

"She pushed me aside and went upstairs and started packing. She wanted to go to her parents' house... here," Mason gestured around the room, "and I was trying to convince her not to. It was too late, and it was raining too hard." He paused, reluctant to reveal the rest. The others waited in rapt silence. He licked his lips nervously and continued.

"She, uh, said she didn't want to spend another night with me in our house. She wanted to end things." The words tasted like chalk in his mouth. In his periphery, Mark and Meena nodded angrily, satisfied with their daughter's judgment. His parents were silent, but he could feel their disappointment.

"You said she pushed you," Hoxton prompted. "Were you physical back?"

"No."

Hoxton studied him closely. Mason forced himself to sit still under her scrutiny. "Did she say anything else?" she finally asked.

"She said a few more... colorful things."

"Such as?"

Mason chewed the inside of his cheek. "Like what a wonderful husband and person I am," he finally replied, tasting blood. A tiny smile tugged at Hoxton's lips. Mason couldn't tell if it was amusement or sympathy, but it gave him hope that she might be on his side.

"Alright," Hoxton suddenly declared, standing up. "Do you mind if we take a look at your house?"

By the window, Mason's father, Steve, finally spoke up. "Is that necessary at this point? What for?"

Hoxton shrugged. "Standard procedure. There may be something in the house that your son missed that could indicate where she was headed."

"I'm fine with that," Mason answered before his father could protest, getting to his feet as well. "I have nothing to hide."

"Fine," Steve relented. "But I'm going with you."

"That's fine," Hoxton agreed. "You guys can ride over with Martinez. I'll follow."

Steve cast a dubious eye at Martinez, who grinned back at him. "Why don't we just follow in Mason's truck?" he suggested.

"Actually, sir, it would be helpful if we could take a quick look at that, too," Martinez said. His tone was helpful, but Mason took one look at him and wished his father would stop talking. Hoxton seemed like she was still making up her mind about Mason, but Martinez had clearly already drawn his conclusions.

Kris stood up and placed a protective hand on Mason's shoulder. "Why do you need to look in his car?"

"My son's pregnant wife goes missing, and you're already treating him like he's some kind of criminal," Steve bristled. "They had a fight. She's probably just hiding out somewhere, perfectly fine."

Meena's bitter laughter pierced the air. "Oh yes, I'm sure she's perfectly fine after what your son has put her through tonight." This seemed to quench some of Steve's fire.

"Meena, I only mean—"

"Dad," Mason spoke up, silencing everyone.

As they all turned to him, Mason suddenly felt very alone, and a little afraid. He knew how this looked for him, and the way his parents and in-laws were behaving was only going to make things worse. His life depended on getting through this ordeal with composure and clear-headedness—something no one around him seemed capable of right now. Mark, Meena, Kris, and Steve were all completely overwhelmed by fear, anger, and stress. Mason felt all of that, too. He just didn't have the luxury of giving in to it.

Meanwhile, Detective Hoxton waited patiently, her nonchalant posture betrayed by the sharpness in those bright, eagle eyes. Mason knew she was watching for him to break, but he didn't get the sense that she was rooting for it. It was too soon to trust her completely, but the fact that she hadn't yet condemned him gave Mason a boost of confidence. Maybe he was a "person of interest" right now, but if those nails and that perfume were anything to go by, there was a woman in there that Mason knew how to win over.

"It's fine," he asserted. He took his keys from his pocket and removed the remote for his truck. "Here," he tossed it to Martinez, who caught it with one hand. "Do whatever you have to do. I have nothing to hide."

CHAPTER 15

Detective Hoxton prided herself on her uncanny ability to read people, but she wasn't sure what to make of Mason Goodridge yet. She'd watched him closely all morning for any sign that he knew more than he was telling about his wife's disappearance, but he seemed to hold back very little. His vulnerability intrigued her.

As they wrapped their initial interview at his in-law's, he'd looked so lonely and afraid. To Hoxton's surprise, she felt her heart go out to him. Mason Goodridge was either very stupid and hapless or incredibly smart and manipulative, and it frustrated Hoxton that she couldn't tell which by now. She hoped this tour of his home would reveal more about who he was.

The neighborhood was eerily still as she and her partner made their way up the driveway of the Goodridge home, following Mason and his father. Hoxton noticed the absence of birdsong and glanced through the tall trees surrounding them—even the wind rustling through their leaves had stilled, leaving behind a weighty silence. Last night's rain was long gone, but thick, somber clouds still blanketed the mid-morning sky. The pale gray light seemed to wash all the color out of their surroundings. Despite the apparent absence of any other living presence, Hoxton had a sense they were being watched.

The house loomed large ahead of them, both beckoning and imposing. It was unnaturally chilly on the shaded porch where Mason waited with his father to unlock the door. Hoxton felt goosebumps on her skin as she and Martinez climbed the steps to join him.

"Pretty roses," she remarked, nodding at the trellis of giant, bright pink flowers. "You've got quite the green thumb."

"I'm in landscaping, but I'm afraid I can't take credit for those," Mason replied, concentrating on his keys. "My wife looks after them." He unlocked the door and stepped aside, motioning to Hoxton. "Please, ladies first. It's cold out here."

Hoxton crossed the threshold, her senses keen. She stopped in the entryway to take in the house's layout while the others trailed in behind her. It was a beautiful, Craftsman-style family home. To her right, a broad staircase led to the second floor, where several bedrooms were visible through an open rail that circled the entire upper level. She wondered how two people utilized all this space. From where they stood, she could also see straight through to the kitchen in the back of the house, which was lined with sliding glass doors. Despite the open layout and the abundance of natural light, the house felt gloomy.

"Where would you like to start?" Mason asked, interrupting her study. "Can I get you anything before we begin?"

Hoxton's reply was interrupted by a small, insistent *meow!* Something bumped against her leg. She looked down to find a black cat with bright, yellow-green eyes sniffing tentatively at her shoes.

"Well, hello there, little guy." Hoxton crouched to offer her knuckles for the cat to sniff. He nosed her curiously, then dipped his head, granting permission to scratch his ears. She obliged, then glanced up at Mason. "Who's this?"

"Otis." Mason tsked. "Shit, I forgot about him. It's Mari's cat."

"Only hers?" Hoxton asked.

"She found him hiding under the house a few months ago," Mason explained, eyeing the animal disdainfully. "I didn't want to keep him, but she did. So, yeah, hers."

"Mari can be quite a soft touch," Steve murmured as Otis wove himself between everyone's legs.

"I'm surprised she left him behind, then," Martinez muttered quietly.

"He's probably hungry," Steve said, not hearing him. "Mase, when's the last time he was fed?"

"How should I know?" Mason asked, then softened, remembering. "Oh," he whispered. "Mari gave him dinner." With a pensive expression, he reached for the cat, but before he could touch him, Otis hissed and lashed out with his claws. Mason jerked his hand back, looking betrayed.

"You two always this chummy?" Martinez asked.

"Best fucking friends," Mason muttered with a self-deprecating half-smile. "Can't you tell?"

"Our fault," Steve explained, laughing it off. "We never allowed pets when Mason was growing up." He scooped Otis up with ease and cradled him in his arms. Otis licked Steve's chin affectionately.

Hoxton kept her expression neutral as she watched Mason with Otis, but internally, her frustration grew. Everything about this encounter was pretty damning under the current circumstances, yet Mason did not attempt to minimize his and Otis' obvious contempt for each other. Perhaps he was unaware of how bad it made him look, but she had a hard time believing he was that naïve.

"Why don't we start in the kitchen, and we can sort Otis out at the same time?" Hoxton offered, scratching the bridge of Otis' nose with one finger while Steve held him. The cat closed his eyes and purred. Hoxton glanced at Mason, who looked on resentfully while Otis accepted everyone's affection but his. She almost felt sorry for him.

Mason quickly rearranged his expression when he realized Hoxton was looking at him. "Sure. Right this way."

Hoxton, Martinez, and Steve followed Mason on a tour of the previous night's events with his wife, starting in the kitchen with their conversation before he left, then the office where they had picked up after he returned.

"This your laptop?" Hoxton asked, gesturing towards the desk.

"Yeah. Do you need to take that, too?"

"Too?"

"You took my truck."

"Ah, no. The truck is still at your in-laws. We're just looking it over, not taking it anywhere. I wouldn't worry about that."

Mason shrugged. "I'm not worried."

Hoxton felt Martinez side-eyeing her and spared him a curious glance.

Noticing their exchange, Mason quickly clarified, "About my stuff. Obviously, I am worried about Mari, but you can take whatever you want. I don't care."

"Good to know," Hoxton replied. "Shall we continue?"

As they went through the rest of the house, Hoxton noted that the place was comfortable and well put-together, but the longer they were there, the more despondent she began to feel. She couldn't explain it. She had never met this missing woman, but as she walked through her home, she was over-come with empathy for the pain and betrayal Marilys Goodridge must've felt here last night. She fought to remain neutral and observe the house objectively, but the feeling was inescapable. It was practically bleeding through the walls, which seemed to expand and contract as Mason entered and exited each room.

When he showed them the empty nursery, lovingly deco-rated and waiting for its occupant, Hoxton's stomach felt hollow. She'd never been interested in having kids of her own, but in this room, she felt an intense longing for motherhood. Grief poured over her, thick and sticky like bitter honey. In all her years of police work, she'd never felt anything like this.

Finally, they reached the master bedroom, where Hoxton felt an inexplicable swell of anger. She pushed it aside and listened while Mason explained how Mari had packed her things and delivered her final, brutal words to him. Her eyes swept the room meticulously. Everything was neat and orderly, except for the bed, which was made but mussed.

"Did you sleep here last night?" she asked.

"No," Mason replied. "Everything in here is how Mari left it. I didn't come in here at all after she was gone. I waited up in the living room to make sure she got to her parents. I fell asleep on the couch for a bit, but I didn't exactly sleep well."

Hoxton detected a hint of regret in Mason's voice and wondered what it was for—falling asleep or not sleeping well? The amity she'd felt toward Mason earlier was slowly morphing into contempt. She fought to control it, unsure of the cause. He hadn't done anything since they arrived to warrant it. On the contrary—he'd been generous, cooperative, and hospitable.

"What all did she take?" she asked, moving toward the closet to distance herself from him. Mason began listing off what he could recall.

"Her weekend bag—a black leather Louis Vuitton. She grabbed some clothes from over there," he said, nodding towards the dresser, "and a few things from the closet. I think mostly leggings and sweats."

"Phone charger's still here," Martinez noted, peering behind each nightstand. "Both of them." He looked at Mason, who merely shrugged. Hoxton noticed Mason kept his hands in his pockets once they entered this room, not touching anything.

"Bathroom through there?" she asked, indicating a half-closed door.

Mason nodded. "Yeah. She went in there and pretty much told me to get lost while she finished packing."

"And you did?" Hoxton asked.

Mason nodded again. "I went downstairs and left her alone after she slammed the door in my face. I figured it was better than staying and arguing more. I didn't want to over-upset her."

"More than cheating on her while pregnant would, huh?" Hoxton retorted, bringing the conversation to a sudden halt. Martinez's mouth fell open in surprise. Mason looked away, his face flushed with embarrassment.

"That's a little uncalled for, Detective," Steve reprimanded on his son's behalf. "Marital issues aren't criminal, so unless you have something more direct to say, I suggest you watch yourself."

Martinez stiffened in Hoxton's defense. "I suggest you do the same, *sir*," he returned, squaring off with the senior Goodridge.

"Alright, everyone," Hoxton intervened, raising both hands in surrender. "Let's all calm down. Mr. Goodridge, fair enough. I rescind the comment." She waited for Steve to accept her apology before moving forward again.

Flicking on the light, Mason led the group into the spacious bathroom. It was cozy and spa-like, with fluffy, cream-colored bath mats and a wall of floating shelves displaying candles and neatly rolled towels. A soaker tub and towel warmer stood in one corner of the room, and on the opposite side was a marble-tiled walk-in shower. Hoxton didn't see any personal items except for a toothbrush stand, which held only one toothbrush.

"Pretty clean," remarked Martinez. "My lady has bottles all over our bathroom." He looked expectantly at Hoxton, who merely shrugged, unable to relate. She kept her bathroom at home equally pristine. She sniffed the air, searching for the tell-tale odor of cleaning products recently used. All she detected was a soothing blend of eucalyptus and vanilla.

"We keep our stuff under the sinks," Mason explained, gesturing to the tidy dual vanity. "Mari's is on the right."

Hoxton opened the cabinet and leaned down to examine its contents. There were spaces where several bottles appeared to have been removed. She recognized a few products she used herself.

"Alright, I think we've seen enough in here," Hoxton declared, straightening.

As she and Martinez turned to leave, they were stopped in their tracks by a long, high-pitched whine coming from behind the walls, followed by a low, angry burble. Slowly, they turned to examine the toilet, which was gurgling urgently. Hoxton glanced back at Mason, who was also staring at the toilet with a curious expression. As suddenly as the noise started, it disappeared, leaving the four of them in stunned silence.

"Sounds like you need a plumber, Mr. Goodridge," Hoxton finally said, going over and lifting the lid. Before Mason could reply, the toilet released a demonic growl from somewhere deep in the pipes, causing Hoxton to jump backward in alarm. Murky, gray water began choking into the bowl.

Mason stepped forward and pushed the lever, frowning. With a whoosh, the water disappeared and refilled normally. He, Hoxton, Martinez, and Steve looked on bewildered as the toilet settled. Finally, Steve broke the silence.

"Uh…shall we?" he asked. Slowly, the other three followed him out of the room.

"We have your statement and your wife's description, and there's an APB out on her car," Hoxton recapped as they made their way back down to the front entry. "Her parents mentioned contacting the media, so it sounds like all our bases are covered."

"That's good, right?" Steve asked. "Hopefully, that means we'll have some good news sooner rather than later."

"You're in good hands, especially with this one," Martinez replied, pointing to Hoxton. "You've got the most experienced detective on the force working for you. There's a reason we call her 'Closed Case Cora.'" He looked pointedly at Mason. "We'll find your wife, one way or another. Don't worry."

"Thank you, detective. I hope so," Mason replied, sounding relieved. He smiled hopefully at Hoxton, who was momentarily taken aback by his good looks. Mason's smile was dazzling—like watching the sun come out. She cleared her throat.

"If you think of anything else, this is my cell." She handed Mason her card. "Will you be heading back to your in-laws now?"

Mason didn't reply, but the look on his face answered for him.

"That's probably for the best," Hoxton agreed, feeling surprisingly sympathetic. "In the event she comes back here, someone should be home. Stay put."

"I don't plan on going anywhere," Mason promised.

In an attempt to get a final read on him, Hoxton willed herself to look into his eyes again. Mason appeared exhausted and concerned, but not tense. He'd cooperated willingly and sincerely, but she wasn't ready to count him out, especially after the strange feelings that had come over her in this house. "If you hear from her, call us."

"Will do."

Mason opened the front door to let the detectives out, but they were blocked by someone else standing there. Hoxton watched Mason's face transform with fury as he processed this newcomer.

"What the fuck are you doing here?" he scowled.

CHAPTER 16

"Mason!" the newcomer exclaimed. He was panting, and Hoxton noticed sweat stains forming in the armpits of his dress shirt. "I was on my way to a showing when Mar's parents called. I canceled it and rushed over here as fast as I could. Hi, Steve. Nice to see you again, sir."

Mason moved in front of his father defensively. "I thought I was clear you weren't welcome here after last night," he sneered.

The other man narrowed his eyes at Mason. He seemed to have something combative prepared but changed his mind when he noticed Hoxton standing there with her partner.

"Hi, I'm Ryan Marsden," he said smoothly, offering his hand. Hoxton detected a sour note underneath his cologne as he leaned toward her. "I own Ryan Marsden Realty—"

"Yes, detectives, please meet Ryan, Mari's aspiring husband," Mason sniped, cutting Ryan off.

"Detective Cora Hoxton." Hoxton accepted Ryan's handshake, concealing her astonishment at Mason's open hostility. "This is my partner, Detective Adam Martinez."

Martinez gripped Ryan's hand firmly. "Hey. I've seen your bus benches."

"Ah, Eastview's finest knows my name. Thank you, thank

you." Ryan placed a hand over his chest and bowed. Hoxton nodded politely, trying to mask her growing distaste for him.

"So, exactly how do you two know each other?" Martinez asked.

"I'm a good friend of Mari's. Actually, we've been best friends since college," Ryan added, eyeing Mason defiantly. "Now we work together."

"I see." Hoxton glanced at Mason, who looked like he was sucking on a lemon. "Either of you care to elaborate on the 'aspiring husband' thing?"

"No," both men replied in unison.

"Detectives, what's happened?" Ryan asked, changing the subject. "Where's Mar?"

"We don't know yet," Mason answered irritably. "Why don't *you* tell *us* since you know her so well? Why would you come here?"

"Where else would I go?" Ryan retorted. "Anyway, the important thing is to find her." He dismissed Mason and turned back to Hoxton and Martinez. "I'm here to help any way I can. Is she answering her cell?"

"I don't know, Ryan," Mason sniped again before the detectives could respond. "Since you're the very first person to think of that today, why don't you try her?"

Steve put a calming hand on his son's shoulder. "Easy Mase. He's only here to help."

Mason rolled his eyes. "You wouldn't be saying that if you saw how he embarrassed himself here last night."

Hoxton watched Ryan and Mason go at each other without intervening. They struck her as similar, in equal but opposite ways. They were close in height and build, though Ryan's dark hair and eyes were a direct contrast to Mason's fair features. They both carried a certain charm, though Ryan's felt much more practiced, whereas Mason's seemed innate. They exuded an equally potent hatred toward each other. It was easy to imagine these two holding a lifelong grudge for simply existing in the same circle, let alone loving the same woman. Hoxton wondered who Ryan harbored stronger feelings for—Mason or his wife? Both men suddenly seemed to realize how closely they were being observed and clammed up.

"My apologies, detectives," Ryan said. "You were saying?"

"We were called several hours ago to look into Mrs. Goodridge's whereabouts," Hoxton explained. "She was expected at her parents' home around 1 a.m. but hasn't been seen since she left here. Do you have any idea where she might've gone?"

"1 a.m.?" Ryan repeated, confused. "Why was she out at 1 a.m.?" Another awkward silence followed as the detectives deferred to Mason, who remained stubbornly tight-lipped.

"Do you have any idea where Mrs. Goodridge might be?" Hoxton repeated. "Is there somewhere she perhaps likes to go when she wants to be alone, to think?" She watched Ryan's concern morph into darkened satisfaction.

"No," he replied, glowering at Mason. "She's not the type to go off alone. She would've called one of us—one of her friends, I mean." He let that hang in the air for a moment. "She's really important to me. If there's anything I can do to help, please let me know. None of this sounds good for her in her condition."

"Rest assured, we are treating this with the utmost urgency," Hoxton replied, signaling to Martinez that it was time to go.

"Thank you. I'm happy to hear that. And I mean it. Anything I can do, please call me."

"We'll do that," Hoxton promised, hastening away. The combination of Ryan's cloying cologne and smarmy attitude was beginning to make her nauseous. As they moved to depart, she noticed him glance at Mason with a sly, satisfied expression that turned her right back around.

"Oops, I almost forgot. Mr. Goodridge, we'll need the name of your, ah… mistress."

Mason's eyes narrowed into icy jade slits. The look of betrayal on his face made her feel slightly guilty. When he finally answered, his voice was rough and low. "Jeanine... Jeanine Alder."

Out of the corner of her eye, Hoxton saw Ryan's jaw drop. The man began to sputter unintelligibly. She nodded in a business-like manner. "We'll need her contact information as well."

Recovering, Ryan stepped forward, placing himself between Mason and the detectives. "I can give you that," he fumed. "She's Mari and I's assistant. Well, *was*, after today."

"I see," Hoxton replied. She had taken Mason's affair in stride as part of the investigation, but hearing that it was with his wife's assistant disappointed her for some reason. "Thank you. In that case, goodbye, Mr. Goodridge."

Without another word, Mason retreated into his house with his father, slamming the door behind him. Ryan followed the detectives closely down the driveway. Unable to get past her distaste for him, Hoxton let Martinez to do the talking.

"So, Mrs. Goodridge and this Miss Alder both work for you?" Martinez asked.

"Mari and I started the firm; we're partners," Ryan said. "I couldn't have done any of it without her. We hired Jeanine as our assistant last year. She was supposed to make things easier for her," he grumbled.

"The two of them get along?" Martinez asked.

"Mari and Jeanine? Sure, yeah. I mean, they weren't close, but they seemed fine. Mari's pretty amenable to most people, and Jeanine is a certified people pleaser."

"So, not the type to hurt anyone?" Martinez asked pointedly.

Ryan snorted. "No way. Not possible. Jeanine's an attention whore, but I doubt she'd ever physically hurt someone, let alone Mari. She's not exactly the sharpest tool in the shed. It's shocking enough that she's been cheating with Mason. I'm willing to bet that was all his doing."

"Any idea when they might've become acquainted?" Hoxton asked. Without Mason present, she found herself warming up to Ryan.

Ryan thought for a moment. "I don't know. Mason attended some work events with Mari... our Christmas party, a few happy hours here and there. I never noticed him with Jeanine, but yeah, I guess there would've been opportunities." He made a disgusted noise. "I cannot believe this. What a fucking asshole."

"Mr. Goodridge alluded to a conflict between the two of you here last night," Martinez remarked. "I assume that was over Mrs. Goodridge... 'aspiring husband'?"

Ryan's cheeks reddened. "He thinks I'm in love with her..." He shook his head, avoiding eye contact with the detectives, who simply waited for him to continue.

"Look, it's no secret that I used to have feelings for Mari, but she chose *him*," Ryan jerked his head toward the house, "and I have always respected that. I don't understand it," he clarified sourly, "but I respected it."

"Until last night?" Hoxton asked.

Ryan nodded. "You have to understand. Mari was—I mean *is*—dedicated to her marriage. She worked really hard to be a great wife, especially after she got pregnant, but... it's hard to explain. He never did anything to her, but the way she described it, it was like he was playing with her, I could tell. He's got everyone convinced he's this awesome guy, but he isn't, and I finally told him so last night. He didn't like that."

"How so?" Hoxton asked.

"How did I tell him, or how could I tell he wasn't perfect?"

"Both," Martinez replied.

Ryan glanced around the neighborhood while he spoke. "He's just... selfish. He thinks he can get away with anything because he's good-looking and charming, but if anyone sees through his act, he becomes a totally different person."

"Can you offer any proof of this?" Hoxton asked, hiding her concern. If what Ryan was saying was true, that would mean she had also fallen for Mason's dual nature this morning, which would be an alarming first. She was usually good at seeing through those types.

"Well, not exactly," Ryan faltered, "but trust me, he's not as perfect as he'd have you believe. Don't let him fool you, too."

"Mr. Goodridge didn't attempt to hide his affair from us when he reported his wife missing this morning," Hoxton countered.

"Yeah, but he was having an *affair*, for Christ's sake!" Ryan guffawed. "Isn't that proof enough?"

By now, they had reached Ryan's car. Hoxton opened the door for him.

"If your friendship with Mrs. Goodridge is as intimate as you say, it seems odd to me that she hasn't contacted you for support after last night or that you haven't tried to contact her yourself yet."

Ryan shifted apprehensively. "Well, it's like you said, Detective, maybe she wants to be alone to think."

"You said yourself that she's not likely to do that," Hoxton reminded him. "Given your argument with Mr. Goodridge last night and your apparent history, it's surprising that you came here first this morning."

"I came here because I think *he* probably knows exactly what's happened and is going to try to lie about it," Ryan countered angrily. "Don't let yourselves be fooled. That's exactly what he wants."

With an irritated sigh, Ryan pulled out a business card and pen, then took out his phone to scroll through his contacts. He scribbled something on the card before shoving it into Hoxton's hands.

"This is my contact info. Jeanine's number is on the back. But the person you should be focusing on is right there behind you in that house."

Hoxton accepted the card quietly.

"Thanks for your time and the information," Martinez replied. "We'll be in touch if we have any more questions."

"Yeah, well, like I said, anything I can do to help," Ryan begrudged. As he turned to get into his car, he stopped and did a double-take at the house. Hoxton and Martinez followed his gaze to a large picture window on the second floor.

"Baby room, right?" Martinez mused. "They showed it to us."

Hoxton felt that sick, hollow feeling in her stomach again.

"Is it?" Ryan asked, his gaze fixed on the house. "I wouldn't know. I haven't seen it. For a second, I thought I saw..." He noticed Hoxton and Martinez studying him skeptically and shook his head. "Never mind," he muttered. He went back to gazing tenderly at the house.

"You know, she fell in love with this house at first sight; it's got her touch all over it," he murmured. "She had big dreams for this place... and he's destroyed them all." Ryan locked eyes with Hoxton. "Don't let him get away with it."

CHAPTER 17

As Hoxton pulled into the parking lot at the police station, Martinez waited anxiously for her by her usual spot. He bounced on his heels like a puppy anticipating his owner's return. Hoxton sighed affectionately. She liked having Martinez as a partner; he was young and eager to learn from her, but sometimes, his unfiltered energy was exhausting and a little too familiar. He had held it together well enough all morning, but now, he looked ready to combust.

"So, what do you think?" he asked as soon she was out of the vehicle. "Something's up there, right?"

"Up?" she repeated.

"Oh, come on!" Martinez groaned. "You don't think so? By all accounts, this is highly unusual behavior for the woman."

Hoxton didn't disagree, but Martinez's eagerness to jump to conclusions tempered her own. "Our whole job is dealing with people in highly unusual situations," she replied evenly as they walked across the parking lot together.

"Maybe, but you've got to admit, the husband's a jerk."

"Partner, it was pretty obvious from the moment you met him that you didn't like him," Hoxton admonished. "You tend to be a little less sympathetic with the privileged. You should work on that."

"Whatever." Martinez shrugged. "I may not be as experienced as you, but I've seen enough to know it's almost always the husband, and Goodridge does not look good. Personally, if my pregnant wife went missing, I'd have gone full Liam Neeson by now trying to find her, no matter what we were arguing about."

Hoxton considered this as they walked into the station together. Martinez was right—assuming Marilys Goodridge wasn't a runaway, which was still a possibility at this point, the first person of interest was typically the husband, but Mason wasn't like other husbands she'd seen. He seemed as intelligent as he did clueless, as beguiling as he was disturbing. She felt like she was seeing him through a mirrored kaleidoscope—every facet reflected a slightly different man, which was highly frustrating. On top of that, the unprecedented emotional reactions he elicited from her were deeply concerning. In her life and work, Hoxton spent all day, every day, managing men who tried to manipulate her in all kinds of ways, but none had ever managed to root themselves in her psyche like Mason Goodridge had today.

"I'm sorry," Martinez suddenly concluded, interrupting her train of thought. Hoxton realized he'd carried on extrapolating while she was zoned out.

"Huh?" she asked.

"Good guys don't cheat on their pregnant wives," he said, repeating himself. "I'm sorry. They just don't. Period."

"Oh." Hoxton nodded. "Yeah. It's shitty as hell, but it's not illegal, and it doesn't make him a criminal."

"Come on, Closed Case Cora. You're telling me those famous female-intuition Spidey senses of yours aren't screaming foul play here?"

Hoxton rolled her eyes. "The only superpower I have is

common sense, and if you have any, you'll cut it out with that stupid nickname before I toss you off my team," she growled.

"Okay, boss." Martinez backed off but remained annoyingly unintimidated. "I meant it as a compliment, though. Is it the worst thing in the world to be so good at your job that your colleagues think you're psychic?"

Hoxton stopped walking and squared off with her young partner in the hallway. Other officers passing by moved warily around her.

"It's not a fucking compliment," she asserted. "I'm good at my job because I spent the last twenty-five years working hard and honing my skills as a detective. When I started out, everyone here acted like I wasn't worth a damn because I was young, Black, and female, and now that I've proven myself, those same boneheads want to say it's only because of some uncanny feminine intuition. That's a put-down disguised as a compliment, and my tolerance policy for that shit is zero. Got it?"

"Okay, got it. Jeez," Martinez exclaimed. "Punch me in the mouth, why don't you?"

Huffing, Hoxton marched into the breakroom with Martinez trailing closely behind. He leaned against the worn countertop with his arms folded and studied her while she poured herself a cup of coffee.

"At the risk of being beheaded," he began carefully, "I've never seen you this reactive, so clearly your instincts—" he put both hands up in mock surrender at the sharp look Hoxton gave him. "I said *instincts*, not intuition," he clarified. He waited for Hoxton to ease up before continuing. "Something about this guy is clearly bothering you," he concluded.

"I'm just not getting a clear read off him," she sighed, chiding herself for not concealing her emotions better.

Martinez raised his eyebrows in astonishment. "You like him!" he exclaimed.

"Excuse me?" Hoxton retorted. "Just because I don't hate him as much as you—"

"Nah," Martinez's eyes widened. "You *like* him!"

Hoxton shot him a dangerous look, but he carried on, undeterred.

"I didn't think blond, white boys were your type," he chuckled. "Man, Cora, I know you're a bit of a cougar, but I'd nip that shit in the bud if I were you. A soft spot for the suspect won't—"

"You're the one who needs to nip it in the bud," Hoxton warned, cutting him off. "Don't forget who you're talking to. You say one more inappropriate word to me, and I will personally shove the employee conduct handbook up your unlubricated ass. Now shut the fuck up."

Martinez wisely kept silent while Hoxton violently shook two sugar packets and poured them into her cup.

"I suppose he's been cooperative, which, I guess, he might not be if he did do something," Martinez offered. "Can you believe he just straight up admitted to having an affair like that? In front of their parents, too? Oof. I thought the windows were going to ice over the way the girl's dad looked, not to mention the outraged friend… I can't believe you outed the husband in front of him like that, *chismosa*!" He chuckled. "What was that all about?"

Hoxton winced at the memory of her clumsy reveal. "I dunno. I caught a look on the other guy's face when he thought we weren't looking. I had a feeling he came there just to piss off the husband, and maybe he knew more than he let on, so I dropped the bomb to test him, but he seemed genuinely surprised."

"And the husband was genuinely pissed," Martinez added. "I doubt he'll be helpful to us now."

"Maybe… but Goodridge never hesitated to talk about the affair. So maybe he really does have nothing to hide."

"Or maybe he's trying to throw us off by being overly honest?" Martinez hypothesized.

"Maybe," Hoxton shrugged. "Maybe he'll crack and just tell us what he knows and save us a bunch of paperwork... *if* there's anything to know. Or maybe this *is* just a case of a wife ditching her piece-of-shit husband. That's possible at this point, too. We won't know more until we know more... you know?" She smiled at her wordplay.

"You have to think he's guilty of something. Otherwise, why search the car and the house already? That could be considered premature."

Hoxton sipped her coffee, testing the bitterness on her tongue before she replied. "I only asked. They didn't say no, so we might as well take a look while we can. It shouldn't complicate things later on... if it comes to that." Her voice was light, but the keen look in her eye betrayed her nonchalance. "I don't disagree with you," she finally admitted. "Something definitely feels off here. And that house..."

"That house feels like something terrible happened there," Martinez finished. "I've never felt more depressed. I thought I was possessed or something. And what the hell was going on with the toilet?"

"Yeah, that was weird," Hoxton agreed. "I'm surprised you felt that too, though. I thought I was just empathizing with the wife for being cheated on, woman to woman, you know?"

"Men feel that shit too, you know," Martinez replied.

"You're right," she acquiesced, "but regardless of what we felt, there was no physical evidence of a crime, and we can't do much more based on just a hunch. Heebie-jeebies won't stand up in court, even if they're coming from me," she relented with a small smile. "We have to follow where the evidence leads, not the other way around; otherwise, everyone loses. I don't like the real estate guy either—showing up and putting on a show like that. As far as anyone knows, the woman is just off somewhere contemplating life, but he shows up screaming foul play and pointing the finger right at the husband less than twelve hours after they fight over her?"

"I agree; he was... slimy," Martinez grimaced. "Definitely gave off whiny, jealous boyfriend vibes. You think he knows more than he's telling? Harboring her, maybe?"

"Maybe. I think he's worth a closer look if she doesn't turn up in the next day or two."

"I'll keep tabs. You want me to get into it with the girlfriend, too? Miss... Alder?" Martinez asked, checking his notes.

Hoxton shook her head. "Nah, I'll take the girlfriend and the husband. You stay on top of the other guy and locating the wife's vehicle."

"You got it, boss lady," Martinez affirmed with a casual salute. "Hey, gun to temple—which one would you put money on right now?"

"Hard to say at this point," Hoxton replied. She paused to mull over all she'd learned that morning. She had a feeling she already knew exactly where things were headed; it was just a matter of time and evidence. "In my experience, the simplest explanation is almost always the right one."

CHAPTER 18

Hoxton rocked herself on the Goodridge's porch swing, admiring the neighborhood. Twilight was falling around her, bringing a sense of tranquility to the scene. A warm breeze blew the scent of roses her way from Mari's trellis. Above her, a full moon rose steadily.

"I get why you love this place," Hoxton said, smiling.

"It's so peaceful at this hour," Mari agreed. She reached for Hoxton's hand and squeezed it. "Detective Hoxton, I can't thank you enough for all you've done for us."

"Please, call me Cora." By now, it felt strange to keep using titles.

"Cora then," Mari accepted warmly. "How long has it been now?"

"Hmm." Cora paused to count. "A couple days?"

"Wow. Time flies, doesn't it? I wish we'd met sooner," Mari added, laughing. "Something tells me we would've made great friends."

Cora laughed with her, but not as heartily. "Me too." Their laughter died out, and they rocked together in silence.

"Would you like me to hold him for a little while?" Cora finally asked.

Mari gazed lovingly at the bundle in her arms. "Absolutely not," she cooed.

Cora watched her wistfully. "Everyone's worried about you," she finally said. "I don't think your parents are doing well."

"Mmhmm. I know," Mari sighed. "I'll speak to my mom." She shrugged apologetically. "I just can't yet."

Cora wanted to offer something encouraging, but all she could muster was, "I understand."

Mari nodded appreciatively, then stared out at the neighborhood. Nighttime had fallen quickly while they were talking, much faster than Cora expected. Around them, things were getting dark and very, very cold. A clap of thunder sounded overhead, startling her. In an instant, a heavy, steady rain broke loose.

"Should we go inside?" Cora asked, mildly alarmed.

Mari shook her head. "You can't. But I will soon," she promised, her tone taking on a darker edge.

Cora heard a splashing sound nearby and realized small waves of water were lapping urgently at the porch steps. She stood up and looked around uneasily—the place was flooding. She turned back to Mari.

"Will you at least tell me where you are?" she asked.

Mari remained on the swing, rocking her baby in her arms. "You'll find me soon enough."

"Before it's too late?" Cora cried.

"It was too late before you even started." Mari smiled at the distressed look on Cora's face. "Don't worry. It's not your fault," she comforted. "He's so easy to fall for."

As the water swirled higher on her calves, Cora stared at Mari in frustrated disbelief. Mari remained calm, in total acceptance of their surroundings. With a sinking heart, Cora realized there was nothing more she could do for her. She dropped her shoulders, defeated. "What will you do?" she asked.

Mari looked at the sky, inhaling resolutely. "I have to make things right." Her voice was soft, but her eyes were full of fire.

"I can help you!" Cora cried. "I can help make it right!"

Mari shook her head. "No one can help me now."

The water was above Cora's waist now. She felt her feet float off the ground. Mari remained rooted on the porch swing as the water rose over her shoulders. She still held the baby firmly to her chest, fully submerged, though she didn't appear concerned.

"Time for us to say goodbye, I think," she said softly. She eased herself to her feet, taking care not to jostle the bundle in her arms. "Thank you again, detective—I mean Cora." She smiled. "Thank you."

"No! Wait!"

Cora's mouth filled with water as she was swept off the porch by a rip current. The last thing she saw was Mari disappearing into her house as the swirling tide pulled the door closed behind her. Cora fought like hell to swim down to her, but the rising water kept taking her higher. Blinding flashes of lightning cracked the clouds above her while screaming winds buffeted her around on the waves.

Cora squeezed her eyes shut, bracing for the bolt that would inevitably strike her. When she opened them again, all was quiet. Outside her bedroom window, dawn was just beginning to break. She lay in bed, on top of the covers, still wearing yesterday's clothes—the same way she'd fallen asleep every night since Marilys Goodridge went missing a little over a week ago. As the investigation progressed, Mari had begun appearing in her dreams. Hoxton closed her eyes again so she could examine this most recent one, scouring for details that might finally help her solve this, but it was too late. The dream was already fading from memory.

Something vibrated underneath her, breaking her concentration. With an irritated huff, she opened her eyes and shifted to retrieve her ringing cell phone.

"Hoxton," she answered gruffly, swinging her feet to the floor. "What is it?"

"We found her," Martinez replied on the other end, equally terse but energized.

Hoxton shot up as if she'd been electrocuted. "Where?"

"We're at the quarry lake, below the overlook off Eastview Highway. You'd better hurry. Word's already getting out."

Without saying goodbye, Hoxton hung up the phone, grabbed her keys, and raced to the scene ahead of the media vans already en route. She marveled at how the news always managed to be barely one step behind them. She beat them to the site by minutes. As she exited the car and looked around, she realized grimly that their nationwide search net had been for nothing. In the end, Marilys Goodridge hadn't gone far at all.

The scene was surreal on the secluded, rocky beach where a recovery team had dragged the wreckage on shore. Water dripped from the vehicle's sides in small streams. Hoxton had pictured that car so often in her mind that it felt strange to lay eyes on it in real life. She had hoped they would find it in better condition.

Her heart broke when she clocked the zipped-up body bag on the ground nearby.

"Park maintenance called it in just before dawn after one of their guys noticed some broken railing up there," Martinez explained as he approached.

He gestured upwards, and they both turned their eyes to the cliff face towering above them. At the top was a popular lookout spot that most people in town either knew as a local lover's lane or a great place to think. Now, Hoxton realized, it would be known as a grave site.

"When he looked over the edge, he saw the car down below, just under the water." Martinez went on. When Hoxton looked confused, he added, "It's only about fifteen or twenty feet deep a few yards from the edge here. It's lucky the car was white. Any other color might've been harder to spot."

"Lucky," Hoxton echoed darkly.

"Well, you know." Martinez shrugged. He paused, then added, "She was inside when they pulled it out... across the dash."

"Jesus Christ," Hoxton murmured as her eyes traced the rocky façade from the water's surface up several stories to the cliff's edge above.

"Jesus Christ," Martinez agreed. "I'm surprised she wasn't in worse shape, though, to be honest. Nasty bash on the forehead and bloated from the water, of course, but considering she wasn't buckled in... I would've expected a lot worse."

"No seatbelt?" Hoxton asked, surprised.

"No seatbelt."

"You'd think a pregnant lady would be a little more careful," Hoxton mused. "Precious cargo, you know?"

"You'd think," Martinez tsked. "My wife hated wearing the seatbelt while she was pregnant, too, though. She said it was too uncomfortable when I'd get on her about it. I guess it's not that farfetched that she wouldn't have it on."

Together, they watched as the coroner and a few others raised the gurney carrying Mari's remains and began to pick their way back over the rocks to a nearby van. As they passed her water-logged SUV, Hoxton noticed the driver's side window was gone.

"Did they smash the window to get her out?" she asked, confused.

Martinez followed his partner's gaze. "No, it was rolled down."

Hoxton frowned at this odd detail. "Have you been up there yet?" she asked, indicating the overlook above.

"Not yet. We've got it cordoned off, though. Shall we?"

Hoxton nodded gloomily. They left the scene and drove together, following the road as it curved and sloped up to the overlook. They parked on the shoulder near the turnoff and made their way on foot to a wooden barricade. An officer standing guard lifted it out of the way for them to pass through.

Unlike the damp and rocky little beach they'd just come

from, the quarry lake overlook was a bright, open, and well-traf-ficked dirt parking lot directly off the main road that faced west, allowing for uninterrupted vistas of the entire lake and surrounding trees, all the way to the distant horizon. Hoxton herself had been here on a couple of dates—a far cry from the reason that brought her here now.

"Been a while since I came up here," she murmured.

"Not me," said Martinez. "In my rookie days, we were constantly busting freaky teens for parking up here after dark." He shook his head in disgust. "Hmph. Nasty."

Hoxton studied the area in detail. The cliff's edge was barri-caded by a brittle wooden rail, gray with age and dotted with rusting signs warning people to keep back. The rail spanned all but the furthest parking space, leaving an open path to the precipice beyond and a steep drop straight down to the lake's surface below.

Hoxton nodded towards the unguarded space. "Why didn't they extend the rail out to there? I'm surprised no one's had an accident like this before."

"They did," Martinez answered. "Her car went right through it and made a clean break. I guess that's how nobody noticed it until today… that and the fact that it's at the far end. Hardly any tracks, either. The rain must've washed most of them away that night."

Hoxton squinted at their surroundings. "It was raining that night…" she repeated, trying to picture the place under those conditions.

"Yeah, pretty hard," Martinez affirmed. "I'm guessing she detoured out here to think about things and went over acciden-tally. All this dirt would've made for some slippery mud. It would've been pretty deadly up here. And," he gestured above them, "no lights. It would've been tough to see. One false move…"

"Don't they gate this place at night?" Hoxton suddenly

asked, angry over the number of common-sense failures that led to this.

Martinez tsked regretfully. "Yes, there is a gate, but no, they're not strict about locking it. People around here see the place as a rite of passage for kids in town, so the city is kind of whatever about it. I guess that'll change now."

Hoxton peered over the cliff's edge with a dissatisfied expression. "Why would she have rolled down the window in the rain?"

"Maybe she rolled it down trying to get out, down there?"

"She would've had to have done it up here," Hoxton disputed. "No way could she have survived that impact and opened it down there. She'd be dead already."

Martinez shrugged. "After a night like she had, maybe she needed some air. I know I would've," he added sympathetically.

"Yeah... maybe..." Hoxton murmured.

"You don't think so?"

"I don't know what I think," Hoxton replied, looking out at the horizon. The sun was starting to break through the morning fog, turning the low-hanging clouds a burnished gold as they burned away above the misty forest. It was going to be an unjustly pretty day.

"I guess I was expecting something different," she sighed. "It's hard to believe after everything... this is it. Just an accident."

Martinez nodded. "The husband's been shitty, but like you pointed out, we can't arrest someone for that, and so far, we don't have any evidence to indicate otherwise. We spoke to the neighbors; we checked home surveillance footage. He was the only one to go into the house that night, and he never left. We saw her leave the house in *that* car." He nodded to the beach down below. "I don't like it either, but it's like you said... sometimes, the simplest explanation is the right one."

Hoxton wrestled with that for a long time. Martinez was making sense, but this didn't feel simple at all. She couldn't shake her dreams about Mari. There was more here that she just couldn't see yet.

"Let's wait and see what the autopsy says," she finally said. "Hopefully, they can get to it quickly."

"I think that won't be a problem," Martinez mused, looking back at the crowd of press growing just beyond the police barricades.

CHAPTER 19

The summary of Marilys Goodridge's autopsy named her official cause of death as *'drowning as a result of a motor vehicle accident involving a body of water.'*

The condition of the body suggests the victim was submerged in water for approximately 8-10 days before remains were recovered. Epidermal tissue is extremely waterlogged, though there appears to be minimal effect on the body from wildlife (fish, insects, etc.) known to be in those waters. There is a large gash surrounded by bruised tissue on the forehead, as well as a bar-shaped bruise across the upper-back and fractures to the back ribs, attributable to reports that the victim was not wearing a seatbelt at the time. Victim is missing three anterior teeth—one canine, two incisors on the right side— indicating an impact to the face, consistent with a car crash with no seatbelt. There are additional contusions covering the torso, arms, and legs, consistent with a car crash with no seatbelt. Fractured vertebrae of the cervical spine, surrounded by bruised neck tissue, suggest whiplash, also consistent with a car crash with no seatbelt. Water was found in the lungs, indicating that the victim was alive, but likely unconscious (given the severity of the wounds to the head and face) as the vehicle sank. At the family's request, the unborn

fetus has been removed from the mother's remains to be prepared
separately for burial.

These words burned themselves into Hoxton's memory as she reviewed the final autopsy report and closed the investigation into Mari's disappearance. They swam across her vision now as she sat in a wooden pew reading her funeral program, the clinical phrasing juxtaposed coldly against the words lovingly put together by her family.

Marilys Mina Daniels Goodridge
Beloved Daughter, Wife, Mother, and Friend.
Your light will shine forever in our hearts.
Rest peacefully among angels with your cherished baby boy.
We will carry the memory of your love
Until we meet again in Heaven.

Mari's loved ones were gathered in a large, sun-filled funeral home cathedral with tall, stained-glass windows. Bitter regret mingled with the scent of lilies above the crowd of mourners, their grief swelling and crashing around Hoxton like black waves on a somber sea. It was a smaller funeral than most had anticipated, given the frenzy surrounding Mari's disappearance. Once her death was confirmed an accident, the hordes of caring strangers quickly dissipated. Hoxton was relieved to see less than a hundred people gathered for the final service, knowing those who remained were genuinely devoted to upholding Mari's memory with dignity.

At the front of the room, a single closed casket rested on a curtained platform. On top of it sat two sprays of white flowers, one larger and one heartbreakingly small, held together with a delicate, pale blue bow. A tiny teddy bear was nestled among the blooms of the smaller arrangement. It was an agonizing reminder of what lay inside—excruciating to look at but impossible to look away from. An enlarged photo of a very pregnant

Marylis sat on an easel nearby, also wreathed with white flowers. She beamed at the mourners, cradling her rounded belly with both hands.

Sitting in the front row, directly under their daughter's gaze, Meena and Mark clung to each other, inconsolable. Kris and Steve sat across the aisle from them, also at a loss, though composed enough to acknowledge sympathetic guests. Hoxton noticed the two couples barely acknowledged each other.

The Daniels and the senior Goodridges had been united in their focus on the quick and safe recovery of their daughter and grandchild, but as the investigation wore on, relations between the two families crumbled. Kris and Steve had done their best to save face amid the onslaught of public opinions vilifying their son, but by the time the case was closed, they struggled to remain on speaking terms with Meena and Mark.

Mason sat on the other side of his parents, as far as possible from his grieving in-laws, in a world of his own. Hoxton studied him openly. If the rest of the attendees were an ocean of grief, Mason towered above them like a darkened lighthouse, offering no comfort. He spoke little and mostly stared into space, avoiding all eye contact. His lack of presence was further indictment to Hoxton and many others in attendance—not that he seemed to care. As far as Hoxton could tell, he'd been checked out since the day he received the news about his wife and child's fate.

After leaving the scene at the lake, Hoxton and Martinez went straight to the Daniels' home where the families had gathered, to deliver the update in person. Both detectives had watched Mason closely for any sign suggesting his involvement, but the man never flinched. He sat perfectly still as he took in the news, his green eyes going gray while his in-laws broke down sobbing across from him. After a few minutes, Mason looked up and asked one question: "Where is she now?"

From there, Mason and his father had dutifully gone to identify the body. At the morgue, they stood quietly over Mari's bloated remains, with the lab's fluorescent lights buzzing insistently overhead. As Mason regarded his wife's lifeless figure on the cold, metal table, Hoxton watched his eyes wander to the place in her torso where his son used to be. His shoulders slumped a fraction of an inch.

"Do you want to see him?" she asked softly.

Mason shook his head, apparently unable to speak.

"Mase, are you sure?" his father pressed gently.

Mason had only closed his eyes and nodded in silent affirmation. He let his father do the talking as they signed the necessary forms and departed without a single utterance.

"You think that's suspicious?" Martinez later asked, his tone hopeful.

"I don't know," Hoxton sighed. "I don't know if I'd have the strength to see that either."

"I guess so," Martinez conceded. "But there's still something about him I don't trust."

Hoxton was tired of having this conversation. From the moment their investigation began, she felt strong emotional pulls to both Mari and Mason and was weary of feeling stuck between them. Her failure to find any evidence to support what her instincts were screaming was killing her. Rehashing things over and over with Martinez only sharpened the ache. She was ready to let it all go.

"There's nothing here to suggest foul play," she reminded him grimly.

"Isn't there?" Martinez persisted. "How would you get a bruise like that across the back in a car accident?"

Hoxton had shrugged at that, too. "Car landed upside down in the water. Who knows how many times it flipped on the way down? She would've been tossed all over the place inside."

When Martinez refused to accept this, Hoxton added, "I get why you don't like him. No good guy cheats on his pregnant wife, right? But being an asshole is not the same as being a murderer, and in the eyes of the law, he's clean."

He's clean. Hoxton's words echoed in her mind as she
returned to the present and watched Mason now at the funeral.
He was dressed in a well-fitting, pressed black suit, freshly
shaved, with his blonde hair combed into smooth waves.
Although neatly presented, it was clear the investigation into his
wife's disappearance and the ensuing hurricane of negative
public opinion had taken its toll on him. He had lost weight. His
face was hollow, with deep shadows unded his eyes, which were
glazed over like he hadn't slept in days. His haunted expression
gave Hoxton a minor sense of satisfaction.

"She's gotta have a brass pair, right?" Martinez whispered
beside her, nudging her with his elbow.

Confused, Hoxton followed his gaze to an attractive blonde
woman seated directly behind Mason, whom she recognized as
Jeanine Alder. Jeanine sat forward in her pew as if she were
magnetized to him, though Mason did not acknowledge her.

"What's different about her?" Martinez whispered.

"The hair. It's blonder... highlights," Hoxton whispered back.

Jeanine appeared to have gotten a makeover since Hoxton
first met her. She had become the subject of some public fasci-
nation and seemed to be making the most of her fifteen minutes
of fame. It was clear she had gotten extra done up for today,
which struck Hoxton as diabolical. She shook her head in
disgust.

When the officiant invited Mari's parents to speak, they stood
up together, holding hands. Mark kept a supportive arm
wrapped around his wife as they approached the podium.
Unfolding a piece of paper from his breast pocket, he cleared his
throat and began.

"I want to thank everyone for the love and support you have
shown my family during this time. We don't have words to
describe the pain of this loss or what it feels like to endure a
moment like this for a second time as parents."

Meena's pale face grew paler as she listened to her husband.
She squeezed her eyes shut, pressing a wad of tissues she was

clutching to the space between her brows. Hoxton's heart went out to her. Mark tightened his arm around Meena and continued.

"Marilys was the brightest light. She was the most important, most precious thing in the world to us." His voice breaking, he paused to collect himself.

"Equally precious was the son she carried, our grandson… our last child's only child. We cannot describe how much it hurts that we will never have a chance to meet you or hold you in our arms. We were prepared to love you to heaven and back, but we never expected to have to do that literally." Mark's composure wavered again, but he persevered, his voice shaking.

"Our Marilys was a beautiful person, inside and out. Warm, funny, caring, fiercely loving—she gave everything she had to the people she loved. She would've been the most incredible mother. She deserved a much longer life." His voice became more assertive, and he looked pointedly at his son-in-law. "She deserved so much more than she got."

Hoxton glanced at Mason, who stared at the floor.

"We will love our daughter and grandson to our last breath, and we will carry their memory in our hearts until we are all together again someday. To my Mari, being your father was the greatest honor of my life, and I thank God for that privilege every day, even now, because I know this pain is only proof of the love we shared. I miss you terribly, and I will love you forever."

Keeping one arm around his wife, Mark shifted so that Meena was in front of the microphone. She stood frozen for several moments, looking down at the podium, taking small gulps of air. The crowd waited for her in rapt silence.

"Marilys was my daughter," she began, her voice barely above a whisper. "She was my best friend." Her face screwed up tightly again, and she whimpered and pressed a balled fist to her forehead. "I'm so sorry, I'm so sorry," she breathed. "It's hard to find the words…" she trailed off, hyperventilating.

Hoxton shifted uncomfortably as a dull ache bloomed in her

chest. She wanted to get up and run from the room. A few muffled sobs sounded around her. She noticed Kris Goodridge tighten her grip on her son's arm as she dabbed at her tears. Mason clasped his hands together so tightly his knuckles were white.

Catching her breath, Meena began again. "I had a dream about Marilys. She came to me, and I held her in my arms, and she told me she would be alright. My beautiful girl..." Meena let her tears fall. "I wish so many things were different. I wish both my children were here. I wish we were celebrating our beautiful new arrival, our sweet grandson, instead of saying goodbye, again." She swallowed a sob, then turned to her husband and buried her face in his chest.

It was a heart-wrenching picture: Meena and Mark, aged with grief and rocking each other like children as they stood beside their daughter and grandson's coffin. Some dropped their eyes to the floor, unable to bear the sight of them. Others seemed unable to look away. Finally, the officiant stepped in to relieve them. They returned to their seats without ever acknowledging their son-in-law.

While the service went on, Hoxton returned to studying Mason. As other friends and family members spoke, his nostrils would occasionally flare at their remembrances, but Hoxton couldn't tell if it was from grief or anger. Before bringing the ceremony to a close, the officiant opened the floor one last time to anyone else who would like to offer a few words. A palpable resentment began to simmer as people realized Mason would not be speaking. A young woman Hoxton recognized as Mari's friend, Amanda, turned in her seat to glare at him expectantly. Mason remained stoic, avoiding everyone.

Nodding once, the officiant offered closing remarks and a final prayer. Hoxton steeled herself to interact with Meena and Mark as she made her way out in the receiving line.

"I'm so terribly sorry for this outcome. I pray you and your family find peace." Hoxton clasped their hands as they tearfully accepted her words.

"Will you be staying for some refreshments?" Meena asked in a small voice. She gestured through a wide archway where guests had already begun to help themselves to finger sandwiches and lemonade.

Hoxton shook her head. "I'm afraid I can't stay. You all take good care of yourselves." She stepped to Mason next and offered her hand. "You too."

Mason took her hand automatically and mumbled his gratitude. When it was time to let go, she held on, sensing for one last inkling of the truth in his touch, but Mason remained indifferent. When Hoxton finally moved on, he turned to offer Martinez an equally robotic farewell.

"If we can't bust him for anything, at least we never have to deal with him again," Martinez muttered as they walked back to the car.

Hoxton grunted her half-hearted agreement as she opened the car door and dropped into her seat, exhausted and dissatisfied. Perhaps it was wishful thinking, but something told her they hadn't seen the last of Mason Goodridge. If that turned out to be true, she'd make sure he got what was coming to him.

CHAPTER 20

Mason felt the muscles in his neck finally relax as he watched the two detectives depart. He could feel Hoxton studying him all morning, like an ant under a magnifying glass, but Mason refused to give in to the heat. As the investigation continued, she had proven to be such a disappointment, incapable of deciding which side she was on. Mason savored her and her partner's dissatisfaction when the evidence cleared him of any wrongdoing. He was glad to finally be rid of them.

He quickly refortified himself for the next fake exchange in this hellish receiving line. Everyone took his hand and offered their condolences, but Mason could feel their contempt for him crackling like electricity in their palms. He could see it in their hardened eyes. The feeling was mutual—he hated everyone here just as much as they hated him, if not more. He hated how capricious and sheeplike they all were, how quickly they'd jumped to conclusions and judgment, and how they circled like vultures around him now in the wake of his tragedy.

He'd never felt so attacked in his life. Since that final night with Mari, when she called forth his greatest insecurities and named his most painful shortcomings, her words had echoed over and over from every direction—from the detectives, the media, his community, and even his own family. Even if someone was careful with what they said, no one could conceal the hatred in their eyes. It was almost comical now to think that just weeks ago, he'd been carefully planning a marital exit strategy that he thought would minimize their judgment to a level he believed he could withstand. He'd been a fool, and an arrogant one, at that.

The only way Mason knew to cope with the tidal waves of emotion from the people surrounding him now was to disassociate behind a completely stony exterior. No matter what he thought or felt inside, he reacted to nothing and no one. He knew his parents and friends were desperate for any sign of life from him, but it paled in comparison to how desperate he was just to be left alone. It was like he was living in a fishbowl, and someone was constantly tapping on the glass to get a reaction from him.

Kris and Meena's tearful eyes sought him out constantly, hungry for a glimpse of accountability, begging him to shed tears that would validate their own. Everything they did, everything they saw and heard reminded them of the loss of Mari and the baby they'd never get to meet, and their aching hearts couldn't bear it. They were utterly incapable of controlling or containing their pain, and it hung around them, humming like a sorrowful swarm of bees. Mason couldn't stand to be near either one of them.

Meanwhile, so many others were full of anger and resentment. He had betrayed their friend, neglected her, and broken promises to her, and now she was gone, and he was to blame. Aside from wishing that final night with Mari had never happened in the first place, Mason hadn't had a moment to unpack the rest of his feelings because he was so busy being battered by everyone else's. He certainly couldn't express any of it, knowing it would only be twisted into more ammunition against him.

He floated through the rest of the funeral in a daze. He resented having to sit there and listen to everyone talk about what a perfect person Mari was. Mari was far from perfect. He might not have loved her anymore, but that final night was the first time he'd felt hate for her, and now he couldn't make it go away. He wondered what people would think if they could've seen her that night, sobbing and screaming and storming around like a hysterical banshee.

"Hey, baby," a woman's voice purred in his ear, interrupting Mason's thoughts. He flinched as a freshly manicured, feminine hand slid around his waist from behind.

A fresh wave of exhaustion threatened to take Mason off his feet. Jeanine had been an incessant presence in the last few weeks. Once Mari's remains were discovered, she'd wasted no time attempting to be by his side despite everyone's objections, including his own.

He remembered the stunned look on his mother's face the first time she'd answered the door at his house to find Jeanine standing there with two armfuls of grocery bags and an idiotic grin. The rest of her face was obscured by giant sunglasses and a sunhat with a brim so wide it flopped against one of her shoulders. Mason had rushed to the door himself the moment he heard her voice, but he was too late.

"You must be Kris!" she declared, breathless. "I'm so sorry we're meeting for the first time like *this*." She jerked her head back to the gang of photographers at the end of the driveway.

Mason and Kris had just stared at her, dumbstruck.

"We haven't been properly introduced, but I'm Jeanine Alder," she persevered. "I used to work with Mari, and, well, I'm sure you know about Mason and me by now." Jeanine smiled sheepishly, as if she and Mason were a couple of teens who got caught necking rather than two full-blown adulterers.

"Your son is a wonderful man," she gushed, with a loving

glance at Mason, who looked on, aghast. He could hear cameras clicking furiously from the end of the driveway and felt a migraine coming on as he imagined the next day's headlines. Kris made no move to invite her in. After several awkward seconds, Jeanine piped up again.

"I brought groceries!" she announced, lifting her heavily laden arms. "I figured you guys might have a hard time getting in and out, what with the mob out there. Mase, I got some of your favorites!"

Mason could've strangled her. He was grateful Meena and Mark were not present at the time, or the media would have had one hell of a show. To Kris' credit, she had politely accepted the bags but let Jeanine know in no uncertain terms that company was not welcome at the moment. Then, she'd brought her son back inside for an earful about his recklessness and utter disregard for the optics of the situation. Later, he found Jeanine's groceries in the trash, unopened.

"Jeanine," Mason warned through gritted teeth, his eyes darting warily around the reception. "I told you to leave after the service."

"I know, I know," she replied, smoothing a stray hair off his forehead. "You just looked so far away all day. I wanted to check on you."

"Of fucking course I look far away!" he hissed, batting her hand away. "This is my wife's funeral! I told you not to come here!" He could see his words stung her, but Jeanine held her ground.

"Mason, I've been your girlfriend for the past year," she replied. "Today is the hardest day of your life. They can't expect the woman who loves you to—"

"You shouldn't be here," he whispered angrily, cutting her off. "I've told you a million times. Look at my in-laws right now. Think of what this looks like!"

"I *am* thinking," she hissed back. "I'm the only one thinking about *us*, Mason! About our future. It would look worse if I *didn't* pay my respects to Mari. Future honoring the past, hello?"

It was such a delusional take that Mason struggled to comprehend it well enough to argue. "You need to go," he ordered in a low, threatening voice.

"Mason, it's *me*," Jeanine implored. "Let me be your safe space today."

Mason let out an exasperated sigh. "Look," he began, softening his tone in an attempt to reason with her. "I know you are just trying to have my back, but your being here is hurting me. That can't be what you want."

"People will have to get used to us eventually. The more they see us together, the faster that will happen. It'll be tough at first, but after all we've been through..." She reached for him again.

"Stop it!" Mason swatted her hands aside and then pressed his palms together. "I'm begging you, Jeanine. I can't do this right now. *Please*. Please, just go home, and we can talk later. I promise."

Jeanine was about to insist again when another female voice interrupted her.

"I think my son has made himself clear," Kris declared in a low but firm voice, appearing at Mason's side.

"Mrs. Goodridge, hello!" Jeanine was polite but undeterred. "I'm sorry. It wasn't my intention to cause a scene. How are you? Please accept my sincerest condolences." She offered her hand, but Kris eyed it distastefully. Jeanine's confidence wavered.

"I—I know this is a tough time," she stammered. "But I just want you to know that I care very deeply for your son, and in the future, I hope that—"

"If you care at all about my son or the impression you are making on his family, you will leave *right now* and not show your face again until someone invites you."

Mason rarely saw his mother lose her temper, but he could feel intense anger rolling off her now as she processed Jeanine's audacity. He feared what she might say next, but thankfully, Jeanine backed down immediately.

"Yes, of course, I didn't mean to intrude," she whispered, shrinking under Kris's glare. She glanced at Mason, who refused to make eye contact. "I'll call you." She reached for him one last time.

Mason clenched his jaw to keep himself from slapping her hand away again. With that, Jeanine made her way out, weaving through funeral guests who stared after her in disbelief. Kris remained at Mason's side, watching her go.

"Mom, I—"

"Don't." Kris looked up at her son sternly. He watched her regret-filled eyes trace the waves in his dark golden hair. The tips of his ears burned with shame.

"Mason, I don't know what's happening in your head right now. And obviously, I have no idea what the past few months were like for you at home. But none of that justifies you and *that woman* disrespecting your wife and the mother of your child at her own goddamned funeral!" Kris scolded in a hushed voice. "Look at her parents right now!"

Mason refused to look at Meena and Mark, but Kris didn't let up.

"They are devastated, and you are humiliating them! We raised you better than this! Do you have any idea how much it hurts to see you behave this way?" she asked.

Mason's cheeks reddened. "Mom, I don't need this right now."

"None of us needed any of this right now," she replied. "We are all hurting. I know you are too, more than any of us."

Mason pressed his lips together tightly. He saw his father approaching, pushing past several funeral guests who were fully tuned in to their conversation.

"Son, I love you," Kris sighed. "I always will. We've already lost so much as a family. I just don't want to see you lose anymore."

"Everything okay here?" Steve placed a hand on his wife and son, concern etched across his face. Kris looked to Mason, who straightened his shoulders.

"We'll be fine," he promised, looking his mother in the eye. She squeezed his hands reassuringly. The Goodridge family stood together, holding each other and ignoring their guests, who finally gave them some space.

CHAPTER 21

Kris and Steve moved in with Mason indefinitely after the funeral, intending to support him as he found his way forward, but instead, they watched helplessly as their boy retreated further inward, alienating himself from the world. His stoicism after everything he'd been through was frightening—Kris knew he had to be heartbroken inside. When he informed them of his plans to put the house up for sale immediately, they tried to talk him out of it, worried that he was behaving rashly.

"Don't you think it might be a little soon?" Steve asked, searching Mason's expression carefully across the dinner table.

"Why on earth would I want to stay here?" Mason sneered. "I hate it here. This house feels like a fucking tomb."

Kris couldn't help but agree. When Mari was here, the place always felt so inviting, but now, the atmosphere was somber. Everywhere she looked, she saw longer, deeper shadows where there were none before. Still, after losing so much already, she wasn't sure uprooting himself from his home so abruptly was the healthiest thing.

"It's true, there's a lot of sadness here," Kris acknowledged, "but there are a lot of good memories too, aren't there?"

Mason's expression darkened. "Not enough of them."

Kris waited for him to elaborate, but he resumed eating his dinner in grumpy silence. Once more, she found herself wondering exactly what had gone on between Mari and Mason before things came to an end. She couldn't recall anything that suggested they were this unhappy.

Then again, what would she have done if she knew then what she did now? Kris hated to admit that she probably wouldn't have intervened, but perhaps Mari and the baby would be alive today if only she had...

No. She stopped herself from going further down that road, just as she had every day since Mari disappeared.

"I may not know the details of what happened between you two," she began, "but I know that Mari loved you—"

"Mari hated me!" Mason sniped, cutting her off. "She was trying to leave me when—" he stopped short and pressed his lips together. Kris didn't move a muscle. This was the first time Mason had opened up about that day, she didn't want to spook him into silence. He dropped his eyes to his plate.

"It's just too much here," he finally muttered.

Kris's heart went out to him. "I understand, honey," she replied gently. "You wanna hear something silly? The other day, I could've sworn I heard the glider rocking in the nursery. At first, I thought it was you, until I realized you and your dad were watching TV downstairs. And of course, when I went to check, nobody was there. The chair wasn't even moving!" she laughed, but stopped when she saw Mason's stony expression.

"My point is grief can really throw us off balance sometimes. Maybe if you let yourself let go a little, things around here wouldn't feel so painful. You don't have to worry about us. You can cry, or scream, or do anything you want. We're here for—"

"What I want is to get the hell out of here," Mason replied. Kris looked to her husband for help.

"Mase, we just don't want you to do anything hasty," Steve

reasoned. "I agree, it doesn't make sense for you to stay here long term—"

"I'm selling," Mason said over him. "End of discussion."

Unfortunately, once the house was listed, it attracted more people who were interested in seeing inside the infamous Goodridge home rather than buying it. Their morbid curiosity was frustratingly obvious the moment they walked through the door. The house seemed to respond in kind, reflecting exactly what its audience hoped to see: Tragedy. With every walk-through, it took on a more unwelcoming air. Even if someone genuinely interested showed up, nobody wanted to linger there after spending just a few minutes inside.

Eventually, Mason was desperate enough to allow Kris and Steve to seek Ryan's help in pushing a sale. Enticed by the idea that it would get Mason out of town and out of their lives faster, Ryan agreed to help, but it made no difference.

"How long am I supposed to be punished?" Mason grumbled as he stood on the front porch with Kris and Ryan, watching another prospective buyer depart. It was a rhetorical question, but Ryan answered anyway.

"Forever sounds about right," he muttered.

Mason rolled his eyes.

"Boys, let's please not do this right now," Kris sighed.

"Eastview's number one realtor," Mason fumed, ignoring her. "Give me a fucking break. This is one of the most desirable streets in one of the most desirable neighborhoods in town. We're priced below market, and you still can't move it."

"The most desirable street in the most desirable part of town, owned by the most hated man in Eastview," Ryan sneered. "The house is not the problem, *you* are."

"Boys…" Kris warned.

"Maybe if you spent more time doing your job instead of buying up bus benches and inviting every asshole in town to sit on your fucking face—"

"Mason!" Kris exclaimed. "That is enough!"

"He started it!" Mason objected.

"Enough!" she repeated.

Ryan watched their petulant exchange with a smug smile. "It's alright, Mrs. Goodridge," he said evenly. "That's not a bad idea, Mason; why don't you just sit on it for a while? The house, I mean," he clarified to Kris.

"Is there anything else we can do at this point to make it more attractive to a buyer?" Kris asked, ignoring the covert middle finger Ryan offered her son.

Ryan surveyed Kris with a look of pity and skepticism. "Honestly, I don't know. You could drop the price more, but even then, people are just really hesitant when it comes to murder houses—"

Kris gasped sharply as Mason began to shout.

"It's not a fucking murder house! I did not kill my wife! She left this house alive!"

"Try putting that in the listing," Ryan clipped dryly. "See how that works out. I'm done here. Goodbye, Mrs. Goodridge, you have my sympathy."

With that, Ryan left the Goodridge house for the last time. After further urging from his parents, Mason begrudgingly took the house off the market and resigned himself to being a prisoner there.

Kris attempted to draw him out by recruiting sweet Greg, Mason's last and probably only real friend, to show up at the house. Since Mason now spent most of his time hiding in the back of the house, it was Kris who answered the door.

"Hi, Mrs. Goodridge. Is Mason here?" Greg asked loudly, just as they'd rehearsed. Kris instructed him to wait, then sought out her son, who pleaded with her to make an excuse for him. Kris refused, and after a brief standoff, he trudged to the front door, looking dour. Kris listened from the hall while poor Greg did his best to act normal.

"Hey, bud. I thought we could grab a beer."

Mason declined and exchanged a few words but refused to

invite his friend inside. Eventually, Greg seemed to get the message and excused himself forever with a soft, sad, "See you around." It pained Kris to see him go, but her pleas for Mason to go after him went ignored.

Meena and Mark, on the other hand, were all too eager to move on with their lives without Mason. Working through Kris, they arranged to come to the house and collect their daughter's most precious possessions while Mason was out with his father.

"Are you sure you don't want to take it all?" Kris asked as she walked them to their car.

"And do your son the favor of erasing her from his life?" Meena sneered. "No."

Kris struggled to find the words to respond. "I think about Marilys all the time," she blurted as they loaded the last box. Meena's hand froze on the trunk she had just closed.

"I hope that's okay to say," Kris added quickly. "I want to say I'm sorry for all that's happened, but I know that doesn't even begin to…" she trailed off, knowing 'sorry' would never be enough.

"Marilys was like a daughter to me, too," she began again. "Not like she was for you, of course, but… our family was never close the way you were, and she brought that to us. She was… well… I was looking forward to the future with her as my daughter-in-law." Kris' throat tightened. She swallowed hard, forcing back tears.

Meena pressed her lips together and looked to Mark, who answered for both of them.

"Thank you, Kris," he accepted formally. "And thank you for being good to our daughter. She always spoke well of you."

"I have no idea how people move forward in times like these," Kris admitted, twisting her fingers together anxiously, "but I hope you won't be strangers."

Mark hesitated. "I think that might be hard," he finally said.

"Well, at the very least, we'll see each other again when we spread the ashes, right? Please keep us posted on your plans for that. We'll make sure we're there."

Meena and Mark exchanged wary glances.

"Actually," Mark said quietly, "we were planning to take Mar and the baby's ashes and scatter them in Lake Michigan, where we spread our son's ashes. We have good memories there. It seemed like the right way to bring this to a close for our family."

"That's a beautiful idea. We can make it out anytime—"

"No," Meena said.

Kris blinked. "No?" she echoed.

"We intend to do this, just the two of us," Mark said delicately. "We... don't want Mason there."

Kris took a moment to digest this. "I... understand," she began slowly. She did understand, but she also wanted to point out that Mason had a right to be present for that moment, especially because of the baby, and she didn't want to see him robbed of it. She also knew that advocating for him directly would only fuel their anger, so she tried a different tactic.

"Would you also stop Steve and I from trying to be there for our grandson? I understand why you wouldn't want Mason there, but please, at least let us represent him. I know it would mean a lot to him."

"Your son doesn't give a shit about being there," Meena scoffed. "He doesn't give a shit about anyone but himself, and I'll be damned if this family makes one more concession for that selfish, lying, cheating, monster sack of shit."

Kris flinched at her words but wisely held her tongue. Mark put a calming hand on his wife's shoulder, but she shrugged it off. The floodgates were open, and Meena was far from finished.

"You're right," she continued. "My daughter brought a lot to your family. She gave *everything* to your family, and look how she was repaid. I know you're his mother, and I believe you are a good person, Kris, but not him. Not him." Meena looked balefully back at the house.

"She was supposed to have a good life here. A long, happy, *full* life," she mourned, tears filling her eyes. "Now, I look at this house, and I see nothing but my daughter's pain—pain *your son* caused. I felt it the moment I walked through that door today; the walls are practically bleeding with it. Even her roses are dying."

Kris followed Meena's gaze to the trellis of roses Mari had planted on the porch, which had begun to wilt from neglect. Seeing them like that sent a dull stab through Kris' already aching heart. She looked back at Meena, whose eyes were full of fury.

"He deserves to rot for what he did to her. I pray every day that he gets what's coming to him. I hope he never finds another moment's peace. I hope I never have to lay eyes on any of you ever again." With that, Meena turned her back on Kris and got in the car, slamming the door.

Mark spared a regretful look for Kris, whose face had gone pale. "I can't say I disagree with her," he murmured. "You and Steve take care."

Kris withdrew to the porch, holding back tears while she watched Mark get in the car with his wife, start the engine, and slowly pull away. She waited until their taillights disappeared around the corner before retreating inside to huddle on the stairs, where she finally let her tears fall.

Meena's words had cut deep, but Kris couldn't deny them, and her guilt over that was like salt in the wound. She loved her son, but it was becoming increasingly difficult to defend him. Mason had done a terrible thing that led to horrible consequences. It would've helped if he had shown any interest in redeeming himself, but he remained stubbornly apathetic. Harboring unconditional love for someone the entire world hated was hard enough, but when that person didn't seem to care, it added a layer of shame that was difficult to endure.

Mason's reluctance to open up also made Kris feel paranoid—like there was a massive piece of the puzzle she was missing. She sat there, torturing herself until her cell phone buzzed with an incoming text from her husband.

> Heading home in 15. Coast clear?

Kris replied with a simple thumbs up and started pulling herself together, rolling her shoulders as she made her way upstairs. In the bathroom, she caught her reflection in the mirror and hardly recognized herself. Her eyes and nose were swollen from crying, and her cheeks were flushed bright red, but it was her grief that had taken the more serious toll.

Kris prided herself on looking younger than her years, but now, her face appeared worn. Underneath the splotchy redness, she saw long shadows in the new hollows under her eyes and cheekbones. Fresh worry lines had etched themselves into the space between her brows and around her mouth. Kris put a trembling hand to her cheek—her skin felt hot.

Taking a breath, she turned the taps at the sink, but there was no water. Frowning, she tried both sides again, then tested the toilet and shower, but nothing worked. Grabbing a tissue, she dried her eyes and went to check Mason's bathroom, where she found everything running normally. She washed her face, feeling her mind clear as the cold water splashed her skin. She dried off, inhaling deeply through her newly restored sinuses.

After rearranging the towel neatly on its hook, Kris turned off the lights and was about to leave the bathroom when she heard a soft gurgling behind her. With one foot over the threshold, she turned back and listened. She detected a slight whining, no louder than a whisper, singing through the pipes behind the toilet. As she focused her attention there, she also became aware of a faint skittering, like pearls, bouncing across the tiles.

Kris stared at the floor, searching for the source of the noise. The sound echoed in the back of her skull, and she resisted the urge to shudder. Her eyes traced the tiles as some invisible thing skittered toward her until the noise suddenly disappeared beneath her feet. A tremor went up her legs, but she remained rooted to the spot.

In the silence that followed, Kris released the breath she'd been holding. She waited, listening, but when all remained still, she turned away, eager to escape the creepy atmosphere that had settled around her. As soon as she moved, a faint knocking began, starting at the baseboard where the skittering had started and making its way up the wall.

Flicking the lights back on, Kris went toward the toilet, her eyes moving up the wall as the soft knocking morphed into what sounded like a fingernail tapping and scratching on the other side. The toilet belched, startling her backward, then began to gurgle aggressively. Kris had had enough. With an impatient huff, she marched over and threw back the lid. The bowl was filled nearly to the brim with murky water, which was now receding in great, halting gulps as though it were being chugged away by something inside the pipes. Transfixed, Kris watched the water disappear, inch by inch, until it was gone. In the ensuing stillness, she became aware of her heart thumping fast and heavy in her chest.

Finally, she reached for the lever and flushed. Swirls of clean, clear water washed into the bowl. As the water stilled, a small, misshapen mass at the bottom of the bowl caught her eye.

Squinting, Kris leaned down for a closer look. The small, ivory-colored rock was difficult to distinguish from the surrounding white porcelain. It had smooth sides and was slightly ridged along its edges. Unable to tear her eyes away, Kris fumbled with one hand for the nearby toilet brush. Using the handle, she poked gently at the rock, causing it to separate into three tiny, distinct shapes. She peered at them closely and, upon recognition, gasped and stumbled backward, catching herself against the bathtub's edge to keep from tumbling in. There, at the bottom of the toilet, retched up from some deep recess, lay three pearly-white teeth.

CHAPTER 22

"Mase... Maaase... still sleeping?"

Mason groaned in response to his name. He heard a woman giggle affectionately. Her breath was warm against his ear.

"Maaaason," she sang playfully, her lips brushing his temple. A delicate finger traced a line from his forehead to the tip of his nose. He twitched it away. The laughter came again.

"Wake up, sleepy head!"

"Mhhmpff." Mason frowned and turned away from her, nuzzling deeper into his pillow.

"Mason!" she whispered urgently. "Wake up!"

Mason sighed and squeezed his eyes shut tighter. He didn't want to wake up. It was his first morning alone in forever. His parents had finally gone back to their place yesterday, and he'd gone to sleep last night with a profound sense of relief.

"Maaase. Where are you, baby? Come back to me."

Mason felt that light touch again, this time along his hairline, fingers curling into the waves above his forehead.

"Mhmm," he hummed sleepily. That felt nice. He always liked it when Mari did that, but couldn't she give him five more minutes?

Something in him snapped to attention. *Mari is dead. Someone else is here.*

Mason tried to lift his head but found that he couldn't. The nerves in the back of his neck quivered at the command, but his muscles wouldn't obey. He became aware of a great weight on top of him, pressing him down into the mattress, squeezing the air out of his lungs. His heart started beating fast. He willed his eyes to open, but his eyeballs only rolled frantically under closed lids.

Panic welled up in Mason as he thrashed in his mind, fighting to move his leaden body under motionless sheets. All the while, he was aware of feminine laughter echoing nearby. The more he fought, the more delighted she sounded. While he struggled, the laughter grew louder, until he felt it booming in his ribcage.

"WAKE UUUUUUUUP!!!!!!!!!!!!!!!!!!!!!"

The harsh scream sent a stab of hot pain through Mason's ear canal. He felt something brush his cheek—the sensation caused whatever was holding him down to instantly release. Mason's eyes snapped open. He pushed himself to his knees, his shoulders heaving with rage.

"Who's there!" he shouted, looking around wildly for his tormentor. There was no reply.

Tossing the covers away, Mason bounded out of bed and stormed into the hallway. He went to the railing and looked down into the foyer. The front door was locked. Cocking his ear, Mason listened intently for another presence in his house.

"JEANINE?" he thundered. "You'd better not let me catch you here!" He heard nothing in response but his own hammering pulse.

Mason swallowed, then winced at the roughness in his vocal cords. He realized the scream that had broken his sleep paralysis was his own. Still, he refused to believe he'd been dreaming. Someone had touched him, *whispered* to him, but as he stood there surveying his home, he couldn't deny that he was alone.

He shivered and looked down at his bare chest, slick with cold sweat. His heart rate slowed as adrenaline receded from his veins, replaced by a groggy wave of exhaustion.

Mason returned to his bedroom, hoping to climb back under the covers, but found Otis curled up comfortably in the spot he had just vacated. The cat snored softly, his furry back rising and falling with each gentle purr.

Mason leaned against the door frame and watched Otis sleep. He used to come out of the shower in the mornings to find Mari in a similar position—nuzzled affectionately into his pillow. As Mason marveled at how much his life had changed so quickly, a strange emotion began to take hold. It took him a moment to recognize it. He hadn't felt it in so long that he had started to believe he never would again. For the first time in months, Mason felt happy. He smiled.

Nestled in bed, Otis blinked his eyes open, sensing the change in Mason's mood. They held each other's gazes, grinning and glaring at each other, respectively.

"Good morning, fucker!" Mason laughed, breaking the standoff. "Breakfast?"

Otis refused to dignify him with a response.

Mason stretched his arms up high, hooking his fingers on the door frame above him. He hung there for a long, delicious moment, feeling his spine decompress, then clasped his hands behind his head, puffing out his chest.

"Suit yourself," he exhaled.

Leaving Otis behind, he headed downstairs with a plan to make himself a big breakfast to eat in front of the TV, whistling while he worked over a pile of cheesy scrambled eggs, toast, and bacon. When Otis finally joined him, he tossed him an opened can of food without a grudge.

Mason couldn't remember the last time he felt this good. The weight of the world seemed to have suddenly been lifted off his shoulders. He spent two leisurely hours eating breakfast and watching TV before he felt like getting up and taking a long, hot shower. He left his dirty dishes on the coffee table and sauntered out of the room.

He was at the foot of the stairs when he remembered his cell phone, left behind in the kitchen. He went back for it, smiling at the fact that he no longer had to keep such close track of it. A notification popped up on the screen as he picked it up, reminding him that today was his seventh wedding anniversary. Before he could react, the phone buzzed with an incoming call from an unknown number. Ignoring it, he cleared both notifications and continued upstairs to shower, taking the steps two at a time.

As the hot water cascaded down his back, Mason felt the last of his worries melt from his shoulders. He finally understood why Mari always took such infuriatingly long showers. He helped himself to one of the pressed shower tablets she kept in a sealed glass jar and dropped it in the water between his feet. The scent of eucalyptus permeated the steam. Mason breathed it in, feeling his lungs expand and his mind clear. As he dried himself with a towel fresh off the warming rack, he not only felt clean but cleansed.

"Thank you, Mar," he chuckled.

The house phone suddenly rang from the nightstand outside. Mason went to answer, relishing the freedom of walking around naked, but by the time he reached the phone, the ringing had stopped. He checked the receiver—the caller ID read "Unknown." As he placed it back on its charging stand, his cell phone buzzed in the bathroom, but by the time he went back for it, the caller had hung up. The caller ID, again, read "Unknown."

Mason stared at the cell phone in his hand, wondering who was trying to reach him so urgently. He waited for a follow-up text or voicemail, but none came. Annoyed, he tossed his cell onto the unmade bed and went to get dressed.

As he opened the closet, he paused to silently thank his mom for reorganizing it for him. All his clothes were now spread out and easily accessible, while Mari's belongings were packed in sealed, neatly labeled boxes tucked at the back of the narrow space.

"You can deal with them whenever you're ready," Kris had said when she showed him the changes.

Mason had no plans to ever touch those boxes. Now that Mari's belongings were out of sight, he considered them dealt with. He looked at the racks around him, mulling over what to put on. He'd spent half his day in pajamas and didn't feel like getting back into sweats. He was already beginning to feel a little stir-crazy all by himself. He'd spent the last few weeks wishing for nothing but solitude, and now, after just a few hours of it, he was bored.

Struck by an idea, he went back to the bedroom and retrieved his cell phone from the bed where he'd chucked it. He opened his texts and scrolled until he found the contact he was looking for: Greg.

Mason thought back to his last conversation with Greg on the front porch. He knew he'd acted like a jerk and debated briefly about how to pick things back up before settling on something simple.

> Hey bud, feel like grabbing a beer?

He threw the phone back on the bed and returned to the closet. He grabbed a pair of black track pants, then rummaged through a neatly folded stack of t-shirts until he found what he was looking for: a dark green polo with "Goodridge Land-scaping Services" emblazoned across the back. He shook it open and threw it over his head, smoothing his hand affectionately over the logo on the front.

In the initial days of Mari's disappearance, Mason's business was inundated with inquiries from new clients who were eager to support him. His parents had warned him that the majority might just be voyeurs, but Mason didn't let that bother him. Voyeurs could still become paying customers. As the investigation played out, though, Goodridge Landscaping Services was reduced to nothing more than a hotline for people to call and express their outrage and dismay over Mason's character, and he was forced to shutter indefinitely. It felt good to wear his name on his chest again. He looked at himself in the mirror.

"You're still you," he murmured, squaring his shoulders. He was distracted by the sound of an incoming text and left the closet to check his phone.

> Hi honey, checking in. Okay today? It's your
> anni. Love u – mom.

As if Mason didn't know what day it was. He didn't care to be reminded. He suppressed his irritation and tapped out a reply.

> All good. Doing fine, don't worry. Love you too.

The phone buzzed again as he threw it away, forcing him to do a clumsy little dive after it, in case it was Greg.

> Dad says hi and love you.

Frustrated, Mason kept his reply short.

> Okay, tell him hi.

He held on to the phone this time, certain his mom would follow up again, but she didn't. Mason puttered around the house, waiting to hear back from Greg. Finally, he decided to distract himself by going out on his own for a while. He collected his keys from the front entry table and automatically reached for the well-worn, plain, black baseball cap he now kept there, but stopped before he put it on his head.

Mason had only left the house a handful of times since Mari died, and for those rare occasions, he'd taken to wearing this black cap to shield himself from prying news outlets and judg-mental onlookers. Today, it felt heavy in his hand. He didn't want to hide anymore. He didn't have to. He tossed the hat on the table and walked out the door.

Feeling liberated, he hopped into his truck and fired up the ignition, enjoying the familiar rumble from the engine beneath him as he pulled out of the driveway and headed off on his first solo excursion.

CHAPTER 23

Mason drove aimlessly until finally settling on the hardware store as a suitable destination. There would be people, but not too many, and none who were likely to care about his ordeal. It was the perfect place to dip his toe in and reintroduce himself to the world—or so he thought.

He wasn't prepared for the astonished stares his highly recognizable pickup attracted the moment he pulled into the parking lot, nor did he expect the shifty glances he caught out of the corner of his eye as he meandered through the wide aisles, perusing tool sets and industrial cleaning supplies. He offered friendly nods to people who passed by but noticed they gave him a wide berth and avoided eye contact. In a place that used to feel like home, Mason suddenly felt like an unwelcome stranger.

He was examining a roll of heavy-duty plastic tarp when he felt eyes boring into the side of his face and glanced up. A woman was glaring suspiciously between him and the tarp he held in his hands. They stared each other down for a moment before she scoffed, then walked away, muttering.

Mason felt heat rising in his face. He dropped the tarp and

strode out of the store with his hands stuffed in his pockets. Back at his truck, he wasted no time starting the ignition and peeling out of there. He fumed as he drove. It had been almost three months since Mari's passing, and people who had never even met her were still holding a grudge.

Mason hadn't been convicted of any crime, yet everyone in that store acted like he was a danger to society. *He* was the one under attack! Adultery was not a crime! He was not the first, nor would he be the last husband in the world to cheat on their spouse. Not to mention, Mari was alive the last time he saw her, and whatever transpired after she left their house that night was not on his hands! If the cops had found anything to suggest otherwise, he'd be in a jail cell right now. He was not a bad guy!

Mason's phone vibrated in the cupholder, and he snatched it up. "Mom, I'm fine," he answered impatiently.

There was no response on the other end. Mason held the phone away to check the caller ID, which read, "Unknown." He put the phone back to his ear.

"Hello? Hello? Greg?"

The line crackled lightly. Mason put the phone on speaker and held it closer to his mouth.

"You're breaking up, I can't hear you." He listened again. "Greg, if this is you, just text me back. I can't hear a thing."

The crackling faded, giving way to the distinct sound of heavy breathing. Mason listened to it, confused. "Greg?"

The breathing stopped. A raspy voice began calling his name. "Masonnn… Maaason… mmMaason." It had a sinister quality, though the tone was disturbingly intimate. It made Mason's skin crawl.

"Who the fuck is this!" he demanded.

The caller hung up, laughing. Mason slammed the phone back into the cupholder, not caring if he damaged it. This was the last thing he needed right now. That raspy moan echoed in his ears, sending a creepy-crawly sensation up the back of his neck. He shuddered, then gripped the steering wheel with both hands, tightening and twisting his fingers like he meant to strangle it.

He stopped at a red light and reached up instinctively to adjust the baseball cap lower on his forehead, then berated himself for leaving it at home. He slumped in his seat, grateful that his truck was too high for anyone nearby to get a good look at him. He glanced around furtively, debating his next move.

"Come on, Mase," he muttered. "You've got this."

The light turned green and Mason stepped on the gas, determined to stay out and about. He checked his tank, thinking he could at least stop to fill up, then grimly remembered his father had filled it for him before leaving yesterday.

Mason slowed to a stop at another red light, grateful for the delay. In seconds, it blinked green again, forcing him forward. The truck bucked as he hit the gas. He suddenly remembered the winding Eastview Highway. That drive never failed to improve his mood *and* clear his mind. With renewed optimism, Mason veered sharply into the left lane and swung the first available U-turn toward the woods, ignoring the honking minivan he cut off in the process.

As he eased onto the highway's familiar curves, Mason rolled the windows down to savor the evening autumn breeze. It rushed in, sharp and cold, buffeting his hair and raising goosebumps on his arms. He let it drown out his thoughts and allowed muscle memory to guide his steering along the highway's bends. Treetops above him stood in silhouette against a darkening blue sky, edged with pale yellow where daylight was just beginning to disappear. He could barely see into the woods on either side of him, but it was not yet dark enough for the street lamps to begin flickering on. He glanced down and noticed that his cell was lit up with another incoming call from "Unknown." Mason realized he probably wouldn't be hearing from Greg.

"Fuck 'em all," he muttered as he flipped the phone facedown.

He looked back at the road just in time to violently swerve, barely missing a small figure crouched on the shoulder, just off the pavement. He swore aloud as he righted the steering wheel and pulled over, looking frantically in the rearview mirror. To his horror, he saw a limp little body lying face down on the side of the road, wearing jeans and a light-colored sweatshirt with the hood pulled up, both smeared with dirt. On their feet were a tiny pair of white sneakers with bright blue laces.

Mason gripped the steering wheel so hard that his fingers went numb. A tingling, icy-hot wave of fear washed over him. He'd just killed someone... no, not just someone. He forced his gaze back to the rearview. The body reflected in the mirror looked terrifyingly small.

Mason's mind raced to come up with a plan. He had only been stopped for a few seconds, tops. There were no lights or traffic cameras here. Nobody could tie him to this if he left now, but if he was going to make that choice, he had to do it quickly. Someone else could be along any minute and see his license plate or, hell, the truck with his name in big-ass, stupid letters on the side. Was his reckless U-turn earlier near a camera? He couldn't remember.

Mason looked again at the limp, motionless body in his rearview, bathed in the red glare of his brake lights. He felt sick to his stomach. He'd just gotten his life back—there was no way he'd survive another incident, especially if the victim were a child...

He frowned. Something about this wasn't right. Mason cut the ignition, suddenly on alert. He got out of the truck and approached the body slowly.

"Hello?" he called softly.

Crickets chirped back at him from the surrounding woods. Overhead, a single crow punctured the air with its harsh call, then snickered.

As Mason edged closer, suspicion morphed into confusion. The figure on the ground was the general size and shape of a child, but there was something unnatural about it. The head was misshapen, the limbs too rounded. It lacked the heaviness of a human body. He rolled it over with his foot.

"Mother fucker."

Mason's stomach dropped when he realized he had been scared shitless by a life-sized teddy bear wearing a hoodie and jeans on the side of the road, but that was nothing compared to the explosive feeling that came over him when he realized where it came from. A short distance away, one of the streetlamps flickered on in the dark, revealing a roadside memorial dedicated to Mari and their unborn son at its base.

He swore and snatched up the teddy at his feet. Dragging the bear by one arm, its little sneakers making tracks in the grit, he went closer, as if in a trance. A small mountain of flowers, signage, and toys had collected around the base of the lamp post, left there by strangers who had been affected by Mari's death.

Why here? Mason wondered, peering around in the dusk. He wasn't familiar with this area, but he knew it was miles away from the overlook where she'd gone over.

A car drove by in the opposite direction, its headlights illuminating weathered caution tape on the other side of the road, blocking a small, graveled turn-off. The entrance there was also lined with flowers and marked with two small, white crosses. Mason realized this was the beach where the cops had dragged Mari's car out of the water. A heaviness settled on his chest as he turned back to the memorial on his side of the street. He scanned the messages that were left there.

Psalm 34:18 — The Lord is close to the broken hearted
Rest Peacefully Mari! You deserved better.
Rest in Peace Marilys and Baby Daniels ♡

Another set of passing headlights lit up the last sign as it went by, revealing a crude addendum someone had scribbled in black marker.

Burn in Hell Mason Goodridge!

With a guttural scream, Mason lifted the bear over his head and spiked it on the ground as hard as he could. He snatched up the sign, tore it to shreds, and threw the pieces in the air like confetti. As they fluttered down around him, he kicked at the flower bouquets, crushing their delicate blooms under his heels. Every offering at this memorial represented someone who hated him, and he hated them all right back. He wanted to punish them the way they were all punishing him. He pictured their faces under his feet and stomped on them with a force that made his ankles ache.

Another car went by, but Mason no longer cared who saw him. He marched back to where he had abandoned the teddy, skidding clumsily on a scrap of cellophane. Freshly enraged, he snatched up the oversized bear and hurled it into the woods, listening with satisfaction as it crashed through the dry brush. With a caveman-like grunt, he resumed his desecration of the memorial.

"Hey! Hey! Sir!"

Mason heard the authoritative voice shouting at him, but chose to ignore it.

"Sir, I order you to cease!" A strong hand grabbed Mason's arm and twisted it painfully behind his back, forcing him to his knees.

"Stay down!" the voice ordered. Mason had no choice but to obey. A bright light flashed in his eyes. "Hey man, what the hell is wrong with—Mason Goodridge?"

Mason scowled past the flashlight's blinding beam, trying to make out the face behind it. "Do I know you?"

"It's Eric... Boyer. From high school? We played football together."

The flashlight was making Mason's eyeballs throb. He had no recollection of any Eric Boyer from high school. He dropped his gaze to the ground.

"Oh. Right," he muttered.

"Mason, I'm going to help you to your feet. When I release you, I need you to turn around and keep your hands in the air. Do you understand?"

Mason resisted the urge to roll his eyes. "Yep."

Eric hoisted him clumsily off the ground. He kept one hand on his weapon as Mason turned to face him with both hands in the air.

"Do you know where you are?" He addressed Mason as if he were a wild animal.

"Yes," Mason replied with a withering glare. His answer seemed to surprise Eric, who paused uncertainly.

"Well, uh… Okay. Then, uh… I need to see your license and registration."

Mason regarded him coolly. "They're in my truck," he replied, nudging his head toward his vehicle. "Back there."

"Fine," Eric said. "Walk that way, slowly, and keep your hands up."

Mason shrugged and did as he was told. When they got back to his truck, he narrated his movements as he retrieved his ID from his wallet and the registration from the glove box. Eric accepted both and told Mason to wait with his hands on the vehicle while he looked them over.

"Alright, you can relax," Eric finally said, handing back the documents. Mason turned around to accept them, tossed them back in the truck, then leaned against the open doorframe while Eric studied him.

"What the hell are you doing?" he finally asked.

Mason lifted his chin defiantly. "Are you going to arrest me?"

Eric raised his eyebrow. "For this?" he asked, gesturing around. "Technically, vandalism is a crime, so yes, I could arrest you, but more than that, it's just… shitty."

Mason snorted. "Well. I'm a shitty guy, Eric. Haven't you heard?"

Eric processed this silently. "Okay," he said gently. "I'm going to let you off with a warning this time, but don't let us catch you out here doing this again. We've got officers driving by here all the time."

It was Mason's turn to look bewildered. "Why?" he asked.

Eric shrugged, looking across the way to the graveled turnoff. A ragged piece of crime scene tape left behind on the gate fluttered gently in the breeze.

"People are strange." Eric glanced at the destroyed memorial, then looked meaningfully at Mason. "Case in point."

Mason rolled his eyes. "Can I go now?"

Eric studied him a moment longer. Mason shifted under his scrutiny.

"Hey, man… are you okay?"

Mason's eyes snapped up. "What is that supposed to mean?" he scowled.

"It means what it sounds like," Eric shrugged. "This… this…" he waved his hand at the torn signage and destroyed flowers in their wake. "This doesn't look good for you," he finally said.

Mason felt something in him soften unwillingly. This was precisely what he needed right now—a friend—but Eric's sympathy made him uncomfortable.

"Look, Mase, I know we weren't exactly friends in high school," Eric said, "but if you ever need someone to talk to—"

Suddenly, Eric's kindness was too much to bear. Whatever had softened in Mason a moment ago hardened in an instant.

"Either charge me for something or let me go," he snapped. "I don't need your pity."

Mason meant to shut Eric out, but he got the sense his reaction had only further exposed him to the other man, who was eyeing him again with too much understanding. Mason crossed his arms and stared stubbornly into the woods.

"Okay," Eric finally declared. "You can go."

He stepped back to allow Mason to enter his truck. Without another word, Mason got in the driver's seat and slammed the door shut, avoiding Eric's gaze as the engine roared to life. As he drove away, he spared one last look in his rearview for Eric, who had already begun to clean up the mess Mason left behind.

CHAPTER 24

The warm, turquoise water swished softly as Mason moved through it. He took in a mouthful, bracing for the briny flavor, but was surprised that it tasted sweet and fresh.

He floated on the surface, allowing himself to be rocked by the ocean's gentle waves. He closed his eyes and let the sun warm his face. When he opened them again, he saw nothing but sky and water. The world around him was all vibrant shades of blue. Birds called to him from high above, too far away to see. He dove under the surface. Beneath the waves, sunlight rippled in circles above him, casting bright patterns on his skin.

A low, keening sound vibrated the water around him, drawing Mason's attention to the depths below his feet. He looked back to the surface, thinking he should take another breath before diving down to investigate, and realized he didn't need to. He'd been breathing underwater this whole time. Delighted at the discovery, he swam around, relishing his newfound freedom. The keening came again, reminding Mason of his intentions to explore. He swam down, following the sound.

The water down here was darker and less clear. It got colder, raising goosebumps on his bare skin, but since he could still breathe comfortably, Mason didn't mind. The keening grew louder and more urgent, and in the depths, he saw a pale shape rising to meet him—a white whale. He felt pressure building in his head as he swam deeper, but he didn't slow down. The whale was closer now, but it looked strange—too wide, and too square. Its mouth was small, and it smiled at Mason with long, irregular teeth. Something wasn't right.

It was getting harder to breathe, and sensing that the whale had sinister intentions, Mason reversed course. He pulled hard with his arms but found himself swimming in place, trapped in the pull of the black ocean below him.

The white shape continued to rise out of the dark, coming into focus to reveal a white SUV. The small mouth was a license plate, dirty and scratched, so it gave the impression of broken teeth.

Mason hung suspended in the water above the SUV, unable to look away. Through the back windshield, he could see someone floating inside, asleep, like an embryo in the womb. Her shape was distended, and her hair waved around her head in the currents that passed through the open window. Sensing his presence, her head suddenly jerked unnaturally in his direction. Mason felt electrified as familiar dark eyes locked onto him. *Mari.* She smiled and mouthed something. The water muffled her voice, but the words went off like a bomb in his head: *You're mine.*

Mason struggled against the force dragging him down, trying to fight his way back to the surface, back to the warmth and the light, and away from Mari's baleful glare. His fear seemed to energize her; she drifted higher and faster toward him with her hands outstretched. Her rage billowed like blood in the water as it swelled up to devour him.

Mason could no longer breathe, and his limbs and lungs burned for oxygen. He tried to scream, but the sound was muffled. He clawed upward, his hands finding nothing but empty air. He was lying on something familiar—his couch. Mason was relieved to know it was just a dream, but the moment was brief. He was still being smothered. He grunted and began to fight back.

Mason thrashed like a wild animal, trying to throw off his attacker, who pressed something against his face with unwavering strength, crushing his nose and sealing his lips. He tasted blood as the soft tissue in his mouth split against his teeth. Bright spots flashed against the insides of his eyelids.

Mason punched and grabbed at his opponent, but they evaded his touch. Furious, his mind raced to figure out who was doing this, and why. He'd covered all his bases; the police had cleared him. Was there something he'd missed? As his energy faded, hot rage gave way to cold fear and a panicked realization: *Someone knew.*

With an explosive gasp, Mason rolled off the couch and landed hard on all fours on the carpet. He scrambled to his feet, ready to continue the fight. Something jingled behind him.

Mason whipped around to confront Otis, who had leaped onto the coffee table and was weaving through the obstacle course of empty beer bottles Mason had left there earlier, after returning from his memorial massacre.

A sudden, aching dizziness forced Mason back down on the sofa. He shivered, his T-shirt soaked with sweat, and cradled his throbbing head in his hands while he waited for his heart to slow. It was just a bad dream.

He sat back and surveyed the room again. The sofa's throw pillows had taken a beating during his struggle and now lay strewn about on the floor. He looked at the one closest to him, remembering the sensation of something pressed painfully against his face. Mason licked his lips, then winced when he felt a stinging cut. The taste of blood brought back a flash of memory. With trembling fingers, he reached for the throw pillow and flipped it over—there was a tiny smear of blood and spittle.

Swearing, Mason stood up and began scouring his house,

screaming violent threats as he turned on lights and flung open doors, checking for an intruder. There was no sign of anyone.

Returning to the living room, he collapsed on the sofa again and pressed his fists to his eye sockets. In his mind, he saw Mari rising to devour him from that dark water again. He blinked his eyes open frantically.

"Fuck you, Mari," he muttered.

His cell rang in response, startling him as it buzzed on the coffee table, vibrating the empty bottles. Mason watched it ring, wondering who could be calling at this hour.

"Hello?"

"Maaaase." A voice purred his name on the other end. Mason's blood returned to a boil.

"Who the fuck is this!" he shouted. "What the hell do you want!"

"Oh my God, what is the matter with you?" the caller demanded.

Mason frowned, confused. "Who is this?"

"Babe, are you serious? It's *Jeanine*. Geez… are you okay?"

Mason held the phone away to recheck the caller ID, then remembered he had never saved her number.

"What the hell is wrong with you?" she asked again.

Mason put the phone on speaker and dropped his head back in his hands. "Nothing… I was just… hey, wait. Did you call me a bunch of times today?"

"No, why?"

"Are you sure about that?" he pressed. "I got a bunch of calls from an unknown number today, and when I answered, it was just heavy breathing…"

"Maybe it was one of your other bitches," Jeanine sniped.

"Bye." Mason started to hang up the phone, but Jeanine begged him to wait.

"I'm sorry, I'm sorry, don't hang up. I didn't call you today, but why would you answer unknown calls with everything going on anyway? It could've been a reporter or something! Come on, babe, you know better than that."

"Of course I do. I'm not a fucking idiot, Jeanine. You have no idea what today has been like for me," Mason snapped. "Don't be a bitch."

"Don't call me a bitch," Jeanine snapped back. "Don't you dare talk to me like that!"

Mason was in no mood to argue. He closed his eyes and counted to five. "Alright, alright," he sighed, defeated. "What do you want?"

"Well, first of all, I want you to say you're sorry for calling me a bitch."

Mason rolled his eyes. "Fine. Sorry."

"Thank you, baby. I'm sorry too," Jeanine purred in a baby voice. "I heard the coast is finally clear. Want some company?"

Mason looked at the time. "Jeanine, it's two in the morning."

"Mmhmm, I know. Nothing good happens at this hour… so should I come over?"

Mason did not feel like dealing with Jeanine right now, but he also understood that even though she was asking, she was really calling to announce she was coming. He wondered how she even knew his parents were gone. He didn't have the energy to fend her off, and if he was being honest, he still felt a little shaken. He'd take a warm body right now, and there were worse ones to cling to than Jeanine's.

"Well?" Jeanine prompted.

"Yeah."

He could practically hear Jeanine grinning on the other end of the phone. "That's what I thought. I'll be there in twenty. Don't fall asleep."

"Make it fifteen," Mason replied, then hung up.

Ten minutes later, Mason opened his door to find Jeanine leaning against the frame in the sluttiest nurse costume he'd ever seen. The sheer, white collared dress was so tight it looked like it had been painted on, and the first few buttons were undone to reveal a sheer red bra that barely contained her cleavage. Two red, X-shaped patches were sewn right over where her nipples would be. Mason's eyeballs nearly popped out of his skull.

"What the hell do you have on?" he guffawed.

"Oh, just testing out my Halloween costume," she said airily, doing a slow turn.

The dress barely covered her behind, and his eyes followed the lines of a red garter belt that held up red tights as they disappeared under the hem. She had incredible legs, made even more shapely by the white platform pumps she wore.

"Just a dry run," she winked, "but I'm kinda feeling the opposite, you know what I mean?"

Mason felt like he was going to pass out. A cool breeze picked up at that moment, thankfully restoring his senses. He caught the scent of Jeanine's candy perfume mingled with something bitter and moldy-sick-sweet. Distracted by the odor, Mason looked away, trying to find its source. He didn't have to look far.

The vibrant pink roses that crept along the trellis by his front door—Mari's roses—were almost completely rotted. The stench they gave off was impossible to ignore. He stared at them, bewildered. When he came home earlier that evening, they were wilted, but nowhere near this level of decay. Perplexed, Mason's eyes followed the blackened vines down to their planters, which were standing in a growing puddle of fetid, dark water. A spark of recognition sent a jolt of fear and confusion through him. Mason bit back a curse.

"Ahem." Jeanine cleared her throat, but he paid her no mind. She repositioned herself in Mason's sightline. "Should I leave?" she pouted flirtatiously.

Mason wanted to say no. He knew if he let her in now, there would be no getting rid of her, but over Jeanine's shoulder, the roses came back into focus, looking and smelling like pure death.

Mason looked back at Jeanine, who had folded her arms and was tapping her foot impatiently, causing her boosted cleavage to jiggle like a cartoon. She looked ridiculous; inviting her here had been a mistake. He was about to send her away when he heard a strange noise behind him. He looked back and saw the nursery door slowly creaking open on the second floor. The hairs on the back of his neck stood on end.

Jeanine narrowed her eyes suspiciously. "Is someone else here with you?" She attempted to peer around Mason into the house.

A chill went down Mason's spine. Logic told him it was probably just Otis wandering around, but his instincts screamed something different. In an instant, his mind was made up. He grabbed Jeanine and kissed her hard on the lips.

"Get inside," he growled.

Jeanine wasted no time obeying. Within seconds, Mason had torn her flimsy costume apart and was thrusting into her on the stairs. Hours later, he succumbed to his exhaustion and passed out in the bed he once shared with Mari, entangled in Jeanine's tightly wrapped limbs.

CHAPTER 25

October 25, 2022

Dear Diary – IT'S HAPPENING!!! Mase and I are FINALLY moving toward our destiny—our DREAM LIFE! Together!!! Ugh. My heart is EXPLODING. I knew if I was patient, we would get here eventually. All my baby needed was a little push at juuust the right moment, and what can I say? I made him an offer he couldn't refuse, hehe.

It's been almost a week since I moved in here, and I'm happy to report that living together so far has been pretty seamless. I guess it didn't hurt that this place was already set up for two. I know that's bc it all used to be hers (ew, lol), but that's okay. Little by little, I'm adding my own touches, and soon it'll all just be mine, and mine ONLY!

Case in point – this morning, I helped Mase finally get rid of those disgusting, tacky roses that were on the front porch. Can you believe it! Me?! Manual labor???

*They smelled like death, it was sooo gross, but I did it!
Actually, it was kind of nice doing something physical
together other than fucking haha. I always thought
this suburban housewife shit would be boring, but so
far, I'm enjoying being domesticated. I guess I just
needed the right guy to settle down for. If only we'd
found each other before he ended up with HER. We all
could've been happier sooner, and probably no one
would've died...*

J eanine lay sprawled across the bed, scribbling in her diary while she waited for Mason to finish showering. She would've preferred to be in there with him, but he had locked the bathroom door. She considered picking the lock and letting herself in, but decided to use the time to journal instead—she'd fallen behind since moving in. She kicked her feet idly in the air behind her while she practiced signing "Jeanine Goodridge" in the page's margins. When she was finished, she snapped the diary shut and rolled onto her back, hugging it to her chest. She'd been dreaming of this moment for over a year, ever since the day she met Mason.

Their attraction to each other had been undeniable from the start; Jeanine couldn't have resisted it, even if she wanted to. She remembered how he reached over his wife just to touch her through the car window that afternoon. His hand had engulfed hers completely. When he fixed those stunning green eyes on her, Jeanine nearly orgasmed on the spot.

From that moment on, she thought about Mason constantly. She was desperate to know more about him. How had he ended up with someone like Marilys? What had attracted them to each other? Not that the girl didn't have a lot going for her, but Mason seemed like he'd prefer someone more… exciting—someone like herself.

They reconnected a few weeks later when he came to an office happy hour for Mari's birthday. Jeanine was at the bar with her back to the door, but she felt his presence the moment he walked in. It was as if her body recognized its match was nearby. Like a hunter sizing up their prey, she'd watched him hungrily over the rim of her martini.

Mason walked through the place with unshakeable confidence. He kissed his wife, shook a few hands, then approached the bar to order a drink. He didn't acknowledge Jeanine, but she knew he had seen her. He was playing hard to get, which only excited Jeanine more. She listened patiently while he ordered for himself and his wife, then made her move.

"Well, hello there again, handsome stranger. How's the modeling career?" Jeanine leaned forward so he could get a glimpse of her cleavage. To her satisfaction, Mason glanced down, then chuckled.

"Hi there… Jeanine, right?"

He'd remembered her name! One look confirmed to Jeanine that he'd been thinking about her as much as she'd been thinking of him. The bartender suddenly returned with Mason's drinks. Jeanine gestured to the one for his wife.

"I guess you should probably go deliver that," she purred, daring him to leave.

Mason had looked down at the drink, then smiled. "I'll get her a new one later," he winked, pushing it toward Jeanine. "She won't miss it."

Jeanine pushed it back. "Margaritas aren't my style, babe."

Mason raised one amused eyebrow. "So, what is?"

Jeanine waved the bartender over. "I'll have another martini…on him. Extra dirty, please."

The bartender nodded. "So, three olives? Four?"

Keeping her eyes on Mason, she'd replied, "As filthy you're willing to go."

Jeanine opened her eyes and smiled to herself, remembering that night. It was some of her finest work. She rolled back onto her stomach and reopened her diary, flipping through the pages until she found her entry from that evening.

May 18, 2021

> *Dear Diary – I think I've met my soul mate!!!! I have never, ever, EVER encountered a man like Mason Goodridge ♡ I have NEVER felt feelings like I felt tonight. The way he looked at me, the way he smiled, the way those goddamn gorgeous green eyes moved all over my body, UGH. He's so sexy I could die! I must've asked him a thousand questions, but it was like he wanted me to! I wonder if he's a little bit starved for attention. If that's the case, his wife is a fucking idiot... How could you even think of anything else if you lived with a man like that? Honestly, if she wasn't standing a few feet away, I would've jumped him right there at the bar. I get the feeling he wouldn't have minded, lol.*
> *AHHHH!!!!!! I NEED to see him again!*

As soon as she got home that night, Jeanine found Mason online and sent him a message. Steamy DMs quickly turned into a constant volley of sexy texts until, eventually, the distant exchanges became too much to bear.

A week later, she took a half day at work to meet him at her apartment for the most intense sex she'd ever experienced. Jeanine's skills in the bedroom were a point of personal pride, but with Mason, she'd finally met her match. He took control of their bodies in a way that made her want to surrender to him completely, unleashing himself on her as though he were a storm trapped in a bottle, and she was the only one with the power to release him. It wasn't just their powerful physical chemistry that swept her up, though. In between their intense rendezvous, they would talk.

Mason confided in her about how unsatisfied he was at home. He'd been happy... at first. Marilys was a good person and a good wife, but somehow, it just wasn't what he wanted anymore. They had a good home, good friends, and a baby on the way, but he felt there was more out there for him. He didn't know what that might be, but Jeanine understood. She'd felt the same hunger her whole life.

Mason also revealed his belief that trying to have a baby had been the nail in the coffin for his marriage.

"I was on board! At first..." he insisted once, as they lay in her bed with the afternoon sun dappling across their naked bodies.

He thought he wanted a family, but as they began to try, something about it didn't sit right with him. After a while, he began to question Mari's attraction to him. It broke Jeanine's heart, and pissed her off.

June 27, 2022

Dear Diary,

I just spent the most glorious afternoon with my love, but my heart is so sad. Every time he has to go back to her, my heart breaks for him, knowing what he's walking into. I honestly don't get it! At work, she's little Miss Perfect, but I swear to God, she is the dumbest bitch alive not to know what she has. I would never take him for granted like that! Clearly, her baby fever has taken over, and MY baby is paying the price!! UGH, I've seen it a million times. Those bitches never learn. That's how their husbands always find their way

to me. Thank God I've been able to learn from their
mistakes.

Ughhhh. It's so frustrating! I'm ~~beautiful~~... no. I'm
FUCKING HOT! I'm successful and sexy and indepen-
dent. I have way more to offer than she does, and I
deserve him more! He deserves me, too. Every single
second we spend together is just more proof that we are
meant for each other. He might be married to her right
now, but I have his heart, and I know we are meant to
be together. He's too good of a person to leave her with
a baby, but I just know there's a way. I'll find it for us.

Jeanine was proud of herself as she read her words from just four months ago. Though she could not have predicted how much things would change in such a short time, she sent a silent thank you to the Universe for bringing her to this moment. What happened to Marilys and her baby was terrible, but that whole mess made it possible for her dreams to come true.

The bathroom door suddenly opened, and Mason emerged in a cloud of steam, looking and smelling absolutely delicious. Jeanine quickly shoved the diary under the pillows.

"Finally!" she exclaimed.

Mason didn't acknowledge her. Jeanine crawled across the mattress toward him as he went to the dresser.

"Mmmm. You smell yummy." She reached for him, but he moved away.

"I gotta go out for a bit," he said, throwing on some clothes.

Jeanine sat back on the bed, pouting. "Where? Why?" she demanded.

"Jeanine, please don't start," Mason sighed. "I just need to run a few errands."

"Well, why don't I come with you?" Jeanine offered. "We can get some coffee and—"

"It's not going to take that long," Mason clipped. "Besides, don't you still have to shower?" He paused and looked her up and down. "Have you been rolling all over the bed in those clothes?"

Jeanine looked down at her sweaty gym clothes, smudged with dirt from the gardening they'd been doing. "Whatever. Just give me a second to change, and I'll—"

"Too late," Mason cut her off and started toward the door. "I'm already gone." He paused, then came back and kissed her. "Go enjoy your shower," he purred, rubbing the tip of his nose against hers. He flicked his tongue languidly against her lips. Jeanine felt her insides liquify.

"I'll be back soon," he promised. Before she could muster a response, he was gone.

Breathless, Jeanine steadied herself against the bed and waited for her head to stop spinning. Mason was pure magic; she marveled at his ability to make her feel so many things with one touch. She put a hand to her suddenly parched throat and caressed her neck, allowing her fingers to brush lower over her chest. She sighed out her frustration, wishing Mason had stayed to finish what he'd started. He was so hot and cold. It was the only shadow over their otherwise glowing existence together.

Jeanine knew he would need time to process what happened. Mason had a long journey ahead as he came to terms with the loss of his ex-wife and unborn child, even though before they were gone, he'd been terrified at the thought of being trapped with them for a lifetime. Jeanine was prepared to love him patiently through all of this, for however long it would take. She wasn't prepared for how often he would retreat into his head about it and shut her out.

Mason was an open book at the beginning of their relationship, but now, he rarely shared what he was thinking. Even just now, as he kissed her, seducing her with those beautiful eyes and golden-boy smile, she knew she was being denied access to his inner world.

Heaving herself off the bed, Jeanine made her way to the shower, stripping off her dirty clothes and dropping them on the ground in her wake. She turned the water on its coldest setting, then stepped under the shower head without flinching. The freezing temperature did nothing to cool her libido—she'd make sure Mason took care of that when he got back—but it helped clear her mind. By the time she was finished, she was back in control of her senses.

If history had taught her anything, when it came to her and Mason, she had the power to shape their future as long as she let him feel like he was in charge. She'd let him have his little mood swings while he worked through his feelings. It was only fair, and what a good, devoted partner would do. At the end of it all, though, they'd have their happily ever after, exactly as Jeanine envisioned it.

CHAPTER 26

Since moving in with Mason, Jeanine was used to starting her day with sex, followed by a leisurely shower together, but when she reached for him that morning, she found him already wide awake and staring moodily at the ceiling.

"Boo!" she whispered, nibbling his ear. "Happy Halloween, baby."

"Mm hmm." Mason twisted away from her to gaze out the window. It had rained heavily through the night and the early morning gloom reflected in his green eyes, making them appear gray.

Jeanine scooted closer and planted several more kisses on his face and neck. She put a hand to his cheek and tried to bring his lips to hers, wrapping one leg around him, but he remained aloof.

"What's wrong?" she finally asked.

Mason ignored her.

"Talk to me, baby," Jeanine purred, brushing her fingers along his hairline. He usually responded favorably to that, but this time, it seemed to annoy him. He extricated himself from her arms and swung his legs over the side of the bed. Jeanine reached for him again, but he stood up before she could touch him.

"I'm gonna go for a jog," he announced, then went into the closet.

Jeanine propped herself up on one elbow, pulling the sheets closer around her nude body. "Okay, how long will you be gone? I can have breakfast ready when you come back."

"I dunno." Mason emerged from the closet fully dressed and headed for the door. "Probably an hour or so. Later."

Jeanine listened to him go downstairs and out the front door, slamming it behind him.

"Okay then," she sighed irritably, plopping back against the pillows. She studied the ceiling, bored.

She and Mason had been living together for almost two weeks, and his behavior had yet to improve. Jeanine was trying hard to be patient with him, but she could feel herself inching closer to snapping every day. She had come too far to give up on their relationship now, but Mason was testing her limits. To soothe her frustration, she bounded out of bed and retrieved her diary from its hiding place. Nestling herself back under the covers, she flipped to a particularly worn, tear-splashed page.

August 12, 2022

Ahhhhhhh I am SO fucking mad and sad and frustrated and... I never knew it was possible to feel so much love and so much hate at the same time for the same person! Mason wants to end things. I can't believe I'm even writing these words!

Something must have happened, but he won't tell me what. He just keeps saying this isn't what he wants, but I KNOW that's not true. I know it because of the way he touches me, and the way he kisses me, and the way he looks at me when we're making love. How could he do

this to me??? I HATE HER!!!! I know she's the reason.
She must've said or done something that scared him.
Why do we even care if she finds out at this point?
FUCK HER! She's in the way!
NO!!!!

I am not letting it end like this. The universe
brought us together for a reason. I have to fight for us.
He is scared and under way too much pressure from her
to do the hard things... The RIGHT thing!!! All he can
think about is what everyone else will think, but those
people are too selfish to see how unhappy he is. I see it.
I LOVE HIM. I loved him before I even knew him. I
know that now. My soul and my body recognized him
right away because he's MINE. This is just a test.

I will be strong for both of us. I will fight for both
of us, for as long as it takes, until we are free to love
each other the way we both deserve to be loved.

As she lay alone in Mason's bed re-reading her words, Jeanine felt her fervor for her relationship return. This entry reminded her of her power—her prayers had been answered the very next day. Jeanine got out of bed, reenergized. She took a shower and dressed quickly, then hurried downstairs to have breakfast ready by the time Mason returned. On the way, she almost tripped over Otis, who lay sprawled across one of the steps, blocking her path.

"Oops, sorry, kitty!" She reached down to pet him, but he leaned away and hissed defiantly. "You know you'd better start being nicer to me," she admonished. "I'm the only one who feeds you around here."

Unbothered, Otis stood up and stretched languidly, offering Jeanine a generous view of his butt hole, then trotted away.

"Like father, like son, I see," she muttered, following him down the rest of the stairs.

She found Otis curled up expectantly near his food bowl in the kitchen. She fed him, then turned the coffee pot on and started cutting fruit into a bowl for herself and Mason. She'd wait until he was back to scramble some eggs, so they'd be hot when they sat down together.

As she hulled and quartered a carton of strawberries, Jeanine thought about how they would spend the rest of the day. It's not like she had a job to go to, or other friends to hang out with. Her world consisted entirely of Mason, which was fine by her, but she needed to think of something that would entice him to stay with her. She was beginning to loathe being left alone for long stretches in this creepy old house.

The house phone rang and Jeanine went to check the caller ID, wiping her hands on a kitchen towel.

"Hi Kris, how are you?" she answered cheerfully, placing the phone against her shoulder and returning to her strawberries.

"Uh... hello. Who is this?" Kris asked.

"It's Jeanine! Sorry, I thought you would recognize my voice."

"I see. No... I didn't realize you'd still be there."

"Well, yeah, of course I am," Jeanine said brightly, ignoring the dismay in Kris' voice. "I'm just getting breakfast together for me and Mason. How are you? How is Steve?"

"Is my son there?"

"No, he's out for a run, but he has his cell with him. Have you tried it?"

"Yes, of course I have," Kris clipped. "He's not answering."

She sounded just like Mason when he was annoyed. Jeanine smiled at this little insight into his character. "Oh, yeah, he does that sometimes, huh?" she offered commiseratively. "I'll tell him you called. What's it about?" There was another long pause on the phone.

"Please tell him I called to see how he's doing," Kris finally said. "Today would've been his and Marilys' due date. For their baby," she added pointedly. "I'm sure it's at the top of his mind."

"Oh, wow, is that today?" Jeanine asked, genuinely surprised. "I had no idea."

"It's on their calendar on the fridge," Kris replied icily.

Jeanine didn't bother to inform Kris that she had thrown out that calendar, along with the ultrasound photo clipped to it, the day she moved in.

"I see," she replied instead. "Well, I will definitely have him get back to you. You are so sweet to check on him. Hey! By the way, I don't know what plans you have today, but if you're free, would you like to hang out with us? You could come to the house... hello? Hello, Kris?"

The line was dead. Jeanine shrugged and put the phone back on its base. She wasn't offended by the older woman's rudeness. She knew her and Mason's relationship would take some getting used to, and she wasn't going anywhere anytime soon. Eventually, his mother would come around. Until then, she would just continue to kill the old bitch with kindness.

Humming to herself, Jeanine finished the berries, set the table for two, placed eggs and butter next to the stove, and settled in to wait for Mason. She was on her second cup of coffee when she decided to text him and check in. When he didn't respond, she tried calling, but his phone went straight to voicemail. She waited a few minutes, then called him again. This time, he picked up.

"What's up?"

"Hey babe, when are you coming back for breakfast?"

"Oh, I forgot and grabbed something already. I'm gonna run a couple of errands; I don't know how long it'll take."

"Oh. Okay." Jeanine felt a flash of irritation but forced herself to get over it. "What errands?"

"What?"

"What errands are you running? Are you going to the grocery store?"

"Jeanine, I don't have time for this right now," Mason sighed.

Jeanine bit back a bitchy retort. Given what day it was, she guessed it wouldn't take much for him to shut down on her, and she didn't feel like fighting.

"Never mind," she replied. "But if you were planning to go to the store, don't. I'll go. Your mom told me what day it was... I thought I could make something special for us for dinner and try to take your mind off things."

Mason was silent for a moment. "Okay, sure. Thanks."

"Is there anything special that you want?"

"I'm sure whatever you make will be fine."

Jeanine smiled. "Nothing but the best for you, my love. What time do you think you'll be back?"

"I'm not sure, but I'll let you know. Listen, I gotta go. I'll see you later."

"Okay, babe, see you soon. Hey! Wait! Do you get trick-or-treaters here? We don't have any candy. I was wondering if I should get some in case anyone comes by... Mason?"

The line was dead.

"Like mother, like son, I see," Jeanine grumbled. She slumped in her chair and glanced around the empty kitchen, feeling dissatisfied. Her stomach growled uneasily, reminding her that she hadn't eaten yet. Shaking off her misgivings, she busied herself by scrambling two eggs, then quickly finished eating and tidied up the kitchen.

Knowing she probably had hours to kill before Mason returned, she decided to go to the grocery store and take her time shopping. Once there, she realized she had no idea what Mason's favorite meal was. She considered calling Kris to ask but decided against it. Figuring steak was a safe bet, she wandered over to the butcher section. As she perused the chilled cases, her eyes fell on a package of ground chuck, giving her a brilliant idea.

Jeanine grabbed the meat, then hurried around the store, collecting the rest of what she needed. She scooped up a big bag of candy and a pumpkin for carving before rushing home to put together a Halloween night for two that Mason would never forget.

Several hours later, Jeanine sat half-naked at the kitchen table, which she'd set with wine, candles, and burgers. As an extra naughty surprise, she'd donned the same sheer red tights and matching lingerie set she'd worn the night she arrived, but swapped out the nurse's dress for a festive pair of devil horns. She'd carved the pumpkin and left it in the front hall at the head of a trail of more candles and Halloween candy that would lead Mason straight to her when he walked in.

Jeanine was on her second glass of wine when she finally heard his keys jingling in the door. She straightened, listening excitedly while Mason emptied his pockets and discovered the trail she'd left for him. It seemed to take him ages to follow it to the kitchen. When he finally came into view, he looked nervous.

"Surprise!" Jeanine threw her arms over her head so he could get a good look at her costume. "Happy Halloween, you handsome Devil."

Mason froze, taking in the scene. He looked over his shoulder at the jack-o-lantern and trail of candy, bewildered. "What are you doing?"

Jeanine sashayed toward him, took his hand, and led him back to the table while she explained. "You were so out of it this morning, and when your mom told me about the due date, it made perfect sense.

"Baby, I'm so sorry if today was hard for you. I thought we could have a little Halloween celebration of our own to take your mind off things and make some new, good memories." She gestured to the plates on the table. "Look, I recreated the burger from the bar where we had our first date."

"Date?" Mason repeated dumbly.

"Well, the happy hour," Jeanine laughed. "I count it as a date." She pecked him on the lips. "Come! Sit! The food's getting cold." She tugged Mason to his seat, but he kept his feet planted.

"Oh... unless you'd rather have dessert first?" She pressed herself to him, but Mason held her at bay.

"Baby, what is it?" Jeanine searched his eyes, trying to read his expression. "Tell me, let me fix it."

Mason sighed. "Jeanine, I appreciate what you've done here, but I'm really not in the mood for all of this."

Jeanine's face fell. "What do you mean?" she demanded. "Why not?"

"Why not?" Mason repeated.

"Yes, Mason." Jeanine's blood came to a simmer. "Why not?"

Mason's nostrils flared impatiently. "Jeanine, you found out that today is the day my dead wife would've delivered our dead child, and you thought the best thing to do was put on this getup, carve a pumpkin, and make me a burger, and that would make everything okay? Are you stupid?"

Jeanine flinched at his words.

"Are *you*?" she fought back. "Don't you dare speak to me that way! Not after all I've done for you."

Mason gazed at her with sudden interest. "What exactly have you done, Jeanine?"

"What *haven't* I done at this point?" Jeanine challenged. "Don't underestimate me."

"What did you think was going to happen here, Jeanine?" Mason sneered. "You thought I was going to come in here, eat this burger, and then throw you across the table like there was nothing else going on?"

"Uh. Yeah! *Hello*?" Jeanine shouted, gesturing to her outfit. "Obviously, that was the plan."

Mason tightened his fists like he wanted to throttle her. Jeanine could see him counting in his mind. After ten seconds, he deflated, dropping his hands at his sides.

"Then you're an even bigger idiot than I thought," he muttered. "I'm not doing this with you right now." He attempted to leave the kitchen.

"Oh no, you don't." Jeanine grabbed Mason's arm and spun

him back around. "You're not dealing with your wife anymore. I will not stand for your bullshit."

Mason looked at her condescendingly, but she carried on.

"I put this together because I imagined today *would* be difficult for you. But actually, why don't we examine that for a second?" Jeanine put her hands on her hips and puffed out her scantily clad chest.

"How hard was today for you, *really*, Mason? Huh? Was it hard?" she patronized in a baby voice. Mason's jaw twitched with anger, but she kept going.

"And before you answer that, honey, don't forget who you're talking to. I know you, Mason. Don't think for a second that *I'm* gonna buy this 'poor me with my dead baby and my dead wife' act," she mocked. "You didn't care about them before, and you don't care about them now. If they were alive and today had gone the way everyone thought it would, we both know that *I'm* the first person you would've been calling to escape from it all."

Jeanine could feel that she was toeing a dangerous line. Mason's expression was murderous. He had lowered his chin and was looking at her like he was about to charge. She lowered her voice and changed tactics.

"Look. I'm not her, okay? I don't care where you've been today. All that matters to me is you're here now."

Mason's expression didn't soften, but Jeanine persisted. She took a step closer, pressing herself against him again.

"Why are we even pretending to care about them right now?" she said, rubbing his arms. "This is *me*. Let's just focus on us and what we do best."

Jeanine snaked her arms around Mason's shoulders, curled her fingers in his hair, and pulled him in for a kiss. Mason was spellbound, but as soon as their lips brushed, he pushed her away again.

"Jesus Christ, Jeanine, don't you have any self-respect?"

Jeanine stumbled away as if he'd slapped her. She reached for him again, but he batted her hands aside and left the kitchen.

She watched him storm away to the office, flinching as he slammed the door shut behind him.

Jeanine stood there, heaving with anger. She wanted to follow him, smash down the office door, and scratch his eyes out. Instead, she kicked off her shoes, poured herself another glass of wine, and cleaned the kitchen until she felt calm again. Leaving Mason's burger in Otis' bowl, she went upstairs to get ready for bed. After slamming him in a scathing diary entry, she passed out, her anger spent. She wasn't sure how long she'd been asleep when she felt his hand on her shoulder.

"What?" she demanded.

Without saying anything, Mason pulled her close and kissed her roughly. Jeanine fought against him at first, then let go and gave in.

Mason was never exactly tender, but he was rougher than usual tonight. Jeanine let him tear off her clothes, paying no attention to where they fell. As he moved inside her, he wound his fingers through her hair and pulled, hard. Her neck twisted uncomfortably, but she didn't resist. His other hand moved to her throat and began to apply pressure. Jeanine closed her eyes and arched, pressing into his palm. Mason's fingers tightened, and she whimpered as he began to thrust harder.

Jeanine took shallow breaths. She felt pressure in her temples as her blood pumped harder, building heat. Mason's lip was curled in a sneer; perspiration shone on his forehead. He grunted, his pace intensifying. Jeanine looked into his eyes, feeling a thrill as she registered their color. That mesmerizing green had darkened to almost black. It was like looking at two people in one body.

Mason's image began to swim above her. It suddenly occurred to Jeanine that she hadn't taken a breath in a while. White spots obscured his face as the blood vessels behind her eyes began to throb. She felt an unexpected flash of fear. She brought her hands to her throat, her fingers prying at Mason's, but he didn't let up. He adjusted his grip on her hair and pulled again, driving into her while his other hand tightened like a vice around her neck.

Jeanine bucked and writhed underneath him. Her mouth opened and closed like a fish, gasping for air. She hit her palms against him, trying to distract him, trying to scream, but it was no use. As Jeanine's strength waned, her terror grew.

Mason's whole body suddenly seized, his eyes boring into hers for several long, agonizing seconds. Jeanine felt herself fading; her peripheral vision going dark. Without warning, Mason's fingers slackened. He collapsed on top of her, and Jeanine gasped as air rushed back into her lungs. They lay together, limp and panting, not saying a word.

"Mase?"

At the sound of his name, Mason inhaled sharply, then rolled off of her to stare at the ceiling, mute. His eyes were their normal color again, and totally blank. Jeanine waited, but he didn't speak. Rolling toward him, she propped her head on one hand, wincing at the pain in her neck, and rubbed his chest.

"Mase... are you okay?"

Mason had barely moved, yet he seemed to freeze at her question. He frowned, then removed her hand from his chest.

"Yep. That was great." Then, just as he had that morning, he threw his legs over the side of the bed and stood up before Jeanine could touch him again.

"I'm gonna take a shower," he said over his shoulder. He went into the bathroom and locked the door with a firm *click*.

Jeanine stared after him, perplexed. Mason had choked her during sex before, but it had never gone that far. She sighed and rolled onto her back, testing the bruises she felt blooming on her neck. She wondered how she'd explain if anyone saw them, and then realized she wouldn't have to. They were in a bubble all their own—no coworkers, no friends, barely any family, just each other.

Jeanine got up to look for her clothes, straightening the bed covers as she searched. She redressed and got back into bed. As she settled against the pillows, afterglow settled into her body. She stretched languidly, humming to herself. Caressing her neck again, she recalled Mason's intense expression while he'd been inside her; the way he had looked at her—*into* her—at the moment of his release. She'd do anything to make him look at her like that for the rest of their lives.

Jeanine pressed her fingers lightly against the tender tissue on her neck, savoring the pain. Smiling, she closed her eyes and waited for Mason to return, dozing off to dreamy thoughts of her tortured romance with this brooding and complex man.

When he came to bed, smelling tantalizingly fresh, she curled her limbs around him possessively and breathed him in. They fell asleep without exchanging another word.

CHAPTER 27

Mason was awakened a few hours later by Jeanine jostling her way out of bed. She padded around to his side, leaned over, and nuzzled his cheek, announcing her intentions to go to the bathroom. He grunted dismissively, trying to hold on to sleep. Moments later, she returned and gently shook his shoulder.

Half-awake and fully annoyed, Mason grunted again. "What."

"I'm going to get some water. Do you want some?"

"No."

"Okay, honey. I'll be right back." With another peck on his cheek, she tiptoed out of the room.

Mason kept his eyes closed as Jeanine's footsteps disappeared, but he struggled to fall back asleep. The harder he tried, the more irritable he became. He knew the source of his frustration: Jeanine. It wasn't the first time he'd lost sleep worrying about how he would get himself out of this thing with her. He kicked himself for letting his fear get the best of him and allowing her through the door that night.

His affair with Jeanine had been a complete accident. He wasn't looking for it, and he certainly wasn't trying to escape his marriage only to get tangled up with someone else, but Jeanine had been impossible to say no to. He'd told her he was only interested in sex, and she'd assured him she only wanted the same. After that, he got so caught up in enjoying his forbidden fruit that he didn't realize the extent of her attachment until it was too late.

Now that they were under the same roof, Jeanine was constantly in his face, wanting things from him that he resented being forced to give. Like a boa constrictor, the more he struggled against her, the tighter she squeezed. If he didn't resist, she squeezed anyway. She seemed determined to devour him whole one way or another. He hated that the quality of both their days depended entirely on his treatment of her. At least Mari had had her own sense of identity.

Frustrated, Mason rolled away, as far as possible, from Jeanine's side of the bed. He closed his eyes and focused on his breathing to calm down. Just when he began to feel drowsy, he felt Jeanine climb back into bed beside him. Mason held still so as not to attract her attention. He listened carefully for her breathing to slow, indicating she was finally asleep.

Jeanine's breath flowed in and out, in sync with his own. After a while, Mason realized she was keeping pace with him, matching the length of his inhales and exhales like an obnoxious copycat. He began to breathe irregularly to throw her off, but she matched him with irritating accuracy.

"Quit it, Jeanine," he muttered grumpily, but she didn't.

Finally, he drew in a quick, sharp breath and held it. Jeanine gasped too, then giggled. Exhausted and fed up with this ridiculous game, he flipped over to tell her to stop it, but the bed was empty.

Mason sat up warily. "Jeanine?"

There was no answer.

He peered around in the dark. A shadowy figure stood in the corner, waiting to be noticed. Mason fumbled to turn on the bedside lamp, then turned back. The figure was gone.

A familiar uneasiness crept across Mason's shoulders, but he dismissed it as nothing more than extreme exhaustion and irritability. He turned out the light, settled his head against his pillow, and closed his eyes again with determination. Just as his body began to relax, the breathing returned, faint but distinct, and very close by. Mason opened his eyes and listened, not moving a muscle. The breathing was soft but soon became ragged. Every once in a while, there was a stifled whimper, like crying.

Huffing, Mason threw the sheets back and marched around to the other side of the bed, expecting to find Jeanine crouched there, but she wasn't. Another soft sob came from the empty space he was looking at. Perplexed, Mason stood with his hands on his hips, closed his eyes, and listened. The sound was coming from the nightstand.

Scowling, Mason yanked open the drawers. The first one was empty, but when he opened the second, a baby monitor receiver slid forward on the empty wooden surface. A row of three tiny green lights ebbed and flickered as sound came through the speaker.

Mason picked up the receiver and switched it off, then stared at it curiously. He hadn't even realized it was still in there, let alone turned on. Why would it have been? As he considered the possibilities, it dawned on him that he was hearing it now because someone was in the nursery. With another exasperated groan, he realized that someone was Jeanine, probably waiting for him to come check on her in another of her random, deranged tests.

Mason looked up as the crying reached his ears from down the hall. He had half a mind to ignore it and get back into bed, but he knew the longer he kept her waiting, the more difficult Jeanine would be later. With a defeated sigh, he made his way down the hall to the closed nursery door. He grasped the doorknob, which was surprisingly cool to the touch, only to discover it was locked.

"For fuck's sake." Mason rapped on the door. "Jeanine!"

There was no answer. He put his ear to the door and listened. The crying had ceased. Jiggling the doorknob, he called out louder.

"Jeanine! What the hell are you doing?"

She still wouldn't answer.

Mason had had enough of Jeanine's nonsense. He didn't care what she might do or say, or that it was the middle of the night, or if she had anywhere to go. It was time to get her out of his house and his life for good—*tonight*. He pounded angrily on the nursery door.

"Jeanine, get your fucking ass out of there *right now*!"

When she still didn't answer, Mason gathered his strength to break down the door. As soon as his shoulder made contact, the latch clicked softly. He stumbled into the room, knocking the door aside so hard it rebounded against the wall with a *BANG!* Enraged, he flipped on the lights, hunting wildly for Jeanine, but the room was empty.

Mason stormed over to the baby monitor, snatched it up, and switched it off, then reached behind the dresser and yanked out the plug for good measure. He whipped around again, searching for Jeanine. He stomped over to the closet and shoved the folding doors apart, but there was nothing inside except baby clothes, swinging on hangers with their tags still attached. He slammed the doors shut, marched back to the middle of the room, and surveyed his surroundings.

Mason hadn't set foot in this room since before Mari died. He had hoped his parents would empty it for him while they were here, but Kris insisted he be part of the process, which Mason had stubbornly refused. As a result, it remained untouched, exactly as Mari had left it.

Memories of them putting it together replayed in his mind. He saw her flop into the glider after they'd hauled it upstairs, and remembered the way she rocked in it while he and Mark assembled the crib. It had only been a few months, but it felt like years had passed since that day.

Mari's touch was all over this room, her presence so palpable that he could almost feel her standing there beside him. A shiver went up Mason's spine. A vision of Mari's waterlogged corpse suddenly flashed to the front of his mind while a low, throaty laugh echoed in his ears. Instinctively, Mason looked down at the baby monitor, still in his hands, but it hadn't come from there.

Mason closed his eyes and listened. The laughter came again from behind him, lifting the hairs on the back of his neck. He opened his eyes and whirled around, but there was no one there. Mason's heart began to pound. Looking around in disbelief, he whispered her name.

"Mari?"

The laughter stopped, giving way to dead silence. A soft, cold breeze ruffled his hair, raising goosebumps on his flesh. Mason stood like a statue, frozen with fear, bracing for whatever came next.

RRRrrAAOW!

He nearly jumped out of his skin as Otis yowled and dashed out from underneath the crib like he'd been shot from a cannon. His fur brushed Mason's legs as he darted out of the room in a little black blur.

"Jesus Fucking Christ, Otis!" Mason shouted after him. He put a hand to his chest and steadied himself against the furniture. How had that dumb cat managed to lock himself in here? Mason realized he must've been the source of the crying he'd heard on the baby monitor.

"Stupid fucking mangey cat," Mason fumed. He made up his mind to find a shelter to take Otis to in the morning—if he could get his hands on him without being scratched. He heard the distant sound of the air conditioner turning off in the house, explaining the cold breeze he'd felt a moment ago. Exhaustion washed over him again; he suddenly felt as if he hadn't slept in years.

He trudged back to the master bedroom to find Jeanine sound asleep and blissfully unaware of the commotion in the baby's room. He slumped miserably when he saw the unwanted glass of water she had placed at his bedside. As he got back into bed, her body drew toward him like a magnet; one leg and one arm crept across him like a stubborn vine. Too weary to resist, Mason surrendered to her affections and finally passed out.

CHAPTER 28

"You selfish motherfucker! This is not over!" Jeanine shouted as Mason backed out of his driveway, maneuvering his giant truck as quickly as possible to escape her wrath. He clipped his mailbox as he turned into the street, then sped off without looking back.

Mason had experienced his share of bad days since his wife died, but when he opened his eyes on the morning of his 37th birthday, something told him this would be the worst one yet.

Jeanine had woken him up with a blow job followed by breakfast in bed, which he'd endured with brittle patience. He managed to talk her out of joining him in the shower, then made up an excuse about seeing his parents for lunch, thinking she wouldn't try to accompany him. He was dead wrong.

"Oh, is it somewhere nice? How long do I have to get ready?" Jeanine asked eagerly. "Eek! It's going to be our first proper sit down with your parents! Finally!" she squealed, wriggling with excitement. "I need to make sure I make the right impression, you know?"

When Mason delicately informed her that it would only be himself and his parents, her fuse was lit. He ran out of the house before things could escalate further, then called his mom from the road to cover his bases.

"Hi honey, happy birthday!" Kris was overjoyed to receive his call; she'd gotten used to him dodging her these days. Mason cringed guiltily.

"Hey, Mom. Thank you."

"What are you up to today? Do you want to meet us for lunch? Our treat."

"No, thanks," Mason declined. "I'm just going to hang out and keep it low-key."

"Okay, sure, Mase, if that's what you want. What about dinner tonight?" Kris persevered. "You could come over. Your dad and I would be so happy to—"

"I can't, sorry."

Kris was silent on the other end. Mason could practically hear her wheels turning as she debated whether or not to say what was on her mind. "Please don't tell me you're having dinner with that ridiculous woman," she finally said.

"Okay."

"Oh, Mason!" The disappointment in her voice filled Mason's mouth with ash.

"Mom, please don't start," he muttered. He hated the idea of dinner with Jeanine just as much as his mother did, but he didn't have much choice in the matter. She'd be there when he got home no matter what—ready to fight, or fuck, or most likely, both. Things would be even worse for him if he stood her up. He couldn't explain any of that to Kris, though.

"I just don't understand what you could possibly see in her," she groaned. "I've never encountered someone so idiotic."

"Mom!" Mason wasn't expecting many gifts for this birthday, but hearing his mom call Jeanine an idiot felt like one.

"Please don't tell me you're serious about her," Kris begged. "You can't be!"

"Mom, I don't want to talk about this right now."

Kris sighed into the phone. Mason waited stonily for her to move on.

"Fine," she relented. "Here, talk to your dad…" After a moment of fumbling, Mason heard his father's voice.

"Mase? Son? Hey, it's the birthday boy!"

Mason rolled his eyes at Steve's patronizing tone. Since Mari's passing, he had reverted to treating Mason like he was twelve again.

"Are you coming over?" he asked eagerly.

"Hey, Dad. No, not today."

"Oh… well, that's alright, my boy," Steve soldiered on. Mason's stomach twisted guiltily at the disappointment in his voice. "I'm sure you've got big plans of your own, right? Where are you off to?"

Mason looked around. He had no idea where he was or where he was headed. He hadn't planned beyond getting out of the house and away from Jeanine as quickly as possible. "I've got a couple of things going today."

"Of course you do, atta boy… See? I told you so!" Mason heard his dad whisper to his mom and realized she was still listening in.

"Okay, guys, I gotta run. I'll talk to you later." He hung up quickly as his parents wished him one more "Happy Birthday!" in unison, then turned his attention back to the road.

He drove aimlessly for the next two hours, just killing time. To amuse himself, he made up a game of coming up with turn patterns and following them until he was forced in a different direction. *Right, right, left. Right, right, left. Right, left, right. Right, left, right.*

When that finally got boring, Mason decided to brave the mall, thinking the weekday afternoon crowd would be sparse enough to manage a low-key stroll.

It was early November, but the mall was already decked out for the holidays, and the cheerful, festive atmosphere helped lift Mason's spirits. He considered buying himself a birthday gift, but nothing appealed to him. Finally, he decided to treat himself to a warm pretzel.

He was about to settle in at the food court when he spotted Jeanine wandering out of a lingerie shop nearby. Ducking and pulling his black baseball cap low—he never forgot it again after that first terrible solo outing—he waited until she moved on, then speedwalked out of there, clutching his pretzel so tightly it was crushed to pieces by the time he reached his truck. After that, Mason gave up on stopping anywhere.

Now, he was once again cruising the Eastview Highway, calculating how much longer he could stall before heading home. A car honked impatiently behind him, then cut around his truck and zoomed off. Mason checked his speed—nearly twenty below the limit—and heaved a long, depressed sigh.

The late afternoon sun beaming through the windshield made Mason feel warm and drowsy, and he let himself drift into a daydream about Jeanine getting amnesia and forgetting he ever existed. His eyelids drooped heavily, his grip on the steering wheel relaxed, and he began to float into the oncoming lane of traffic. A horn blared from an approaching car, jolting him awake just in time to swerve into his lane and avoid impact. Though Mason kept his eyes fixed firmly ahead, he could not miss the other driver's middle finger waving at him as they passed by.

Mason slapped his face firmly to wake himself up. He hadn't had a decent night's sleep since Halloween. His dreams about that dark ocean and Mari reaching for him from its depths had returned. With Jeanine sleeping soundly beside him, he'd wake up in a cold sweat and see Mari standing in the shadows, waiting for him to fall back asleep and return to her. Sometimes, he could blink and make her disappear, but not always. If she remained, he'd squeeze his eyes shut and lie still until her presence faded with the morning light.

He tried to tell himself it wasn't real, that the only unwanted presence in his home was Jeanine, but it was getting harder to ignore the increasing malevolence in the atmosphere, especially around the nursery. Before the incident on Halloween night, he'd kept the door to that room closed so he could forget about its existence, but now, it was always wide open, so he never had to imagine some unseen hostile presence hiding within, waiting to catch him by surprise.

Mason knew these thoughts were absurd, and he was annoyed at himself for having them. The lack of sleep was only making him more unhinged, more vulnerable, but he couldn't help it. He thought about drinking or drugging himself to sleep but feared not being able to wake up from his nightmares.

To make matters worse, Jeanine seemed utterly oblivious to everything Mason was experiencing. When he tried talking to her about it, she called him paranoid and said that if he would just commit to their relationship and stop torturing himself, all his bad feelings would go away. Mason marveled at how she managed to be so devoted to him, and yet somehow so incredibly self-centered.

To placate him, she had initiated a nightly routine of canvassing the house and double-checking the locks before they went to sleep, but this only pissed Mason off more. He didn't need her to check for monsters under the bed. He needed to know he wasn't losing his mind.

Mason's cell phone vibrated in the cupholder beside him—the caller ID read "Unknown." With a disgusted noise, he threw the phone into the back seat. Since his anniversary, Mason had continued to receive countless calls from an unknown number. He did his best to ignore them, but when he couldn't take it anymore and answered, it was always the same: some creepy, ragged breathing coming through a crackling line while a hoarse, menacing voice croaked his name. It was unnerving, incessant, and unstoppable.

He'd done everything he could think of to try and block the calls, but they would not stop. They came every day, several times a day, to both his cell and the landline at home. According to Jeanine, they never happened when he was out of the house. He still harbored suspicion that she was the one placing them but stopped accusing her after she suggested reporting them to the police. The last thing he wanted was to deal with the cops again, so he gave up and accepted the calls as yet another piece of garbage on the trash pile of his miserable life.

Mason looked ahead and saw that he was coming to a point in the road where he could either turn away from the lake and head home or keep going for another lap. He checked the time— it was almost five and getting dark. Rolling his neck and shoulders, he continued straight, away from home, committing to one more go around the lake. He looked out over the expanse of water, remembering how his father had once convinced him that alligators lived in its depths.

Mason had been obsessed with reptiles as a youngster. The year he turned seven, the local aquarium hosted a special exhibit of a rare albino alligator, which Mason's parents took him to see for his birthday.

He'd stood at eye-level with the creature, watching it through a thick sheet of glass as it drifted in its tank, occasionally treading water with lethal-looking claws. The alligator's skin was ivory, but the swampy water gave it a neon-greenish glow. Its pink eyes seemed to hold unfathomable power, their dark vertical pupils dilating as they settled on Mason, who sensed a strange telepathy from this animal. His dad had shared his awe and wondered aloud what the alligator must be thinking as it floated past its audience in the murky green water.

"It's probably gone insane from captivity," Kris replied with an equal measure of sadness and pragmatism. "Imagine if it was you."

Her words struck a chord in young Mason, who pressed his forehead to the tank in solidarity. With a lazy swish of its tail, the gator floated away. Moments later, without warning, it swam straight and fast at the glass a few feet away, smashing its snout on the hard surface right where a little girl was standing.

Frightened, the girl began to wail, and her parents whisked her away while the rest of the crowd jeered angrily at the gator before also dispersing. Mason stayed where he was, stunned by the animal's speed and strength. He watched it resume its idle drifting, a lonely prisoner deprived of its morsel.

He pictured the albino alligator's rosy eyes now as he drove, imagining them in such detail that they eventually became his own. He looked through them, not seeing the road he was driving on, but that little girl the gator had lunged for, distorted through the sheet of glass that separated them. He understood the appeal; she would've made a tasty snack.

Another blaring car horn snapped him back to the present, where he realized he had drifted out of his lane again. He cursed and swerved away.

"Shit! Come on, Mase, wake up," he muttered, shaking his head violently.

He looked in the rearview mirror, half expecting to see the whites of his own eyes turned pink, his pupils elongated to slits. Instead, a pair of warm brown eyes glinted at him.

Startled, Mason yelped and veered right, then slammed on his brakes, coming to a screeching halt on the side of the road. He sat there panting and shuddering. A familiar unease crept up the back of his neck. When he finally worked up the courage to look in the mirror again, all he saw was his own reflection, his green eyes wide with fear. He collapsed against his seat and breathed a sigh of relief. His eyelids drooped heavily, telling him it was time to go home. He couldn't put it off any longer.

Checking his rearview, he pulled onto the road again, searching for a safe place to turn around. The steering wheel jerked in his hands, causing him to veer into the oncoming lane before he righted it again, barely avoiding a collision.

"Whoa," he breathed, relief mingling with confusion.

Mason tightened his grip on the wheel, feeling freshly alert. He checked his rearview, thinking maybe his tires had skidded on something, but saw nothing.

Mason sat up straighter. He checked his gauges, then rolled down the windows and blasted the AC, aiming the vents directly at his face. He drove cautiously, feeling for any resistance from his truck. The wheel jerked mutinously again, and he wrestled it back to a straightened position.

"What the..." he muttered, frowning at the dash.

He decided to pull over, calm himself down, and then swing around as soon as the coast was clear. He pressed the brake pedal, but the truck didn't slow. Confused, Mason lifted his foot and pressed down again, testing his brakes, but they didn't respond. Instead, the truck seemed to accelerate. Mason checked the speedometer—slowly but surely, the needle was rising.

Trying not to panic, Mason pushed down hard on the brake, but it was no use. Fumbling, he located the switch for the parking brake and pressed it until he felt pain in the tip of his fingernail, but his speed continued to climb.

"Hey! Whoa!"

Mason grabbed the wheel with both hands as if trying to subdue a bucking bronco. He wrestled it back and forth, but it remained locked in place. Up ahead, the road bowed to the left. His stomach lurched as he imagined sailing past the barrier and crashing into the trees beyond. His eyes widened as he neared the turn at breakneck speed. He struggled desperately to turn the wheel, which stubbornly resisted his efforts.

Just as Mason could make out the bark on the trees ahead of him, the wheel spun sharply, whipping him around the curve. At the same time, he heard a *click* and felt his seatbelt come loose. Mason flailed as he slid unrestrained against the leather upholstery. He scrambled to right himself and buckle the seatbelt again, but it jerked against the retractor, refusing to be pulled back down.

"Stop! Stop!" Mason yelled at his truck, which sped recklessly around the highway's twists, beyond his control.

He wrenched at the wheel, stomped on the pedals, and clawed at every dial he could while fighting to stay in his seat, but nothing helped him regain control; the truck had a mind of its own. Afraid to take his eyes off the road, he clutched his seat with one hand and scrabbled in the backseat with his other, trying to locate his cell phone to call for help. Every time his fingers brushed against it, the truck swerved again, sending it flying out of reach.

Mason screamed in terror. "Stop it! Stop! Please! What do you want!"

A familiar, feminine laughter crackled through the truck's radio.

"Please... Please!" he begged. "Stop!"

In one final act of desperation, Mason grabbed the wheel and wrenched it as hard as he could to the right. Whatever was holding it in place suddenly gave way, and the steering wheel spun in his grip. He felt a sharp pain in his shoulder as his whole body twisted with it. His tires screeched as the truck slid against the asphalt and veered into the trees. The last thing he saw was the rough face of a thick tree trunk, illuminated by his head-lights, speeding towards him through a spray of leaves and brush.

CHAPTER 29

BANG!

Mari gasped and looked up in the mirror as the bathroom door flew open behind her. Her reflection was distorted with grief, her cheeks stained with tears.

Mason stood in the mirror behind her, taking her in with a dark, wild expression. He seemed gratified by her anguish, though it did not temper his fury. His green eyes had narrowed into glittering black slits; they bore into her with the look of a man possessed. His shoulders heaved with rage. His chin was lowered as if he were about to charge.

Mari's pulse quickened. She felt a sudden instinct to run. She whipped around to confront him. "Mason," she warned, "I'm serious—"

Mason took one stride forward and clapped both hands around her neck, cutting off her speech.

Mari reached up, trying to pry her fingers under his to loosen his grip. Unable to communicate with words, she looked into his eyes, but he wasn't there.

As her husband bore down on her, Mari went from disbelief to confusion, then fear, then fury. Gritting her teeth, she grunted and began to fight, wrenching her pregnant body back and forth as she tried to twist out of Mason's clutches. She clawed at his hands, digging her nails into the sides of his palms, hoping that the pain would distract him.

Her fight fueled Mason's fire. He tightened his grip on her neck, flexing his biceps, relishing his strength. Mari sensed an unfamiliar power surging through him. She searched his expression desperately, but the Mason she knew, her only hope for salvation, was gone. Something fierce and animalistic had been unleashed in him, and he had given it free reign.

Mari felt a pinch in her lower spine as Mason bent her backward over the vanity, his hands squeezing like a vice around her windpipe. Black and white spots popped against her vision as her eyes rolled back to the ceiling. She felt herself floating up toward it. The tip of her nose turned cold, and her eyelids grew heavy. Her lungs burned. Her limbs felt like lead. She wasn't sure how much longer she could fight. Mason's face swam above her as hot tears stung her eyes. He was going to kill her, and the life inside of her.

I'm sorry, she thought to the baby boy curled up in her center. She wondered if he knew what was happening—if it was getting dark for him, too. She felt for him in her body and sensed him nestled against her side, helpless against his father—this wild, cruel, heartless monster. He didn't deserve this. She'd fought, begged, and bargained with God to give her this little life. She'd promised to care for him and raise him into a good man, and now he would be snuffed out like one of those colorful little birthday candles before he was even born.

Mari felt her resolve return, locking in like iron armor to defend her. Summoning her strength, she snapped back into her body and twisted out from under Mason's weight as he crushed her against the marble countertop. Something popped in her lower back as she fell away from him. She gasped raggedly as oxygen seared her lungs. She was only free for a moment before Mason lunged at her again, but it was enough time to prepare. She pushed both arms out to stop him before he could reach for her throat again.

"Mason!" She shouted his name as he caught her in a bear grip, and together, they tumbled to the side, crashing over the toilet and landing on the cold tiles.

She knew he hadn't heard her; he was too blinded by rage. They wrestled on the floor—Mari clawed towards the bathroom door while Mason grabbed for her clothes, her limbs, anything his hands could find to drag her back into his clutches. She was almost free when he caught her by the hair.

Mari felt herself whipped up and backward. She spun on her knees, bringing her hands up just in time as Mason lunged again, grabbing her wrists. She heard a sickening crunch as her back slammed against the bathtub's edge. A cocktail of pain radiated across her shoulder blades.

Stunned, Mari shook her head, trying to regain focus, but the pain seared away any coherent thought. Her vision cleared just in time to see Mason's closed fist coming straight at her face. Everything went black, then exploded with popping, white stars. She heard skittering, like pearls bouncing across the bathroom tiles. Her mouth filled with blood, hot and metallic, and she realized he had knocked her teeth out. She felt the wind go out of her as she crashed back down to the floor. She lifted her arms, but the pain, like cold fire in her nerve endings, forced them down again.

Mason climbed on top of Mari, pinning her down. His hands closed around her throat again. She grabbed his forearms and squeezed, but she was so weak that her touch was more like a caress. She batted at his face, and her fingers caught briefly in the hair at his temples before dropping to the floor. Her knuckles knocked painfully against the tiles.

Mari's head throbbed from the pressure as her face flushed with blood. She bucked weakly, kicking her legs, but her socks scrabbled uselessly against the tiles. She looked into Mason's eyes, begging him to stop, but her mouth just opened and closed without making a sound.

Mason looked on with ravenous delight as darkness closed in around her periphery. With a final burst of effort, choking on her own blood, Mari gurgled her last words.

"Please... please..."

They fell on deaf ears. Eventually, her feet slowed their kicking. Her mouth stopped moving. Moments later, she was gone.

———

From the moment Mari slammed the bathroom door in his face, Mason had heard nothing but roaring, seen nothing but red, and felt nothing but white-hot fury. Now, it all disappeared as suddenly as it came. He released her and sat back against the shower, bracing his elbows against his knees while he caught his breath. He closed his eyes and pressed his knuckles into his eye sockets. When he opened them again, she was still there, lying at his feet. If he didn't know better, he'd have thought she was asleep.

Squeezing his eyes shut, Mason shivered, then began to convulse. He hugged himself tight, willing his body to stop shaking. The trembling intensified, thundering in his ears. He recalled the feeling he'd had just before he entered the bathroom—a rumbling at the base of his spine, followed by a wash of heat searing up his back. He remembered feeling the blood recede from in his body, gathering like a tidal wave behind his eyes, turning his vision red, and then...

Mason opened his eyes again, suddenly calm. He remembered it all—her tear-stained reflection in the mirror, the way their bodies had crashed against each other, the way she writhed underneath him, begging and pleading for release. He'd never felt power like that before… and then it was over.

He stared at his wife, lying motionless at his feet, and waited for remorse to set in. All he heard was Mari's voice echoing in his head, clanging against his skull.

I SEE YOU!

How dare she speak to him that way? Who the fuck did she think he was? Who the fuck did she think *she* was? Mason felt his blood temperature rising again. He savored its heat and the clarity it brought to his mind. It was no use wringing his hands over what he'd done. The more pressing issue was what to do next. Bracing himself against the shower, he pushed himself to his feet, then nudged her with his toe.

"Mari," he murmured. She didn't respond.

Mason looked around. Considering the intensity of their struggle, the bathroom was surprisingly in order. A few things were knocked over, and the bathmats slid around as they wrestled, but nothing was broken. He stepped over Mari's body and checked the bathroom door. By some miracle, it was also undamaged from being punched open moments ago. As he stood there surveying the room, with Mari lying in the middle of it all, he caught sight of her half-packed bag sitting on the bed and immediately knew what to do.

Mason hurried back to the kitchen to retrieve his cell phone. As he picked it up, it rang with an incoming call. He answered immediately.

"Thank God for you, Jeanine," he breathed. "Hey, listen to me—"

"No, Mason, *you* listen to *me*," Jeanine shouted into the phone.

"Jeanine, shut the fuck up and listen to me right now. We can't talk for long, but I need you to come here, to the house, *now*. Do you have cash?"

Jeanine was taken aback. "…Yes, but—"

"Good. Call a cab, tell them to drop you at the grocery store near me, pay cash, and walk the rest of the way. Use a fake name if they ask for one. When you get to my street, stay on the opposite side until you get to number 27, then cross and come around the left side of the house to the back patio. Make sure nobody sees you, and don't tell anyone you're coming here."

"Mason, what's going on?" Jeanine demanded. "It's raining like crazy! I can't just walk—"

"Just do as I say and get your ass over here." He started to hang up but paused, adding, "Please, baby. I need you."

He didn't wait for her to respond before ending the call. He hurried back to the bedroom in an adrenaline-fueled daze, half expecting to see Mari on her feet and ready for round two, but to his relief, she remained right where he had left her on the bathroom floor. While he waited for Jeanine to arrive, he quickly finished packing Mari's bag. He dragged her out to the bedroom and tied her sneakers onto her feet, then straightened up the bathroom and meticulously wiped up the small amount of blood that had spilled when he'd knocked her teeth out.

Frowning, Mason looked around again to see where her teeth had fallen and found all three in a neglected corner near the toilet. He picked them up carefully with a tissue and flushed them away, pushing the handle twice for good measure. Finally, he stepped back to check his handiwork—the bathroom was in perfect, lived-in order. He heard Jeanine rapping on the patio doors downstairs and hurried to let her inside.

He slid open the heavy glass door, pulled her into his arms, and planted a long, heady kiss on her before breaking free. "Jeanine, baby, thank God you're here."

Jeanine had arrived ready for a fight, but Mason's kiss completely disarmed her. "Mason! Baby, what is going on? Are you okay? Where is your wife?"

Mason hushed her and took her face in his hands, talking fast. "Look, baby, I know I said that we were done, and I'm sorry for that, okay?" He kissed her again and guided her to the kitchen table, holding her hands tightly. "I'm going to tell you something, and I need you to be on my side. You're all that I have right now. I *need* you."

Mason's heart was hammering as he delivered his lines. He hoped Jeanine would pick up on his desperation and succumb to her instinct to please him. This would only work if he kept her focused on saving him.

"Baby, I'm here," Jeanine assured him, her expression ablaze with ardent care. "I'm sorry, too. I love you. What's happening?"

"I love you, too." Mason breathed, allowing relief to flood his features. "I need you to do something for me. My life—our life together—is going to depend on it, okay?"

Jeanine nodded eagerly. "Okay."

Mason took a deep breath. "Mari and I had a huge fight when I got back here. She went through my stuff and found out about you. She was acting insane! I didn't know what to do."

"Oh my God." Jeanine squeezed his hands. "Are you okay? Where is she now?"

Mason swallowed hard. "She's upstairs... Jeanine... it's bad."

Jeanine nodded slowly as comprehension bloomed. "Tell me what happened, Mase."

"She started screaming, then she pushed me and went upstairs, saying she was going to pack up her stuff and go to her parent's house. I tried to talk her down! I told her it was too late and the weather was crazy. I told her it's not safe! But she wouldn't listen. She said horrible, nasty things. I never saw her like that before." He shook his head and stared at the ground in manufactured awe.

Jeanine pulled Mason into her arms and held him tightly. "Shhh. It's okay, baby. It's okay." He allowed her to rock him for a bit before disengaging to finish his story.

"I tried to physically stop her. I had to! But it was nothing, I swear! I just grabbed her arm like this." Mason demonstrated by gripping Jeanine's upper arm with a firm but gentle hand.

"Of course, Mase, I know. What happened when you did that?" She spoke to him as if he were a frightened child.

"Jeanine, she *attacked* me. It was crazy! She was like a wild animal. I tried to fend her off, but she just kept coming. I was so worried that she'd hurt the baby… it was so… intense…"

Mason trailed off, recalling the power that flowed through him while he wrestled with Mari. The memory sent a warm wave of pleasure through him, and his hands tightened instinctively around Jeanine's.

"What happened next?" Jeanine whispered, calling him back.

Mason blinked as if coming out of a trance. "We… we went down to the floor," he began softly, then cleared his throat. "She knocked her head against the bathtub, and the next thing I knew… she was gone."

Mason and Jeanine sat at the kitchen table, clutching each other as they processed their situation. The rain falling outside filled the silence, punctuated by droplets splashing on the kitchen tiles from Jeanine's drenched overcoat.

"She's dead?" Jeanine finally asked.

Mason nodded. Jeanine looked at the ground. When she raised her head again, her expression was determined.

"What do you need me to do?" she asked.

Mason exhaled his relief. "Jeanine. I fucking love you."

"Tell me what to do," she repeated.

"She's dressed, and the bag she was planning to take is all packed. I think we can make it look like she left here alive and had an accident on the way to her parents. The weather is bad, and I can prove she was distraught. It would basically be like the thing I warned her might happen, happened. Baby, that's where you come in."

Jeanine waited eagerly for him to go on.

"I need you to drive her, in her car, to the quarry overlook and make it look like she drove over the edge in the storm," Mason explained. "But you'll have to do it alone."

Jeanine blanched. "Why?"

"While you're gone, I'm going to call her parents and tell them she's on the way to them. When she doesn't show, I'm sure they'll call me back, and then we'll call the police and report her missing... I'm going to have to admit to our affair, though."

A spark of excitement flashed in Jeanine's eyes, followed by a concerned look. "Isn't that going to make you look worse, though?"

Mason shook his head. "I have to give them a compelling enough reason for her to leave in the middle of the night and show what state of mind she was in. It's better if I'm honest about the affair from the beginning. They're going to look into me and find out anyway. If I don't admit it myself, I'll look like a liar."

Jeanine blinked several times while she considered this. "We're more than just an affair, Mase," she finally said.

"You know what I mean, baby. Stay with me here," Mason pleaded.

"Mason, even if I do this, how am I supposed to get home from the overlook on foot?"

"Hike to that picnic area where you and I met up that one time." Mason licked his lips and brushed them against Jeanine's. She moaned softly and tried to kiss him back, but he pulled away. "Wait there for me. On my way to her parent's place, I'll pick you up and drop you close enough to walk the rest of the way home."

"Mason, this is insane! And exactly how am I supposed to explain a random cab trip to the grocery store in the middle of the night if anyone asks?"

"If we do this right, nobody will ask. Cops are idiots. They'll follow the evidence they have—the evidence we give them. You didn't give the cab company your name, right? You paid cash? Nobody saw you leave your place?"

"Right," Jeanine repeated skeptically, "but..."

"That's good," Mason assured her. "No trail. You went home and stayed there. No one can prove otherwise. We can do this!"

Jeanine slowly got to her feet as she turned Mason's proposal over in her mind. Mason followed and took her face in his hands.

"Jeanine, listen to me. We can do this. If you can pull this part off, and if we stick together, this will look like nothing more than a terrible accident. There won't *be* an investigation."

Jeanine looked at Mason dubiously. Sensing she was teetering, he played his final ace.

"Jeanine. I never meant for this to happen, but now that it has... I see now that my marriage was never going to end any other way. Mari was too volatile; she would've destroyed me before she let me walk away from her. As soon as I got back here, I knew I'd made a mistake. I wanted to come back to you, but she was never going to let that happen. You are the strongest, sexiest, most beautiful, incredible person I have ever met. This is our chance to be together with nothing standing in our way! I'll do everything. All you have to do is the last step... Can you do that? For us?"

Mason stared into Jeanine's eyes without blinking, allowing her to search him for as long as she needed. He watched as something in her ignited. She nodded wordlessly.

"Good girl." He kissed her again. "Come on."

It took them much longer than he would've liked to carry Mari's body downstairs to the garage, and almost more patience than he possessed to coach Jeanine through the process.

"Why can't she be in the trunk?" she whined when Mason opened the passenger door. "I'm just supposed to drive with a dead body next to me?"

"She needs to be in the front when the car goes over, so it looks like she was driving," Mason explained while he adjusted the seat. "Do you want to move her by yourself when you get there?"

At that suggestion, Jeanine quit complaining. As they hoisted her into the seat, Mari's head lolled to one side, and a soft breath escaped her parted lips. Mason and Jeanine froze.

"You said she was dead!" Jeanine gasped.

Mason peered at his wife closely. She was pale, the muscles in her face completely slack. He put his ear to her lips, feeling for breath. There was barely any warmth emanating from her skin. A soft whoosh of air tingled against his cheek.

"Well?" Jeanine hissed.

"Shut up for a second," Mason hissed back. He closed his eyes. In a final moment of intimacy, Mason tuned all of his senses into his wife's body, feeling for signs of life. Pressing his thumb to her neck, he felt for a pulse but could only feel his own panicked heartbeat thudding through his fingertips.

"Mar?" he whispered her name one last time.

"Mason? What's going on?" Jeanine whispered frantically. "Is she dead or not? Oh my God…" She began to jump up and down, panicking.

Mason made up his mind quickly. "She's gone," he declared, ducking out of the car. "But let's not waste any more time."

"Agreed."

Together, they removed Mari's sweatshirt, folded her body forward, and covered her with a blanket. As they walked around to the driver's side, Jeanine threw the sweatshirt over her head.

"Ugh, it's still warm," she grimaced.

As she was about to climb into the driver's seat, Mason pushed her up against the side of the SUV and planted a dizzying kiss that left her breathless.

"Last but not least," he murmured, placing one of Mari's old baseball caps on Jeanine's head and pulling the brim down. "Don't take this off until you get there, and keep your head low at the lights."

"I will," Jeanine promised.

"You don't know what this means to me."

"To us," she whispered, looking into his eyes. "And yes, I do."

Mason's instincts sharpened at her words. He had seen Jeanine in a heightened state of desire many times, but for the first time, he noticed an intensity in her expression that gave him pause, like there was some obscured fine print to their agreement that he didn't yet understand. He pulled back, attempting to read her, but as he did, his eyes flicked past her to Mari, moments from death underneath the blanket in the passenger seat.

There wasn't time to deal with this now. He needed to get them both out of here, fast. It brought him some comfort, knowing Jeanine would unwittingly deal the final blow. At least now, he could honestly say he wasn't a murderer, and after the way he'd convinced her tonight, he was confident he could handle Jeanine with ease when the dust settled.

"Go now, and hurry," he said. "And don't call me until I call you."

———

August 14, 2022

Dear Diary – I have just had the most INSANE twenty-four hours of my life! The things you do for love!! When Mason called me over last night, never in my wildest dreams would I have expected what was waiting for me at his house! I'll never forget the look in his eyes when he told me what happened. He looked so scared. The way she acted out on him tells me everything I need to know about what kind of person she was. I wish I could've stayed with him to make sure he was okay! I keep checking the news, but so far, nothing is out yet. I'm going crazy worrying about how he's handling all of this right now!! I wish I could tell him everything is going to be okay, that everything went according to plan... well. Mostly.

First of all, it's hard keeping your head down with half your face covered while you're driving! How are you supposed to know when the lights change if you can't look up at them?? Anyway. We made it. They should really be better about locking the gate to that overlook. I guess they will be now. I think the fact that it was open for me was a sign.

Second of all, disposing of a body is totally disgusting and way harder than it looks in the movies. Honestly, the size of her was grosser than the fact that she was dead. I swear she weighed like 300 pounds. Reason #1568 why I'll never get pregnant. Ugh. I've taken like three showers today already, and I still feel like she's on me, yuck!

Anyway, Mason's idea was to unbuckle her seatbelt and then use a rock or something to weigh down the gas pedal and send her over the edge. My poor baby, I will give him a pass since he was in panic mode, but that was the stupidest idea ever. First of all, it took me forever to find a rock big enough, slipping around in the mud, and second, the dummy forgot that I would have to press the brake to change gears. That's not even the worst part! After all that, she wasn't even dead!

I mean, she was pretty close, but definitely not dead yet. I should've known when she sighed back in the garage. I should've checked myself instead of taking his word for it. But I guess we were both panicking, and she looked pretty fucking dead... Plus, I've heard dead bodies fart and sigh and stuff, so he totally could've been right, but he wasn't! I almost had everything ready to go when the bitch woke up! JFC. I swear I almost had a heart attack when she started to make those creepy noises. She looked god awful, with her face all bruised and her teeth knocked out. This is why he needs me – to do the hard things he can't.

I mean, what was I supposed to do? Call Mase? Take her back to him so he could kill her again properly this time? He already looked so traumatized. I couldn't do that to him. Plus, he already botched it once.

I guess I could've just hurried up and sent her over, but I don't know. Something in me just felt like there was the tiniest chance she could survive. In horror movies, you have to make SURE the villain is DEAD. Headshot. Soooo... I did what I had to do. Honestly, it was kind of fitting. If this is really what I want – to be with him forever – then this is on me. Like when the Universe tests you to see how far you're willing to go and what you're willing to do to manifest. I think it's safe to say I passed my test with flying colors.

It was easier than I thought it would be, but also harder at the same time. She was already so weak, I figured if I just plugged her nose for a bit, she'd suffocate, but she actually tried to fight me! I mean, it wasn't much of a fight, she was already halfway gone, but I have to admit, I got scared for a second. She almost scratched my face! It honestly was like a lucky break that I was able to slam her head against the dash and knock her out. I was shaking so bad after that I could barely finish. I can't imagine what I would've done next if she woke up again. Thank God.

It is the bravest, scariest thing I have ever done. I felt like I was in an action movie or something. I backed *up the car, put it in drive, told myself it was now or never, baby girl, then took my foot off the brake, tucked and rolled, and slammed the door behind me, and that was it! I'll never forget what it looked like. Her car busted through that wooden rail like it was made of toothpicks and just disappeared over the edge. The end.*

I'm not going to tell him that I had to kill her in the end. Maybe one day in the future, when we're old and gray, but for now, I'll let my baby keep his conscience clean. It was meant to be me. I believe that. The next few days are going to be so hard, just waiting (ahhh!!!!!), but I know that the life of our dreams is on the other side, and I'll hold on to that to keep me going until we get there.

———

Mari felt like she was dying, but that didn't make sense. She was supposed to be dead already. She'd felt herself go as she looked into Mason's eyes, watching him disappear above her while everything went dark… but now she was remembering other things—being dragged, then pushed into a small, dark space filled with the cloying scent of candy mixed with something sour. Jeanine's face flashed before her, then exploded in bright, white stars. Mari remembered flying. Then everything went black. Now she was dying again, but where?

Unable to open her eyes, Mari used her other senses to ascertain her situation. Her body burned in agony at the mere thought of moving, but her skin felt like ice. Water was spilling in all around her, freezing cold and rising fast. The air smelled acrid and metallic. Something warm and sticky dripped into her mouth—blood. Her heart pounded feebly in her chest.

Don't be afraid, Mar, a voice echoed in her head. It sounded familiar, though she hadn't heard it in years, not since she was a kid. She could hardly believe it was real.

"Mikey?" she croaked in disbelief. The effort set her insides on fire. It hurt to breathe.

I'm here, he replied. *Don't be afraid.*

Mari didn't dare speak again—the pain was too much. *Is this Hell?* she thought fearfully.

Though she couldn't see him, she could feel her brother's sympathy when he answered her. *No. Just hold on to my voice. This will be over soon.*

Where am I? she asked. He didn't answer.

For a brief moment, all of Mari's pain disappeared. She felt herself lift out of her body. Her head bobbed forward, plunging her face into ice-cold water, and all physical sensation came rushing back. Her sinuses stung as water went up her nose, and she coughed again, sputtering and moaning in anguish at the effort. She wanted to weep from the pain, but her sobs remained lodged in her chest, aggravating her torment. Suddenly, it all clicked. She was in her car, and she was drowning.

This was the end.

Time to go, Mar. It was Mikey again, calling her away.

Wait, no, this isn't right! Mari insisted as the water inched higher around her. If she could just get to the door… but her limbs were paralyzed. *This can't be the end,* she pleaded, *not like this.* The water closed over her head, and everything went quiet. That peaceful floating sensation returned.

It's alright, Marylis. Let go.

There were more voices now, all whispering to her at once. She didn't recognize them all, but she could feel she was surrounded by love.

We're here, they soothed. *You're not alone.*

Mari sensed them nearby, waiting to embrace her in the light and warmth. She wanted to go to them but was stopped by the sound of two heartbeats, still echoing in her body. She paused and listened as they slowed together—the larger one, hers, keeping time while her baby's thumped softly alongside it. Even after her heart beat its last, her son's kept going, blissfully unaware that the end was near. Unable to save him, Mari listened helplessly until it finally stilled, and he was gone. She felt herself drawn toward the light. The voices urged her to give in, to let go, but she couldn't.

There's nothing left for you here, Mar, Mikey said, but he was wrong. Everything she ever wanted had been right here. Why was it being taken from her? She didn't understand.

It doesn't matter anymore. You're free. Let go! Her brother and the other voices pleaded with her, begging her to join them, but she pushed them all away. How could she ever be free knowing all that she'd lost?

Suspended in the void between life and death, Mari howled her grief and betrayal. *How could this happen? I was good to him! I did everything I was supposed to do! I loved him with everything I had, even when I shouldn't have. I loved him...* she mourned. *Why did I deserve this?*

There was no answer. The warmth, the light, and the voices were all gone. She was utterly alone, empty, and lost as she relived every moment she'd ever had with Mason, starting with that magical first kiss years ago. She'd believed it was fate that brought them together, and love that would keep them that way forever. She'd been so wrong.

Mari never imagined it was possible to feel this much love and hate for the same person at once. She'd given all of herself to Mason, and he'd repaid her with violent, brutal death, then gave her body away to be disposed of like trash. If this was love, if this was fate, she refused to accept either. She refused to go quietly into oblivion. She was done playing by the rules.

Out of the darkness, Mari felt herself ignite and expand, like a phoenix spreading its wings above an inferno. Rage billowed from her like blood in the water, and she used it to soar out of the depths that had nearly consumed her. Mikey and the others who called to her were long gone, but they were right about one thing: she was finally free. Nothing would ever hurt her again. Not even *him*.

He wouldn't get away with this. Piece by piece, she would destroy everything he held dear until there was nothing left but his pathetic, empty husk. Even if it meant abandoning Heaven and condemning herself to Hell alongside him, she would make sure Mason got what was coming to him.

CHAPTER 30

Jeanine sat in her robe on the stairs, pouting over the chocolate birthday cake she'd spent the afternoon making for Mason. By now, he should've come through the front door and discovered her with nothing but this cake in her lap and a smile on her face. Instead, she'd posed there for over an hour, avoiding Otis' judgmental stares as he occasionally wandered past.

Fed up, Jeanine got dressed and started trying to reach her annoyingly enigmatic boyfriend. When she couldn't get through, she tried his parents, but unsurprisingly, they didn't answer either. Of course not—they'd probably spent their little lunch together brainwashing Mason against her, which was why he wasn't back yet.

Fuming, she stomped to her purse and dug out the burner phone she'd been using to call him anonymously. It began as a simple insurance measure to spook him into believing someone else knew what they'd done, so he stayed close to her. It worked like a charm, and Jeanine meant to stop until she realized it was also a relatively harmless way for her to blow off steam whenever he was a jerk to her. She'd place a call and have some fun getting under his skin, but tonight, satisfaction evaded her.

She tried him two more times and imagined the distressed look on his face as he screened his "Unknown Caller." She hoped it ruined his night, wherever he was. Then, she took the chocolate cake to bed with her, dusting all her crumbs into his side as she ate. Finally, exhausted by anger, she passed out. When she woke up alone the next morning, depression set in.

November 9, 2022

Dear Diary – Mason never came home last night, and he hasn't answered my calls or texts. I don't know what to do. Everything is going so wrong. I feel so alone. I swear, sometimes it feels like the entire world is against me. Now, I'm losing him too. I can't believe I'm even saying these words!

I have no clue where he might be. I know he's not cheating on me. No other woman in town would touch him right now, lol. I know we've had our problems lately. I wish he would just talk to me like he used to. I never know what he's thinking anymore. Oh my God. What if he couldn't take it anymore and decided to confess??

Lol JK. He couldn't do that to me without fucking things up for himself. Besides, police would be kicking the door down by now if he did, and they're not. He'd have another fucking thing coming if he thought he could get away with that shit. I told him I wasn't like his wife, and I fucking meant it. In fact, the next time I see his sorry ass, I think I should remind him of that. If he keeps this up, maybe I'll be the one to go to the police.

Jeanine snapped her journal shut and forced herself out of bed. Downstairs, she threw away what was left of Mason's cake, made herself breakfast, and flipped on the TV, hoping to find something distracting. She froze when she saw a reporter standing in front of a wrecked white pickup truck bearing a familiar green logo. Forgiving and forgetting all, she got dressed and rushed out of the house.

———

"Are you family?" a steely-haired, older woman behind the nurse's station asked. She looked Jeanine up and down over large, wire-rimmed reading glasses.

"I'm the only family he's got left!" Jeanine wailed, frustrated. She's already lost too much time visiting different hospitals to find out which one Mason was at. She had none left to waste on this mean, old hag.

The nurse regarded her disdainfully but seemed to decide Jeanine was not worth arguing with. She directed her to another floor where Mason was recovering. Paramedics had brought him in the night before all banged up—a broken arm, a dislocated knee, and several torn muscles. The airbags had burned part of his face when they deployed in the crash. Jeanine rushed into his room, took one look at his disfigured form, and covered her mouth with a desperate sob.

"Baby! Oh my God, I was so scared!" she cried, throwing herself on top of him. "I was sick all night wondering what happened to you! Are you okay? How do you feel?"

"How do you think he feels?" a woman's voice asked sharply. "He's been in a car accident. He's lucky to be alive. Please get off of him."

Jeanine was so focused on Mason that she completely missed his parents hovering nearby. Kris was looking at her with barely concealed disgust.

"Of course, you're so right," Jeanine agreed, swallowing her tears. She eased herself off Mason's hospital bed. "I was just so worried."

She wiped her face and went towards Kris with open arms but stopped short when the older woman took a step back. Jeanine dropped her arms, then awkwardly hugged herself. Her whole body was trembling.

"You two must be exhausted. I can sit with him while you get some sleep," she offered. When neither of Mason's parents responded, she tried a different tactic. "Or, I can bring us some coffee? Have you eaten breakfast? I can see what the cafeteria has."

Kris exchanged a telepathic look with her husband. "I think Mason's father and I can handle it from here," she clipped.

Jeanine stared at her, dumbfounded. "I—I don't understand," she finally said, though she did perfectly well. She watched Kris wearily gather her patience and suppressed an urge to roll her eyes. When the older woman spoke again, her voice dripped with condescension.

"What I mean is, we don't want you here. We will take care of our son. You can leave."

"Kris…" Steve admonished gently, but she held up her hand to silence him.

Jeanine felt the color rising in her face. She glanced at Mason, who was watching the exchange, mute. His face was so swollen and bruised, she couldn't read his expression, but she could feel his apathy.

"Why do you hate me?" she whispered.

"This isn't about hate," Kris replied. "It's about what's right."

"I love this man, and he loves me!" Jeanine insisted. "What is wrong about that?"

"Honey, if I have to explain that to you, we've got bigger problems," Kris scoffed.

Jeanine was about to go off when Mason finally spoke.

"Mom…" he muttered quietly. Just as she'd done to her husband before, Kris held up a hand to silence her son.

"Mason is going to need time to recover, and I intend to make sure he does that without any… distractions." She eyed Jeanine up and down. "In the meantime, I suggest you go back to wherever you live. If he wants to see you when he's better, that's up to him, but until then, I would ask you to respectfully keep your distance and let my family heal *properly*."

Jeanine's blood began to simmer. She'd had enough of the Goodridges and their condescending bullshit. They walked around thinking they were untouchable, but she held cards that could destroy them all in an instant. She looked pointedly at Mason, who seemed to know exactly what she was thinking. He shook his head ever so slightly, pleading with her.

A small smile tugged at Jeanine's lips. She lifted her chin defiantly. She would not be put down and ordered around by this old bitch. Maybe Kris was used to that with Mason's last partner, but she was dealing with someone new now—someone who wasn't going anywhere.

"No one in the world understands what Mason needs better than me," Jeanine replied calmly. "But as his mother, if you want to be the one to look after him, go right ahead. I'll go back to *our* house and make sure it's ready for when he comes home."

With Kris watching, Jeanine went to Mason, leaned down, and brushed her lips against his. He eyed her like she was venomous.

"Take all the time you need, baby," Jeanine cooed, stroking his hair. "I love you, and I'm not going anywhere." She leaned closer and whispered, "You won't get rid of me so easily." With that, she turned her back on all three Goodridges and left the hospital with her head high.

Jeanine visited Mason daily after that, ignoring Kris' mandate for space. Her persistence paid off. Eventually, Kris and Steve would begrudgingly depart whenever she showed up, leaving her and Mason alone to talk.

"I can't take this anymore!" he fretted one afternoon as soon as they were out of earshot. Jeanine sat with him on his hospital bed, massaging his thigh. "They're always watching me! My mom... I think she knows..."

Jeanine's hand stilled, her fingers tightening on his knee. "Knows what?"

They stared wordlessly at each other; Jeanine's eyes narrowed as she took in Mason's wide, panicked ones.

"I need to get out of here!" he breathed.

"Hush, baby." Jeanine resumed rubbing his leg. "The doctor said just a few more days."

"No, you don't understand, Jeanine. I need to get *away*."

"From the hospital?"

Mason shook his head. "No! No…"

"From your parents?" Jeanine paused, then scowled. "You better not mean from me…"

Mason made a frustrated noise. "Jeanine! Shut up and listen to me!"

Jeanine was about to escalate, but Mason's frantic expression gave her pause. "Okay. I'm listening."

Mason collapsed against his pillow with relief. "My parents want to take me home with them after I get out of here… you can't let them. I don't think I can hide it from them much longer. My head is all…" His gaze went cloudy as he stared at the blankets covering his body.

"All what, baby?" Jeanine asked. "Is your head hurting? You want me to get the nurse?"

Mason shook his head. "Jeanine… I'm not crazy. You have to believe me. I can't tell anyone else."

"Tell anyone what, baby?"

Mason's voice shook. "That day… in my truck… it wasn't an accident. She's trying to hurt me… I think she wants to kill me!"

A tidal wave of anger and jealousy swept over Jeanine. She leaped to her feet. "Who the fuck are you talking about right now, Mason? Have you been messing around with someone else? After everything? Are you fucking stunted?"

"Jeanine, please! Please!" Mason begged. "You don't understand! It's Mari!"

Jeanine froze, confused. "Mari?"

Mason teared up. "I know how it sounds, but it's true. I've seen her..." His eyes darted around the room. "I see her all the time. When I'm sleeping... sometimes when I'm awake... I heard her voice in my truck," he whimpered. "She wants to punish us for what we did."

"We didn't do *anything*, Mason," Jeanine asserted. She sat down again and took his hands in hers. "She had an accident. Okay?"

"Okay," he agreed shakily. He tried to nod but was trembling so much that his head just bobbled feebly. "But... you believe me, right? We have to stop her! She wants to kill me! I know it was her. Please! You have to believe me!"

Jeanine sat back and studied Mason, unsure how to respond. His face was hollow, with deep shadows visible under the bruises around his eyes. He had lost weight on bed rest, but it was his cowardly expression that made him appear truly diminished. She searched him for any sign of the confident, charismatic man she'd fallen in love with but came up empty.

"Jeanine, please!" Mason begged, interrupting her thoughts. "I need you!"

Jeanine used to dream about hearing these words from Mason, but coming from this desperate, mewling version of him, she suddenly felt repulsed. She squeezed his hands, pushing away her discomfort.

"Baby. Your ex is gone. She can't hurt you, or us, ever again."

Mason tried to protest, but Jeanine shushed him, balking internally at his pathetic expression.

"As long as we're together, nothing can touch us. I'm not afraid of her, and you don't need to be either. Please, baby, try to remember who you are!"

"No!" Mason moaned. "You're not listening!" He looked like a scared little boy, shrinking under the covers of his hospitable bed while Jeanine tried to convince him there were no monsters underneath it. She bit back her frustration.

"Alright, alright. Just try to rest now," she soothed.

"Will you stay with me while I sleep?" he asked in a small voice.

Jeanine wrestled with herself as she took in his anxious expression. She still loved Mason, but the life she'd imagined for them wouldn't be possible with this version of him. Hopefully, this was temporary—he was probably just depleted from his accident. For both their sakes, Jeanine resolved to do whatever was necessary to bring the old Mason back as quickly as possible.

"I'm not going anywhere," she promised.

Jeanine watched Mason's body relax as he finally succumbed to his painkillers and fell asleep, clinging to her hand like a baby. She waited until he was out cold, then let go, grimacing as she slid her fingers out of his clammy grip.

CHAPTER 31

November 18, 2022

Dear Diary — Mason is FINALLY coming home!!!!!
I finally get my man back, and the first order of business will be getting him back to who he was, so we can get back to being US.

I wish I could've picked him up from the hospital, but I knew his parents would make a stink about it, so I just have to sit here and be patient while he ditches them. I guess I could've picked him up from their house, but I just know his mom would get all weepy and try to convince him to stay with her. It's so annoying how she's made this whole thing all about herself. Ugh!

At least now she knows she can't push ME around. She can think or say whatever she wants about me, but at the end of the day, her son is coming home to ME, so guess who won!!! That's right. ME! I won!

Jeanine carried out her domestic duties victoriously in anticipation of Mason's return later that afternoon. She straightened up their bedroom and changed the sheets, dreaming of the day they could move to a new house in a new town and finally begin a new life, together.

From down the hall, the dryer's digital chimes pierced the air, beckoning her to the laundry room. Jeanine followed the sound, quickening her pace as she passed the closed nursery door. She hated that room. When she first moved in, Mason acted as if the nursery simply didn't exist, which Jeanine was happy to go along with. It gave her the creeps, the way everything in there was kept exactly as *she* had left it.

Then, the morning after their fight on Halloween, Jeanine noticed the door standing wide open. She'd closed it, but Mason freaked and insisted it remain open at all times without explaining why. Jeanine was going to suggest they convert it into a workout room, but he ended up in the hospital before she could broach the subject. After he shared his little ghost story with her, she'd returned home, shut that door, and vowed to make Mason empty that room as soon as possible.

She was a few feet past the nursery when she heard the latch click and the door creak open behind her. Confused, she backed up, coming to stand in front of the half-open door. She heard a soft, irregular bumping coming from inside. Tentatively, she placed her fingers on the knob, which was surprisingly cool to the touch, and pushed it all the way open.

The bright afternoon sun streamed through the open curtains, bathing the empty crib in warm light and adding a soft glow to a white knitted blanket draped over its side. A floppy, stuffed rabbit slumped lamely in one corner of the crib, assessing her with beady, black eyes. A slight motion drew Jeanine's attention to the glider, bumping lightly against the wall. She went over and stilled it with her hand, then looked around to see what had disturbed it.

"Otis?" she called. "Are you in here?"

She checked under the furniture, but he was nowhere to be found. Standing alone in the middle of the room, Jeanine shivered. The air in here was colder than the rest of the house.

Probably because the door is always closed, she reasoned. Still, she felt a sudden urge to get out of there as quickly as possible. She forced herself to leave calmly, pausing to check behind the door on her way out for anything that might have caused it to open on its own. She found nothing. Frowning, she stepped back into the hall and pulled the door shut. As soon as she turned away, the latch clicked, and the door creaked open again.

Frustrated, Jeanine grasped the knob and twisted it back and forth, testing the latch. She pulled the door shut again, jiggled the knob for good measure, then stepped back and waited. This time, it stayed closed. With a satisfied "Hmph," she continued to the laundry room.

As she emptied the dryer, she pressed her face to one of the warmed towels, inhaling the scent of fresh laundry, but the fragrance suddenly made her ill. She grimaced, then glanced at the nearly empty gallon of detergent on the counter nearby. They hadn't replaced it since she'd moved in... this was the last of what was left from *her*. The thought had never occurred to her before.

Jeanine held the towel away from her and shook it so hard that it snapped, then vigorously folded the entire pile of laundry, growing more ill-tempered as she handled each item—items that had been selected by *her*, that reeked of the detergent *she* picked. Even the laundry basket Jeanine was using used to be *hers*. When it was full, she snatched it up, set it against her hip, and headed for the linen closet.

"*Her* linen closet," Jeanine grumbled. She didn't know why Mason's ex was suddenly front and center in her mind. Her mood was souring, and she didn't want that today. Mason would be home in a matter of hours, and she needed her game face on when he arrived. Whatever this was, she needed to shake it off. She stopped short as she came back down the hall and saw the damn nursery door swinging open again.

"For fuck's sake!" Jeanine dropped the laundry basket, stomped over to the door, and slammed it shut. "Quit!"

She snatched up the laundry basket and marched away. She put the sheets in the linen closet, slamming those doors too, then continued to their bedroom. Lifting the folded towels out with one hand, she kicked open the door to the walk-in closet and tossed the empty basket inside, then, hugging the towels under her arm, stomped to the bathroom. As she extended her hand to push open the door, it floated away from her touch.

Jeanine drew her fingers back in surprise. While she stood there contemplating how that happened, another sound drew her attention. Jeanine leaned closer and listened through the half-open door. She heard a skittering noise, like tiny pearls, bouncing across the tiles toward her. As she pushed the door open all the way, a small, dark shape darted behind the tub.

"Otis?" Jeanine called, peering into the darkened bathroom. "Where are you, you little fucker?" She glanced in the mirror and gasped.

A woman stood at the vanity, silhouetted against the light reflecting through the open door. Jeanine's blood turned cold as she recognized *her* olive features and dark eyes, radiating pure rage.

Frightened, Jeanine dropped the towels and fumbled for the light switch. When she turned back, the woman in the mirror was gone. Jeanine blinked at her own reflection.

"Get a grip, girl," she muttered, shaking her head. She scooped up the towels, straightened their folds, and placed them on the shelf. Her heart was still racing as she left the bathroom, and the hairs on the back of her neck stood on end.

Jeanine slumped against the bed with a sigh, feeling suddenly wiped. As she rolled the tension out of her neck, her eyes fell on Mason's nightstand. Jeanine idly traced her fingers across its empty surface, down to the top drawer. She opened it, then casually began snooping through his things.

As she felt towards the back of the drawer, her fingers brushed against something soft. With a tiny gasp, Jeanine drew her hand back as if she'd been bitten, then eagerly resumed her expedition. She felt giddy as she drew out a velvet ring box. She cradled it with trembling palms, her eyes filling with tears of joy.

She knew she shouldn't open it. She wanted to be surprised, but her excitement was hard to contain. She set the box down on the nightstand and tore her eyes away, hoping to break its spell on her, but it didn't work. The box, and whatever lay inside, called to her. Unable to resist, Jeanine snatched up the ring box and cracked it open. Against the deep blue velvet, an oval-shaped diamond solitaire glinted on a simple yellow-gold band.

Jeanine stared at the ring for a long time, trying to dispel her disappointment. It was a good-sized stone but plain for her taste, although she supposed some might call it timeless. It was nothing like the platinum, diamond-encrusted showpiece she'd envisioned for herself.

Never mind, she reasoned. She was confident that when the time came, it would be easy to convince Mason to exchange the ring for something more her style. If she started dropping hints now, he might even fix it before he proposed. Plucking the ring out of the box, she held it up to the window, letting the diamond catch the light. An engraving on the inside band caught her eye: $M \infty M$.

Jeanine's heart sank. She should've known this boring thing was *hers*. She felt her temper heating up again, though she wasn't sure where to direct her anger. At Mason for holding on to it without telling her? At herself for foolishly believing this box held something for her? At *her* for somehow always managing to get in the way despite being dead for months?

Jeanine stood up and tossed the ring on the bed, then began to pace angrily. The diamond twinkled innocently against the bedspread, catching her eye again. Entranced, she stretched across the bed to retrieve it. She lay on her stomach and stared into the diamond's facets, watching them gleam.

"Fuck it," she whispered, then slipped the ring onto her finger. It caught against her knuckle, but with one deft push, it was all the way on—and a near-perfect fit.

Enthralled, Jeanine rolled onto her back and stretched her hand above her, admiring the ring's sparkle. Maybe it wasn't her style, but it looked damn good on her. The longer she wore it, the more it seemed to take hold of her, filling her mind with dreamy pictures of her and Mason's future together. Like a movie, scenes flashed before her eyes of a proposal against a vivid sunset, followed by a romantic elopement to some far-flung, exotic place where they could stay for the honeymoon. Maybe they would have a family after all—a boy first, then a girl.

Actually, no. Jeanine shook the image away, revising it. They would have a girl… two girls… twins! Not just sisters but best friends, so neither would ever be lonely. The three of them would have Mason completely wrapped around their fingers. Jeanine saw it all so clearly, as if they were memories she'd already lived rather than visions of what was to come.

A low, menacing yowl startled her out of her reverie. Jeanine quickly rolled to her stomach. Through the fingers of her still outstretched hand, she saw Otis crouched at the threshold, watching her with those blazing yellow eyes.

Jeanine curled her bejeweled hand underneath her, out of sight. She pushed herself off the mattress as Otis stalked into the room. He leaped silently onto the bed, making himself comfortable in the place she'd just vacated. Before Jeanine could decide what to do next, the cat suddenly seemed to lose interest in her. He began licking his paw as if to say, "You're dismissed."

Her cheeks reddening, Jeanine quickly pulled the engagement ring off her finger and put it back in the drawer. She slammed it shut, hoping to startle Otis, but he didn't flinch.

Fighting the urge to throw something at him, she took a deep breath to calm herself and checked the time. Mason would be home soon. Where had the day gone? She glanced back at the closed drawer and marveled at how quickly she'd forgotten herself the moment she put that godforsaken, ugly ring on—how quickly she'd turned into *her*. She shuddered, suddenly feeling the need to cleanse herself with a long, luxurious bath.

CHAPTER 32

Mason winced at the pain in his shoulder as he clumsily guided the steering wheel with his good arm. He glanced longingly at his hospital bag in the passenger seat, and the zippered compartment that held his prescription painkillers. He reached for it, but the ensuing ache in his side stopped him from going further. With a regretful sigh, he resigned himself to the pain until he got back to his house.

He tensed anxiously as another car passed him on the road. He shouldn't have been driving, but he had to get away from his parents. Kris and Steve begged him not to go, but after seeing how worked up he became, they'd quickly caved to avoid distressing him further. After lunch, Steve had taken him to get a rental car and, with one final plea that went ignored, reluctantly let him go.

Now, Mason was slowly making his way around the lake along the Eastview Highway toward home. He wasn't looking forward to going back there either, but it was easier than being with his parents, whose constant, close attention was making him paranoid. He could see in her eyes that his mother was burning with questions. It was only a matter of time until she asked them, and he knew that in his diminished state, he wouldn't be able to fend her off.

For better or worse, Jeanine was the only person who understood what he was going through right now. He didn't have anyone else. He knew she didn't believe him about Mari, but he would find a way to convince her. Once again, despite not wanting her, he was stuck needing her.

Mason gritted his teeth as he drove over a bump that jostled him roughly in his seat. Hot, throbbing pain seared his entire right side as a high-pitched ringing screamed in his ears. Through watery eyes, he spied a turn-off to his right, quickly pulled into it, and parked. He cut the ignition and pressed his head against the steering wheel, focusing on his breath until his agony finally began to subside.

Twisting uncomfortably, Mason fumbled to retrieve his painkillers, shook a few into his mouth, and gulped them down dry. Finally, he leaned back against the headrest, closed his eyes, and surrendered.

He was startled awake an hour later by a car door slamming nearby. Groggy and disoriented, Mason lifted his head, squinting into the late afternoon sun that was setting directly in front of him. Voices drew his attention to a young couple passing by. Mason slumped in his seat and watched them walk arm-in-arm towards the setting sun, stopping at a thick, newly-built wooden rail. A sick feeling settled in his stomach as he realized he'd been asleep for an hour at the quarry lake overlook.

With shaking hands, Mason sat up and buckled his seatbelt, pushing down firmly to make sure it was securely in place. Without a second glance at the beautiful sunset happening in front of him, he restarted the ignition and headed for home.

CHAPTER 33

J eanine turned on the bathroom light and stared defiantly at the mirror. It was bad enough that *she* was in Mason's head, eating away at him, but Jeanine would not surrender to irrational hallucinations from a guilty conscience. She had nothing to feel guilty about—they'd done what they had to do!

She waited, daring the wretched figure from earlier to return, but only saw herself. With a satisfied nod, she marched over to the tub and turned on the taps. While she waited for the water to fill, she undressed and brushed out her long, blonde hair.

"*She* could never," Jeanine preened, admiring her naked form in the mirror. As she turned to blow a kiss over her shoulder, she noticed the tub was ready. She shut the door so Otis couldn't sneak up on her again, then eased herself into the water, exhaling as her muscles melted in the heat. Finally, she let her head fall back, closed her eyes, and surrendered.

Jeanine sank deeper until only her face remained above the surface. Under the water, she could hear her heartbeat echoing in her ears. Like a cat purring, she began to hum along. Her voice reverberated back through the water in a lower register. Playfully, she hummed lower, harmonizing with herself as the sound deepened and returned to her. In her relaxed, half-dreaming state, she imagined the echo came from a mermaid, or a memory, or herself, happily humming in a parallel universe.

As her lungs emptied, Jeanine paused to inhale and was surprised to hear the humming continue without her. The voice was faint but distinct... and utterly hypnotizing. She let go and listened to the humming as it grew louder and lower, vibrating the water around her in a pleasant way.

Slipping deeper into her subconscious, Jeanine imagined she was a baby in the womb, floating weightlessly in warm darkness while she listened to her mother's voice sing to her from somewhere far away. No, not far away... the voice was closer now, beneath her.

Jeanine let herself sink down to it. She extended her consciousness until her mind brushed against something swirling and dark. It seemed to come alive with the contact. The low hum shifted to a soft, menacing growl.

Jeanine suddenly felt afraid. The growling intensified, feeding on her fear. Under the water, something cold slithered across her tailbone. Jeanine flailed her arms wildly, her hands eventually finding the edges of the bathtub, then pulled herself up in a rush of water, gasping for breath. She looked down frantically, but saw only her legs against the tub's white porcelain, distorted under the rippling bathwater. Gripping the tub's sides with white knuckles, she shut her eyes again and listened, but the growling was gone. All she heard now was the water dripping out of her soaked hair.

"Fuck," Jeanine chuckled to herself. She rarely had bad dreams—she'd forgotten what it was like. As the adrenaline receded from her limbs, she let out a deep, regretful sigh, remembering how relaxed she'd been just a few moments ago. Determined to recapture the feeling, she dried her face and settled back into the water. This time, instead of floating, she kept her arms draped over the sides of the tub. Within minutes, she dozed off, snoring softly. Moments later, something impacted against the side of the tub with a loud *BANG!*

The sound pierced Jeanine's consciousness like a gunshot. She reared up, screaming and sloshing bathwater all over the floor. Still sputtering, she leaned over to see what had caused the commotion. There was nothing there but the soaked bathmat. Jeanine stared at the floor, confused. A cold draft on her shoulder drew her attention to the door, which was now wide open behind her.

"Hello?" she called, leaning further out of the tub. "Mason? Are you here?" There was no reply.

Jeanine considered the possibility that Otis had somehow managed to open the door and make that sound against the tub but quickly dismissed it as impossible. Muttering impatiently, she abandoned her bath. She needed time to prepare for the evening ahead with Mason anyway. She put in her headphones and listened to music while she performed an intensive skin-care routine, followed by a luxurious, full-body self-massage with her favorite candy-scented lotion.

Singing offkey, Jeanine strutted to the closet and put on lingerie, topped off with one of Mason's shirts. She was returning to the bathroom for a final spritz of perfume and a slick of lip gloss when her eyes fell on his nightstand again. The top drawer was partially open.

Jeanine removed her headphones and stared at the drawer. She definitely remembered slamming it shut. As she went to close it again, her eyes caught a glimpse of blue velvet. She reached for it automatically, took out the ring, and slipped it onto her finger.

The gold band was cold against her skin and sent an illicit shiver through Jeanine's entire body. Transfixed, she held the ring at arm's length, admiring the diamond's sparkle once more. It really did look stunning on her. Jeanine suddenly didn't care who it belonged to before—she didn't want to take it off. She decided to wear it until Mason came home, then put it back later while he was asleep. He'd never know.

With the ring on her finger, Jeanine popped her earbuds back in, finished getting ready, and sashayed out of the bedroom and down the hall with renewed energy. She danced past the nursery, giving the offending door a bold knock to the beat of her music. At her touch, the door flew open with a *BANG!*

Jeanine screamed and stumbled backward, catching herself against the railing behind her. Her earbuds flew out of her ears and fell to the front foyer, clattering against the floorboards below. She stared into the nursery with saucer-wide eyes, her chest heaving.

"H-Hello?" she called out. She couldn't see anyone through the open doorway, but as her heart slowed, she detected a soft, steady creaking coming from inside. Unwilling to go closer, Jeanine kept hold of the railing and leaned forward, craning her neck to see inside the nursery.

The creaking intensified, and Jeanine finally recognized the sound. Someone was rocking, fast and hard, in the glider. Keeping both hands and her hips pressed against the banister, Jeanine slid closer. From her new vantage point, she could see the back of the glider, which had been rotated so its occupant could look out the window while they rocked.

"...Mason?" Jeanine called out, confused. "Babe? What are you doing in there?"

He didn't reply. The glider continued to rock without slowing.

"Mason?" she repeated. "Are you okay?" When there was still no answer, she followed up with a tentative, "How are you feeling?" but he still wouldn't respond. Jeanine felt her temper rising again. If this was his idea of a joke, she wasn't laughing.

"Mase." She stepped into the doorway to confront him. "What the hell are you doing in here? Why didn't you tell me you were back?"

Mason continued to ignore her. Jeanine rolled her eyes. This was not the sexy reunion she had in mind.

"Mason, can we please not do this right now?" she sighed. "Will you at least turn around, please? Mason? Mason!" Fed up, Jeanine stomped over to the glider and swung it around to face her.

"Mason, what the fu—" She gasped and stumbled backward as dark eyes circled to meet hers.

Mari sat in the glider with her hands resting on her swollen belly. Her once warm, brown eyes were black against her pallid skin and fixed singly, hungrily, on Jeanine.

"No," Jeanine whispered, squeezing her eyes shut. She shook her head. "This isn't real. You're not real." When she opened her eyes again, Mari was still there, regarding her in hard judgment. Her eyes flicked sharply to the diamond on Jeanine's ring finger. Jeanine covered her hand instinctively, shrinking under the dead woman's glare.

"...Marilys?" Her name escaped Jeanine's lips in a whisper. At the sound of it, Mari rose to her feet weightlessly, lifted by some unseen force.

Jeanine stumbled backward as Mari advanced on her. They moved together like a dance until Jeanine finally found her feet and fled toward the open door. In an explosion of rage, Mari reached out with both hands, grabbing Jeanine from behind as the nursery door slammed shut, trapping her inside.

Jeanine's wretched screams echoed throughout the house, which stood in silent sentinel, impassive to the slamming and wailing in the nursery as she met her fate. With a final *BANG!* the door flew open again, and Jeanine's limp, weary body sailed through it. Her spine crunched as she slammed against the upper-floor railing. The sound of cracking bone mingled with splintering wood as the barrier gave way and Jeanine came crashing down, landing with a heavy, lifeless thud on the first-floor entryway.

CHAPTER 34

Mason braced his good elbow on the hard metal table in front of him and covered his face with one hand. His eyes throbbed from the harsh fluorescent lights; he struggled to distinguish the buzzing in his brain from the noise they made overhead. His whole body hurt; he was thirsty, hungry, and in desperate need of painkillers. He was living in a nightmare. Across from him, a familiar, gravelly voice called his name.

"Mr. Goodridge," Detective Hoxton said, "please pay attention."

Mason felt someone rubbing his back. "Son?" Steve prompted. His voice was gentle but serious.

Mason pressed his palm into his eye socket, trying to numb the dull ache in his head. Two weeks ago, he'd returned home to find Jeanine lying dead in a pool of blood and broken wood in his foyer. His first thought had been to get rid of her and scrub the place clean, but he dismissed the idea just as quickly. He was in no physical condition to handle a situation like this without an accomplice, and the person most likely to help him was currently sprawled at his feet. He called his father instead, who picked up on the first ring.

"Son? Everything okay?"

"Yeah, yeah, I'm fine," Mason assured him. "Dad… Jeanine's dead."

"Dead?" Steve repeated dumbly. "What do you mean dead?"

Sitting on his porch steps, Mason looked back to where Jeanine lay like a broken doll with her limbs askew. Her neck was twisted unnaturally towards the front door, her glassy eyes fixed accusingly on him. Mason shuddered and turned away.

"I don't know," he replied, his voice cracking. "I just got here, and she was lying on the ground, all beat up."

There was a long pause on the other line. "Mase," Steve asked quietly, "did something happen between you two?"

"No!" Mason exclaimed. "I just got here! I swear!"

"Where did you go before?" Steve asked carefully. "After you left us, I mean…"

Mason's jaw went slack as he processed his father's insinuation.

"Mase," Steve continued, "if something happened, you can tell me. I'm always on your side."

"Dad, I *swear*. I didn't do this!"

"Well, do you have any idea who did?"

"I…" Mason closed his eyes and willed himself to stop shaking. He knew exactly who was responsible for this, and that no one would believe him. "I'm not sure," he finished lamely.

"Mason, that doesn't sound good!"

"Dad, *please*!" Mason gritted through his teeth. "I need your help!"

"Okay, okay, I'm sorry," Steve yielded, clocking the fear in his son's voice. "Can you tell what happened?"

Mason leaned back and studied the scene through the front door. Avoiding Jeanine, his gaze traveled up to the broken second-floor railing. When he saw the closed nursery door just beyond it, he quickly moved out of sight.

"It… it looks like she fell over the banister," he stammered. "Dad, there's a lot of blood. What should I do?"

"Have you called the police?" Steve asked.

"I called *you*, Dad."

"Mason. Hang up and call the police *now*," Steve replied sharply. "I'll be there as fast as I can... and don't touch anything."

"What should I say when they get here?" Mason heard his father slam his car door and start buckling his seatbelt.

"What do you mean?" Steve asked distractedly.

"What should I tell them? About what happened?"

Steve paused. "Mason," he said in disbelief. "Tell them the truth."

"Mr. Goodridge?" Detective Hoxton called Mason back to the present in the police interrogation room. As he lifted his head to respond, he caught a whiff of her perfume and nearly retched. She was wearing the same scent as Mari. He dropped his gaze again, fearful of who he might see if he looked at her face.

"What's wrong with him?" Martinez asked.

"Just give him a moment, please," Steve replied. He squeezed Mason's shoulder.

"Mr. Goodridge?" Hoxton repeated. Her voice was gentler this time. Steeling himself, Mason forced his eyes up.

Hoxton was peering at him with those gold, eagle eyes, her expression a mix of concern and curiosity. She'd changed her hair since Mari's funeral—the softer style made her appear younger, though she seemed older at the same time. Mason glanced at her hands, expecting those long, red nails, but instead, they were painted blue-black... like the depths Mari emerged from in his dreams...

"Mr. Goodridge!" Hoxton rapped her knuckles on the table, startling him.

"I already told you," Mason sighed impatiently. "I opened the door, and she was just lying there, dead." He met Hoxton's intense gaze. "I called you guys right away. That's it."

WHAT'S COMING TO YOU   265

"What was the nature of your last conversation with Miss Alder?"

Mason tried to recall his last moments with Jeanine, but all he could picture was her bloodied face, her lifeless eyes gaping at him through the open door while he waited for police to arrive. The image had burned itself into his brain, eclipsing every other memory he had of her.

"It wasn't really a conversation," he said. "We texted that morning before my parents picked me up from the hospital. I told her I'd come home after I spent some time with them."

"And you didn't communicate again at all before you discovered her body in your home?" Hoxton asked. Before Mason could respond, his attorney, Jonathan Spetzler, spoke up beside him.

"Detectives, my client has been over this with you twice already. Once on the day Miss Alder was discovered, and again when you visited him unannounced at his parents' home—both times without counsel, I might add. He's been fully cooperative, and we've obliged your request to come here for further questioning, but unless you have something new to discuss, we're under no obligation to stay."

Mason regarded Spetzler coolly as he spoke on his behalf. He was an aggressive, confident lawyer with a proven track record of successfully representing unlikeable defendants. Mason resented relying on him for something he didn't even do, but his father had insisted they hire him after he was called in for questioning again. Spetzler was about Mason's age, and remarkably close in appearance, down to his stunning green eyes, though he had dark, chestnut hair. They could've been mistaken for brothers, which somehow made Mason dislike him even more.

"Jon…" Hoxton began.

"Cora?" Spetzler returned defiantly. Mason grimaced at their familiarity.

"There are some discrepancies in the timelines your client and his father outlined from that day," Hoxton explained, unfazed. "As well as some autopsy findings that we'd like to discuss."

She addressed the young attorney patiently, but her tone suggested little tolerance for any further lip. Mason watched them size each other up for a long, tense moment. Despite the circumstances, he found himself rooting for Hoxton.

"Go on then," Spetzler finally conceded.

Hoxton indicated for Martinez, who had been sitting quietly beside her with his arms folded, to take over. He leaned forward, resting his elbows on top of a closed accordion folder on the table.

"Mr. Goodridge, when we spoke at the scene, you indicated your parents picked you up from the hospital around 11 a.m. and that you were with them until 3:30 p.m. You returned to your residence shortly after 5 p.m., where you discovered Miss Alder's body. Is that correct?"

Mason shrugged obstinately. His dislike for Martinez had only intensified since they'd been reunited. Martinez ignored Mason's attitude and continued.

"When we interviewed Mr. Goodridge Sr. the same evening, sir," he inclined his head towards Steve, "you indicated that your son left your home at 2:30 p.m., but in the follow-up interview, you stated he left at 3:30 p.m. We conducted a separate interview with Mrs. Goodridge, who also stated that he left at 2:30 p.m. We're trying to account for that extra hour and the discrepancy in your stories."

"How dare you attempt to play my wife and I against each other!" Steve stood up to object. "This is ridiculous! This is entrapment!" he sputtered.

Martinez and Spetzler both stood up to subdue him. Hoxton remained seated but spoke up over all the commotion.

"Mr. Goodridge, we've allowed you to sit in on this meeting, but if you're unable to maintain your composure, we can escort you to the lobby to wait until we're done." Her voice was calm, but her expression was severe.

Steve returned to his seat, fuming. Hoxton spared one last meaningful glance at him, then turned back to Mason. "Please answer the question."

"The question being...?" Mason grumbled.

"Please account for your whereabouts between 2:30 p.m., when you left your parent's home, and 5 p.m., when you returned to yours," Hoxton reiterated. "And before you answer, you should know we have surveillance footage from a neighbor that confirms you left your parents at 2:30 p.m. and not 3:30 p.m."

"Then you should also have surveillance footage from *my* neighbors showing that I arrived home at five, like I told you," Mason retorted.

"We contacted the two neighbors we spoke to when your wife died, who provided surveillance footage in her case," Martinez jumped in. "It appears their cameras weren't working this time."

A cold pit formed in Mason's stomach as he processed this revelation.

"That's awfully convenient," Spetzler muttered.

"An unfortunate coincidence," Martinez replied dryly. "But the point is there's no proof other than your word that you arrived at the time you said. Ninety minutes in traffic from your parent's home to yours is feasible, but two and a half hours is not."

"Are you people crazy?" Mason exploded. "*I'm* the one who called *you guys*! Look at me!" He lifted his casted arm. "How could I have done all that to her with one arm? I was even worse off then than I am now! Someone is trying to frame me!"

"Who?" Hoxton asked, honing in. Mason froze, his eyes darting around the table.

"Mase," Spetzler murmured, "Let me handle this."

Mason felt Hoxton's scrutiny of him intensify. He pressed his lips together and begrudgingly allowed his attorney to proceed.

"My client has a point, detectives," Spetzler resumed. "He

was discharged from the hospital that day after spending nearly two weeks in bed, recovering from a near-fatal car wreck. He was in no condition to withstand any kind of physical altercation, let alone cause the type of injuries Miss Alder sustained. Not to mention, he drove himself home, *alone,* in that condition. It's reasonable to expect he might have driven slower than usual, given his injuries."

"You're suggesting that it took your client two and a half hours to drive 45 miles?" Martinez asked.

"I'm saying the burden lies with you to prove he didn't show up at home when he says he did," Spetzler asserted. "Your inability to find evidence doesn't make him a liar."

"Fine," Martinez replied. "Speaking of, we'd like to discuss some additional evidence from the scene, including findings from Miss Alder's autopsy." He opened the folder he'd been resting his elbows on, pulled out a blown-up photograph, and slid it toward Mason, whose eyes flicked down to assess, then away when he realized what it was.

"This image was captured during Miss Alder's autopsy," Martinez explained to the others. "There wasn't a part of her body that *wasn't* completely bruised up, but the coroner found this particular injury interesting." With his finger, Martinez traced a line across a blackened, bar-shaped bruise that extended across Jeanine's upper back.

"The coroner who performed Miss Alder's autopsy is the same one who performed the autopsy for the late Mrs. Goodridge." Martinez reached into the folder again and produced a second image, laying it on the table next to the first one. It was a picture of Mari, showing a nearly identical, bar-shaped bruise across her upper back.

Mason stared at the two photos side by side. His eyes wandered to the space between them, where the cold steel tabletop shone through. It wasn't that long ago that he'd stood around a metal table in much the same company, looking down at the bloated remains of his wife's corpse. For a moment, he entertained the morbid idea that this was the same table from the morgue where Mari's body had lain, brought in just to fuck with him.

"It's quite a distinct mark, don't you think?" Martinez asked, interrupting Mason's train of thought. "Coroner also noted that Miss Alder had a bash to the forehead in the same spot as your wife, as well as some teeth knocked out... 'three anteriors, one canine, two incisors on the right side,'" Martinez recited the quote from both autopsy reports. "Curious that both women would have the exact same injuries, even though they died under such different circumstances..."

"Mrs. Goodridge's death was ruled a tragic accident," Spetzler replied, unperturbed. "Her autopsy listed several injuries consistent with her car wreck, and I believe my client was cleared of any wrongdoing in that instance by none other than yourselves. Miss Alder was lying on top of a section of the upper floor railing that included several pieces of wood that could match this bruise. You found no blood on my client's clothing, whereas the victim was covered in it. This is an embarrassing reach, detective," he finished, chuckling dismissively.

Hoxton ignored him. "Mr. Goodridge, do you have anything to add?"

Mason stared at the two images before him. In his mind, he heard the crunching sound Mari's bones made as she landed against the edge of the tub. He felt the energy leave her body when she realized it was over for her. He saw Jeanine's empty eyes ogling him through the front door and suppressed an urge to shudder. He looked up and saw Hoxton waiting patiently for him to respond.

"No." He gulped as his stomach did a backflip.

"Okay then," Martinez clipped. "How about this." He reached into the folder, removing a plastic evidence bag containing a flip-style cell phone. He laid it on the table in front of Mason. "Recognize that?" he asked.

"No."

"This was found in Miss Alder's handbag. It's a burner," Martinez explained, pausing for effect. Mason, Steve, and Spetzler waited blankly for him to continue. "There's only one contact in here—yours. Call logs show she was calling you several times a day, every day. Sometimes multiple times in succession."

Mason stared in shock at the cell phone sitting before him. As comprehension dawned, he felt a familiar trembling in his core, a furious heat gathering at the base of his spine. Under the table, he tightened his fists.

"Fucking bitch," he whispered under his breath.

"What was that?" Martinez asked.

Mason glanced up. "I didn't know about this," he said through clenched teeth.

"You're telling us you lived with her for nearly two months and had no idea that she had this in her possession, or that she was using it to call you constantly?"

Mason suddenly had a sense that the walls were closing in on him. He needed to calm down before he said the wrong thing. He released his clenched fists under the table and laid his hands flat on its surface. The cool metal against his palms helped ground him. He took a deep breath.

"I'd been getting prank calls for a while now, ever since my wife died," he explained, his voice no longer shaking. "I had no idea they were coming from her."

"Why would she do this?" Hoxton asked.

"I have no idea," he repeated. He sensed Hoxton attempting to read him one last time and forced himself to hold still under her scrutiny.

"I see," she murmured. "Well. That will be all for now," she suddenly concluded.

Mason, his father, and his lawyer all frowned suspiciously.

"That's it?" Spetzler asked.

"For now," Hoxton repeated, her voice uncharacteristically light. "You're free to go."

Across from her, all three men hesitated before slowly getting to their feet.

"Thanks for your time, gentlemen," she called as they turned to leave. "And Mason?"

Mason turned back automatically, surprised to hear his first name.

Hoxton nodded pleasantly. "Enjoy your Christmas. We'll be seeing you again soon."

CHAPTER 35

K ris curled into an even tighter ball and pushed herself deeper into the couch where she huddled. She wrapped her hands around her coffee cup, trying to warm her fingers, but nothing could relieve the chill that had settled into her bones these last few weeks. She shivered involuntarily, but thankfully, neither her husband nor her son noticed.

Steve was engrossed in the black and white version of *Miracle on 34th Street* playing on TV, while Mason slumped miserably in his chair and stared into their Christmas tree, lost in its twinkling lights.

Kris fought back tears as she studied him. It was his first Christmas back in his childhood home in years, although the circumstances that brought him there were nothing to celebrate. His house was now a designated crime scene, and although he was recovering physically from his accident under their care, his spirit was declining rapidly. He'd regained some weight, so his face was no longer as gaunt, but he wasn't sleeping well, and his expression still carried long, deep shadows.

Kris watched Mason's eyes unfocus; his eyelids drooped heavily. She held her breath and silently willed him to surrender to sleep, but the moment his chin touched his chest, he jerked himself awake again. Kris quickly dropped her gaze so he wouldn't catch her staring and get upset—he was so sensitive to attention these days.

"Maybe I didn't do such a wonderful thing after all..." he said.

Kris's head shot up. "What did you say?"

Mason frowned, then pointed to the TV, where cheerful, jingling holiday music swelled over the movie's final line.

"Oh," she nodded, avoiding his narrow stare.

Steve exited the movie and sat back on the other end of the sofa. He looked around affectionately at his family, his smile faltering as he noticed their pensive moods. After several minutes of silence, he attempted to break the ice.

"So, Mase. Did Santa bring you everything you wanted?"

Kris smiled ruefully. Despite all they'd been dealing with, or more likely because of it, Steve had insisted on going all out for Christmas. They'd decorated the house, had a lavish breakfast, and exchanged a mountain of gifts, most of which were for Mason.

Mason curled his lip in a meager half-smile. "Santa, huh?"

"Yeah, why not?" Steve winked, but there was a hint of sadness in his voice. Kris's heart ached for him. He was trying so hard to keep everyone's spirits up.

Mason laughed humorlessly. "I don't think elves make the things I need right now, Dad."

Steve tutted sympathetically. "You're a good boy, Mase," he said. "You've just been through some tough times. This time next year, everything will be different. You'll see. Right, honey?" He looked at Kris, whose stomach went hollow at his optimism.

"Right." She smiled tightly at Mason, whose expression turned bitter. Kris focused on the mug in her hands.

"Something you want to say, Mom?" Mason asked.

Kris looked up in surprise to see her son glaring at her. She shook her head. "Do either of you want any more coffee?" she asked, unfolding her legs to stand.

"No, thank you, dear," Steve replied.

"Running away?" Mason pressed.

"Mason…" Steve admonished their son while Kris froze, wondering what had suddenly gotten into him.

"If you have something to say to me, Mom, just spit it out," he challenged.

"I don't have anything to say, Mason," she replied calmly. "All I care about is making sure you are okay."

Mason spread his arms wide, showing off his braced arm and diminished form. "I'm just perfect," he sneered. "Can't you tell?"

Kris was stunned. They'd had their moments over the years like any mother and son, but she'd never felt contempt like this from him before. Frustrated tears gathered behind her eyes. "Mason, what is wrong with you?"

"What's wrong with me?" Mason mocked. "Well, gee, Mom, let's think. I'm being investigated for murder. I'm about to lose my entire life—"

"Now hold on, Mase," Steve interjected. "That's not going to happen. Jon said—"

"Fuck what *Jon* says, Dad!" Mason suddenly shouted.

"Stop it!" Kris cried. "Don't talk to him like that! You have no idea the lengths your father is going to help you right now! He believes in you!"

"And what about you, Mom?" Mason asked quietly. "What do you believe?"

Kris pressed her lips together.

Mason nodded gravely. "You think I did this."

"Of course she doesn't," Steve insisted.

"I can't fucking believe this," Mason exclaimed. "I am your son! How could you even think that about me?"

"I don't know what I'm supposed to think!" Kris suddenly cried.

Steve looked at her in shock. "Kris, you can't—" he began, but she stopped him.

She'd had enough. She'd been at war with herself for months

trying to reconcile the boy she raised with this cold, distant stranger. Since Mari's death, Kris had been fighting against increasingly insurmountable odds for her son, but the time for coddling him was over, especially if he was going to treat her like this. There were way too many more questions than answers at this point. She couldn't fight for him anymore without knowing the truth.

"Mason, I love you," she began fervently. "I will *always* love you, no matter what. You *are* my son, but I don't recognize you anymore. You've been through so much, more than anyone could bear, but I don't understand your behavior for the last few months, even before Mari died!"

Steve tried to gently interrupt. "Kris, honey—"

"No." She stopped him again. "He has to hear this. We never talked about it because we were all grieving, but I don't understand how you could have cheated on her while she was carrying your child!"

Kris could hardly believe these words were coming out of her mouth, but she couldn't stop them any more than she could stop her tears from flowing. "That's not how we raised you! You should've come to us if you were that unhappy."

Mason rolled his eyes dismissively, but she refused to let up.

"Maybe you felt like that wasn't our business, that's fine, but what about now, Mason? Look around you. It's Christmas! Your first Christmas without your wife and child, and that hasn't come up *once* since we brought you back here!

"I know you did not love that other woman," Kris said fiercely, "and I can even understand why you might not bring up Mari—barely, but I do—but we haven't even mentioned the fact that this would've been *your son's* first Christmas!" Her voice broke at the thought.

"That, I do not understand at all! Doesn't that matter to you? I miss them so much!" she sobbed. "I think about them all the time. Your father and I both do! We want to talk about it, but it's like we can't with you! You act like they never even existed, and

I don't understand *why*. Did you and Mari hate each other that much?"

Mason's face had gone pale. "You don't know the half of it," he muttered wretchedly.

Kris softened as her maternal, protective instincts automatically kicked in. She knelt in front of him, taking his hands.

"Mason, you know you can tell us anything, right?" She tried to look into his eyes, but he stared stubbornly out the window. "There's nothing you can do or say that will change the fact that we are your parents and we love you."

Mason knitted his brow together as if he were trying to concentrate on something else. His lips quivered as he fought to hold in his emotions. Kris squeezed his hands supportively.

"Is there anything you want to tell us, baby?" she asked.

Mason shook his head firmly.

"Son, are you sure?" Steve leaned forward on the sofa nearby.

Mason refused to look at either of them. "Like what?" he asked densely.

"Like anything!" Kris implored. "Anything at all, sweetheart. We love you. *No matter what*," she emphasized. "We'll stand by you."

Mason was quiet for a long time. Kris held her breath and watched him wrestle with himself.

"You won't," he finally whispered. "I can't."

"You *can*, baby," Kris urged. "As long as you do the right thing, you have nothing to fear."

Mason released a hollow laugh. "I guess I'm all kinds of wrong then, huh?" Before Kris could ask him what he meant, he shrugged her off. "I don't know what else there is to tell you."

"What happened to Mari?" Kris asked. The question burst from her, startling all three of them, but she concealed her surprise and braced for the answer.

Mason looked at her sharply. The light from the window reflected in his green eyes—her eyes—turning them a brilliant emerald. For a brief moment, she saw her son staring back at her, in desperate need of something, but a second later, he was gone.

"She had an accident," he said robotically.

"Where?" Kris breathed, refusing to give up on him. Mason's hardened exterior wavered for a fraction of a second. At that moment, Kris knew the truth. Her hands, still gripping Mason's, turned cold. "What happened to her teeth?" she whispered.

Mason suddenly pushed her away and stood up. As Kris landed on her bottom, Steve rushed to help her to her feet.

"Fuck you, Mom," Mason muttered as he limped out of the room, leaving both of them to stare after him, horrorstruck.

CHAPTER 36

Mason slammed his bedroom door, then flopped onto the bed and stared angrily at the ceiling. He was out of breath, not just from his hasty retreat upstairs but also from outrage.

He would never forgive his mother for what she'd just done. As if his life wasn't enough of a nightmare, being abandoned by the one woman who was supposed to love him unconditionally finally pushed Mason out of feeling sorry for himself and back to hating the entire world, which now included Kris.

She was supposed to be on his side! She had no proof or reason to think he had done anything wrong but apparently had doubted him behind his back this entire time! Her desperate declarations of love and support while trying to con him into confessing replayed in his head, echoing like empty lies. Even his father could barely pretend to disagree with her. They had both betrayed him. He had no one.

Mason pressed a pillow to his face and screamed until his throat felt raw. Exhausted, he sank to the floor and dropped his head back against the bed. The moment he closed his eyes, he saw Jeanine's broken body lying at his feet. He opened his eyes, feeling numb. On an impulse, he pulled out his phone and opened Instagram to search for Jeanine's handle, then held his breath while he waited for her image to load.

Within seconds, the small screen was filled with pictures of Jeanine, neatly arranged in tidy little squares. Like taking a walk down a twisted memory lane, he scrolled through endless selfies of Jeanine looking sexy at the gym, in the pool, at a nightclub, and more until they overshadowed his nightmarish visions of her. She was always alone in her photos—something Mason never noticed until now. He wondered who else had been in her life.

Curious, he went back to the most recent photo of her and clicked on the comments, bracing to see disparaging remarks from her loved ones about his involvement in her death, but there was nothing about him or even the fact that she was gone. Mason frowned, trying to recall what he knew of Jeanine's people. She never talked about anyone else, and he'd never asked. To his knowledge, no one had come forward after her death. What would happen to her body?

"Dammit, Jeanine," he muttered, suddenly irritated. Getting mixed up with her was the very first domino he'd unwittingly knocked over—everything started to topple after that. If only he could go back in time and tell himself to walk away from the bar that day... or go even further and walk away from that restaurant all those years ago. Now, both women were gone, and each had taken a massive chunk of the only thing he really cared about with them—his freedom. He had no idea how he would get it back.

Mason began to feel short of breath. Sweat beaded at his temples, and he shivered, suddenly cold. A powerful wave of nausea threatened to bring up the contents of his stomach. He staggered to his feet as the walls began to spin and close in on him.

His parents called to him as he hobbled downstairs, but he didn't answer. He grabbed his cap and jacket and stumbled out the front door, slamming it behind him. He made it to the side of the house before doubling over.

Mason heaved several times as his stomach emptied, trying his best to be quiet so his parents wouldn't hear. When it was over, he sat back on his haunches and spat disgustedly. He took a deep breath, relishing the cold air in his lungs. When he finally felt better, he straightened, put his hat and jacket on, and started walking. With his hands stuffed in his pockets, Mason focused on putting one foot in front of the other.

This wasn't how his life was supposed to be. He didn't understand how things had taken such a turn. He'd done every-thing he was supposed to—success should've been his. It was!... until Mari turned everything upside down.

Mason exhaled a thick cloud of condensation, watching it dissipate as he walked through it. Now, he was probably going to end up dead or in prison, all because of *her*. He wished he could show people the truth about Mari. She wasn't perfect. She'd made mistakes, too. She was a killer, too! There had to be a way to put the blame for Jeanine's death where it really belonged…

Mason froze on the sidewalk, struck by a sudden bolt of inspiration. He stood there, turning an idea over in his mind until a plan began to form. He reached into his pocket for his wallet and fumbled with frozen fingers to pull out a business card he'd stuck there months ago. He held the card between his teeth as he put his wallet away, then took out his phone.

Can we talk 1-1? – Mason G.

He hit send, dropped the phone back in his pocket, and kept walking. He was surprised when a call came through moments later. He checked the ID, then answered.

"That was fast," he said pleasantly. "I wouldn't have expected a reply on Christmas."

"What can I say?" Detective Hoxton replied. "I'm married to

my work. And I couldn't resist finding out why Mason Goodridge wanted a one-on-one with me, of all people, on Christmas."

"It can wait until tomorrow if you'd like to get back to your family," Mason offered. There was a short pause on the other end as Detective Hoxton processed the surprising warmth in his voice.

"What can I do for you, Mr. Goodridge?" she asked.

"I… there's something I want to tell you that I haven't mentioned before," Mason began carefully. "I didn't because, well, I didn't think anyone would believe me, but given how things are going, I think it's time to tell someone. I'm hoping you can help."

This time, Detective Hoxton was silent for so long that Mason had to check if the call was still connected.

"Hello? Detective, are you still there?"

"Mr. Goodridge, are you sure you wouldn't rather confide in your lawyer?" Hoxton asked.

"No. I don't need him. I need *you*."

Hoxton deliberated silently. "Okay," she finally said. "You're aware that this conversation will be on the record?"

"Yes, yes. I'm aware," Mason replied impatiently.

"Okay. Go ahead."

Mason smiled at the thinly-veiled anticipation in her voice. He licked his lips and began.

"I think someone has been stalking me. It's been going on for a while, ever since my wife died. I think someone is angry at me for what happened to her, and I think they're trying to frame me for Jeanine's death so that I get what they think I deserve."

Detective Hoxton took her time processing this. "You think someone is stalking you…" she repeated slowly.

"Yes," Mason affirmed. Technically, it was the truth, though he didn't plan on adding that the culprit was supernatural.

"Go on," Hoxton finally replied with interest. Mason

breathed a silent sigh of relief and quickly constructed the rest of his story.

"After Mari died, I got a lot of threats from people who blamed me for her accident," he explained. "I understand it was wrong to cheat on her, and I accepted all the hate that came my way afterward. I deserved some of it." He paused contritely, but Hoxton offered nothing, so he went on. "Eventually, most of it died down, but not all of it…"

"You're saying someone has continued to threaten you?"

"My crash was no accident," Mason replied. "Something was done to my truck. And there have been a few occasions since Mari's death where I believe there might've been someone in my house."

"And you never reported those instances to the police…" Hoxton said dryly.

"Would you have helped me if I had?" Mason asked. She didn't answer. "I just wasn't sure," he resumed. "But when your partner mentioned my neighbor's cameras not working, it seemed too big a coincidence. I think it's all the same person."

"Has someone made themselves known to you? Do you have any proof that someone has been, as you say, stalking you?"

"You have the burner phone that proves someone was," Mason pointed out. "You say you found it in Jeanine's possession, but couldn't the same person who killed her have planted it there? You said it yourselves—it doesn't make sense that she would've been calling me so much without my knowledge. When I answered those calls, someone was on the other end. I would have recognized Jeanine's voice if it was her. I don't think it was."

"Look, this is a lot of information to come forward with now," Hoxton replied, sounding slightly annoyed. "Frankly, I'm not sure why you kept it to yourself this long. It would've helped you."

"I'm sorry I don't have a better answer for that," Mason repented. "But I'm here now, and I need you."

Hoxton, again, fell silent for a very long time. Mason held his breath and waited.

"Alright, Mason," she finally sighed. "Is there anything else you need me to know?"

Mason felt something in him relax at the sound of his name. That was a good sign. "I didn't do this," he said fervently. "You know that. There was no blood on me."

"Okay. Thank you for sharing this. I highly suggest you do the same with your attorney."

"Thank you, detective! Thank you!" Mason replied, breathless. He felt like kissing her. "If there's anything else I can do to help, please let me know."

"Okay, sure… actually, there is one thing," she suddenly said.

Mason frowned uncertainly. "Yes?"

"We're having some trouble locating Miss Alder's next of kin," she explained. "Did she ever mention anyone? Any family members or other friends we could contact?"

Mason had no idea, but he worried that being unhelpful might tarnish the delicate connection he'd just nurtured between them.

"I'm not sure," he said slowly, racking his brain. "She definitely didn't have many friends," he chuckled. "I actually think the only friend she had was—" He stopped himself, stunned by a sudden realization.

"Was?" Hoxton prompted. "Hello?"

Mason hardly heard her. His mind was too busy racing over the possibilities of what he'd just remembered.

"Hello?" Hoxton repeated.

"Yes… sorry, yes. I'm here," Mason recovered. "I, uh… I think the only friend she had was me," he finished apologetically.

"Ah," Hoxton said quietly. "That's too bad." They fell into an impromptu moment of silence for Jeanine.

"Detective?" Mason suddenly asked.

"Yeah?"

"What happens if you don't find anyone? For Jeanine, I mean. What'll happen to her?"

"They hold the unclaimed for ninety days at the morgue," Hoxton explained. "After that, they'll cremate, then dispose of the remains. Basically, you just... disappear."

Mason contemplated this. "Thank you for your time, detective," he finally replied. "If I think of anything else, I'll be sure to call. Merry Christmas."

He heard a *click,* and the call ended. Mason put his phone away and started walking home with renewed energy. He hoped that his stalker story would be enough to cast reasonable doubt, but that paled in comparison to the anxiety he now felt over the one detail he had suddenly remembered. Hoxton had asked him if Jeanine had any friends. He never saw her with any real people, but she had regularly confided in her diary. He couldn't believe he hadn't thought of it until now.

He'd seen her scribbling in it with that silly feather pen, but he never concerned himself with what she was writing, he was just grateful she had the distraction. Jeanine was such a simple creature, he assumed there was nothing in there but vapid nonsense. It never occurred to him that she might've been stupid enough to write about their misdeeds in it, but now that he considered it, of *course* she would have, along with God knows what else. It was a miracle the police hadn't found it yet. He was sure if they had, he'd be in jail right now. So where the hell was it?

It had to be in his house, which, unfortunately, was still a designated crime scene. He'd seen her with it in the bedroom and knew she sometimes stuffed it between the mattress, but if it were that simple, it would've been found by now.

Mason racked his brain for other hiding places in his house that Jeanine might've used. He had no idea how he would get back in there to search without arousing suspicion or inviting questions he didn't want to answer. He'd have to be careful not to tip anyone off that there was something there he needed. Maybe he could convince Hoxton to help him…

For a moment, Mason was so overwhelmed by obstacles he nearly fell to his knees. He held himself together, determined to get to that diary before anyone else discovered its existence. If Jeanine's journal held the keys to his damnation, finding it might mean his salvation.

A lightness returned to Mason's step as he continued down the sidewalk. For the first time in a long time, he felt some semblance of control and, with it, a sense of hope. Freedom and a second chance were within reach again, and he was going to fight for it or die trying. He wouldn't disappear into dust like Mari and Jeanine. Men like him didn't go out like that.

"Fuck you, Mari," he spat aloud in a revived battle cry.

A gust of bitterly cold wind blew at Mason's back, forcing him forward. He stumbled to regain balance, grabbing his cap before it was whipped off his head. He shoved it down and scowled defiantly as the wind howled through the bare tree branches above him.

"So come and get me already, bitch!" he shouted. The wind died away as quickly as it came. Mason looked around victoriously. "That's what I fucking thought," he muttered, resuming his journey home.

This wasn't over.

CHAPTER 37

BOOM!!!

Lightning pierced the air, followed by an ear-split-ting roll of thunder that rumbled Mason's bones. He yelped, then peered apprehensively at the midday sky through the windshield. It was blinding white and mottled with steely, angry-looking gray clouds, but the storm they heralded had yet to arrive.

"Ughhhh, hurry up, Dad!" he muttered impatiently. He had borrowed his mom's car and was now sitting in the driveway of his former home, waiting for Steve to meet him there. It was the last place Mason wanted to be, but he told himself that once he got through this, he'd never have to think about this godfor-saken place again.

Just after Christmas, the Goodridges received a lucky phone call from the police letting them know that they had finished processing Jeanine's crime scene and were releasing the property back to the family. It was nothing short of a miracle for Mason, who'd spent that time anxiously scheming over how to break back into his own home. When the call came in, his knees nearly buckled with relief. The police had not recovered Jeanine's diary. It seemed his luck was finally beginning to change.

Wanting to give his son peace of mind, Steve wasted no time or expense calling in resources to clean the house up, empty it out, and get it ready for sale as quickly as possible in the new year. He suggested they sell to the first buyer who came along to get the cursed place off their hands. Mason wholeheartedly agreed, as long as he could go in and retrieve any last personal effects first. All that was left for him to do now was find the diary. After that, a packing crew would box up what remained of his old life and haul it away—he didn't care where.

However, in his desperate haste to get into the house, Mason had forgotten entirely about Mari and what she had done to Jeanine there. It didn't occur to him until now that it might be unsafe for him to be here alone. As a bit of last-minute insurance, he'd asked his father to join him, using his bum arm and shoulder as an excuse. Steve promised to meet him there shortly after he handled some work obligations of his own, but some last-minute emergency had delayed him. Now he was half an hour late, and counting.

While he waited for his father, Mason watched the storm intensify, becoming increasingly agitated himself. Although it was barely past noon, the sky was darkening steadily, which meant the house would be dark inside, too. He sized up the gloomy windows from the safety of his mom's car. The sooner they got this over with, the better.

His cell phone rang, startling him again.

"For fuck's sake! Come on, Mase. Keep it together." He saw it was his father calling and hurried to answer. "Dad, where are you?"

"Sorry, son. It's kind of a hair-on-fire situation here," Steve replied. "I'm gonna be stuck for at least another hour or two... they're ordering lunch," he added regretfully.

"Can't you get out of it?" Mason whined. "Aren't you every-one's boss? Tell them to handle it without you."

"It's *because* I'm the boss that I need to be here," Steve

explained patiently. "Why don't we just shoot for four o'clock? You can head home now, and we'll go back to the house later."

Mason leaned forward again and surveyed the sky. By four, it would probably be pitch black, and the rain would've started. He didn't want to be here then, even with his dad by his side. Steve took Mason's silence as an invitation to troubleshoot.

"What about tomorrow?" he asked. "I'm paying the hauling crew extra to get started early in the morning. You'd just have to work around them."

Mason picked miserably at the drawstrings of his hoodie. More people around would only make his job harder, and there was the risk of someone else finding the diary before he got to it.

"Or, if you want to do it today, I'm sure your mom can head over there and help you," Steve proposed.

"No way." Mason shut down that suggestion stubbornly.

"Okay, okay, fine," Steve conceded. "I get it, but listen, I need you to give your mom a break, okay? She's trying her best."

Mason scoffed, but Steve ignored him and continued. "Listen, I have to jump soon, but these are going to be your options: We can go together tonight at four, or tomorrow at the crack of dawn. Or you can try to do it yourself now, or you can call your mom. What's it gonna be, my boy?"

Mason jumped as another crack of lightning split the sky above him. "I'll just figure it out myself," he muttered. Hearing the distress in his son's voice, Steve tried to be reassuring.

"Hey, bud, listen. It'll be okay. I know it's a hard task, but it's the last one, right? The day after tomorrow is the start of a brand-new year, and all of this will be behind you. We're gonna be okay, okay?"

Mason listened to his father with a sullen expression. There was so much his father didn't understand, and probably never would. Once again, Mason was on his own.

"Okay," he grumbled resentfully.

"Okay," Steve affirmed. "You've got this. I'll see you at home."

"Okay."

"I love you."

"Yeah. You too." Mason hung up the phone and chucked it into the passenger seat. He dropped his head back and stared at the car's upholstered ceiling. Another ominous roll of thunder sounded softly above him, reminding him of the danger that lurked ahead. Was that diary worth his life?

Yes. The answer came to him before he even finished thinking the question. That diary could *mean* his life. Unless he personally retrieved it and saw to its destruction, he'd spend the rest of his days living in fear. This was his last chance to get his life back. If Mari was in there waiting for him, he'd fight. He was stronger than Jeanine, and he'd defeated Mari before. He would do it again or die trying. He had nothing left to lose.

As the thunder grumbled overhead, Mason grabbed his phone and made a list of every hiding place he could think of, then reorganized it based on their locations. He would go room by room, searching efficiently, and then get the hell out of there as soon as he found what he was looking for. If he pushed himself, he could be in and out in thirty minutes or less, then put this place behind him and never look back.

When he was satisfied with his list, he looked up at the sky. The thunder had calmed, and the clouds had lightened to an even, silvery color. It made Mason feel hopeful—perhaps luck would continue to be on his side today. He sent a quick text to his dad.

> I'm going into the house. Check on me in 15?

Mason waited until a small 'thumbs up' appeared on his message. Then, steeling himself, he got out of the car, jogged up the front steps, and unlocked the door.

CHAPTER 38

"You're never going to believe this."

Hoxton looked up from her desk as Martinez's shadow fell across it. She'd been so lost in thought that she didn't sense him approaching, though she should have, by the looks of him. Martinez was practically vibrating with excitement.

"Believe what?" she asked wearily. It was the day before New Year's Eve, and everyone at the station was doing overtime fielding calls as people celebrated the holidays. It was a tiresome end to a year that had been especially draining after the emotional toll the Goodridge case had taken. She was still recovering from the vexing phone call she'd had with Mason on Christmas.

She'd called him back hoping she was about to get a confession; that the holiday spirit had perhaps softened him into coming clean. In hindsight, she wanted to kick herself for her naivete. She knew in her heart that Mason was responsible for everything that had happened since they met, yet, for reasons she couldn't explain, she still held out hope that he was the kind of guy who would eventually do the right thing. Instead, he'd fed her that random stalker nonsense like she was born yesterday. It killed her that they didn't have enough to arrest him yet.

"Buckle up, my friend, you're going to love this," Martinez said, making himself comfortable on the edge of Hoxton's desk.

"Well, don't keep me in suspense," she groused.

"A call came in on the tip line yesterday," Martinez began. "Some cab driver saw something on TV yesterday about Jeanine Alder's murder and got in touch with us. Said he remembered something about her from a few months ago."

Goosebumps rippled across Hoxton's skin. She leaned forward, breathless. "What?"

Martinez chuckled at her disbelief. "I know. Apparently, he was visiting family in Manila for the last few months and just got back, so he had no idea what was going on here. Really sweet guy." He smirked mischievously. "Super, duper helpful…"

Hoxton was leaning so far forward that she was on the verge of toppling off her chair. "Adam!" she demanded. "Spill!"

"He says he dropped her off at a grocery store one night last August. It stuck with him because of the late hour and the fact that it was storming pretty bad. She paid cash and asked him to drop her at the back of the parking lot, which he thought was weird. He asked her if she was sure, and she said yeah, and then he said he watched her walk off in the rain, *away* from the store."

Hoxton's heart hammered in her chest. "Where'd she go?"

"I looked up the store. It's less than a mile from Mason Goodridge's home, but that's not even the best part. She gave the cab driver a pseudonym—Britney Spears."

"Jesus Christ…" Hoxton collapsed in her chair, then began barking with laughter. Martinez joined in until they were both doubled over.

"Wait, wait. Hold on a second." Hoxton waved her hands, collecting herself. "What can we do with this? We closed Marilys Goodridge's case as an accident. This only suggests Alder was in the vicinity, but it doesn't prove she went to the home or committed a crime."

"Mhmm, mhmm," Martinez nodded thoughtfully. "You're right about that... which is why I took the liberty of reviewing the neighborhood security footage around the Goodridge home that night, starting from the time she was dropped off at the store..."

"Kid, stop playing games and just tell me what you've got."

"Alright, alright, you ready for this?" Martinez asked, barely containing his glee. Hoxton responded with a threatening glare. He wisely launched into the rest of his story.

"I went back through the neighborhood security cams. One of them picked up a very blurry shape moving in the direction of the Goodridge home from across the street. Between the heavy rain, the fact that it was dark, and the fact that *whoever* it was stayed on the opposite side of the street and far away from the shitty camera, we missed it the first time. You would've had to know it was there to notice it. It's almost as if whoever it was knew which houses with cameras to avoid."

"That's not nearly enough!" Hoxton replied, frustrated. "Not as evidence..."

"Agreed. Now, will you let me finish?" Martinez asked. He waited for her to concede. "Thank you. Now, I agree with you; the footage is not useful that way, but on a hunch, I decided to review the footage of Mrs. Goodridge that was captured as she was driving to the overlook. She was wearing that ball cap, and for most of the ride, she never stopped. She got pretty lucky with green lights almost the whole way. Can you believe that? Talk about your Green Mile, eh?"

"Get to where you're going, Martinez," Hoxton growled.

"Right, sorry, where was I?" Martinez paused to think. Hoxton wanted to shake him.

"Oh, yes!" he exclaimed. "Luckily for us, mama did get caught briefly at one red light... and she glanced up."

"*Adam*," Hoxton exclaimed. In a rare display of affection, Hoxton reached for her partner's hands and squeezed them tight.

"Check your email," Martinez winked. "I sent you something on my way over here."

Hoxton turned to her computer and logged in, drumming her fingers against the desktop while she waited for her email to open. An email from Martinez with the subject line, *Evening, Ma'am*, was at the top of her inbox with a photo attached. Martinez continued to explain while she downloaded it.

"It's only a partial, and the traffic cam footage was a bit blurred because of the rain. Another lucky stroke for them until now. See anyone you recognize?"

Hoxton leaned so close to her screen that the tip of her nose nearly brushed against it. The image wasn't clear, and the baseball cap she was wearing concealed her eyes, but the woman behind the wheel, once presumed to be Marilys Goodridge, suddenly didn't match any of the photos she'd ever seen of her. This woman's face was thinner, the jawline more angular than the pregnant woman's whose face she had gotten to know. The lips were a different shape. The nose was slightly upturned.

"How did we miss this?" Hoxton murmured, astonished.

Martinez shrugged. "Everyone missed it. This still is a fraction of a second. I was up forensics' ass all night trying to get it enhanced juuuust right. We owe them lunch, by the way. Actually, since I did all this work, you owe them lunch."

"I owe them a year of lunches," Hoxton exclaimed, hugging him. "And you."

"I'll take it," Martinez beamed proudly. "Thanks, boss."

"I can't believe we missed this," she repeated in awe.

Martinez shrugged again. "All the evidence at the time suggested that Marilys was the driver. We interviewed Jeanine, but she said she went home and stayed there all night. We had no reason to think otherwise. After we found the wife in her own car, we didn't need to dig any further. We followed the evidence we had, like you said."

"We're idiots," Hoxton muttered.

"By the way, if you look here," Martinez added, pointing to

the partially visible passenger seat in the image. "You see that dark shape?" Hoxton followed his finger, peering at the grainy, half-concealed mass. "I'll bet that's the body..."

The two detectives stared solemnly at the pixelated shadow of Marilys Goodridge's form as they processed the reality of her final moments—not an accident, but murdered and deliberately disposed of with her unborn child still in her body. Hoxton's sorrow quickly gave way to anger toward Mason, along with the deep satisfaction of knowing he was finally about to get what was coming to him. She vowed to have him behind bars before this day was over.

"Partner, I'm getting you promoted. This is excellent, excellent work." Hoxton smiled, shaking Martinez's shoulders. "This is the best belated Christmas gift I could've asked for. How soon can we pay our good friend Mason a visit?" she asked giddily.

"Warrant's on its way," Martinez grinned. "He's got a few hours, tops."

CHAPTER 39

The first thing Mason noticed was the smell—despite being turned upside-down by the police, the house still held onto the familiar scent of home. It beckoned him inside.

With one hand still gripping the front door, Mason leaned over the threshold and listened. His stomach sank when he noticed the patch of missing floorboards where Jeanine's body had lain. He closed his eyes briefly, feeling for Mari's presence, but sensed nothing. Outside, a soft roll of thunder urged him to hurry up.

"Let's get this over with."

Mason stepped inside and closed the door behind him, leaving it unlocked in case he needed a quick getaway. Immediately, something slithered around his calves. Mason jumped a foot in the air, then stumbled over Otis, who barely avoided being squashed under his sneakers.

"Holy shit!" Mason exclaimed, clutching his chest. "Where've you been hiding?"

Otis meowed indignantly. He was skinnier than Mason remembered, but otherwise fine, if a bit feral. He butted his head insistently against Mason's leg.

"I figured you ran away, you little idiot," Mason laughed, collecting himself. He squatted down, offering his knuckles to Otis, who sniffed at him, then allowed him to scratch his ears.

"I guess when you're hungry, we're friends," Mason mused. He looked across the foyer, eyeing the missing floorboards. "I bet you saw what happened there."

Otis lifted his head to gaze disconcertingly at Mason, who suddenly realized that the cat was the only living witness to *everything* that had happened in this house. He straightened, considering Otis carefully.

"Come on," he murmured. "I'll get you something to eat."

Otis's eyes dilated with comprehension. Together, they set off to the kitchen. Mason opened the fridge and nearly retched as the stench of rotted food hit him square in the face. Covering his nose with one elbow, he reached in, grabbed a can of cat food and quickly closed the door. Gagging, Mason peeled off the lid and dropped the can in front of Otis, who buried his nose in it eagerly.

Mason felt an unexpected pang of guilt as he watched him eat. Tearing his eyes away, he leaned against the counter and surveyed the kitchen. Despite the mess, a nostalgic heaviness settled in his heart. Maybe his mom was right—there were some good memories here, even if they were all tarnished now...

Through the patio doors, another bright flash of lightning illuminated the rain, which had started falling. Remembering his mission, Mason straightened and got to work, leaving Otis to his meal.

He made good time executing the search plan he'd mapped out in the driveway, taking care to turn on as few lights as possible to avoid attracting attention from neighbors. In the gloom, shadows seemed to move around him, but when he looked directly at them, there was nothing to see. Mason resisted the urge to give in to his fear and flee. He couldn't afford to.

He froze as he entered his old master bedroom. The place was completely ransacked—every drawer was opened, and in the closet, every piece of clothing ripped from its hanger. The boxes Kris had packed and sealed with Mari's belongings were cut open and emptied, their contents dumped in a pile in the middle of the room along with all of Mason's and Jeanine's things.

Battling a crushing sense of defeat, Mason forced his feet forward. The mattress had been stripped of its linens and pushed aside, but he started there anyway, running his fingers along the bedframe, searching for any unfastened seams that might reveal a hidden compartment. He did the same to both nightstands and the dresser, hoping to discover a loose bottom or backing.

Coming up empty, he picked over the tangles of clothing strewn across the carpet to reach the closet. Inside, the cardboard boxes that housed Mari's things had been broken down and left in a haphazard stack in the middle of the tight space. Mason pushed them aside and began searching the built-ins. He was on his knees, peering at the underside of some shelving, when he felt something brush against his pant leg.

Mason yelped and attempted to stand, knocking his head against the shelf above him. He grunted and stumbled backward, crashing into the pile of boxes behind him. As he fell, he heard a frantic meow from Otis, who dodged out from under him and scampered away.

"Otis! You… *fucker!*" Mason screamed, spraying spittle through his clenched lips. He was distracted by a throbbing pain on the top of his head. He put a hand up, feeling the beginnings of a huge, tender goose egg forming on his crown.

"I'm gonna fucking kill that cat."

Mason kicked at a nearby cardboard box, sending it flying. Giving into his anger, he kicked and punched at every box within reach until he'd thrown them all out of the closet. His tantrum spent, he collapsed onto the carpet.

It was over. He hadn't found the diary, and there was nowhere left to look. He was going to prison for the rest of his life. It would be better to just lie there and let Mari take him out now. Tears gathered behind Mason's eyes.

"You win, Mar," he whispered. "Come and get me."

Mason closed his eyes and waited. Apart from the rain pounding outside, the ensuing stillness was deafening. He willed Mari to come and put him out of his misery, but she didn't appear.

Feeling utterly abandoned, Mason curled into a fetal position and wept until he couldn't anymore, soaking the carpet with his tears. He wiped his nose with his sleeve, then lay on his side, staring morosely into the corner. He noticed that the rug near the baseboard there was slightly lifted, as if it had been pulled loose.

Mason felt the tiniest spark of hope ignite in his belly. He flipped onto his stomach and pressed his cheek against the floor. There was something underneath the carpet. Shimmying closer, Mason scratched near the baseboard and felt the rug lift under his fingertips. Digging his nails in, he pulled harder until the edge came out completely. His heart nearly stopped when he caught a flash of pink glitter.

Mason extracted Jeanine's diary from it's hiding place, laughing and crying hysterically. He couldn't believe the lengths she'd gone to conceal something nobody in the world cared about, although he was grateful, given the circumstances.

"God bless you, Jeanine," he chuckled, swallowing his tears.

Electricity coursed through Mason's body as he left the closet, clutching the diary. Breathless, he collapsed against the bed and opened the journal with shaking hands. Jeanine's voice flooded his mind.

Mason thumbed through the pages, engrossed in Jeanine's account of their affair from the moment they met to the morning before she was killed. Her infatuation with him was mesmerizing; he was shocked to see how often he'd been a pawn in her obsessive quest to be with him. When he finished her final entry, Mason closed the diary and hugged it thoughtfully to his chest.

Jeanine's perspective was so different from his experience.

For him, the stakes couldn't have been higher, but she made it all sound like just a game.

A fresh idea began to take root in Mason's mind. He'd assumed this diary would condemn him to a lifetime in prison or worse, but Jeanine often credited herself as the mastermind behind everything that happened. Why not let her be? Perhaps he and Mari were both victims of Jeanine's obsessive insanity. He began brainstorming ways to have the diary discovered with only certain pages intact, until he was interrupted by a text message from his dad.

> Checking in, doing okay?

For the first time in weeks, Mason cracked a genuine smile. He'd found the key to his freedom. Everything would be okay. He tapped out a quick reply.

> Doing great! Heading home now.

He was about to leave the bedroom when he was stopped by a loud, distressed yowl coming from the bathroom.

"What the hell?" He'd never heard Otis make a noise like that before. Mason stood at the threshold, debating whether he should get the hell out of there or check to see if the cat was okay. His head still hurt from when he'd bumped it in the closet, but had that not happened, he might not have discovered the diary. He owed Otis for that.

"Fine," Mason sighed, poking his head into the bathroom. The cabinets had all been emptied; the floor was strewn with cosmetic bottles and hair tools. "Where are you, you little fuck-er?" He turned on the lights, then picked his way through the clutter to peer behind the bathtub. "Otis?" he called. "Are you dead?"

Behind him, he heard another foreign sound: a deep gurgling that seemed to be coming from the toilet. Mason turned around, his attention now focused on what sounded like a portal to Hell opening in the plumbing. As he drew closer, he saw water welling up in the bowl, speckled with rotten, stinking debris.

"Ugh, for fuck's sake." Grimacing, he reached for the lever and flushed, but that only made things worse. The water rose higher, but just when he feared it would overflow, it stopped.

Mason was about to abandon the scene when the water began to recede, disappearing in great, halting gulps. Covering his nose, he moved closer and watched the mess disappear. When it was almost completely gone, he reached for the lever again and flushed. Clean, clear water swirled into the bowl. As it stilled, something at the bottom caught his eye—three tiny, white pieces of gravel.

Frowning, Mason leaned down for a closer look. In a flash of horror, he recognized Mari's teeth, but before he could react, he was hit square in the face with an explosive spray of sewage. Sputtering, he threw up his braced arm and fell backward, bumping his already tender head against the bathtub behind him. Mason roared in pain.

"*Motherfucker!*" he yelled, picking up a nearby bottle and chucking it at the wall. He spat, then gagged and swore again. Desperate to get clean, he peeled off his soiled brace and soaked clothes, then stumbled into the shower.

As Mason scrubbed his skin, the soothing hot water melted the adrenaline out of his body. He leaned against the warm marble tiles, feeling dizzy. Outside, he heard a crack of lightning, followed by a boom of thunder so earthquakingly loud he feared it would shatter the glass around him. In an instant, he was plunged into darkness as the power went out.

Fighting against the sudden terror that seized his whole body, Mason fumbled for the shower door but found it was stuck, trapping him inside. He pushed and pulled at the handle, but it refused to budge. Outside, he heard the bedroom door slam shut.

Despite the hot water still streaming from the showerhead

above him, Mason felt a chill race up his spine. Through the steamy glass, he spied a sliver of light as the door opened, and someone entered the bathroom. Mason's heart began to pound.

"... Dad?"

The bathroom door slammed shut. Mason strained to hear over the rushing showerhead, the rain outside, and his own thudding heart. Out of the dark, a familiar, feminine laughter echoed. Mason clapped his hands over his ears.

"Go away!" he shouted, his voice quivering. The laughter rang louder, vibrating his skull—she was in his head. Shaking with terror, Mason shuffled backward until he was pressed against the tiles, then crossed his arms defensively in front of him.

Fingernails tapped a broken rhythm along the outside of the shower glass, circling Mason. His eyes followed the sound as it moved around him in the dark. Just as the tapping reached the door, it stopped. Mason contemplated flinging himself at the glass head first, just to put an end to his torment.

Beside him, the showerhead faucet squeaked, tightened by an unseen hand. Mason shivered as the hot water slowed to a rhythmless *drip... drip... drip.* He wanted to scream, but his vocal cords were paralyzed, along with the rest of him.

Something cold slithered across his bare torso. A scream burst from Mason's lungs as he flailed and began to fight for his life. He felt hands all over him, clawing at his naked body as he struggled to tear himself away. Meanwhile, the entity seemed to draw energy from his terror; it shrieked and growled with delight as it attempted to take him off his feet.

"Please... Please!" As Mason screamed and begged for release, Mari's laughter rang in his ears.

In one final, desperate move, Mason threw himself in what he hoped was the direction of the shower door and felt it give way. He crashed to the littered bathroom floor, banging both knees against the unforgiving tile, then scrambled to stand. Slipping on wet feet, he wrenched open the door, catching his hip against the frame. Something foreign brushed against his bare back.

Without missing a beat, Mason launched himself out of the bathroom and snatched a pair of shorts off the floor, jumping into them as he raced down the stairs and sprinted to the car.

His hands shook violently as he fumbled to start the ignition. He glanced frantically at the open front door for signs his attacker was following. Finally, the engine roared to life. Without a look back, Mason threw the car into gear and sped off.

CHAPTER 40

oxton and Martinez visited Mason's parents first, where his mother tearfully informed them where her son could be found. Hoxton's heart went out to her—Kris Goodridge's grief was unfathomable as she gave up her son. It infuriated Hoxton to see yet another person damaged by Mason's lies, but she admired Kris for doing the right thing.

They had arrived at his marital home a few moments ago and were now parked across the street, observing the house through the rain.

"Looks pretty quiet," Martinez mused. "I wonder what he's doing in there."

Before Hoxton could reply, Mason dashed through the front door in a wild panic, leaving it wide open behind him. He dove headfirst into his car and sped off, tires screeching as they skidded, then straightened on the wet road. The two detectives exchanged a bewildered look.

"So… you want the car chase or the house?" Martinez asked. "Rock-paper-scissors?" He held up his hands, ready to play.

"I'm tired of chasing him," Hoxton sighed. "I'll stay and clear the house. You can get after him. I'll call it in for you, but be careful," she warned, looking up at the sky. "This storm looks deadly."

"Yeah… you too," Martinez murmured.

Hoxton took in her partner's puzzled expression. "What is it?"

Slowly, Martinez turned to her. "Was he barefoot?"

CHAPTER 41

Mason's heart didn't slow until he reached the Eastview Highway, signaling the halfway point to his parents' house. It was only then that he realized he'd been holding his breath. He exhaled shakily. Tears sprang to his eyes as he recalled the terror he felt in the shower. He clenched his jaw, trying to hold them back, but it was no use. He let loose a wretched wail and began to cry.

Rain fell in icy sheets as he drove, and between his tears and the windshield wipers sweeping furiously, he could barely see where he was going. He shivered against the freezing cold, wishing he'd grabbed a shirt during his escape.

Mason heard sirens and checked his rearview mirror, where he saw red and blue lights flashing. Relieved, he pressed the brakes to slow down, intending to pull over. He didn't care if he was arrested for speeding—or anything else for that matter. At least in a jail cell, he'd be safe. As he attempted to guide the car onto the shoulder, the steering wheel jerked out of his hands.

"No," he sobbed, "Please… no." Gritting his teeth, Mason locked out his arms and tightened his hands in a death grip around the wheel, but it was no use. He was no longer in control.

For several agonizing minutes, he wrestled with an invisible force as the wheel jerked again and again out of his grasp. The tires screeched as they fought for grip on the wet road. Mason stomped on the brake pedals, but the car would not slow. As he accelerated, the police cars behind him multiplied.

Depleted and exhausted, Mason felt his will crumbling. He was tired of fighting. He was in so much pain, mentally and physically. There would be no surviving this ordeal. He understood that now. He had nothing left to fight for, or with.

"Fine. Fuck you, Mari." He let go of the wheel and threw his hands in the air. His tires screeched as the car veered off the road and into the trees.

"Mase, baby. Wake up."

"Mmm, mmm," Mason groaned. He didn't want to wake up. This was the best sleep he'd had in months. He heard Mari's gentle giggle. Her lips were warm against his forehead.

"Wake up, sleepy," she whispered, "you're gonna miss it! The baby's kicking!"

In his half-conscious state, Mason felt Mari gently squeeze his hand. He had forgotten how small hers were. Her skin was so soft.

Mason felt himself rocking. It was soothing, like being asleep on a boat. He listened for the gentle lapping of waves against the hull. Instead, he heard a slow, metallic creaking. Rain pounded on metal above him, and the temperature dropped, raising goosebumps on his flesh. The warm sensation on his forehead dripped down and stung his eyes. It smelled coppery—blood. He tasted it, too.

Mason jerked himself awake and looked around in a panic. He was in his mom's car, which had crashed into the trees and was now teetering somewhere. His seatbelt cut painfully into his neck, strapping him to his seat. Blood was falling into his eye from a wound on his forehead. He raised his hand to wipe it away, but someone squeezed it tight, sending a sharp pain through his fractured wrist bones. In a daze, he looked to his right.

Mari sat beside him in the passenger seat, looking more beautiful and terrifying than he'd ever seen her before. She smiled radiantly; her cheeks flushed with life. Mason's heart and his stomach leaped in unison. He threw himself away from her and struggled to pull his hand out of her grasp. He heard that metallic creaking again as the car lurched dangerously forward and down. Mason saw the quarry lake sway below him.

"Don't you want to feel the baby?" Mari asked. Afraid to shift his weight, Mason turned carefully toward her.

"Mari," he begged. "I'm sorry, okay? Please... Please help me! I don't want to die!"

"Neither did we," she whispered, still gripping his hand.

The car swayed downward again. Mason whimpered and pressed himself against his seatback. With his free hand, he fumbled for the door handle, wrapped his trembling fingers around the lever, and pulled, but the latch wouldn't open. Mari threaded her fingers through his and squeezed again.

"Mari." Mason glanced back at her with pleading eyes. "I loved you once, and I know you loved me. You're a good person, Mari. Don't let me die!"

Mari gazed uncertainly at Mason. "I loved you once," she repeated.

"You did. I know you did! Tell me you did!" Mason cried, his voice cracking. Facing death, he suddenly needed to hear that above all else. "Please," he bleated.

Mason heard whispers all around him, though he couldn't understand what they were saying. Other voices shouted over them from a distance. As they got closer, he recognized one.

"Mason Goodridge!" Martinez shouted. "Eastview Police! Someone call an ambulance!"

Mason prayed they would reach him in time. He glanced at Mari, who kept hold of his hand, and realized they wouldn't. A feeling of weightlessness took over as the car rocked forward one final time.

Mason watched Mari's hair float around her face in slow motion, her expression perfectly at peace. He'd forgotten how beautiful she was. He lost himself in her dark eyes; their hands intertwined stirred a memory of a feeling he'd had years ago, outside of a restaurant, under a full moon, when the air was warm and smelled like jasmine.

"Time to let go," Mari said. Mason remained helplessly fixated on her face as the car slammed into the lake's frigid surface.

In an explosive, blinding white flash, she was gone, leaving him to die alone. Paralyzed and still strapped to his seat, Mason watched helplessly as ice-cold water poured in all around him, sealing him inside the car. As it closed over his head, the last thing he heard was his heart pounding furiously, fighting to live while his body was dragged down into the cold, black void.

www.ingramcontent.com/pod-product-compliance
Lightning Source LLC
Chambersburg PA
CBHW021407110726
47901CB00008B/2094